DETROIT PUBLIC LIBRARY

W9-BVO-120

DETROIT PUBLIC LIBRARY

Browsing Library

DATE DUE

APR 1 8 1998

JUN 2 7 1998

JUL 2 9 1998

BC-3

MAR 2 1 1998

THREE
QUARTERS

THREE
QUARTERS

DENIS HAMILL

POCKET BOOKS

New York   London   Toronto   Sydney   Tokyo   Singapore

M

This book is a work of fiction. Names, characters, places and incidents are products of the author's imagination or are used fictitiously. Any resemblance to actual events or locales or persons, living or dead, is entirely coincidental.

POCKET BOOKS, a division of Simon & Schuster Inc.
1230 Avenue of the Americas, New York, NY 10020

Copyright © 1998 by Denis Hamill

All rights reserved, including the right to reproduce
this book or portions thereof in any form whatsoever.
For information address Pocket Books, 1230 Avenue
of the Americas, New York, NY 10020

Library of Congress Cataloging-in-Publication Data

Hamill, Denis.
    Three quarters / Denis Hamill.
      p.   cm.
    ISBN: 0-671-00249-X
    I. Title.
    PS3558.A4217T47   1998
    813'.54—dc21   97-37103
                                                                    CIP

First Pocket Books hardcover printing February 1998

10 9 8 7 6 5 4 3 2 1

POCKET and colophon are registered trademarks of
Simon & Schuster Inc.

Printed in the U.S.A.

MAR 2 1 1998

Browsing Library

This book is for Janet,
for bringing a candle
into my darkened room.
Love always.

Browsing Library

Acknowledgments

I'd like to thank the brilliant Esther Newberg for getting this idea to Dona Chernoff, whose scalpel was sharp and true.

Thanks and love to my kids—Sean, Katie, Nell—for their patience while I was MIA.

THREE
QUARTERS

1

Thursday

Dr. Hector Perez felt sick at the sight of all the blood.

Blood was money for Dr. Hector Perez, the currency of his calling, not something that terrified him, physically or mentally. Until now.

But then he had never awakened, head pounding, mouth a bucket of glue, soaking in the puddled blood of a beautiful, nude, strange young woman before.

He looked at his gold watch: 5:54 AM. Then he looked back at the woman whose jugular vein had been severed, blood still pulsing like a backed-up sink. His clinical eye noticed that it was an arterial purplish red near the deep gash. But as it oxidized in the air and the cells died, the blood turned a brighter, maraschino red on the starched white sheets and pillowcases that were embroidered with the white-on-white legend: Hotel St. Claire. The colors were perversely mesmerizing.

The fuzzy tingling of his arm trapped beneath her body and the soggy warmth of the blood had awakened him. And now he was transfixed by her gaping wound and her half-open blue eyes. Her hair was long and naturally blond, her makeup perfect except for specks of caked blood. His own blood began pounding in his temples, shooting scalding adrenaline through him.

His eyes finally broke contact, and he panned the hotel room: Pigeons cooing on the windowsill. Morning traffic clamoring from the city outside. His clothes scattered all over the floor. Syrupy blood on his skin.

Fucking shit is for real, Perez thought. *I'm in bed with a dead woman.* Murdered. *Did I bang her and then fall asleep? Did she cut her own throat? Did someone else come in when I passed out? What did she give me? Chloral hydrate drops, an old-fashioned Mickey Finn? Or*

1

was it that new date-rape drug the kids called "roofies," Rohypnol? Hits you like a plane crash. Jesus Christ . . .

I should be home in bed with Nydia, Perez thought. *Rubbing her swollen belly. . . .*

Perez pushed himself to a half-seated position and yanked his arm free, recoiling in horror at the flash of gleaming steel. His numb, tingling fingers were stuck to the bloody steel handle of a straight razor.

"No!" Perez shouted in the hotel room and immediately used his left hand to cover his mouth. He glared down at his other hand, which clutched the sticky handle of the razor. A grisly murder weapon gripped between fingers that Perez had spent the last ten years training to save human life.

Only one life still worth saving in this room, he thought, *mine.* As he quickly stood from the bed and backed away from the lifeless woman, his mind worked in freeze-frame stop-action, imagining the forensic photos. Then he thought of the detectives and criminalists who would nibble the room to death for clues.

His clothes were strewn about the floor as if he'd undressed quickly. He saw the room key on the night table on top of the cashier's receipt. He did not touch the receipt but was relieved when he read that the room was rented to a Karen Anders. She'd paid $316.85, *cash.*

Perez carefully used a Kleenex to fasten the chain lock on the hotel room door. Then he took a towel from the bathroom and began wiping every conceivable place he might have left a fingerprint—countertops, TV knobs, remote control, light switches, minibar, champagne glasses, doorframes. Even her earrings. He then walked into the bathroom and used the same towel to wash the blood from his arms and legs and torso and genitals. He washed the straight razor, watching Karen Anders's blood swirling down the drain. He did not shower because he did not want his hair to be discovered in the drain. He pulled the plastic shower curtain down from the bathroom rod and carried it out to the bedroom area and laid it out on the floor.

Ever conscious of the telltale DNA in hair evidence, he used his pocket comb to rake through her pubic hair to remove any trace he might have left of his own. He removed the pillowcase where his head had lain. Then he pulled the fitted sheets free from the corners of the bed. As he tugged the sheet from under the dead woman, she did a half-roll onto the bare blood-soaked mattress. Perez placed the bloody sheets and the pillowcases onto the shower curtain and folded it neatly around them. He then stuffed the plastic-wrapped blood evidence into the clean pillowcase, careful not to soil his hands again.

Then Dr. Perez pulled on his underwear, trousers, shirt. He carefully checked the woman's pocketbook, which was filled with vaginal sprays, mouthwash, dozens of rubbers, a vibrator, butt plugs, handcuffs, and a few other sex toys.

None of his own money or credit cards were missing, everything was intact. He checked her wallet, careful to thumb through it with the Kleenex. No driver's license, credit cards, voting card, Blue Cross card. No identification at all. He decided to remove the five one-hundred-dollar bills, to make it look like a robbery. The only other money consisted of seventy-five cents, three shiny quarters that lay in her half-open right hand. And Dr. Hector Perez didn't know why he noticed such a ridiculous detail—but he was struck that all three quarters looked freshly minted yet were each dated 1991. Odd, he thought and swallowed, trying to summon saliva to his parched mouth. He had no time to contemplate such trivial minutiae. He left the coins alone.

He checked his watch again: 5:57 AM. Jesus! Nydia would be waking up in an hour. To make breakfast. Practice her Lamaze breathing. Sweet, sweet Nydia . . . How could he do this to *her*?

If he drove quickly enough, against the morning rush-hour traffic, he might still be able to cross the Brooklyn Bridge to his new Park Slope brownstone, slip in, hit the couch, and pretend that he got home late. If he could pull that off, his alibi would be solid.

Then later, on the way to work, he could dump the bloody evidence. He knew exactly where to get rid of it, too, where no one would ever discover it. But first he had to get home before Nydia awakened.

Get away, he told himself.

Dr. Hector Perez removed the convention name tag from the lapel of his jacket. Then he picked up the pillowcase with the bloody sheets and the towel he had used to wash himself clean. He made one more inventory of the room, certain that no trace of him was left. He opened the door with a Kleenex and popped his head out into the hallway. Way down the corridor he saw the cart of a Hotel St. Claire maid, but no one was visible.

He stepped out into the hall, hurried to the fire stairs, and, head bowed, took the five flights to the basement and left through an employees entrance, like just one more Hispanic hotel worker.

Perez again checked his watch: 6:01 AM.

2

Bad night in the steel drum.

"Gonna install a tollbooth in your hole and charge for joyrides, you cop motherfucker," came a long shout from down the deafening cellblock. The other cons responded with the ceaseless banging of the steel.

As the cellblock cons continued their all-night jive, Bobby Emmet finished push-up number five hundred and twenty-one and realized that that was one for every day he'd been inside. One for every day he was separated from his fourteen-year-old daughter, Maggie. One for every day he did not know of the true fate of Dorothea Dubrow, the woman he adored, the woman he was convicted of murdering, for which he had been sentenced to fifteen to life.

Bobby Emmet, once proud chief investigator for the Manhattan district attorney's office, was now a cop in the can, pig in a steel blanket: Wallkill State Correction Facility, his fifth joint in eighteen months. Had been here, what, three weeks? Took the mutts three days to learn he was an ex-cop. Then the threats, taunts, and the banging of the steel started. Solitary, twenty-three-hour-a-day lockdown, one daily hour of exercise for a walk to the "car wash" for a shower.

His only recourse was the exercises, dropping to his hands and tippy-toes and starting another set of push-ups, fifty reps at a clip until he'd done a thousand, every morning for the last year and a half. At the rate of a thousand push-ups a day, Bobby figured out that if he did only the minimum fifteen years of his sentence, he would do 5,475,000 jailhouse push-ups. Ditto sit-ups. In the past year and a half he'd done 521,000 of each.

Soon they'd slide breakfast under the cell door.

Before lunch he'd do a thousand sit-ups. And, before dinner, five hundred towel chins, done with his single white towel looped through the upper bars. If the animals banged the steel all night, he did more exercises, squats and isometrics, backward push-ups on the edge of his eighteen-inch concrete bunk to build the triceps and shoulders and forearms. Then more sit-ups and push-ups until sheer muscular exhaustion let him collapse into mindless sleep.

Last night, the exercises had helped him keep *control*. The mutts had been extremely hostile, banging on their cell doors, slamming shivs, spoons, cups, shoes, skulls, anything heavy, against their eight-by-five concrete-and-steel cell doors. They worked in organized, rotating shifts. One crew would scream for an hour about how they were gonna take Bobby's bunghole. Then that crew would take a nod and another would pick up the banging and the mockery, screaming about Emmet the Faggot who was gonna get his throat cut in tomorrow's lockout and how they would all take turns fucking him in the neck. Then that chorus would nod and another crew would pick up the banging rant about castrating Bobby and mailing his balls home to his teenage daughter.

By morning, he'd also done an extra six hundred sit-ups, four hundred leg raises, two hundred towel chins. Keeping count always kept his mind off the screaming and the banging of the steel. When he was busy counting exercises, he maintained an inner *control*. He never let the mutts make him lose count. And in doing his extreme daily workout regime for eighteen months, his body had become rock hard, rippling and in *control*.

Still, it had been the worst night since Bobby Emmet had arrived in Wallkill. He didn't mind the threats so much, even though he knew threats were often carried out. Solitary confinement had not prevented the determined cons in various joints from getting to Bobby during his one-hour-a-day lockout. To date he'd been stabbed twice, had his arm broken once, and received a concussion, all while he was being escorted by uniformed prison hacks to the car wash.

He could deal with the threats, the assaults, and the tedium. The part that bothered him was the banging of the steel. The endless vibrating, tooth-rattling, mind-numbing banging of the steel that reminded him all night long that he was living like one of *them,* one of the mutts, one of the skells he had spent a career taking off the street and vacuum-packing into steel drums like this.

The banging of the steel was the heartbeat of prison life. And Bobby Emmet could never get used to it like the other cons because, unlike them, he did not belong here. The mutts not only accepted the banging, they almost viewed it as a defiant celebration of the life that led them here. This was the tune to which they danced; what the Buddhists called the "om" of their universe.

Yet there was a silver lining to all this; as long as Bobby was bothered by it, he knew he was different. Not one of them. Not a skell, rapist, cold-blooded killer; not a human predator or a scavenger. Bobby had always worked, prided himself in never walking away from a job until it was finished. He was more interested in the intrinsic value of a job well done, done to the very best of his ability, than in the extrinsic monetary rewards. Or the glory of medals or pomp and circumstance. Bobby had always taken pride in protecting the law-abiding taxpayers who maintained a semblance of civilization.

But the noise also endlessly reminded Bobby of what separated him from his daughter, Maggie. And from those who had framed him for killing Dorothea Dubrow. Both of whom he would have laid down his life for. That impotence, that frustration, that bottled-up rage banged home all night long. It was the worst physical burden of doing time.

He wondered how he would tell the story to a stranger. Would he say that while in the midst of investigating a corrupt private-snoop firm owned and staffed by ex-NYPD cops, Bobby had been framed for murder? That he'd worked for the Manhattan DA's office? But it was the Brooklyn DA who'd convinced a jury that Bobby had killed Dorothea with a kitchen carving knife in his Brooklyn apartment and then in the night reduced her body to ash in the crematorium of a local cemetery. Even though he had spent every dime he could borrow to hire Moira Farrell, one of the best trial lawyers in Brooklyn, he was tried and convicted of killing Dorothea Dubrow. The whole thing, from arrest to conviction, took a mere seven months, which he spent in solitary at Riker's Island.

Since they never found a body, just a pile of ash, Bobby Emmet refused to believe that Dorothea was even dead. But he knew that while he was in jail, he would never be sure about what happened to her.

Stop, he thought. *Stop thinking about death and Dorothea and life in here.* He watched the feelers of a large cockroach appear from a crack in the concrete near the ceiling, saw it probe the sour air of the cell. He closed his eyes and conjured Maggie. . . .

An equally torturous emotional horror was not being able to see his daughter, now fourteen years old. She'd visited Bobby twice, at different jails during the winter and spring school breaks, but he didn't want her to come anymore. Didn't like the way the other cons gaped at her now pubescent body. Didn't want her to see him here in this roach-and-vermin-infested shit hole.

The separation after the divorce from Maggie's mother three years ago had been hard enough on the kid. It had devastated all three of them. He and his former wife had once truly loved each other, but life together was never going to work. Connie Mathews Sawyer, his ex-wife, was third-generation rich. The Mathews name was a regular staple of the society pages. Big, inherited cosmetics-industry money. Bobby came from the proud, macho, self-reliant big dreams of the working class. "I'll make my own money, and I'll never take a dime from your old man," was Bobby's constant refrain whenever Connie said she wanted to move away from Brooklyn, to a big estate near the family compound in Connecticut. Maybe Bobby made less money than his father-in-law's chauffeur, but no way was he going to live on what he considered a Mathews family freeload.

Instead, they'd bought a small house in Brooklyn and got a normal mortgage at the Dime Savings Bank like everyone else. Bobby'd told Connie that if she wanted to go to work after Maggie was born, to help pay off the mortgage, that was okay with him. Just no handouts.

They'd married young, against the wishes of Connie's father, who boycotted the wedding. The gossip pages of the daily tabloids had a field day, with headlines like "THE COP AND THE HEIR-ESS" or "LIPSTICK AND NIGHTSTICK."

Bobby got a kick out of the press at first but soon found them hanging out outside his Brooklyn house, pissing off his working-class neighbors. They'd shoot pictures day and night, concoct fictitious domestic squabbles, spreading their lies in the papers and on tabloid TV. Maggie's first step and first tooth made news.

Bobby started hating reporters almost as much as criminals. The publicity made his job increasingly difficult. He had his balls broken constantly on the job, and he transferred from the Harbor Unit, to PAL, to Brooklyn South Narcotics, and finally to the Manhattan DA's detective squad.

The marriage was exciting at first, a raucous, rebellious, randy love affair, blessed with a beautiful daughter. But eventually, as they neared their thirties, the marriage proved to be a bad mix of two good people from different worlds, and the parting was a sad, sorrowful, painful truce. They had driven the marriage as far as it could go before running out of gas. All that remained was Maggie, and they weren't selfish enough to want her to carry a pair of unhappy parents on her back in order to call it a family. So they junked the marriage, promising to remember the good times, still bonded for life by their daughter, who reluctantly moved with Connie to Connecticut and then later to Trump Tower in Manhattan with her new stepfather.

Bobby and Connie would always remember that the last time they made love, on the night they received their divorce papers, it had been the best ever, each taking enough of the other to try to last a lifetime.

Then suddenly they were no longer a family, and it hurt each of them in a lasting, mournful, physically painful way. Bobby thought there should be graveyards for dearly departed marriages, where the forever-wounded could go and have a good cry every once in a while over a marker. The end of a marriage was a burial of a part of your life you would never have back again.

But it wasn't *this*.

Jesus, *this*, this was worse, Bobby thought. Having steel walls between him and his kid was beyond separation. This was like a death between them, a living death that lingered and breathed and could never be mourned away.

Gray morning light now leaked into the cellblock.

"Rumor on the tom-toms upstairs is you might be getting a new trial," said a voice through the bars. It was Morrison, a big, flabby, hound-faced guard who worked Bobby's tier.

"Fat chance," Bobby said.

"That's why the savages are up in arms," Morrison said. "Love to kill them a cop in the joint before you get to leave."

"Rumors," Bobby said, glad for the conversation, even though Morrison could often be a sardonic pain in the ass. "Just the press assholes trying to fill holes in their pages and broadcasts. Rumors . . ."

Bobby's trial, like his marriage, had been a media circus. And ever since, on a slow news day, the press boys always tried to bring the circus back to town: "Hey, what's up with John Gotti?" "What about Robert Chambers?" "Is Son of Sam still alive?" "What about the asshole who shot John Lennon?" "Hey, let's do a Bobby Emmet update."

"Way I hear it, that Izzy Gleason fella came through security a few minutes ago to see you," Morrison said.

"Izzy Gleason is the sleaziest shyster in New York," Bobby said. "Why would he be here to see me?"

"If the shoe fits," Morrison said, giggling, as he continued his patrol.

Bobby closed his eyes and in his mind's eye saw the despicable little lawyer with the red hair and blue eyes, always chewing on a candy bar or sucking on a cigarette, his body as spastic as a puppet's. Over the years, Bobby had often opposed Gleason, investigating and building cases against some of the most dangerous felons in the city, only to watch the notorious lawyer get many of them off with his brilliant, histrionic courtroom antics. Judges, cops, and DAs hated Gleason, but juries loved him because a trial with Izzy Gleason was like a day at the circus.

And now he was coming up to visit him?

Nah, Bobby thought, hitting the floor again to do another set of push-ups.

Gleason was just getting off a one-year bar association ethics committee suspension. And Bobby *had* heard gossip that for his first time at bat in his comeback, Gleason wanted to get Bobby Emmet, his old nemesis from the Manhattan DA's cop shop, out of prison. But he had thought it was just another Gleason attempt to get his name back in the papers. Didn't think the little piglet was serious.

Goddamned press would have a field day with me and Gleason, Bobby thought. The same shit would be dragged through the papers again for Maggie and for Connie and her new husband, who was a decent enough fella but a world-class rich bore. And it wouldn't be easy for Bobby's kid brother, Patrick, the "good" cop in the family. Patrick Pearse Emmet would have to put up with the same old hypocritical shit. The precinct locker-room taunts, the anonymous interoffice notes, the graffiti on the bathroom walls.

Just what I need, Bobby Emmet thought, more sleazy publicity from the man whose past clients included a mass murderer on the Staten Island ferry who had been demanding Staten Island's secession—from the United States; a Westies gang crew charged with burying a city sheriff alive in a mountain of Sanitation Department rock salt after he padlocked their saloon; the owner of a pet cemetery that was really used as a burial ground for mob hits.

And these were just the ones Gleason got off.

Bobby hated everything Sleazy Izzy Gleason—or the Wizard of Iz, as the tabloids called him—stood for. But he couldn't help liking him personally. He could be a generous, comical, self-effacing little sleazoid. The man was a conscious caricature of himself. He'd learned his trade as a Bronx assistant district attorney and was an amazing trial lawyer, with a loud, abrasive, flamboyant style. He thought nothing of exploiting every hole card—race, sex, age, religion—in order to win. In at least three trials for which Bobby had done the investigation and which ended in hung juries, Bobby was certain that Gleason had been sleeping with a female juror who fell for his apparently irresistible combination of Irish blarney and Jewish moxie.

Bobby Emmet and Izzy Gleason were oil and swamp water.

At exactly 7:30 AM, after a very long sleepless night, as he reached rep number thirty-seven in his nineteenth set of pre-breakfast push-ups, Bobby Emmet's cell door slid open and Morrison stood in the corridor, announcing, "You got a visitor, and you smell just about ripe enough for the rotten company."

Bobby strode in front of Morrison, up the tier, getting a good "fuck you" rhythm going with his swinging arms and his powerful legs. He let each work boot heel hammer the concrete with a definitive clack as he moved, his big shoulders back, swollen chest out, head high on the thick neck, large fists opening and closing, making the veins and the muscles in his forearms pop and flex. It was a macho performance, a jailhouse show of force. He let all six foot two, 210 pounds, be known. He was his only weapon. He locked his eyes between half-open and half-closed, seeing all, revealing nothing.

"Hope you believe in mixed marriages, baby, cause I gone marry your ass, pig muthahfuckah," said one black con, who'd reached through the bars, doing sexual pantomimes with his fingers. "You gone to be my Maytag, wash my bloomers and my socks and tell me bedtime stories, baby."

From a cell on the other side of the tier came a long stream of spit, hitting Bobby on the neck with a hot, foul lash. Bobby ignored it, letting it drool down past his sweaty shoulder, over his bulging left pectoral. *Control*, he thought. *These people don't exist. They are* mutts. Skells. *You are Bobby Emmet, father, cop, citizen, honorable man. You have what they don't have—dignity. A dignified man has . . .* control. *Walk on,* he thought, *there will come another day.*

"I gettin' out in three week, Emmet," said a messily tattooed white con who stood in his cell, waving his half-chubbed dick through the bars. He'd spent so much time in jail he spoke with the inflections of the black ghetto. "Heah wha' I sayin', Emmet. Firs', I'm a unna pork you in the car wash. Then when I out, I'm a unna find me that little-titty daughter a yours and I'm a unna make her lick on me. School uniform. K-Y jelly . . ."

The veins popped in Bobby's temples, a blinding rage twisting in his head. He felt himself being sucked close to the edge, almost ready to go hurtling into the rage of what he called *muttdom*. Instead he swallowed, felt the other con's saliva drool down his chest as he balled and unballed his fists, didn't let one click of his boot heels vary. *Control,* Bobby Emmet thought again. *There will come another day.*

Morrison the hack never said a word, just kept walking behind Bobby as he passed the last cell, where Bobby saw an enormous dark-skinned white guy with nappy hair who looked like Bluto from the Popeye cartoons. Bluto stood at the cell bars, just staring. He never said a word. *He's one to worry about,* Bobby thought, and turned right, where he faced another steel door. *Worry about the ones who say nothing.*

Only now, when he was out of view of the other cons, did Bobby Emmet pause to lift his shirttail from his pants and use it to wipe the saliva from his neck and chest. The smell of the other man's spit reeked of tooth decay, cigarettes, mucous, and bile. It was a minor indignity compared to what the system had done to Bobby. The system he once believed in.

"Prisoner with visitor," shouted Morrison, and the loud klunks of the tumblers in the mechanical locks being unfastened echoed through the cellblock.

3

"We'll be the biggest fuckin' thing since Butch and Sundance."

"More like Laurel and Hardy," Bobby said from his rigid plastic chair.

Izzy Gleason's copper-colored hair set off his squinty, red-rimmed, baby blue eyes. He wore a dark blue pinstripe suit that couldn't have cost less than two thousand dollars. Bobby figured Gleason had bought one in every flavor with his share of dirty drug money.

"Look, Izzy," Bobby said from the prisoner's table as Gleason continued to pace. "I'm already doing fifteen to life and—"

"I'm gonna get you a new trial," Gleason screamed, cutting Bobby off in a high-pitched voice that sounded like an IRT subway squealing into Union Square. "With more cameras than Allen Funt."

"In a new trial with you, somehow they might wind up strapping us both into Old Sparky, pull the switch," Bobby said. "Besides, me and you, we're enemies, Izzy, remember? The DA investigator and the bionic mouth for the defense. How would it look if you represented me? I must have helped put a hundred of your clients in places like this!"

"You're forgetting the other two hundred who you collared who should be in here, but who I got off because I'm the best fuckin' trial lawyer in the city of New York," Izzy Gleason said, taking another bite of a Clark bar, the chocolate damming the spaces between the teeth.

"You'll ruin your teeth," Bobby said, shaking his head.

"Caps," Gleason said, chomping the candy bar with the perfect teeth that looked like small tombstones.

"Who paid for *them*," Bobby asked, "that nasty little Albanian hit man from Inwood you walked on that triple homicide at the titty bar?"

"No, he paid for my divorce lawyer," Gleason said. "Now I'd like to use him to whack the divorce lawyer for all the good he did me."

"You're freakin' nuts," Bobby Emmet said.

"I'll tell ya what's fuckin' nuts," Gleason said, circling the table, now lighting a cigarette, ignoring the NO SMOKING sign and Morrison. Gleason took a deep drag of the cigarette, inhaling like a man attached to a life-support system. The smoke puffed out in small clouds as he spoke, like dialogue bubbles in a comic strip. "I'm back from being suspended from the bar for a year. You've been in jail for a year and a half . . ."

"Seventeen months and four days," Bobby Emmet corrected.

"Whatever," Gleason said, blowing a long blue stream of smoke directly at Bobby, who fanned it away. "But in that time, I did a lot of thinking. I need a second act. See, I've had a great first act. Been on TV in all the big trials, on the cover of magazines, did all the talk shows, made all the money. Spent all the money. Romanced tall women. Some of them, with my help, wound up good-looking. Then it all went in the dumper. I lost both my houses, Riverdale and Westhampton. It didn't matter that me and the wife hadn't slept in the same bed for the last ten years. She waited for her best shot and flattened me when I got caught with my pants down in public. . . ."

"You're such a great lawyer that you couldn't hold on to one house?" Bobby asked.

"The IRS glommed the second one," Gleason said with a shrug

and a puff of smoke. "Then I got suspended for helping that damsel in distress. . . ."

Bobby took a deep breath and said, "You stayed in the same Plaza hotel room with your female client for three days when you were supposed to be in court with her."

Bobby knew the details because he'd done the initial investigation and was the one who'd found Gleason with his missing client, a woman who was accused of castrating her sleeping husband with a pair of bolt cutters.

"How did I know the judge would get that pissed off?" Gleason said.

"You didn't think we'd look for you? Didn't think the judge was gonna report you to ethics for not showing up at his trial? Fucking up his calendar and his Caribbean vacation while you were out banging the defendant? The only way he got you and the lady—a man-hating, ice-blooded wannabe killer, I might add—both back in the courtroom was with bench warrants! This woman cut off her husband's nuts in his sleep, Izzy!"

"I was helping her detox," Gleason said. "I couldn't put her on the stand drunk any more than I would go to sleep around her and a pair of sharp scissors. . . ."

"You took advantage of a client with a drinking problem," Bobby said.

"Hey, I was drinking pretty good at the time, too," said Gleason. "But I was helping to wean her off. And I got her off, didn't I? The booze and the attempted murder rap. And then she went back to her husband and his fuckin' loot! Maybe I was wiggling her, but then she *stiffed* me! And my wife got everything I owned. Add insult to injury, a year later I'm suspended. And the headlines were awful. But, Bobby, what a body this broad had. Literally to die a slow death for. . . ."

"Which her husband almost did," Bobby said. "But forget her body. What do you have in *mind* now, Izzy?"

"I need you to listen to me," Gleason said, pacing, smoking, chewing candy with his mouth open, his metabolism running on turbo, legs kicking, heels scraping, arms flailing. Bobby was certain Gleason never used illegal drugs because he'd tailed him in the past. Sugar, caffeine, nicotine, and alcohol were his drugs of choice.

But when you compounded all this with raging testosterone

and a few missing chromosomes, he appeared like someone on high-octane cocaine. He wasn't completely, clinically insane, Bobby thought. But he was more than a half a bubble off plumb. And then there was his problem with women. Gleason was intoxicated by them—big women, small women, skinny, zaftig, white, black, brown, yellow. Worse than booze, the guy was nuts for women. With the exception of his wife, he was, by all reports, very nice to them.

A different guard tapped on the glass door, and Morrison got up and stepped outside to talk to him, leaving Bobby and Izzy alone.

"Okay, I'm listening," Bobby said.

"I need a middle act," Gleason said, taking a puff of his butt and leaning in close to Bobby, talking in a rushed, urgent torrent now. "I'm forty-eight, and except for some pin money, I'm broke. I know I'm considered a rummy and a clown. A has-been. I can read the papers. So can my two daughters. Thank God they're away at school most of the time. But the joke's over. It's humiliating, Bobby, and it's a long road back. I've had a long time to think, look around. When I do, I see that you're in here. Now, I know you never did what they say you did. I can relate to how much you loved that dame of yours."

"I still love Dorothea," Bobby said. "I don't talk about her in the past tense. Yet . . ."

"Good," Gleason said. "Because I need you to either prove she's alive or that someone else killed her."

"You'd probably defend that guy, too," Bobby said.

"Don't get moral on me, asshole," Gleason said, angry, pointing at him with what was left of the candy bar, the cigarette smoke surrounding him.

"I'm sorry," Bobby said. "That was uncalled for."

"I'm here to help *me,* sure, but I can get *you* out of this shit bowl," Gleason said. "If you let me. See, I happen to think your lawyer, Moira Farrell, went in the tank on you . . . By the way, were you banging her?"

"No," Bobby said. "Jesus Christ . . ."

"Too bad, because she sure fucked you," Gleason said. "Worst courtroom defense I've seen since Mike Tyson's. I mean there was never even a body, no corpus delicti, and they convicted you . . ."

Bobby thought about the glamorous red-haired lawyer who wore the tight skirts and high heels and who had made great press copy but a terrible impression on his mostly middle-aged female jury. The trial had been like a slow-motion hallucination.

"Give me your pitch, Izzy," Bobby said softly. "I want to get the hell out of here."

The door opened again and Morrison leaned in and said, "Gleason, you got a fax coming into the administration office. And a phone call, too."

"Okay," Gleason said to Bobby. "Let me go get this, and we'll talk. Think about this, asshole. I'm your only chance. . . ."

At 7:40 AM, Nydia Vargas Perez served her husband a cup of black coffee and a slice of dry toast. Dr. Hector Perez had already showered, shaved, brushed his teeth, changed into a fresh suit. He sipped the coffee with trembling hands, his mouth still dry with fear. She'd asked how the convention had gone the night before. He told her it had been dull, but that a bunch of doctors had sat up late in the lounge discussing how one-man patrol cars lead to police stress, ulcers, sick leaves, and overtime abuses. He hadn't wanted to disturb her when he got home around 1 AM, so he sacked out on the couch.

Nydia barely listened as she rushed into the bathroom and retched with morning sickness. Perez tried to comfort his wife, but all he could think of was the dead woman.

After splashing her face and catching her breath, Nydia walked her husband to the door, kissed him good-bye, and was surprised at the enthusiasm of his embrace. "I adore you," he said, as he rubbed her rotund belly. *"Te adoro . . ."*

Then, crossing the Ninth Street Bridge over the infamous Gowanus Canal, named after an ancient Indian chief and now often used to dump whacked Mafia chieftains, Dr. Perez drove his Lexus 300 down to the Red Hook projects, where he had been born and raised. It was just a ten-minute ride but a social continent away from his brownstone block in Park Slope. The Red Hook projects were the second-largest public housing complex in the nation, marooned between the Gowanus Expressway and the moribund Brooklyn waterfront. The area was a forgotten urban asteroid, lost in its own orbit of deep shadows and high unemployment, fatherless children, rampant drugs, and the crackling automatic weapons of the night.

It bothered Dr. Perez that this wasteland felt more like home than his brownstone.

He knew from a lifetime of experience that the projects' trash was compacted at exactly 8:15 AM every morning and quickly hauled away to prevent roaches, mice, and rats from feeding on it and the homeless from tearing it apart in search of redeemable bottles and cans. If he shoved the pillowcase with the blood evidence down the building trash chute into the compacting room by 8:05 AM, it would be compressed with a ton of other garbage and on its way to the Staten Island landfill by noon, never to be seen again.

He pulled off Columbia Street behind the projects and walked to the rear of the car. With his left hand he clicked the remote, which automatically opened the Lexus trunk. The late-summer early-morning wind was blowing off the harbor, where Lady Liberty looked close enough to scratch. Dr. Perez peered both ways to be certain he was not seen and reached into the trunk to grab the pillowcase.

It was not there.

The trunk was empty and suddenly so was Dr. Hector Perez's future.

Bobby waited anxiously for Gleason's return. His head was pounding with echoes of the steel drum and Gleason's "get out of jail" pitch. Bobby was considering the alternative; there wasn't one.

Gleason reappeared, sipping a can of diet Coke, eating a bag of Raisinets, torching a new cigarette to life.

"Look, okay, I read the file," said Gleason. "The Brooklyn DA's office, FBI, INS, and Interpol were unable to track any birth, family, school, police, or passport records of your girlfriend, Dorothea Dubrow, in the Ukraine, where *you* said *she* said she was from. No record of anyone with her name in Russia, Poland, East Germany, or any of the other former Soviet bloc countries."

"They said the ashes contained DNA," Bobby said.

"Yeah, but she has no medical records or history here in the United States to match it against. The authorities—local, Feds,

Interpol—believe she was using an alias. This Dorothea Dubrow dame of yours, she's a complete enigma.''

"It blew my mind when this came out at trial,'' Bobby said. "All I know is that when I met her, she had been in the country a few months, was living with a girl named Sandy Fraser. Maybe Dorothea's vague background explains why she always avoided setting a wedding date. Maybe she was already married. Maybe she was on the lam. I just don't know.''

"You're missing the point,'' Gleason said. "How can they say you *killed* a woman who doesn't fucking exist?''

"The blood in my apartment,'' Bobby said. "The same as the blood in my car . . .''

"That could be anyone's blood,'' Gleason says. "If they can't prove it was the blood of this cipher named Dorothea Dubrow, where's your motive? There is none. If they can't connect that blood or those ashes to you, this case holds no water.''

"Yeah, and so . . .''

"And so,'' Gleason said, reaching into his inside jacket pocket and removing a sloppily folded, chocolate-smeared sheath of fax papers. "So . . . I almost forgot . . . So, last week I sort of went into the court of appeals, and with your brother Patrick's power of attorney, I filed a brief for a new trial based on lack of evidence and motive.'' He stuffed a Tootsie Roll into his mouth and tried desperately to get it mashed into a manageable wad. Bobby watched him unclog the words from the brown mass in his mouth as Gleason handed him the fax papers. Bobby unfolded them, felt them tremble in his fingers as he saw the seal of the New York State Court of Appeals on the top of the legal document.

Gleason finally said, "This was all done early this morning to avoid a press circus. It just came over the fax. Your conviction has been set aside, and there will be a new trial. You'll be processed out of this shit bucket in less than an hour.''

4

Bobby sauntered with a renewed bounce in his step on his way back up the metal stairs on his last walk to his cell, his final subjection to the banging of the steel.

"Slow down, Emmet," said Morrison the hack. "You're still state property until I get the release papers."

When they reached the tier to walk back to his solitary-confinement cell, it was the middle of the morning lockout, and Bobby passed the immense, silent, glaring Bluto character.

"Morrison, can I talk to you a minute," said Bluto.

Morrison paused in front of Bluto's cell and said, "Get back to your cell and start packing, Emmet. I'll be a sec."

Bobby's and Bluto's eyes met like ice cubes in the same small dirty glass. Bobby held the frozen stare for a long moment. "Move it," Morrison said. Bobby broke the stare and proceeded down the gauntlet of prisoners, who mingled in knots and cliques, smoking and scratching their balls, bullshitting, telling recycled crime stories that predated the Internet.

As Bobby resumed his shoulders-back, chest-out, stomach-in parade down the tier, he saw tension suddenly move from one set of eyes to another, like the rattling of delft before an earthquake. He saw the tattooed ape who had made the vile remarks about his daughter, huddled with his back to him, saw him suddenly spin to face him, a sharpened metal spoon in his hairy right hand. He also saw the black man who had spit on him, saw him step quickly from his opened cell and produce another crude jailhouse shank. Now a third guy, with the mixed-blood features of all the races of the hybrid city of New York—what they called in here a "whorehouse baby"—started walking briskly his way from a distance of five feet, a pointed deadly stick sliding down from his shirtsleeve.

All conversations stopped at once, and an eerie, breath-bated silence fell on the prison corridor, the way the dimming lights in a theater bring a sudden hush just before show time.

Bobby could hear a faint muffled scuffle from behind him. Then he saw Morrison struggling to free himself from the grip of two prisoners, and at that same moment Bobby felt a set of massive arms bear-hug him from behind, two white hands the size of prime ribs clamping together at his sternum. *Bluto,* Bobby thought. *Worry about the ones who say nothing. . . .*

Now Tatoo grinned at him. Bobby blew him a kiss, and the other two snarled, nostrils flaring. *Control,* Bobby thought. *Think, don't panic. I'm better than these mutts. I can't let these lowlives take my life. Not now! I'm getting* out! *I'm gonna see Maggie. I'm going* home *and these cocksuckers are gonna try to kill me . . .*

When in doubt, go for the balls, he thought.

Straining his right arm, he was able to wiggle his probing right hand behind him like a backhoe. He groped until he located Bluto's balls and squeezed them like a fist full of ripe peaches, twisting until Bluto's scream exploded in his ear and echoed through the cellblock.

Then, as the three cons lunged at Bobby, he steered Bluto in front of him by the balls, the way he would a bull by a nose ring. As the three attackers lunged, Bobby yoked his left arm around Bluto's throat and used him as a human shield just as the three attacking cons thrust at him with their crude shanks. The weapons entered Bluto's neck, chest, abdomen, making wet plunging noises. Bobby felt a spasm with each impact. Now the tier was alive with shrill jailhouse screams, whistles, and war whoops, which resembled, Bobby thought, what Purgatory must sound like on Halloween night. With his free hand, Bobby quickly grabbed Tattoo by the left ear, violently whipped his face toward him, and met him halfway with his own head. The impact made a sound like a watermelon falling off a roof to the street, and Tattoo collapsed in a spray of blood. Little ticking noises coming from his throat.

The black man with the bloodied shiv made another lunge at him, and this time Bobby used his massive upper-body strength to heave the bleeding Bluto at him, using him as a battering ram. Bluto collapsed on top of the attacker, pinning him to the floor, a man trapped under a boulder. Bobby kicked him once in the left temple, and his eyes rolled back in his head like a doll's.

The whorehouse baby jumped into his own cell and slammed the door shut with a loud clang. Bobby reached through the bars, grabbed a handful of his hair, and pulled him face-first into the space between the bars, crushing both his cheekbones. The astonished con dissolved to the cell floor like a spreading stain.

Bobby heard the hacks charging, shouting for the cons to return to their cells. Then he heard muffled whispers from Bluto. Bobby crouched and turned him over to listen. Bluto lay on the dirty cellblock floor, gasping and hemorrhaging, his torso a palette of blood.

"You a bad dude," the big man wheezed. "But they gonna get you outside if not here."

"Who?" Bobby said.

"Big people, important people. You bad for bizniz. Only reason I tell you is I respec' that you never dimed inside. Word is, no matter how many beatins in whichever joint, you never dimed. But you're still a fuckin' pig. Now, tell these muddafuckuhs to get me some needle and thread 'fore I die all over the fuckin' floor. You, you're no rat. But you just bad for bizniz. And they gonna git you. . . ."

Bobby looked up and saw a flying wedge of hacks with riot helmets and Plexiglas shields and batons at the ready storming down the tier. Bobby lay down flat, clasped his hands behind his head, and was soon picked up under the arms and dragged on his boot tips down the tier and heaved into his cell. The door slammed shut. For the last time. In less than an hour, Bobby Emmet was going home, where he was most certainly going to be "bad for bizniz."

5

Dr. Benjamin Abrams sat at his large oak desk in his office at the NYPD Medical Board at 1 Lefrak Plaza in Rego Park, Queens, as bright morning sun lanced through half-shut window blinds.

It was 8:45 AM.

Dr. Abrams, a tall, elegant-looking man who was finally losing his proud mane of silver hair at age fifty-one, was going through a stack of police medical-pension applications when Dr. Hector Perez, the new doctor on the medical board, entered the offices. Perez nodded hello to Ms. Burns, the slightly sour, middle-aged civil-service receptionist.

When Dr. Perez walked past Dr. Abrams's open door, he looked ashen and fatigued, shiny with perspiration. Unlike every other Monday and Thursday morning when the medical board met, the young doctor had not even said hello, just stopped to unlock his office door.

"You have a package, Doctor," Dr. Abrams said.

Dr. Perez nervously picked up a thick package bearing a sticker marked URGENT. A little more than a half hour earlier, before Ms. Burns had arrived at 8:10 AM, her usual ten minutes late, Dr. Abrams had signed for the messenger delivery.

Dr. Abrams had taken special notice that the parcel had no return address. A parcel that felt as if it contained a videotape, just like the one he had received two years ago.

All three doctors' offices had TV sets with VCR units, for viewing the latest video pitches from the technology and pharmaceutical companies and taping the news shows that were pertinent to their jobs. But Dr. Abrams could remember only one other videotape that had ever arrived without a return address and was marked URGENT. That one had borne *his* name.

At 9 AM Dr. Abrams stared at his TV screen, looking for clues on the twenty-four-hour all-news TV station. The newscaster mentioned briefly that the body of a murdered woman, suspected of being a prostitute, was found in a hotel room in the Hotel St. Claire. Dr. Abrams knew that the night before the St. Claire had been the site of a convention of the American Association of Police Physicians. He had not accepted their invitation to attend. The last convention he'd gone to had been in Boston two years earlier. The parallels were frightening.

He glanced across the hall into Dr. Perez's office, where pictures of the doctor's beautiful wife and various diplomas and awards decorated the walls. He knew that Dr. Perez had been at last night's gala, so Dr. Abrams had a disturbing idea as to why the young doctor did not look like a happy camper this morning.

Dr. Abrams continued sorting through the paperwork on his desk as if his life depended on it. Which it did. As he had for the past two years, Dr. Abrams separated out those medical-pension applications with a small number 91 penciled onto the upper right-hand corner of the first page. He arranged these in a neat stack on the right-hand side of his desk and dropped all the others in a loose pile on the left. He knew which ones he would approve and which ones he'd reject without even reading them for merit.

Then Dr. Abrams unscrewed the cap of the Montblanc pen. It had been given to him by his now fifteen-year-old daughter, Rebecca, one Father's Day. She was a straight-A student at Dalton and wanted to be a doctor like her dad. He always used his daughter's pen to sign his signature on all the specially coded "91" applications, to remind him of the shame that she would suffer if he did not approve these petitions.

He flashed back to that morning two years ago. Another dead woman. Another package. Marked URGENT. A video clearly showing Dr. Abrams, in a Boston hotel room, sitting up naked in a bloodstained bed, holding a straight razor and hovering over the nude body of a hooker, with three shiny quarters in her open palm, each dated 1991.

The morning after a convention of police doctors in Boston. A murder still unsolved and mostly forgotten. But his blackmailer knew that murder has no statute of limitations. And so Dr. Abrams had been signing his approval signature on the specially coded NYPD medical-pension forms ever since, as instructed.

He looked at the stack on the right-hand side of his desk. There were a few dozen backlogged "91" applications. Full approval of a pension required the signatures of two of the three NYPD doctors. Once you had two, the third doctor always rubber-stamped his approval; easier to join 'em than to fight 'em. Although they had never discussed it, Abrams knew from a simple process of elimination that the second signature on the "91s" had always been supplied by Dr. Frederick Jones, a prominent Harlem physician who had been given this prestigious job by a previous mayor as a payback for his support in the black community.

Then the system was disrupted. Jones was killed in an automobile accident three months ago on the Saw Mill River Parkway, coming into the city in a torrential rainstorm. The "91" applications had piled up, and Abrams had been wondering who the lucky replacement would be.

Dr. Perez appeared in his office door, his face as white as a hockey mask, mumbling about something he ate. But before he left, he asked if there were any applications he should peruse.

Abrams looked him in the stunned eyes. He picked up the thick pile of applications with the "91" codes. "Actually, these look like they need to be expedited," Abrams said. "We're more than a little behind. . . ."

Dr. Perez took the applications and pretended to examine them. His fingers left damp imprints on the crisp pages. He swallowed dryly, grimacing. He blinked twice, and from his suit jacket pocket he produced a gold Mark Cross pen given to him by Nydia to celebrate his appointment to the NYPD Medical Board.

"Nice pen," Dr. Abrams said as Perez signed the forms.

6

Outside the prison gates Gleason handed Bobby a pair of Ray-Ban sunglasses and said, "Hurry up before the fuckin' press descends like seagulls after a Puerto Rican picnic."

"Okay, Izzy, so what do I owe you for you helping me?" Bobby asked, trotting after Gleason, who power-walked across the parking lot. Out of the corner of his eye Bobby noticed a white Ford Taurus parked on the opposite side of the parking lot and saw a long telephoto lens pop out and point in his direction. Then the lens disappeared back behind a partially open tinted window. "You must have an agenda, Izzy; what do I have to do?"

"A little indentured servitude," Gleason said with a wicked smile as the two men hurried toward Gleason's dark blue Jeep Cherokee. "See, the only big cases I ever lost are the ones where *you* collected the evidence against *my* clients. If I have you working for me, I figure I can't lose. I estimate that my complete comeback—to get clients, do investigations, schedule trials, get on the calendars, grease the ·press—will take two years. So, if I get you off this rap, in return, for those two years, you work for *me*. To pay off the legal work I do for *you*. How's it sound so far?"

"Awful, which is heaven compared to life in there," Bobby said.

"I'll provide you with a place to live, an office, wheels, a living allowance plus ten percent of my fee on any case you do investigative work on. You'll have your freedom. You'll see your kid, and I'll defend you in the new trial. Better, with you investigating your own case, I can almost *guarantee* I'll walk you on all charges."

Bobby was feeling excited, his heart thumping with optimism. Then he saw the same long lens reappear from the window of the car on the other side of the lot. "I won't help you defend certain clients, like child molesters," Bobby said. "Or serial killers, drug lords . . . Izzy, you see that white Taurus? Someone is taking pictures of us."

Bobby pointed at the car, and when Gleason looked, it pulled slowly away, turned a corner, and was blocked from view by a collection of two-story administrative buildings.

"Could be a tabloid asshole," Gleason said, kicking a stone as he walked with his hands in his pants pockets. "Let's get moving."

"About these lowlife clients you represent, Izzy . . ."

"Look, in my comeback, I'm thinking of representing more respectable clients," Gleason said, pointing at Bobby. "Like killer cops."

"Cheap shot," Bobby said.

"Yeah, well, you're living proof that sometimes people are wrongly accused. But remember, good lawyers usually make a living defending bad people. So don't get moral on me again. If you need righteousness, remember every client has the constitutional right to a defense. Pretend you're doing it for God, country, the Founding Fathers, blah, blah, blah. And never forget what 'The People' did to you, asshole."

Bobby nodded. "I can walk away from a case I find too reprehensible?"

"Only after you look into it objectively," Gleason said, doing a pirouette, without breaking stride. "Jesus Christ, but you're a picky fuck for a jailbird."

"The deal sounds fair," Bobby said, keeping pace with Gleason.

"Fuck fair," Gleason said. "This is *business*. 'Fair' is someplace you win blue ribbons at for apple pies. 'Fair' is a schoolyard fight without knives. 'Fair' is a two fifty hitter. In a courtroom, a *fair* defense means a prison sentence or the electric chair. So fuck 'fair.' Part of my new act is I still gotta eat, and 'fair' is fuckin' *famine.*"

"What else should I know?"

"Like I said, personally, I think your first lawyer did an Olympic swan dive off the high board," Gleason said, stopping to light a cigarette. "Into an empty pool. There's also a new political climate blowing."

He blew out a long stream of smoke for emphasis. He watched it scatter in the country breeze and said, "This is a gubernatorial election year, and there's a fresh-faced Republican candidate named Gerald Stone running for the statehouse. That primary is thirteen days away."

"Stone . . . I vaguely remember him," Bobby said. "Councilman?"

"Yeah, law-and-order asshole out of Staten Island. Handsome, Vietnam war hero, a real Mr. Family Values. He's got the backing of the toughest power brokers in the city and state. Wall Street loves him, and the polls say the people do, too. They say if he pulls this off, he could eventually grin his way right into the fuckin' White House."

"What the hell does any of this got to do with me?" Bobby asked, feeling silly and out of touch, as they paused before entering the Jeep.

"One of Stone's first and loudest supporters is Sol Diamond," Gleason said, and Bobby's heart sank at the mention of the Brooklyn district attorney whose office prosecuted him. "And since you went away, Cis Tuzio, the assistant district attorney who personally prosecuted you, got promoted to chief assistant district attorney. Your case gave her the bump. If Stone gets nominated and elected, she could get a state supreme court judgeship from him, and Diamond could get appointed to the state appeals court."

"Democracy sure hasn't changed in my absence," Bobby said.

"That's the good news," Gleason said. "The bad news is that Diamond is outraged about your release and has already issued another arrest warrant. I just answered it by phone with the judge's clerk. Stone will probably drag your name into the final days of the primary race. Cis Tuzio is so livid she's going to personally prosecute you all over again. Her political future rests on putting you back inside. I already anticipated that she would ask for a ridiculously high bail, pending trial. More good news. I went panhandling and I secured the quarter-mil bail from an angel who prefers to remain anonymous."

"Don't tell me it's a drug lord or a wise-guy client putting up my bail," said Bobby.

"I'm on a comeback, you jerkoff," Gleason said. "Not a suicide mission. Far's I know, he's as clean as a monk's asshole."

"Jesus Christ, Gleason," Bobby said. "What do I say? How do I call a toad a prince without having to kiss him?"

"Fuck you, too. Well, deal or what?"

"Where do I sign?"

"Uh-uh," Gleason said. "Legal documents can be broken. I want something better than that from you. See, I know you, Emmet, and you're from the Brooklyn streets with a ridiculous, romantic sense of gutter honor—man of his word, and all that cornball corner-boy horseshit. So if you're gonna make a deal with me, I don't want it in writing. I want a fuckin' handshake, your word on your street-honor. This way if you welch, I put it on the street you reneged and your word ain't shit."

"And you think people would take your word over mine?" Bobby said.

"Give it to me, and I can help you straighten out your fucked-up life, if you help me do the same with mine. It won't always be nice or pleasant, and you'll probably hate me more often than you like me. And get it straight: I own at least one of your nuts and half your time. But I can keep you out of here for good, back home with your kid. Back out where you can prove your innocence. Get back your rep. Where you can find out what happened to your dame. All that good shit. Or you can come back here and die. Now, do we have a fucking deal or what?"

Gleason wiped his hand on his pants leg, leaving speed stripes of chocolate on the expensive suit, and held it out.

"Deal," Bobby Emmet said, shaking his hand.

7

Bobby sat next to Izzy in the backseat of the Jeep Cherokee as a silent, overweight Hispanic woman named Venus drove south from the state prison to the New York State Thruway.

Bobby looked over his shoulder and saw the white Ford Taurus tailing them.

He rolled down the Jeep's tinted window and feasted on the

hot, clean country air of late summer as they passed pastures of grazing cattle, farmers driving slow-moving tractors, and fields of bundled hay. Soon it would be fall, the dying season, he thought, the season of the witch.

Occasionally Bobby looked over his shoulder and saw the Taurus following at a discreet distance, a steady white termite munching the road behind them. He kept thinking about Bluto, the big wounded con, talking of big people who wanted him dead.

"Car's following us," Bobby told Gleason. Gleason turned, and the Taurus disappeared from view in a turn in the road.

"You'll be paranoid awhile," Gleason said. "But it's a free country, and we got us a ninety-minute ride. We'll be in the city by ten-thirty, quarter to eleven. Just fuckin' relax."

"I'm free, going home to see my kid, and already I'm being tailed," Bobby said.

"You spent your life tailing people," Gleason said. "Now the fuckin' gumshoe is on the other foot. Deal with it. Unless he starts shooting, don't worry about it."

"It's gonna be a *long* day, with a checklist of people I have to see," Bobby said. "I've waited a long time for this day. And, hey, Izzy, you think it's right to curse in front of the lady like that?"

"Venus is Dominican, five three, twelve, maybe fifteen pounds overweight, only speaks Spanish," Gleason said. "She doesn't understand word fuckin' one of English. This here way, you don't have to watch your fuckin' lingo in front of her. It's like having a human V chip."

"Let me get this straight," Bobby said. "She works for you, but she can't speak English? And you can't speak any Spanish?"

"*Sí,*" Gleason said, "*señor.*"

Venus laughed uproariously, glancing at Bobby in the rearview mirror. She had beautiful pearl-white teeth, flawless nutmeg-colored skin, and gold earrings that sparkled in the sun that blazed in through the side window.

Bobby looked over at Izzy Gleason and realized that the next time he was in a courtroom, his life would be in the hands of a madman. But if someone was following him right now, he wanted to be in *control.*

"Izzy, ask Venus to pull over, will ya?" Bobby said. "I want to drive."

"Venus," Gleason shouted, pointing to the shoulder of the road. "Pull-o over-o."

"*Sí, Señor* Eeezee."

At the Newburg tollbooth, Bobby grabbed the ticket for the thruway south. Gleason was next to him in the passenger seat. Bobby looked in the rearview mirror, searching for a white Taurus. All he saw was Venus sitting in the back wearing headphones, listening to English/Spanish audiotapes Gleason had bought for her. *Inglés Sin Barreras*—"English Without Barriers."

"You sure she can't understand English?" Bobby asked.

"*Nada.*"

"Then what does she do for you?"

"She's losing weight," Gleason said.

"She's losing weight?" Bobby said, nodding. "So . . . you pay her by the hour or the pound for this?"

"See, I like my women a little imperfect," Gleason said. "I'm gonna send her to a fat farm where she'll fast for a week or so and study the English tapes. When she's finished, drops twelve or fifteen pounds, learns some English, she's the perfect gal Friday. I help her improve herself, assimilate into the American Dream. She'll be as loyal as a religious convert. An Izzyette. There used to be legions of them in the good old days. In the end, with a little investment, I'll have a great-looking, well-educated, loyal worker for the new millennium."

"I'm catching on to your game," Bobby said. "You get a jammed-up ex-cop to do investigations for you and an indebted, slimmed-down fat girl to take dictation. On your lap?"

"Or my face, but that would be impractical," Gleason said, grinning. "Until *after* she loses the weight."

"Jesus Christ . . ."

"Get a sense of humor to go with the fuckin' merit badge, will ya, Emmet? Meanwhile, since I have no driver's license, thanks to three DUIs, she drives me around. I pay her. This is evil?"

"With what money?" Bobby asked, and now here came the Taurus, filling his side-view mirror, about a thousand feet behind him. "By the way, the tail is back."

"I told you, I'm a lawyer, not a shamus," Gleason said. "I already got fifty large in advances from clients."

"Any of these clients legit?"

"Christ, I hope not, or they won't be steady customers. Meatball cases. Assault, gun rap, tax evasion, divorce—shit like that. Can't be picky yet. In fact, I'll need your help on a few. But we'll talk about that later. And forget being tailed and *my* woman. Right now, we're gonna use this drive home for you to tell me all about your girl. . . ."

"Dorothea?"

Bobby made a sudden swerve to the shoulder of the road. Gleason grabbed the dashboard as Bobby braked. The white Taurus accelerated and passed them doing eighty.

"John David Francis . . ." Bobby said aloud.

"You losing your marbles?" Gleason asked. "Talkin' to the saints while you're driving . . ."

"JDF, those were the first three letters of the license plate," Bobby said. "I'm out of practice, and he was moving too fast to get the whole plate. I'm gonna chase that bastard."

"Do that, and we'll get pulled over," Gleason said. "And you said you had people to see. Calm down. We don't need attention."

Venus did not seem at all bothered by the commotion, just sat with her eyes closed, mouthing the new English words: "Boy, ball, bleach . . ."

"You know how many white Tauruses there are in New York State?" Gleason asked Bobby. "How do you know it's the same one?"

"I know," Bobby said and slid back onto the road.

Gleason stuffed half an Almond Joy into his mouth.

"How can you eat all that shit?" Bobby asked.

"I'm a sweetheart and a lover, so I think of it as every day is Valentine's Day," Gleason said. "And it makes me fuck like an Easter bunny. I don't know why I crave it. I just got a sweet gene. If I don't eat candy, I start gnawing at the walls of my mouth until they bleed. I am trying to cut down, though. That's why I started smoking again."

"You started smoking to cut down on your candy habit?" Bobby asked, incredulous.

"It's a toss between diabetes and emphysema," Gleason said. "I'm trying to strike a balance. If I can get down to a dozen candy bars and two packs of smokes a day, I think I can find a safe middle ground, live to seventy."

"You ever see a doctor?"

"I went through the whole tune-up, the full physical at the Strang Clinic, and they said I'm fit as a horse," Gleason said.

"I meant a shrink," Bobby said.

"Only as expert witnesses," Gleason said.

Bobby looked at him and blinked. Gleason fired another Almond Joy torpedo into his mouth. *"Bon appétit, Izzy,"* Bobby said. "But chew on this—I'm out an hour and already we're being followed. I don't like it."

"Get used to it," Gleason said. "Gotta be a reporter. . . ."

"How'd they know I was getting out?" Bobby asked, still not trusting Gleason.

"The appeal moved through the courts! No atomic secret, chrissakes. Maybe it's a fuckin' DA's tail, because Cis Tuzio is gonna come after you like she just grew kryptonite balls. Plus the same stooges who set you up before, they might try framing you again. For whacking someone else. This time they might just take you out, period. See, they didn't whack you before because you were a cop. Killing a cop brings big heat. Framing you was better. But you're not a cop anymore. If someone whacks you now, you're just a dead ex-con, shit on the city's shoes. Who gives a fiddler's fuck? So you better carry a piece."

"You know I lost my carry license," Bobby said.

"This time around you're gonna have to think like a cop," Gleason said, "and act like a con."

"I have a checklist," Bobby said. "I have to see Sandy Fraser, Dorothea's friend and old roommate, and find out everything I don't know about Dorothea. I hear she works for a guy named Lou Barnicle, who I think masterminded my frame. I want to know why she's working for him and everything she knows about Dorothea. I want to see my old friend John Shine for some advice and to see what he's heard on the tom-tom's about my case and Lou Barnicle and Dorothea. . . ."

"I know who Shine is," Gleason said. "Good cop."

"I want to find the guy who *found* the body in the crematorium. He must know *something*. Moira Farrell never even subpoenaed him because she thought his testimony would be too gruesome for the jury. I want to pay *her* a visit, too. I gotta look up Tom Larkin, an old cop who was my father's friend, because he knows how to get background information on people inside the NYPD better than anyone. And I'm gonna confront this Cis Tuzio face-to-face. I'm gonna find out why I was framed and why they're trying to kill me. I'm—"

"Hold on, Kemosabe," Gleason said. "You're going too fast for me. Pull Trigger here over at the next rest stop. We need gas, and I don't think too good on an empty stomach."

8

As Venus gassed up the Jeep, Bobby and Gleason ate burgers and fries at McDonald's. Gleason probed Bobby for particulars about how he met Dorothea, their relationship, their plans, how he could not have known that her identity was a mystery. A secret. Or a lie.

"I want details," Gleason said. "If God didn't like details so much, he wouldn't have made so many of them. It's how I choose my women and how I win my cases."

"I'll give you details," Bobby said, biting into a Big Mac and then taking a long drink of orange juice, thinking it had never tasted so good before. "I went over them every day for a year and a half."

"Details leading to the arrest first," Gleason said, opening his Quarter Pounder, dumping half a bag of fries on top of the burger, and placing the bun back on top. His mouth opened wide and snapped down on the sandwich like a bear trap.

Gleason said he also wanted Bobby to form a list of the people he thought he could count on back in the city. And, of course, a list of his enemies. A menu of white hats and black hats and the gray hats who could be used but not fully trusted. "When your life is on the line," Gleason explained, "you can usually count all your true friends in the world by cupping your balls. But lucky people like you might have a few real friends. Most, as

33

you already know from working the other side of the fence, are mutts. Ninety-nine percent of the human race is disappointing."

Bobby laughed. Nothing like becoming a jammed-up cop to teach you that. After he was arrested only three cops stayed in touch with him—John Shine, Tom Larkin, and his kid brother, Patrick. Everyone else avoided him as if he had a flesh-eating bacterium.

"I met Dorothea a little less than two years ago, not long after the divorce," Bobby said. "I was with Shine, who was my training officer when I got on the job. It was at a Christmas party for Brooklyn South Narcotics—where I used to work before going to the Manhattan DA's squad. I had been working on an anonymous tip I received in the mail at the Manhattan DA's office, about an extortion racket involving police medical pensions. The note said the racket was based in Brooklyn, but that some cops were actually paying to get their phony papers approved. I didn't know if it was a crank or not, but I'd heard rumors of it before. So I thought it wouldn't hurt to sniff around at the party, where people would be drinking, tongues wagging—holiday season."

"Biggest loudmouths in the world are cops with a few in 'em," Gleason said.

"That girl I told you about, Sandy Fraser, who worked at the police medical office, showed up at this party and brought Dorothea with her. The whole place seemed to stop at once when Dorothea walked in. She looked out of place. Exotic. Held her head high, shoulders back, like someone who came out of a proud history, a heritage. Different than the relaxed, slouchy style of the women of Brooklyn, especially the policewomen . . ."

"The Dunkin' Donuts Dumper Department," Gleason said. "I never met a policewoman that you couldn't show Panavision movies on her ass after two years on the job."

"That's a cliché," said Bobby. "A lot of them are knockouts. But Dorothea would not have looked right in a police uniform. She didn't even fit into the room, with her long-legged sophisticated walk, big dark eyes, a mane of thick, wavy black hair, full lips, a *Sports Illustrated* swimsuit body . . ."

"I said details, not the whole wet dream," Gleason said.

"I'd just come out of the men's room, where I heard these two ex-cops named Kuzak and Zeke, from a private-snoop firm called Gibraltar Security, talking about the police medical-pension fund. At the urinals, Kuzak and Zeke were asking a cop named O'Brien, who had about ten years on the job, what it would be worth to him to get out on an early disability pension. At first it sounded like idle piss-house banter. O'Brien laughed, said he'd pay a year's salary to get a lifetime three-quarters pension. Then Kuzak mentioned a retired police captain named Lou Barnicle, who I always suspected was dirty—a greedy, brazen, mean, rat bastard. Zeke began checking stalls, and when they saw me, they dummied up fast. Kuzak, a big, tall, muscular guy, not exactly a genius, changes the conversation by saying, 'So what about them Mets . . .' It's December and he's asking about the Mets. The cop they were propositioning, O'Brien was his name—"

"You said that already," Gleason said. "Details, not reruns, I don't forget anything. Ever. Except maybe broads' names. . . ."

"O'Brien was a guy I used to work with in Brooklyn South. He wasn't going to write any dissertations on the missing link of evolution either. We were never pals, but maybe O'Brien knew I worked at the Manhattan DA's office. That's not considered as bad as Internal Affairs, but I'm not a cop's kosher meal either. He saw me and bolted. Kuzak and Zeke just glared at me when I stepped out of the stall. I didn't say a word, made believe I was preoccupied, disinterested."

"These the guys you think set you up later, maybe?" Gleason asked, mumbling through his burger.

"I think so," Bobby said. "Anyway, I go out to the party room, where a band is playing, and I walk directly to John Shine to let him know what I heard. To get a read from him, because he's not your ordinary numb-nuts beat cop. He was my training officer and has better radar than an air-traffic controller. Maybe he thinks it's a bullshit scam, not worth a full investigation. I want to bounce it off him. But when I start telling him, he's distracted, transfixed, like half the guys at the party. Because here comes Sandy from the medical office, looking hot as one of Victoria's Secrets herself. But she's laughing and talking and walking with this . . . this *goddess!* This Dorothea, dressed in a clinging mini-dress. The lead singer fumbled the words of the song. I mean, this wasn't an entrance. It was an *event*. Dorothea didn't mean it to be; it just came with the genes. She was out of place, like Sophia Loren walking into a laundromat. Half the women in

35

the room would have liked to shoot her on the spot for feloni-
ous perfection."

"Or bedded her," Gleason said. "How many broad cops you
figure are moes?"

"John Shine bet me I couldn't get a date with her," Bobby
said, ignoring Gleason. "I had a few cocktails in me, was feeling
my beer balls. I was missing Connie and Maggie something terrible. I knew the worst this dream-in-a-dress could do was say no.
The divorce was much worse than any rejection this woman could
give me. Plus I would have regretted not trying for the rest of
my life. And John bet me; he was egging me on."

"I told ya, I know who John Shine is," Gleason said. "One of
the toughest cops I ever cross-examined. Confident, unflappable,
straight. A defense lawyer's nightmare. Know why? Because he's
one of those rare cops who always tells the fuckin' *truth* on the
stand."

"Johnny Shine ruined his health on the job," Bobby said,
"screwed up four disks in his back, wrestling with a crack dealer.
He was always in pain. But he never complained, kept working.
He helped get me my transfer to the Harbor Unit. Then I made
detective and transferred to the Manhattan DA's squad. We sort
of lost touch. But sometimes the world is perfect. Three years
ago, Shine won the goddamn New York State Lottery for three
million bucks. He retired from the job, opened up a saloon out
in Bay Ridge, but didn't forget where he came from. Later, he
loaned me money for my defense. He offered to help pay for an
appeal, but I couldn't let him throw good money after bad."

"So Shine made you a bet about Dorothea . . ."

"Yeah, so I forgot all about why I was there, about Kuzak and
Zeke and O'Brien and the pension-racket rumor. I walked right
up to Sandy and asked her to introduce me to Dorothea. She
did, and we danced a fast one, a slow one, and sat out the next
one at the bar together," Bobby said as they slowly walked to the
Jeep, his eyes searching the area for the elusive white Taurus. "I
asked her out to dinner the next night. She asked what I had in
the fridge. I told her leftover pasta. She said she'd love some of
that, so we stopped at a liquor store and she bought a bottle of
expensive French wine . . ."

"Oy!" Gleason shouted, fumbling for a smoke. "A first
nighter!"

"I took her home, we drank half a glass each, skipped the pasta, made love all night, and she never left. I gave her my keys when I went to work in the morning, and when I came home, she had unpacked two of her suitcases. She said she had been staying with Sandy, was taking courses at the School of Visual Arts in photography a few days a week. Other than that, she was vague about her life, her background, family, friends. Said Sandy was her only friend in New York. I liked the idea that she was a loner. I was needy. Greedy. Possessive. I didn't want to let her out of my sight. I was afraid someone was going to kidnap her, take her away from me. Not only did I fall in love with her right away, I *wanted* to. I needed to replace Connie. I didn't ask questions about who Dorothea was—until later. It didn't seem to matter. She was beautiful, sweet, smarter than me, better educated, better read . . ."

"Didn't you bother, between rolls in the hay, to ask her who the hell she was?" Gleason asked. "At least proof her for age?"

Bobby paused and stared at Gleason, shook his head, and climbed back into the Jeep, which was parked over by a rank of public telephones. Venus sat in the backseat mouthing the new English words. "Baby, bottle, bird . . ." Gleason handed her a plain salad and water. "Here's your shrubbery, hon, *mangia,*" Gleason said.

"Gracias," said Venus, who began picking at the salad.

"Your welcome-o," Gleason said.

Bobby looked from one to the other, shaking his head, then started the car and pulled back out onto the highway.

"Whenever I did ask Dorothea her background, she'd change the subject—politics, law, history, literature, art, music, fashion, dance, movies, theater, opera, cities, countries I never even heard of," Bobby continued as they moved back into southbound traffic. "Dorothea spoke flawless English and French, some Italian and Spanish, and her native Ukrainian, Russian, Polish, and a few others. She said her mother had been brilliant and taught her all the languages and about world politics and the arts. But she also said her mother had lived a terrible, sad life. As an outcast. That she had died the year before. I guessed the mother was some kind of political dissident back in the old country. I could never get Dorothea to elaborate."

"You were too busy hiding the salami," Gleason said.

37

"She was too busy pleasing me, in a lot of ways," Bobby said, shooting Gleason a disgusted glance. "Dorothea even sat down and read a baseball rulebook because she knew I was a fan. What woman does that? She read through all my old copies of *Ring* magazine because I liked boxing. She even knew how to fix a car, Gleason. A car! I can just about change a friggin' flat, and she can get under the hood, elbow deep in grease. She was the most complete woman of the world I'd ever met. She could put together a gourmet meal in twenty minutes, with veal and mush-rooms and pasta and a salad of greens that I didn't even know grew on planet earth but she found growing wild in Prospect Park on some nature walk she read about on the Key Food bulle-tin board! The second day she was with me, I went to work, came home, and she had her hair in a babushka, was wearing one of my shirts tied at the waist—a woman in a man's shirt drives me crazy—"

"Oh, yeah!" shouted Gleason, interrupting Bobby. "Especially if they wear red heels and thong panties and they bend over to pick up forty-seven cents you just happen to drop on the floor."

". . . She came in and she'd redecorated my entire apartment. It looked like something out of a magazine. My bachelor stuff, same eclectic clutter, rearranged and presented like one of her perfect meals. She took me over to little restaurants in Little Kiev in Alphabet City and ordered piroghis, lamb, borscht, caviar, vodka. She took me to the Ukrainian festival on Seventh Street, into these little Ukrainian saloons where men played cards and bet horses and spoke in whispers as if the KGB was outside the door. *She* showed *me* around *my* city! I was overwhelmed, swal-lowed whole. Then one day she took me into St. Peter's Church on Seventh Street, a gorgeous Ukrainian cathedral, and in front of the altar she looked me in the eyes and whispered, *'Ya tebe kohayu.'* I told her I loved her, too. I asked her to marry me. If I could have, I would have copyrighted her."

"I would have fuckin' *adopted* her," Gleason said, clearing his throat, growling.

"She said she *would* marry me," Bobby said, checking in the rearview mirror. "That Taurus is back."

Gleason turned and looked. "So? Just drive. Keep talking, I'm listening."

"Anyway, I could never get her to commit to a date," Bobby said. "I never doubted her story that she was raised by her outcast mother in the Ukraine. Or that after her mother's death, she came to New York a few months before I met her, on a possible exchange program. That she fell in love with New York and decided to stay. When I pressed her for more details or a marriage date, she simply got undressed and would make love to me and whisper passionately in my ear in a different language every time. I was becoming multilingual in sex!"

"Jesus, the most exotic I ever got was a Panamanian stripper from Washington Heights who used to call me 'Poppi' in the sack," Gleason said.

Venus leaned forward and said, *"Qué?"*

"Nada, sweetheart," Gleason said, waving his hand. *"Nada . . ."*

Venus smiled and sat back and listened to her tapes.

"She stole me, heart and soul, body and mind, inside out," Bobby said, not even hearing Gleason. "When I was with Dorothea, the world didn't seem dirty or corrupt at all. She was the perfect antidote to the job."

"Did she work, get mail, make long-distance phone calls?" Gleason asked.

"Not when she was with me."

"Where did a broad from a commie country get money?"

"She seemed to have plenty of money," Bobby said. "I didn't ask from where or how much. I thought that would be impolite. Especially since she wouldn't take any of mine. She offered to pay half the rent, bills, but—"

"You turned her down? Someone finally found one broad willing to pony up her half of life's fuckin' nut, and you turned her down?"

"Yeah," Bobby said.

"You set men back twenty fuckin' years," Gleason said. "The idea, dickhead, is to clone a broad who actually pays her own freight."

"My daughter, Maggie, who is more protective of me than I am of myself, liked Dorothea right away," Bobby said. "She thought she was perfect for me, and Maggie has a built-in bullshit detector, a human polygraph. Besides my daughter, Dorothea was my lifeline to humankind at its very best, as it's supposed to be. When they charged and convicted me of killing her, I was in a prolonged trance, too stunned at the horror of Dorothea's supposed murder to even comprehend the gravity of being charged with it. I was in jail for six months before I accepted that she wouldn't be coming to visit me.''

"Okay," Gleason said. "I get the picture. You had a storybook ten-week romance with a mystery dame, and you got Shine in your corner. Who else can you count on?"

Bobby told him more about the old cop named Tom Larkin, sixty-one years old, facing mandatory retirement in two years. Because of his age he was now the "house mouse" or "the broom" at the 72nd Precinct in Brooklyn, the glorified porter who swept up around the precinct. Since becoming the house mouse, Larkin had also become something of a computer wizard, surfing the Net and tapping into the NYPD and other law-enforcement databases on the sly. After years in the Stakeout Squad and then the Intelligence Unit, he was one of those nosy old coots who had a dossier on almost everyone on the force. Knew where skeletons were buried, who was banging whom, who took extra days off, who was claiming court appearances that were canceled. He was a human database.

Tom Larkin wasn't muscle, but he was smart, ballsy, and loyal. Larkin had also been there the day Bobby's father was killed in the line of duty.

"Good, we might need an old fuck like him," Gleason said.

Of course, Bobby also counted in his younger brother, Patrick, who ran the Brooklyn Police Athletic League, working with ghetto kids in sports and recreation programs. Bobby never let Patrick come to the trial as a spectator because he didn't want the press or the brass to make a show of him. Didn't want to contaminate him with his scandal.

"Your brother wrote me the letter asking me to look into your case," Gleason said. "Since you gave him power of attorney, he could sign all the documents for me. I know what you said on the stand. Now tell me again. What happened that night?"

"I was in this bar, called The Anchor, in Gerritsen Beach, ass end of Brooklyn, drinking beer with some guys I knew worked for Gibraltar Security. Kuzak and Zeke weren't there. Anyway, I'm working these guys when I see the young cop, O'Brien, the one I used to work with at Brooklyn South walk in. He's the one from the Christmas party. He sneers at me, like he knows something. Now, I always remember this guy O'Brien as a weasel, dumb as a lost cow with a broken bell, one of those guys who became a cop because he got the shit beat out of him for his lunch money every day in the schoolyard and now he needed a gun and a badge to get even with the world."

"Carries his dick in his holster," Gleason said.

"Something like that," Bobby said. "So I'm asking these guys from Gibraltar what exactly goes on behind the black marble, windowless walls of their compound. The place looks like Hitler's bunker, with video cameras scanning the street, razor wire on the roof, gates and alarms. You'd think they had nuclear secrets in there. Then O'Brien buys me a drink, which he never did in ten years of knowing him. The bartender was an old doof, name of Cleary, retired charter fisherman from Sheepshead Bay, who conveniently died in a fall down a flight of stairs before we could subpoena him to trial. So, anyway, I take the beer, a glass of tap. I buy the next round, trying to oil these guys . . . and, man, suddenly, *blanko!*"

"The bartender, the dead fuck, he Mickey-Finned ya," Gleason said. "Rohypnol, probably. Nicknamed *roofies*. The 'date-rape drug.' I almost defended a guy who raped a series of women with Rohypnol. Slip that into someone's drink and good night, Nurse; good morning, Doctor, or undertaker. That rock star, Kurt Cobain—it put him in a coma once. My daughters talked me out of defending this rape suspect because they knew a girl who had been raped with Rohypnol. Ten times stronger than Xanax. Really, really bad shit."

"I have no idea what the hell it was," said Bobby. "But, man, next thing I know I'm being woken up in the early morning in my car by cops, brass, Brooklyn DA investigators. Twirling cop-car lights, flashlights, forensic flashbulbs. I'm parked in Evergreen Cemetery, outside the crematorium, covered in blood. My whole car is soaked in blood. I ask what the fuck is going on, and Cis Tuzio is on the scene herself with a Brooklyn DA detective named Hanratty. She tells me that a body had been illegally cremated in the crematorium last night. Plus, she says, homicide police did a search of my apartment and found it covered in blood. They find a bloody knife in my car. With my prints. They lock me up on suspicion of murder. Say I killed Dorothea in my apartment and transported her to the cemetery in my car, cremated her, and fell asleep."

"Didn't you tell Tuzio or the cops about this O'Brien and Cleary guy who Mickey-Finned you?" Gleason asked.

"Of course I told them I'd been drugged," Bobby said. "But when they went to The Anchor, everyone denied I was ever there that night. I couldn't prove it."

"Then they booked you?"

"Yeah," Bobby said. "It took less than twelve hours to do a positive blood match between the blood in my apartment, my car, and the crematorium. My head was spinning. I never knew what the hell happened. Still don't. And I went over it every night for the past eighteen months."

"Sure you don't want a Kit Kat?" Gleason asked, eating one himself.

Bobby blinked and looked in the rearview mirror. The Taurus was obviously going to follow them all the way into the city. The cat-and-mouse was starting to give him a restless edge. It made him know he had no time to waste. He was *out*, which meant he had to dive right back *in*.

"This newspaper pain-in-the-ass, this Max Roth, can he be trusted?"

"He doesn't like you," Bobby said. "But he likes me. We go back to my Brooklyn College days, before I transferred to John Jay College after I joined the PD. I helped him with stories over the years."

"You mean you leaked him stories," Gleason said. "Your office was a sieve, and your leaks won him awards. I know. Some of them were won on my clients' convictions. The awards got him a fuckin' column. He owes you at least a six-pack of blow jobs. . . ."

Bobby took no offense, knowing that in the tabloid trade a positive story was referred to as a "blow job."

"He has integrity," Bobby said.

" 'Integrity' is just a word sandwiched between 'incest' and 'intoxication' in the dictionary," Gleason said. "But we need a newspaper guy. His readers are my jury pool. Can *you* trust this shifty, ink-stained suckass?"

"Yeah," Bobby said, refraining from telling Gleason what names came to his mind when he looked at him. "But he's no suckass."

"Okay, so you got your brother, a kid, an ex-wife, some nosy old fuckin' flatfoot, a retired-cop-slash-saloon-keeper, and Roth," Gleason said. "That's the whole fan club? You're not too popular."

"Neither are you, Sleazy Izzy," said Bobby, realizing they had just entered the city of New York. He saw a sign for the Triboro Bridge and another for the Henry Hudson Parkway.

"That's why we'll make a great team," said Gleason. "We got nowhere to go but up."

"This isn't a team. This is another bad marriage."

"What's your first move?"

Bobby looked in his rearview mirror, saw that the Taurus was following him onto the Henry Hudson. At the last possible moment Bobby made a hard left and veered across three lanes of traffic for the ramp to the Triboro. Horns honked at him and the Taurus braked suddenly, doing a squealing half spin. Bobby slowed and in the rearview he made out the numerals 682. New York State JDF-682.

Bobby looked over at the Taurus, gave it the finger, and headed over the Triboro.

9

A half hour later Bobby knocked on the big door, feeling the reinforced steel reverberate through his knuckles. After fifteen seconds he rang the bell and then knocked again. He stood outside the polished black marble cube of a building on Gerritsen Avenue, the main boulevard of this low-key, etherized section of Brooklyn. A small brass sign was bolted into the gleaming stone: GIBRALTAR SECURITY.

Bobby had wasted no time, didn't even call Maggie or Patrick to say he was home. No hugs, balloons, welcome-home parties. There was work to do. If he was going to stay out of the joint, he had to go get to the bottom of who framed him. Pronto.

He knew that Sandy Fraser, Dorothea's girlfriend, worked here at Gibraltar.

He needed Sandy to fill in crucial missing blanks about Dorothea's past. He also wanted to jostle the hornet's nest of Gibraltar Security, to make them react, make mistakes.

Bobby knew the area well, had been to a dozen barbecues and christenings out here, knew that a lot of cops, active and retired, lived in the more than ninety percent white Gerritsen Beach, where some would sit around gin mills with neon shamrocks in the windows, overlooking Gerritsen Canal or the creek, lamenting about the slow encroachment of "them." "Them" used to be just the "niggers," but today it was "alla them"—immigrants, "Pakis," "Chinks," "dot heads," "Rooskies," "every kind of spic they make." "These piss-colored people burn canary feathers, drink blood out of eggshells, and want to send their niglets to school with my kids," Bobby remembered one forty-year-old retired cop saying, explaining why he was hammering a FOR SALE sign into his lawn with the handle of his service revolver. "Next stop, Windy Tip."

Windy Tip was a private, closed co-op community on the southern tip of Brooklyn, the last one hundred percent stronghold in the city of New York, where the truly terrified xenophobes took refuge with their backs to the sea. Even a New York Jew had to have the signatures of three prominent white Christian members of the Windy Tip co-op to be allowed to buy there. And the half-dozen Jews who did live there were married to shiksas, daughters of established Christian residents. Windy Tip was pure Pat Buchanan country, a simply breathtaking peninsula of bay and oceanfront property, just a few zip codes from Gerritsen Beach.

Bobby folded a small piece of paper and jammed it into the doorbell so that it would ring continuously. Finally the door opened to reveal Zeke and Kuzak in expensive pastel-colored suits, which probably once fit them well but now barely closed over swelling guts. Zeke pulled the paper out of the doorbell.

Both men had the strong, bulky frames of guys who used to pump iron and then went to suet when they gave up the gym for the oat bag. At the moment they also had the squinty, bloated, unrested look of an all-nighter of booze, maybe a couple of grams of coke, a tag team of high-maintenance bimbos. Guys who lived like that went down like porridge, Bobby thought.

"Ah, the lady-killer," said Kuzak, the big guy, his hair so perfectly cut it looked like a toupee. "Fuck you doin' out?"

"Take me to your sleazeball," Bobby said.

"A comedian," said Zeke, the blocky, shorter man, a strap of hair lashed across his bald dome. "Maybe you should go to open-mike night over Pip's Comedy Club on the bay."

"If your moms is too busy bobbing for someone's apples, I guess your boss will do," Bobby said. He knew that in Brooklyn, especially a time warp like Gerritsen Beach, the best way to make someone lose his cool was to rank on his mother. It was an old and crude approach, but it rarely failed. "Ma" was still a holy word here, like in old gangster movies.

"Say another word about my fuckin' mother, I'll cut your dick off," said Zeke.

"She that hungry?" Bobby said.

Zeke moved for him, but Bobby used a trick he'd learned in the joint when the macho-sissies went after his behind. As Zeke reached toward him, Bobby stepped his way, bringing his work boot down on the man's instep. Zeke howled and a series of spasms erupted in his body, sending him reeling to the side, banging against the doorframe and sliding down the marble wall into a lumpy wedge. Bobby bent toward Zeke and said, "Geez, so sorry, pal. Should I call Ma?"

Kuzak made a two-handed grab at Bobby, who was bent over Zeke. But, as it had always worked in the joint, Bobby straightened at the count of three, coming up fast with the back of his skull, which accidentally on purpose caught Kuzak on the tip of his nose. Kuzak's hands went to his nose, as if he were a Little Leaguer hit by a pop fly, and then he did a pirouette, stamping his feet, skidding on the marble floor, his legs crossing as he fell across Zeke's ruined foot.

With one eye on Kuzak, Bobby reached down and took the .38 Smith and Wesson from the ankle holster just above Zeke's wounded foot. And with Kuzak's back to him, Bobby groped under his suit jacket and removed an all hard-plastic Glock 9 mm. Bobby lifted it to his nose and sniffed. It smelled like a new car, weighed about two and a half pounds, and could stop a charging bull.

Bobby discharged the thirteen-bullet clip from the Glock and emptied the bullets from the chamber of the .38 into his right palm. With his left hand he carried the guns by their trigger guards into Gibraltar Security.

As Bobby passed through a second door, he broke the beam of an electric eye, triggering an alarm, a two-tone blare. Bobby immediately recognized a startled Sandy Fraser, who walked from behind her receptionist's desk to shut off the alarm.

"Jesus Christ, Bobby . . ."

"Hello, Sandy," Bobby said. "We need to talk. About Dorothea . . ."

"She was my friend, Bobby," Sandy whispered, glancing at the closed door to an inner office.

"I didn't kill her, Sandy," Bobby said.

"I believe you, but . . ." Sandy nodded at the door. "It's a freakin' mess. I'm scared. Not just for me. You should be, too."

"I need your help," Bobby said.

"You aren't the only one," Sandy said. "But I can't get involved. I have good reasons, Bobby. I'm sorry. . . ."

Sandy was still beautiful, with her dark fluffy hair, framing a face dominated by two very round blue eyes almost hidden by heavy mascara. She had soft, full lips with too much red lipstick.

"You *are* involved," Bobby said. Sandy walked back around her desk toward her chair. Bobby was aroused by the way her body moved inside the tight black dress. She took a nervous sip of coffee.

"Please, Bobby, we can't talk here," Sandy said, still looking at the door to the inner office as the groans from Kuzak and Zeke came from the outside vestibule.

"Fine," Bobby said. "But soon. *Today.* I'll find you."

Bobby dropped five bullets from Zeke's gun into a heavy glass ashtray on Sandy's desk. He picked up her steaming coffee cup, which was stenciled with her name and rimmed with fresh lipstick. Bobby winked at Sandy, and she half-smiled, then her wide mouth slashed into a thin line when two more Gibraltar goons in expensive summer suits appeared through the door from the inner office. A backup crew. Guys that still went to the gym, Bobby thought.

"Geez, but the service here is great," Bobby said. "After the first two executives literally fall over each other trying to help me, Gibraltar sends a couple of floor attendants to take care of me. Class."

Sandy stifled a laugh and turned away on her swivel chair from the confrontation, pulling open a file drawer behind her.

The two goons looked from Zeke to Kuzak then back at Bobby. The youngest one, about twenty-eight, as cleanly barbered as a marine recruiting poster, began removing his jacket with slow precision.

"My name is Flynn, and my associate here's name is Levin," Marine Poster said. "And you're trespassing, Mr. Emmet."

"Son, in another situation—Last Chance Saloon, three in the morning, John Lennon doing 'Imagine' on the juke, three bikers walk in, jostle my date—I'd welcome you having my back," Bobby said.

He took a sip of the coffee. Sandy's flavored lipstick greased his lip, the taste of a woman tantalizing his mouth. He dangled both pistols. "But I really think you're a little inexperienced for this particular piece of customer service. Maybe you should call inside for a supervisor, huh? Someone a little higher up on the evolutionary scale?"

"I warned you politely," Flynn said. "And you make with the mouth. For that, I'm going to have to snap your fucking spine like a number-two pencil, scumbag."

Bobby turned to Sandy, said, "He pronounces his 'i-n-gs,' and he can count to two? Precocious. But he needs manners, cursing in front of a lady like that shows that he was dragged up."

Kuzak stumbled into the room from the vestibule now, a bloody hankie to his nose. Bobby put the coffee cup down.

"I'm gonna fuckin' kill you," Kuzak said, weakly.

Flynn put a hand up to stop Kuzak. He signaled for Levin, his redheaded partner-in-dumbbells, to flank Bobby from the left side.

Bobby nonchalantly transferred Zeke's .38 to his right hand, sat on the edge of Sandy's desk, and pointed it at them. He stifled a yawn. Flynn looked at the ashtray on Sandy's desk, where the bullets lay amid the dead Carltons.

"Okay, class, let's play count the bullets in the ashtray," Bobby said as Flynn and his partner hesitated. "I count five. That means there's still one in the chamber. Let's see which brave boy wants to count to number six first."

Bobby spun the cylinder, amusing himself with this game of threatened Russian roulette. "Moving on to advanced math, let's see, you two guys can't be more than twenty-eight years old. Tops thirty. Both wearing NYPD rings. But if you work here and also double-date at the gym, it must mean you guys are retired from the job. Medical-disability pensions, I bet.''

He spun the cylinder again, took another sip of the coffee, and said, ''Then you work here, probably off the books, job classi-fication—Prime USDA Beef. Plus, you almost certainly got your papers in for Social Security Insurance, another couple a grand a month. You guys must be good for what . . . six, maybe even seven or eight grand a month. For life, no tax. For two guys who can't count to six? Not bad. New math for a new century.''

''Let's play how many face bones of yours I can break with one punch,'' Flynn said.

''Let's play nice and put your guns on the desktop first,'' said Bobby, waving his gun from one to the other. Sandy sat silently, her hands in front of her on the desk, her nails clicking nervously on the glass top.

''Come on, I only have one bullet,'' Bobby said. ''Who's gonna be the hero that takes it?''

Flynn and Levin reluctantly took out their 9 mm Glocks from back belt holsters and put them on Sandy's desk. Bobby disen-gaged the clips from each one and dropped the guns into a fish tank that graced the reception area, causing a panic among the ravenous piranha. Someone should get a photograph of a school of piranha trying to eat a Glock nine, Bobby thought. Dorothea would have seen it as a microcosmic image of New York City and set up a camera. Bobby also dropped Kuzak's gun into the tank but still held onto Zeke's .38.

The door to the inner office opened, and Lou Barnicle stepped out, wearing Ray-Ban tints, a gold Rolex, and an Armani suit, looking more like a polished machine politician than a retired cop. He smiled, showing off a big row of capped white teeth that perfectly set off his deep tan. The skin on his face was as free of wrinkles as a snare drum, and Bobby was sure he'd had a touch-up job around the eyes and a chin tuck. Good job, too, keeping his age on cruise control, somewhere between forty-five and fifty. His blue pinstripe was a perfect fit, with the beige crewneck silk polo shirt underneath making him look stocky, powerful, a man of stature without a trace of the old police fat. His feet were too wide for the oxblood loafers, but he wore them anyway, probably for the cute little gold bars that told you they were some expensive Italian brand.

"So, what seems to be the problem here, gentlemen?" Barnicle asked, spreading open his arms like a priest giving a blessing.

"Hello, Barnicle," Bobby said with a smirk. "I see you're still spending two hundred bucks a week in the barbershop."

Barnicle had always been the best-shaved cop he'd ever known; no other cop paid to have his face shaved every morning. At the Manhattan DA's office, Bobby had requested the NYPD Internal Affairs Bureau file on Barnicle, and they had a whole section just on his shaving and grooming expenses. And another subsection on his extravagant sartorial spending. When he was on the job, on a captain's pay of under a hundred grand, he had also managed to buy a half-million-dollar, six-bedroom bay-front house in Windy Tip, drive a forty-thousand-dollar BMW, keep a three-hundred-and-fifty-thousand-dollar, forty-five-foot cabin cruiser, and spend at least a month of every winter in the Caribbean. Though they could never prove it, IAB knew he was too clean to be anything but dirty.

"Guns?" Barnicle said rhetorically as he took small confident steps through his outer office, shaking his head as he looked at his men.

"How're the war wounds there, Lou?" Bobby asked. "Looks like a truly anguished retirement."

Barnicle was retired now, another three-quarters disability pension. His private-snoop firm hired nothing but other retired cops, most of them probably on medical pensions. It was all legal. On the close-shaved face of it. But something more than a few scam artists beating the city for pensions was going on here, Bobby thought. Or else they would never have framed him for sniffing around. That's if he was looking in the right place. . . .

"Fellas, guns and violence?" Barnicle said like an uncle settling a family feud. "We need this for Bobby Emmet? I worked with Bobby, on the job, through tough times, when cops were cops. We don't pull guns on our own. We should be celebrating his release."

Barnicle looked at the bloodied Kuzak helping the hobbling Zeke to a chair as Flynn and Levin stood staring at their guns in the fish tank. Barnicle shook his head like a disappointed teacher, but under the veneer, in the cold cobalt eyes, Bobby could see the anger rising like a chronic bile.

"Geez, I heard the welcome-home party was here," Bobby said. "Am I late? Cake all gone?"

"Bobby," Barnicle said, "come inside; we'll talk . . . Sandy? Make some espresso. . . ." He turned to the four men. "There's a backlog of fieldwork. Do it. Plus we need to get five more Gibraltar uniformed guys for the rap concert in Brooklyn College tonight. It's sold out. Maybe oversold. Could be a ruckus. Eight bucks an hour. No OT."

Lou Barnicle held the door to the inner office open, and Bobby placed Sandy's cup back on her desktop. Their eyes met ever so briefly, and then she picked up a ringing phone. Bobby followed Barnicle into his office, still holding on to the .38.

Bobby looked around the oak paneled inner office. There were no windows. He heard the whir of an exhaust fan, sucking out the first smoke from a Havana cigar that Barnicle was now lighting.

"Where you've been, Bobby," Barnicle said, "I guess you'd like a scotch, a vodka . . ."

"No thanks, Lou. Last time I had a drink with someone from this rat's nest, I wound up convicted of murder."

Barnicle feigned offense.

"You're not suggesting I had . . ."

"There was more natural light in my cell than there is in here," Bobby said. "But this is good prep for you, Lou. Like astronaut training. If you can spend eight hours a day in this box, you might be able to handle solitary. Cops like us get twenty-three-hour-a-day lockdown. No hot-towel shaves. No personal tailors. Even the diamond-studded Rolex doesn't improve *time* when you're doing it, Lou."

"You're bitter," Barnicle said evenly. "You have to learn to forgive and forget."

Bobby paced the room, looked at some of the plaques Barnicle had won as a police captain over the years: the Emerald Society, B'nai B'rith, Knights of Columbus.

"Yeah, well, I have Irish Alzheimer's," Bobby said, tapping his temple with his left forefinger. "I forget everything but the fucking grudge."

"You're a courageous man," Barnicle said. "No one can ever say that Bobby Emmet has no balls. Or brains. Too smart to be a cop, I always thought. But you're also reckless. You overstep your bounds. You step on other people's toes. You took a job where you even went after your own kind. What the fuck is that? I mean, IAB tries to run guys out of the department. But you, you tried to put cops in the joint. As you found out, that's not a nice place to be for a cop. And now here you are, as soon as you get out, making waves with me. For what?"

"I think you had me framed," Bobby said. "No use beating around the bush. I think you set me up, and like most red-blooded Americans, I believe in revenge."

"You got no backup, no carry license, no friends, and I'm supposed to gulp Maalox for the puny *agita* you wanna give me?" Barnicle produced a manufactured belch. "There, that's all the gas you give me. You're a burp in the hurricane of my life."

Bobby took a deep breath.

"I'm going to find out what happened to Dorothea Dubrow," Bobby said. "Bet on it."

"Hey, I might be a lot of things," Barnicle said. "But I don't go around killing girls. Especially beautiful ones. . . ."

"Jesus, that is aesthetically discriminating of you," Bobby said.

"I run a legit shop here," Barnicle continued, as if Bobby had not even interrupted. "I take care of guys retired from the job. Even you. That's right." He smiled his toothy smile. "I can offer you twenty-five dollars an hour to start, bodyguarding a few rap stars right now. What do you say?"

"I'm sure you'd like that, having me check IDs and ticket stubs at Brooklyn College," Bobby said. "Better to have me inside the tent pissing out instead of vice versa. But if you didn't help kill her, what makes you so certain Dorothea's even dead?"

"If she's alive," Barnicle said, "why doesn't she come forward?" He stood up, poured a snifter of Rémy Martin cognac, swirled it, sniffed it. "She reads the papers. She knows what happened to you."

"Maybe she's being held against her will," Bobby said.

"Where, in a zoo? Come to think of it, she did have an ass like a jungle beast . . . no offense."

Bobby felt a flare ignite in his head, a fuse of white-hot rage. *Control,* he thought. *Control.* "Offense taken," Bobby said. "And duly noted."

A knock came on the door.

"Come in, babe," Barnicle said, still swirling the cognac in the snifter.

Bobby gripped the .38 by the handle again, behind his back. Sandy carried in a tray with two cups of espresso. Bobby loosened his grip on the gun and palmed it again. He fell silent as Sandy tore open an envelope of Equal and poured it into Barnicle's demitasse cup. As if performing a ritual, she stirred it with a tiny silver spoon, twisted a lemon rind, and skimmed the rim of the ceramic cup with it.

"Real sugar or plastic, Bobby?" Sandy asked, looking at him, her eyes filled with other questions.

Bobby had always been attracted to Sandy—her pleasant manner, sassy sense of humor, street-smart intelligence, her gleaming smile, her unabashed Brooklyn accent—back as far as when she worked over in the NYPD medical office.

All the cops had always wanted Sandy to interview them because she was as easy to talk to as she was to look at. Mid-thirties and she still had a body like that of one of those babes *Playboy* always found in college-campus searches. She'd dated lots of cops. Rumor had it she'd had affairs with married brass who promised to get divorced but only broke her heart. There had always been something hauntingly sad about her, a sense of never being happy, always searching for and never finding her place in life.

"Nothing for me, thanks," Bobby said. Barnicle glanced from one to the other, not liking their eye contact. Sandy lingered for a moment as if awaiting instructions.

"The hell you waitin' for?" Barnicle asked.

"A 'thank you' might be nice," Sandy said.

"I'm the goddamned *boss,*" Barnicle said in an exasperated way.

"I'm a goddamned *lady,*" Sandy said. "A human being. We have these weird customs—'please,' 'thanks,' 'you're welcome.' Like that."

Sandy strode out of the office, Bobby watching her lovely gait until she closed the door behind her.

"That's my honey," Barnicle said, smiling. "Had a baby with her when you were away on your . . . furlough. A son . . ."

He rattled the small cup into the saucer and pushed a framed photo of a baby boy toward Bobby. Jesus Christ, how could Sandy have settled for this miserable prick? he thought. Maybe security was the biggest aphrodisiac.

"They sure shit a lot, don't they?" Barnicle said.

Bobby laughed darkly.

"If shit was gold, only people like you would have assholes, Barnicle," Bobby said, leaning over the desk. "Now, listen to me, *Papa*. I'm gonna find out what happened to my woman. But I'm not a cop anymore. Like you, I don't have to follow any rules. So this is your last chance. If you know what happened to Dorothea, tell me now, and if she's okay, maybe we can go our separate ways. But if you or your goons had anything to do with hurting her in any way, or get in my way again, I'll gladly die killing you. Remember that. I *am* warning you, I am willing to die, but not before I find the truth."

Barnicle stared right back into Bobby's eyes.

"When they send you back, they should make it the fucking puzzle factory this time. Because you are a fuckin' wack," Barnicle said, shaking his head.

Bobby took the last bullet from the .38 and dropped it into the espresso. He smacked the gun onto the desk in front of the picture of the baby boy. Barnicle jumped in his seat as Bobby turned and walked out.

Zeke, Kuzak, and Flynn blocked the front door of Gibraltar Security. Levin was trying to fish the Glock nines out of the fish tank with a wire coat hanger as the piranha bit at the wire. Bobby looked at the three goons in front of the door. *Control.* Once again he picked up Sandy's steaming cup of coffee.

"Okay, which one of you research primates wants to wear this?" Bobby asked.

The ex-cops looked uneasy, glanced at each other, and finally cleared the path for Bobby to pass, carrying the coffee cup with him out the door, sipping it, savoring Sandy's luscious lipstick.

Sandy watched him go, and he wondered what she would tell him when he got her alone.

10

Bobby picked up Gleason and sped the Jeep Cherokee along the Belt Parkway, around the loop of Shore Road, the most magnificent stretch of waterfront in the city. He passed the million-dollar homes of the doctors, lawyers, gangsters, and politicians of Brooklyn. He moved under the pylons of the Verrazano Bridge, breezing by the Narrows, where tugs urged tankers past Staten Island, Brooklyn, and Jersey out to deep sea. Ferries, garbage scows, barges, Coast Guard cutters, police and fire boats, luxury liners, sailboats, and other pleasure craft, all moved through the great port of New York.

Bobby hadn't slept the night before because of the jail noise, but he was feeling absolutely no fatigue. Freedom pumped in his veins like some magical elixir. He had to get settled, see his kid first, and then get quickly to the checklist of his case.

He weaved through stubborn traffic on the Gowanus Expressway and finally burrowed through the Brooklyn Battery Tunnel and jolted up the West Side Highway of Manhattan to the Seventy-ninth Street exit.

The trip took thirty-two minutes, and the dashboard clock told Bobby it was 12:05 PM. It was going to be a very long day, and he looked forward to every minute of it.

Gleason told Bobby to park on the rotunda above the Seventy-ninth Street Boat Basin. The rotunda was a shelf of granite and concrete sitting forty feet above sea level at one of the most beautiful marinas in the water-blessed city.

Although Bobby had once been a Harbor Unit cop, a regular fixture at the marina, he'd always approached it from the river and had never before taken time to see it from this vantage.

The boat basin spread out below them for three city blocks on the banks of the Hudson River, a weather-worn but resilient network of floating walkways and 145 boat slips, serving as home to cabin cruisers, motor sailers, trawlers, houseboats, yachts, fishing skiffs, sailboats, dinghies, speedboats, Jet Skis, and schooners. There was even a Chinese junk moored. The marina resembled the mouth of a small fishing village. "There's only ninety-one year-round slips," Gleason said. "And seventy-six of us are considered 'live-aboards.' My father put my name on the waiting list here the day I got married. He called it divorce insurance. Half the guys here are divorced and wound up with the boat, while the wife got the house. My old man was a half-assed sailor. Me, I need instructions to run a bath and I get seasick watching a bar of Ivory float. But I got a slip and a boat."

The boat basin was a fenced-in public community with a twenty-four-hour dockmaster on duty in a wooden security shack. But it was hardly impregnable. All the residents had keys to the iron security gate and duplicates were given to friends, who made copies for more friends who came to the endless parties in the summer months.

Many New Yorkers had passed the Seventy-ninth Street Boat Basin on the West Side Highway dozens of times without even knowing it was there. If they did notice it while speeding past, they rarely stopped to explore it from the rotunda. It remained nestled there on the banks of the Hudson like a secret little gateway to the great archipelago of New York.

"The waiting list for a slip is as long as your enemies list, but once you get a lease here, you can keep it forever," Gleason said. "The Parks Department is the landlord. I pay three hundred and ninety-five bucks a month rent and another hundred and twenty-five for parking. That's five bills a month it costs to live here on the Yupper West Side. They lose money, but they do a pretty damned good job. A guy can live year round on a boat here and never have to pay property tax because any moveable vehicle is immune to real estate tax laws. Broads love it here. It's a home run. It's like having season tickets to the Knicks. And remember: You gotta say you're living with me because there's no subleasing allowed. Don't get me evicted."

They parked the car in the ancient indoor parking garage, shielding their eyes as they stepped out into the bright sunshine of Riverside Park. Gleason managed to communicate to Venus that he would like her to wait on a park bench while he and

Bobby went into the boat basin. "Bench," Gleason said. "As in warrant. Hang in there, hon, you're doing great."

Gleason unlocked the security gate, and Bobby followed him in, stopping at the security shack inside the gate, a small hut covered inside in nautical maps, with a reception desk and tiny office off to the side. Gleason introduced Bobby to Doug, the dockmaster, the city's parks administrator of the boat basin. There were worse city jobs, Bobby thought, starting with mayor. Bobby recognized Doug first.

"Doug, this is Bobby, Bobby, Doug," Gleason said. "Bobby's gonna be staying with me here awhile, slip ninety-nine-A. Extend all courtesies and Santa will grease your chimney come Christmas."

Doug smiled and shook Bobby's hand. He was a friendly, affable guy with a thick set of arms and a face that had been leathered by twenty-odd years of salt, sun, and sea. His job was to maintain upkeep for the permanent tenants of the boat basin, collect rents, provide minimal security, and to rent temporary space to transient boaters for about a dollar a foot for nightly dockage, one of the great seafaring bargains on the eastern seaboard.

"Anything you need," Doug said, "just call . . . *hey!* Aren't you . . . ?"

"Yeah," Bobby said. "It's been a while."

"You guys know each other?" Gleason asked, surprised.

Now Doug remembered Bobby from the days he worked Harbor Unit and used to moor *Harbor Charlie,* the main NYPD patrol boat, at the boat basin when the cops wanted to stretch their legs or take a hot shower.

"Not for nothing," Doug said. "I never thought you were guilty, Bobby. You were always a gentleman. Welcome back. I hope you feel at home here."

"I appreciate that," Bobby said.

"Keep him low profile," Gleason said.

"You bet," Doug said.

Gleason led Bobby down a slick floating walkway, stepping around heavy ropes, tie-off cleats, barbecues, deck chairs, ice coolers, life preservers. They passed two women in their thirties in cutoff shorts and halter tops who were too engrossed in conversation to pay them much mind. Bobby held his face to the sun and breathed in the river breeze, listening to the honking of boats on the river and the steady whoosh of cars on the highway behind him. Finally they came to slip 99-A.

"It's a nineteen-eighty-seven Silver-some-fucking-thing-or-the-other, and it's seen better days," Gleason said.

Bobby examined the sorrowfully neglected 1987 forty-foot Silverton 34 Express that rocked gently as the Hudson flowed past her, downtown to the sea. The name *The Fifth Amendment* was emblazoned on its dirty stern. A tattered American flag on the cabin roof snapped in the river breeze.

The creaky boat's inside wasn't as bad as the weather-beaten exterior. The galley was a neglected but serviceable stainless-steel compartment with a small refrigerator-freezer, two-burner electric/alcohol stove, Corian-covered countertops, overhead microwave, overhead cabinets, pull-out storage racks, stainless-steel sink. "They teach you how to waltz with a mop upstate?" Gleason asked.

A cherry-wood door led to a nine-by-nine-foot saloon between the kitchen and the master stateroom. The forest green, wall-to-wall carpet needed to be vacuumed and shampooed. The wood-paneled walls were adorned with sepia-colored nautical maps. A cable-wired color TV with built-in VCR dominated the entertainment center, which also included a radio and CD stereo system. The saloon was equipped with a desk and two barrel chairs. Sliding windows with screens faced uptown toward the George Washington Bridge. The convertible sofa was covered with corduroy throw pillows.

Gleason pointed to another wooden door, and Bobby entered the master stateroom, a nine-by-eight-foot cedar-lined affair with a full-sized berth and storage drawers under the bed. The anchored night table next to the bed was equipped with a high-intensity reading lamp. A hanging locker offered ample room for Bobby's few clothes. He slid open a window that looked downtown on the city and let the river air into the room.

"My old man was a real estate lawyer," Gleason said. "Him and his 'clients' used to disappear for whole weekends on this baby. When he came home, my mother used to grill him. That's why he named it *The Fifth Amendment*. Him and his buddies spent more time down here in the basement than they did up on the roof."

"It's called a bridge and a deck," Bobby said, making a mental note to get a new mattress when he could afford one.

"Whole ship needs a good douche," Gleason said, squinting around, unwrapping a Reese's peanut-butter cup, plunging it into his mouth.

"Boat," Bobby said. "A ship is different. . . . Why bother . . ."

Gleason stepped into the master head, a tight, efficient lavatory with a built-in Corian-covered vanity, private head, stall shower. Gleason threw the candy wrapper in the toilet and flushed. It swirled down in a slow, tormented gulp. "A tight squeeze," Gleason said, sitting on the lid of the bowl, measuring the arm room between the wall and shower stall. "Room for the *Daily News* or the *Post,* sure. Don't even try reading the *Times* on this crapper; no room. Small head."

"You finally got a name right," Bobby said.

"I bet I know why they call it that, too," Gleason said. "You bring a broad in there, no room for anything else. . . ."

Bobby took a deep breath, and Gleason turned on the shower. Rusty water exploded with trapped air from the showerhead, and then finally clear water began to drizzle out in a tired stream.

"Shower's like getting pissed on by an infant, but it'll wash the shitty city down the drain," Gleason said.

"You ever consider going into real estate?" Bobby asked. "You give one hell of a sales pitch."

There was another small guest stateroom, big enough for one small person.

Bobby quickly climbed up to the fly deck and scanned the boat basin. Several dozen moored boats lolled gently on the Hudson. He had known cops over the years who had faked overtime, moonlighted on second jobs, taken bribes or loans to buy boats. Highway cops out on patrol were notorious for hiding their patrol car here in the boat basin garage, putting it up on a hydraulic jack, running the motor, and flattening the accelerator with a nightstick to make the wheels spin so that the odometer would show superior officers later that they had cruised the average 120 miles covered on an eight-hour shift. Meanwhile, as Bobby'd heard the stories, they'd be out on a boat, fishing, drinking, playing poker, or getting laid. Most of them wound up living on the boats after their divorces. He always thought of it as guys who left their wives for boats.

Bobby inspected the controls. Like most harbor cops, he was no boating genius. They usually only knew how to start a boat, steer it, and dock it. Bobby didn't know much about mechanical upkeep either, but he could get a feel for a boat by tinkering with the instruments. He felt the play in the helm, working the gyro and the rudder, the hydraulic steering system. The controls seemed to be in working order, just in need of oiling, a hard scrub, a fierce polish, some calibration, and lots of TLC. He was starting to imagine the boat with a major cleaning and a week's attention. It would be a fine flop until he could find something better.

No one would be banging the steel.

"Everything under the hood works," Gleason said. "Thing about boats though, they eat like racehorses. Fuel costs money. Which I don't have a lot of. But I started an account at the fuel dock, and you can take gas and charge it to me when you're using it on my time. Otherwise, I'll rely on your cornball honor to pay for your own time."

"Keys and registration?" Bobby asked, holding out his hand, walking for the exit ramp.

Gleason handed him a set of keys to the boat and the appropriate papers. Then he dangled the keys to the Jeep Cherokee.

"The car is all that's left of my marriage," Gleason said, a tinge of genuine sadness in his voice as he rattled the keys like altar bells. "So take care of it. . . ."

Bobby nodded.

"I'm putting Venus on a bus to the fat farm tonight," Gleason said, brightening again. "The nutritionist says she'll be a size seven when she comes out, and she shows her everlasting appreciation. *Comprendo?*"

"You are one very sick ticket," Bobby said, grabbing Gleason's wrist again to look at the time: 12:21 PM.

As Bobby reached the dock, he suddenly noticed a familiar-looking white Ford Taurus parked on the rotunda above the boat basin. *It can't be,* he thought.

"You got a camera or a pair of binoculars on the boat?" Bobby asked quickly.

"No," Gleason said. "Why?"

Bobby pointed to the car, sitting with its motor idling.

"Whadda you expect? You went into Gibraltar Security, terror-

59

ized the help, and now they aren't allowed to follow you around? You should have spotted the tail on the way up here, Sherlock."

"I checked my rearview all the way," Bobby said. "This guy is good. . . . I have to run that bastard's plate. You have a cell phone?"

"Not here," Gleason said. "In my office . . ."

11

"You have an office in the Empire State Building?" Bobby said, surprised, as he pulled to the curb on Thirty-fourth Street beside the towering skyscraper.

"It's more than a name," Gleason said. "Having an office in the Empire State Building is like being hung like a horse. *Pegasus*. It gives me stature. Professional virility. See, it's a piece of history. It's got ten million fuckin' bricks, twenty-seven miles of elevator rails, sixty-four hundred windows. It's fourteen hundred feet tall and weighs three hundred and sixty-five thousand mother-jumpin' tons. Now, if that ain't hung like the Trojan horse, what the fuck is?"

"Where did you learn all that shit?" Bobby asked as he opened the car door and stepped out into the lunch crowd, craning his neck like everyone else to look up at the building thrown into the sky by immigrant workers in 1931.

"The Jap real estate broker gave me a brochure with every stat in it except the circumference of King Kong's balls," Gleason said. "But I read it, and I thought to myself, if New York is the Cadillac of American cities, then the Empire State Building is the hood ornament. And I'm climbin' in for the ride. Since I'm the best fuckin' lawyer in this city, it makes sense this address is on Izzy Gleason's business card."

Izzy tugged Bobby's sleeve, telling him to park in the garage under the great skyscraper. But Bobby kept staring up at the awesome colossus.

"Wanna buy a fuckin' bridge, too?" Gleason said. "What, you were absent that day in third grade when they had the school trip? Come on, let's go . . ."

Bobby ignored Gleason and instead stood among the tourists with their video cameras and Nikons, staring up at the great spire. *Dorothea. We were here together. And we could see it all the way from Brooklyn. She loved the eternal winking red light at the very top. I told her it was a warning light for low-flying planes. "Be careful," she said. "It's also a warning that I am going to hold you to your promise of marrying me, Bobby Emmet."*

The next day, when they visited the observation deck, Bobby used the binoculars to point out his Brooklyn apartment. He told her to pick a wedding date. Soon. He wanted to have a family and a life together. She grew as excited as a child, making him promise that wherever they bought their house, they'd be able to see the winking red light at the top of the Empire State Building.

"Why?" Bobby had asked her, laughing.

She looked at him on that bright windy day, her eyes filled with childish wonder, her high cheekbones rosy with winter cold, her hair flapping from beneath her beret. "No matter whatever happens," she said, "that red light will always be my heart beating for you. *Ya tebe kohayu.*"

"Then pick a date," Bobby had said.

"I can't," she had said. "Not yet."

And would never tell him why. . . .

"Yo, before a pigeon uses you for target practice," Gleason asked, breaking Bobby's reverie. "Let's go . . ."

"Grab your bag," Gleason said as they found a spot in the underground garage and parked. "I have a terrific shower in my office."

Bobby was impressed that Gleason would use the stairs to keep in some kind of shape. He followed Gleason into the fire stairs and began the slow climb. When they got to the top of the first flight, Gleason was panting. He paused to light a cigarette, then pulled open the door marked in large black letters BASEMENT. It led to a corridor.

"Quitting already?" Bobby mocked, thinking they were walking to an elevator.

"We've arrived," Gleason said as he jingled his keys and walked

down a dingy, fluorescent-lit corridor, past a door marked JANI-
TOR and another marked ELECTRICAL CLOSET. He stopped
in front of a plain black door bearing the simple legend IZZY
GLEASON, ESQ., Room B-378.

"Your office is in the *basement* of the Empire State Building?"
Bobby asked, incredulous. "If you were a duck, you'd fly north
for the winter."

"And still run into jailbird clients like you," Gleason said with
a shrug.

"Actually the basement is a step up in the world for you, Gleason," Bobby said.

"Yeah, and I like the burgers in the coffee shop," Gleason
said, unlocking the door and pushing it open. "Plus, it's centrally
located. The higher the floor, the more the rent. Those high-
roller days are behind and ahead of me. Right now, I'm stuck in
neutral, so I make do. Besides, I don't do any work in the office.
But *you* will."

Gleason switched on the lights. A few rods of overhead fluo-
rescent tubing blinked to life. One bulb remained half-lit and
hummed. Gleason bent and picked up the mail—Con Ed and
NYNEX bills and a large envelope with a Police Athletic League
return address.

"I need the phone," Bobby said. "I want to run that plate."

Gleason tore open his mail as Bobby looked around at the
stacks of newspapers, magazines, and bulging blue-back legal
folders.

"Good thing you are in the basement," Bobby said. "If a client
walked in here, he'd want to jump out the window."

Bobby stepped past a large leather recliner, through the debris
on the floor—old candy wrappers and soda cans, yellowed newspapers. A big, black manual typewriter sat on a gray metal desk;
it looked old enough for Mark Twain to have used it. Boxes of
candy were stacked on both sides of the old typewriter, and Izzy
was already popping chocolates into his mouth.

Gleason handed Bobby the contents of the PAL envelope; it
was an NYPD parking permit, allowing a car to be parked almost
anywhere on city streets. "I told your brother, Patrick, you'd need
it," Gleason said. "It's worth its weight in gold."

Gleason walked behind the desk, sat in an old green leather
swivel chair, unlocked the bottom desk drawer, and pulled it

open. He removed a cellular phone and a Smith and Wesson .38 revolver and placed them on the desktop. He took off his Tag Heuer watch and placed it on the desk, too. Bobby looked from the gun to Gleason, who rocked in the swivel chair.

Bobby dialed a number and asked for John Shine, who was out. He called the 72nd Precinct, asked for Officer Tom Larkin, and the desk sergeant said he was working the four-to-twelve shift. He called Patrick and got an answering machine. He left a message saying he'd call back in a couple of hours. He tried Max Roth at the *Daily News,* hoping he could run the plate with the computer in the newspaper library. The receptionist said Roth was out on assignment, so Bobby was connected to his voice mail. "Max, this is Bobby. I need a couple of favors. I need a license plate run. But in the meantime, could you get an intern to do a 'Where Are They Now' computer search on all the principals in my case? Defense, prosecution, cops, witnesses. Everybody. I just need an update. Thanks. I'll call again later."

Bobby pointed at the items on the desk and said, "The phone and the watch I can use. Not the gun."

"I wanted you to know it's here for when you need it," Gleason said.

"*If* I need it."

"Oh, you'll need it all right," Gleason said.

A twelve-inch color television sat on top of the fridge. Bobby turned it on and heard baseball scores.

"That all we came here for?" Bobby asked. "I got things to do."

"No, to get my messages," Gleason said.

"Your messages?" Bobby said. "You can get them from a pay phone with your remote number."

"I always forget the fuckin' number."

"I'll reset it," Bobby said examining the answering machine. "To the same number as your door. Three-seven-eight. Okay?"

"It's too complicated," Gleason said. "The outgoing message on this machine tells clients to call me at the Chelsea Hotel. The only people I tell to leave messages for me here are *broads.* I don't like them calling me at the hotel, in case I'm there with another broad. So I come by every once in a while and push the play button. That I know how to do. See . . ."

Gleason hit the play button on the answering machine. There

were calls from all the local newspapers and TV and radio news stations, including an earlier one from Max Roth. They all wanted Gleason to set up interviews with Bobby Emmet. Gleason jotted down the names and numbers.

"I already called Associated Press to do a media alert that I'm holding a two-thirty PM horseshit photo-op press conference in front of the Brooklyn district attorney's office," Gleason said. "When Roth calls you, tell him you need a few days before you give him the exclusive."

Bobby nodded. Then he heard his daughter Maggie's voice.

"Hello, Mr. Gleason, this is Maggie Emmet. First, I want to thank you from the bottom of my heart for getting my father out of jail. Second, I'm *looking* for him. If you get this message, will you please tell him that he better call me or he's coming off my Christmas card list. He knows the number. Oh, yeah, tell him I love him to death, too. Thanks."

"Sounds like a good kid," Gleason said. "Be careful they don't try to get to you through her."

Bobby looked at Gleason with haunted dread. "That's crossed my mind."

"These are ruthless motherfuckers we're dealing with," Gleason said and lit another cigarette.

Bobby pulled open the only interior door in the office to reveal the executive bathroom.

He tugged the glow-in-the-dark knob of the light cord, and a bare incandescent bulb popped to life in the high ceiling. The bathroom had old, cracked ceramic fixtures—a bowl, sink, and small shower stall. Everything was spotless. There was a pile of clean white towels on top of a wicker hamper. The medicine cabinet above the sink was filled with deodorant, shaving cream, razors, aftershave lotion, toothpaste, soap. He nodded approval.

"You might have a sleazy reputation, but I don't ever remember you without a shave, a haircut, and a crease in your pants," Bobby said.

"Believe it or not, like you, I do want my daughters to be proud of me . . . again," Gleason said softly. "They will be; just watch me. Just watch. . . ."

Gleason pulled out a large wad of cash from his front right-hand pocket and peeled off five one-hundred-dollar bills, placed them on the desktop next to the watch, the gun and the cell phone. He weighted the bills with a set of office keys.

"Just so you know," Gleason said, "I already applied for a private investigator's license for you, saying you were going to be my chief investigator. Any more questions?"

Bobby put the .38 back in the drawer and locked it. He picked up the money and the watch. It was 1:01 PM.

"Izzy, I'm in a hurry, but answer me this."

"Yeah?"

"If you got this kind of dough," he said, waving the five one-hundred-dollar bills and pointing at the overhead lights, "why can't you get a fucking bulb fixed?"

"Look, you don't like the fuckin' lighting, fix it yourself. I gotta put a broad on a bus. Then I'm gonna do a press conference in time for the six o'clock news. I'm gonna cash in on your sorry ass big time."

Gleason made a move for the door, and Bobby Emmet called to him.

"Izzy," Bobby said softly.

Izzy Gleason turned to him.

"Thanks," Bobby said.

"Give it time and you'll take that back," Gleason said, and then he was gone.

The line echoed in Bobby's head. He wasn't at all sure that Gleason was legit. He still couldn't trust him. Everything in Gleason's past told Bobby the man was a devious bag of shit. Bobby seriously considered the idea that Gleason could be working for the guys who framed him. Guys who failed to have him killed in the joint who now wanted him on the outside, where they could whack him. Gleason could be getting paid to set him up by this anonymous "angel" who put up his bail. Who was this benefactor, anyway? Gleason had stashed Bobby in a boat on a remote marina, an easy place to waste someone. Gave him a car that could already be bugged or wired. Which could account for the white Taurus—that Gleason didn't seem overly concerned about. Even this office could be monitored. Gleason had been a mouthpiece-for-hire for killers all his life; what would one more corpse in his career be? And what about this Venus, whom Gleason claimed didn't speak a word of English? She could probably recite the Constitution backward in English and Spanish. Was she part of some setup, too?

Bobby felt dirty inside and out. Just doing business with Gleason called for a shower.

Alone now as a free man for the first time, Bobby listened to the TV blare a commercial for a limousine service. Then the anchor did an introduction about Bobby being released from prison and segued to old file film footage of himself being led away from the courtroom in handcuffs after the guilty verdict. And there was Moira Farrell, his first lawyer, with her thick mane of red hair, sapphire eyes, and legendary short, tight skirts, which the media loved but had failed to seduce the jury.

The scene shifted to a live interview in Moira Farrell's plush law office. "First, let me say I'm delighted that Bobby Emmet is out of jail and has won a new trial," Farrell said. "And, no, I have not been contacted or consulted by his new attorney. I wouldn't have time these days to involve myself in a criminal trial anyway, since I'm much too busy with other important, exciting matters in my life right now. But I do wish Bobby the very best in his new trial."

Something was wrong, Bobby thought. Not once did she say she thought he was innocent.

Farrell's interview was followed by one with Cis Tuzio, who was now Brooklyn's chief assistant district attorney. "Robert Emmet had better enjoy his short-lived freedom, because he is going straight back to jail like a boomerang," Tuzio said. "This is a classic example of junk justice, a case in which a man violated his position as a police officer and canceled his subscription to the human race when he butchered his lover and *cremated* her. The evidence is overwhelming. This office will not rest until he is back behind bars."

The anchorman said Izzy Gleason, Bobby Emmet's new attorney, was scheduled to hold a two-thirty press conference in front of the Brooklyn district attorney's office in downtown Brooklyn.

The anchor then switched to a story about gubernatorial candidate Gerald Stone chairing a national panel on "The American Family in the 21st Century." Bobby stared at the square-jawed, perfectly groomed candidate with the toothpaste-ad smile. The time was superimposed on the lower left-hand corner of the TV screen: 1:05 PM. Bobby had time for a five-minute shower.

He carried his canvas bag into the bathroom and removed a pair of clean jeans, a sweatshirt, underwear, socks, and a pair of sneakers. He laid them out on top of the wicker hamper. All worn and ragged. He definitely needed new clothes.

He turned on the shower, the nozzle blasting a forceful spray from the great plumbing system of the immense building. He'd been dreaming of this for a long, long time. He got under the spray, then worked up a big lather with the fresh bar of soap, his jail muscles bulging and jumping as he reached around to his back. He vigorously shampooed his close-cropped hair, brushed his teeth under the showerhead, scouring his gums, tongue, the roof of his mouth. He let the very hot water boil him for a good three minutes, his pores oozing eighteen months of prison and scandal.

With his face held directly into the spray, he shut his eyes. He saw the televised faces of Farrell, Tuzio, and Stone, along with Lou Barnicle. Then he willed them all away with a turn of the water faucets. He stepped out and quickly towel-dried and dressed.

He had a much more important face to see.

12

Bobby wanted to walk the twenty city blocks uptown to see Maggie. But his face was all over the news. So he took the Jeep Cherokee, stopping into a costume store called Incognito on West Thirty-seventh Street.

He bought a simple dark fake beard and mustache, a pair of thick, black-rimmed glasses, and a straw fedora hat. The Korean owner let him put on the disguise in front of a small mirror. Bobby was satisfied that it altered his appearance. He paid forty-seven dollars, breaking one of Gleason's hundred-dollar bills, and laughed aloud at his reflection.

He drove uptown in stop-and-go traffic and parked the car in an illegal spot on Fifty-sixth Street near Madison Avenue. He put the Police Parking Permit card in the window. That made it legal.

By 1:26 PM Bobby was waiting for his daughter in the mall of Trump Tower.

Around the corner, on Fifty-sixth Street, he'd passed three TV news crews from local stations, who looked as if they were staking out the residents' entrance of the building for reaction shots or interviews with either Bobby or his ex-wife or Maggie. Security guards had them penned off to the side and wouldn't allow them into the lobby. Bobby had stopped long enough near one of the remote TV news vans to hear the crew talking about his release. *These bastards have been following me since the day I first started dating Connie,* he thought. *They haunted our marriage, made a circus out of the divorce, and a tabloid Olympics out of my trial. They'll never go away.* He took a small victorious delight in the fact that they did not recognize him.

He'd entered the Trump Tower mall, dialed Maggie's number, and told her he was downstairs in the mall in a silly disguise. She told him to wait in front of Harry Winston's jewelers, that she would take an elevator to the basement and transfer to an elevator to the mall to avoid the TV crews.

"Daddy!" Maggie shouted as she ran from the elevators across the waxed marble floor of the mall. Behind her was Connie Mathews Sawyer and her new husband, Trevor Sawyer. Bobby scooped his daughter up in his arms, kissing her once on the lips, realizing she was probably too old for that now. He felt a little funny holding a blossoming fourteen-year-old in his arms, so he put her back on the floor, held her at arm's length, and looked in her moistening eyes.

Maggie was now part girl, part young woman, with long, flowing blond hair, a single-strap metal brace across her front teeth, big earrings in pierced ears, a wad of bubble gum, breasts under a T-shirt, and a sprinkle of Irish freckles across her nose and cheeks. Her skin was as flawless and soft as it was when she was in her crib. Her big, wet green eyes were now dripping mascara.

Bobby bent to her, whispered in her ear, "No tears. I'm home.

I promise you, I am never going back. Today we can talk about anything except jail, okay?"

Maggie nodded silently, choked-up.

Connie Mathews Sawyer and Trevor Sawyer stood looking at Bobby in disbelief.

"Trick or treat," Connie said, laughing at his disguise.

Bobby nodded at Connie with an old, sad fondness, glad she was looking so well. She shimmered with a halo of money.

"Jesus, you could use some new clothes, Roberto," Connie said.

"The shopping isn't great in the north country," Bobby said.

Trevor Sawyer stepped forward, awkwardly extended his right hand to Bobby. "Welcome back," Trevor said. "Good luck. . . ."

"Thanks, Trevor," Bobby said, shaking Trevor's small hand. He'd touched warmer hands in coffins.

"You're going to need it," Trevor added.

Bobby didn't know if it was a warning or a threat.

Trevor was a short, balding man who would have been more relaxed wearing a traditional dark suit and tie with cordovan shoes. But Bobby knew that Connie chose his clothes. Today he was wearing an expensive Italian linen sports jacket, a white Calvin Klein dress T-shirt, fluff-dried Levi's 501 jeans, and oxblood glove-leather loafers with no socks. He looked like a cross between some of the Wall Street and showbiz types he'd busted in big coke deals as a DA cop.

"Thanks for being so good to my kid," Bobby said.

"She's a delight," Trevor said. "You're a lucky guy."

"So are you," Bobby said, nodding toward Connie, who smirked with obvious glee.

"Trevor, you're going to be late for your two o'clock," Connie said, checking her watch.

"What?" Trevor said. *"My* employees are going to fire *me?"*

Connie straightened his jacket, kissed him on the lips, and said, "Bye, Trevor. Bobby and I have kid-chat to do."

Bobby gave him a thumbs-up, and the third-richest cosmetics magnate in America walked out of Trump Tower toward a waiting gray Silver Cloud Rolls-Royce. He looked like an actor playing a corporate honcho.

"Go into Winston's and clean yourself up, sweetheart," Connie said to Maggie, who was wiping mascara from her cheeks. "Your dad and I need to talk a minute. Alone."

Maggie smiled at her father. She turned and blew her nose. Connie put her arm through Bobby's, grabbing the rock-hard bicep in her small, soft hand as she led him on an aimless walk and talk through the atrium, former husband and wife, divided by a few hundred million and yet still joined by the common blood of a child.

"Don't get me wrong, Bobby," Connie said, clearly enjoying the stroll, passing mostly young tourists and affluent New Yorkers who came there to dine in the bistro or shop in the expensive boutiques. "I'm glad you're out. I never thought you killed that woman. You never raised a hand to me, so I just can't imagine you doing it to any other woman. You're too cornball macho to even curse in front of a female, never mind *murder* one. Freud would say that comes from having a mother you adore. That said, I have mixed emotions . . . Why the hell are my emotions always mixed about you?"

"You're looking good, too, Connie," Bobby said, passing a plainclothes security guard, who nodded to Connie. Bobby thought her delicate rose-petal perfume was probably designed specially for her by Daddy's company, or maybe her husband's. She owned half of each now.

"I didn't comment on your looks because you already know, dumb disguise or not, you look like a goddamned Adonis," she said. "You always did. It's what made me abandon all reason and run away with you and your civil-service paycheck to begin with. I'm sure with jail muscles no one'll be throwing you out of bed for eating animal crackers either."

"Geez, and I thought it was my Shakespearian expertise that always turned you on, Con," Bobby said.

"Don't call me *Con*," she said. "It's what they call *you* now. And actually, you also had more brains than anyone as good-looking as you deserves. My ex-con ex-husband . . ."

She stopped and looked him up and down as if at auction and then took off the dopey black-rimmed glasses and looked him in the eyes. Bobby saw her tough facade fracture when she looked too deep, seeing things only they could know about each other. Things so foreign to the world she was born into, the world she again inhabited. He knew she saw summers down on the Jersey shore, nights in the balcony of Brooklyn's Kingsway movie house, afternoons in a leaky rowboat on the lake in Prospect Park, making love in front of the fireplace in the Brooklyn brownstone, a walk in a blizzard on the Coney Island boardwalk, the night he helped her deliver Maggie into the world. That was the night they swore they would never, ever part. The divorce. The awful press. Maggie's broken heart. Picking up the pieces. Then the murder trial. . . .

"Maggie is different," Connie said softly. "She's not a kid anymore. She gets her period. She wears bras. She likes boys. She hates me and adores you. But what happened to you ripped the heart out of our little girl and crushed it. In some ways, it never mended. There wasn't one day she didn't talk about you coming home. 'When Daddy comes home . . .' was the way she started every other sentence."

"Well, I'm home and—"

"Let me finish; then I'll let you two be together," she said. "I know you want to see her regularly. I want that, too. You are a terrific father, no denying that. But you're still facing a murder charge. The press is still going to be all over you. Again. Which means all over Maggie—and me. This woman prosecutor wants you so bad that I bet she dreams about you. Trevor hears things all the time in his political circles about how they're going to make you the law-and-order whipping boy of this guy Stone's governorship campaign—"

"Gubernatorial . . ."

"Don't you dare correct my English, you sanctimonious Brooklyn-bred asswipe," Connie said.

Bobby laughed, and so did she, and then she exhaled deeply. "They're going to make you another Willie Horton," she continued. "They're gonna make you an O.J. Simpson–style 'He Got Away With Murder' poster boy." She stopped, looked him in the eyes, and said, "I don't want Maggie in that poster."

"Con—"

"Constance," she said.

"Get off it, Con," he said. "I don't want to ever hurt Maggie. Believe me."

"If I have to, I'll go into family court to protect her from the media circus," she said. "Ask the judge not to grant you visitation

71

rights until your new trial is over. I could take her to Europe, or up to Connecticut for the duration.''

Bobby looked at her and then over at Maggie, who awaited them as they circled back her way near the elevators.

"Don't kick me when I'm down," Bobby said. "I just want to see my kid. I promise I won't expose her to the media animals."

"When the new trial starts, I don't want her in court," she said, "—for some cheap sympathy trick your new lowlife lawyer might try to use."

"I never let her near the first trial," he said. "I don't even want her to watch any of this one on TV. Use the V chip. On all fourteen TVs."

"Still can't resist sarcasm, can you?" she said. "The only reason I'm keeping Maggie in town is so she can take extra credit in summer school and because she wants—needs—to see you. Here I am feeling sorry for you, and—"

"Don't feel sorry for me," Bobby said. "Just don't make it any harder for me and Maggie."

She shook her head in a subtle way, her diamond earrings clicking, her eyes sparkling, her long lashes blinking. He half expected her to start purring.

"If you need money . . ."

"Thanks, but no thanks."

"Same macho Brooklyn-Irish horseshit," she said. "I could have paid for an appeal. I could have gotten you a real lawyer the first time around and can still get you the best appeals lawyer in America instead of this Izzy Gleason, who looks like something I'd be afraid to step in and who'd probably represent his mother's killer. But you won't have it. No! You're *proud!* You've got your goddamned Irish, macho, working-class-hero dignity. . . ."

"I'll get along fine," Bobby said. "As soon as I get a job, I'll send my support checks right away. Make up the arrears. . . ."

She laughed at the idea and waved her hand.

"I must confess I'm sort of jealous," she said.

"Of what?"

"Of whoever gets the first post-jail tumble with you," Connie said, squeezing his bicep again.

"I have to find Dorothea for that," Bobby said. "Besides, she's at the heart of this mess. My mess . . ."

Connie stared at him and took a deep breath, as if she was

certain Bobby was chasing a ghost. "Maggie liked Dorothea," Connie said, exhaling slowly. "She must have been okay."

"And you have Trevor," he said. "Maggie says he's a . . . nice guy."

"He is a nice guy," Connie said, like someone speaking about her accountant. "He's . . . right for me. He fits. He doesn't always match my mood, but he's devoted."

Bobby nodded.

"Thanks for not making this hard, Con," Bobby said.

"I never had any trouble making it hard for you," she said, squeezing his arm again. Her touch and smell sent involuntary shivers through him. He smiled.

"That was never our problem was it?" he said.

"The problem was that it was never a problem and it still ended," Connie said with a deep sigh. "Just remember, I will make it *difficult*—that's a more appropriate word—for you, if I have to. I won't let Maggie get hurt again."

Connie looked as if she wanted to kiss him good-bye, but she just swallowed, glanced at Maggie, who was rolling her eyes with impatience.

"Maybe we can have lunch sometime," Connie said, shrugging. "And talk, like we used to, when we were best friends."

"Absolutely," Bobby said. "Can I ask you a question?"

"Sure . . ."

"What do you *do* now, exactly?"

"I . . . well . . . I . . . I have absolutely no fucking idea," she said with a baffled smile. "But the checks clear. Have Maggie back in an hour. She'll show you how to leave through the back way of Harry Winston's jewelers, the way Michael Jackson always ducked the press."

As she walked away, Bobby heard her say, sotto voce, "God, you look good . . ." He watched her go and knew why he married her all those years ago. Trevor was one rich and lucky fool.

After successfully dodging the press, Bobby drove with Maggie to Lexington Avenue and parked the car in a bus stop across the street from one of those new computer cafés, where the two of them now sat at a window table, near a bank of computer terminals where people surfed the Internet as they sipped coffee.

Bobby noticed that Maggie was looking at him oddly. He'd left the fake-beard disguise in the car, so it wasn't his appearance that was bothering Maggie. It was something deeper, darker, and scarier.

"What?" Bobby felt self-conscious in front of his kid, whom he'd been separated from for too long.

"That's your third muffin, Dad," Maggie said.

"How's school?"

"Sucks," she said.

"Too bad," Bobby said. "Got a boyfriend?"

"Mom makes it impossible," she said.

"Why?"

"Cause she's Mom."

"Oh," Bobby said. "She doesn't let you date?"

"Not the kind of guys I want to talk to," she said.

"Who does she want you to date?"

"It's not *dating*, Dad," she said, laughing. "You're either *talking* to a guy or *seeing* a guy. Like that."

"Okay," Bobby said. "Who's she want you *talking* to?"

"Money nerds," Maggie said. "Assorted herbs."

Bobby understood immediately. School sucked because it was filled with rich kids, the kind of kids Connie wanted her daughter to date.

"Who do you want to date . . . *talk* to? *See?*"

She shrugged and took a sip of ice tea. "Tell me more about this boat," Maggie said. "When you get it fixed up, can you take me out on it, to Coney Island? Mom says she's afraid I'll catch Ebola down Coney, but I miss Brooklyn *so* much, Dad. I miss living in a neighborhood. Trump Tower isn't a neighborhood; it's a birdcage for exotic pterodactyls. And who has St. Patrick's Cathedral for a parish church? I miss Holy Name. I miss schoolyards, corner pizza joints, hanging out on stoops, street corners, and Prospect Park. My friends . . ."

That was it, he thought. She still missed Brooklyn and the childhood she had before her parents' divorce made her divorce the place and the friends she loved. A kid's divorce was always more painful and complicated than the one the adults went through.

"Yeah," Bobby said. "I'll take you to Brooklyn soon, as long as you don't tell your mother. Would you like that?"

She nodded and then fell into another deep silence, looking

away from her father, as if trying to reestablish the lines of communication that had been silenced by prison.

"Something else is bothering you, kiddo."

She turned and just stared at him, her eyes sad and nervous.

"Just say it," Bobby said. "There are things we both need to say."

"You said not to talk about jail," Maggie said, stabbing her straw into the ice cubes in her glass.

"Well, if you really want to, we can," Bobby said. "I just never liked war stories. But if it makes you feel better, ask me whatever you want."

"I watch the news, Dad," she said, her lower lip trembling. "That awful woman, Cis Tuzio, she's promising to put you back in jail. It scares me. . . ."

"I promised you I'm not going back," Bobby said.

"Then what are you going to do about the murder charge? What about Dorothea?"

Bobby looked his kid in the eye. "I'm gonna find her," he said.

"You think she's alive?"

"I have to believe she is."

"If she is, and you find her, all of this is over?"

"Yes. And I have some ideas about who knows where she is. I have lots to do. And that's why I can't stay long and—"

Bobby abruptly cut himself off as he saw a white Taurus with tinted windows pull into the bus stop behind his Jeep across the avenue. He saw the driver's window open a crack and a camera lens come out and point in his and Maggie's direction as they sat next to the window.

"Son of a bitch," Bobby said, standing to shield Maggie from the photograph. Bobby then ran out the front door of the restaurant, into fast-moving downtown traffic, toward the Taurus.

"Hey! You haven't paid your check!" shouted a harried waitress, who chased Bobby into the street.

"Dad," Maggie shouted as she followed. "What's wrong?"

The camera lens quickly disappeared back behind the tinted window, and the white Taurus made a hasty departure from the bus stop, racing through a red light amid madly honking horns, and then weaved downtown in free-moving traffic. Bobby stood in the middle of the gutter, traffic swerving around him.

Maggie reached her father and gently led him back into the

restaurant. Patrons gaped at him oddly, a few looked as if they recognized him now and whispered furtively. Bobby apologized to the waitress and then unfolded his cell phone and called Max Roth but was once again connected to his voice mail.

"Max, for Christ sakes, this is Bobby again. I need to run a plate! I'll keep trying."

Maggie lifted her knapsack onto the table and unzipped it, took out a small Apple notebook computer, which she left unopened, and searched through a collection of computer disks in a zippered pouch.

"Gimme the plate number," she said. "Why didn't you tell me?"

"What are you going to do with it?"

"Gimme it, Dad," Maggie said, taking the plate number from Bobby as she walked to one of the large phone-rigged café computers and plugged a disk into the floppy-disk drive.

"You can run a license plate?" he asked.

"If it's New York, Jersey, or Connecticut I can because I have a Usenet Warez bootleg copy of the communications software for those DMVs, with the passwords," she said. "So I can dial in and do a search. It's how girls track down cute guys who wave from passing cars."

Bobby watched in amazement as Maggie clicked at the keyboard.

"I remember going out with you on the police boat, Dad," she said as she waited for the computer search to appear. She looked up smiling, and in that tilt of her head Bobby could see her face was maturing into womanhood, saw her mother's disarming feline eyes, and once the little brace came off, that smile would help her win her way with most guys. She looked so much like her mother it was spooky, bringing back haunted memories he didn't want to visit.

"You took me to all those neat little islands in the harbor," she said. "Under the Verrazano Bridge, over to Hoboken, all the way around to Liberty Island and Ellis Island, where Grandma and Grandpa came into the country . . . By the way, she called. She knows you're out. Wants you to call . . ."

"We have to call her together," Bobby said. "Her hearing isn't so hot anymore. And when everything is straightened out for good, maybe we'll go down there together and visit her in Florida, huh?"

"I'd love that," Maggie said. "Can I bring Theresa, from Brooklyn?"

"You're already asking for sleepovers?"

The two of them laughed, because in the old days after the divorce Maggie never once came to Bobby's apartment without having Theresa sleep over.

"I wish I would have known Grandpa before he was killed," Maggie said, tapping a few more keys on the computer.

"He died as bravely as he lived," Bobby said. "My mom never wanted me to join the police force after he was killed. Then after what happened to me, she took it hard, kiddo."

"Dad," she said. "I really like Dorothea. I think she's nice, smart, funny. And she loves you. Not that Mom puts you down. She doesn't. In fact I know Mom still has at least a physical thing for you . . ."

"Maggie, Jesus God," Bobby said, wiping cappuccino cream from his mouth, blushing in front of his kid. Time passes and suddenly your kid was telling *you* about the birds and the bees, he thought.

"Just look at the way she got dressed for you today," Maggie said. "I mean Trevor is okay, a nice enough dude, more money than God's boss, but Mom is incapable of hiding her feelings. I saw the way she looked at you in the lobby, like she wanted to jump your bones . . ."

"Maggie, this is your mom and dad you're talking about here," Bobby said.

"I'm talking the real deal," Maggie said. "You guys were married for twelve years, man. But Dorothea . . . I could tell her stuff. Dorothea was totally cool. If she *is* alive, Dad, please, you got to do whatever it takes to find her."

Bobby touched her hand.

"I fully intend to," Bobby said. "That's why we might not be able to have our weekends together right away. I might be dealing with some bad people. I just can't let you get hurt."

"Cool, but let me help, when I can," she said. "Computers, databases, a little hacking, classified information, legwork, phone stuff, just anything. Dad, I live for something to do. Especially for you. . . ."

"Thanks, Mag," Bobby said. "And thanks for believing in me."

"Know what bothers me, Dad?" Maggie said. "The blood. If it

wasn't Dorothea's blood in your apartment and your car. And if it wasn't her body in the crematorium, then whose *was* it?''

"That's the question that put me in jail," he said.

Maggie circled her finger up in the air as the computer search was completed. She read from the screen and seemed disappointed. "The white Taurus is a lease job," Maggie said. "Leased to, get this, the Stone for Governor Campaign, Inc. The address is Fifteen Court Street, Brooklyn."

"Jesus Christ," Bobby whispered with quiet surprise. It wasn't a DA cop or a paparazzi or one of Lou Barnicle's Gibraltar Security goons who had followed him from prison and all over the city.

Maggie packed up her disks and her laptop and slung the backpack over her shoulders. They stepped out onto the sidewalk, and at the corner Bobby put his arm around his daughter's shoulder. He noticed more than a few people giving him disparaging looks.

"They think you're a pedophile." Maggie laughed.

He took his arm from around his daughter's shoulder and angrily shoved his thumbs into his belt. They'd stolen those few months of their lives, he thought, when he could still walk with his kid without him looking like a pervert sugar daddy.

"Cheer up," she said. "You're free."

"Not yet," he said.

"Is there anything else I can do?" Maggie asked. "Anything on your checklist I can scratch off for you?"

Bobby smiled and said, "Actually there is. Check the old newspaper clips. I need to know more about Cis Tuzio."

"The witch . . ."

"Yeah," Bobby said. "Where she lives. Where she shops. Where she went to law school. Where she socializes. Hobbies. . . ."

"I'll even find out where she buys those brooms she flies around on," Maggie said with a smile.

Bobby smiled again and gave her his new cellular phone number.

"Dad, I don't think you should drop me home," she said. "The press'll still be there, and you have better things to do."

He kissed Maggie on the cheek and checked his new watch, which told him it was almost three o'clock.

"Go find her, Dad," Maggie said. "Go find out what happened to Dorothea."

13

"I can't tell you how thrilled I am you're out," John Shine said. "You said you need to ask me about something?"

"You were assigned to City Hall once," Bobby said. "What do you know about this guy Stone? Gerald Stone, the councilman who's running for governor? Is there a file on him?"

"You don't need a file," said John Shine. "I busted him once. Doing ninety on the Brooklyn Bridge. Half-stoned. Bimbo with him. Claimed she was a campaign worker. Now he's Mr. Family Values."

They were in a window booth of The Winning Ticket saloon on Third Avenue in Bay Ridge, Brooklyn. Shine had bought the place with the winnings from a three-million-dollar New York State Lottery jackpot. Shine watched Bobby devour a chicken breast sandwich, sliding fries into the right corner of his mouth.

Shine had ignored the first few remarks from the two half-drunk off-duty cops standing a dozen feet away at the bar of his restaurant. Bobby seemed almost oblivious when the bigger of the two drunken cops, the one wearing a Giants jacket, said, "I guess when you eat with the jigs in the joint, you rewrite the book of etiquette."

There were only a few men on the opposite side of the horse-shoe bar and a couple at a booth near the back door, out of earshot of the boisterous cops. Bobby noticed just four tables of late-lunch customers in the main dining room, which was separated from the bar by a smoked-glass divider.

"So Stone has an arrest record?" Bobby asked.

"I didn't say that," Shine said. "The duty captain that night squashed the arrest. The captain was from Staten Island, where Stone was a councilman. It helps to have someone who can get you a zoning variance when you need one, so he let him sleep

79

it off without logging the arrest. Pissed me off. But that's life in the PD. The bimbo spent most of the night, behind closed doors, in the captain's office. You get the picture. . . ."

"Fuck the book of etiquette," said the short, squat cop at the bar, talking loud enough for Bobby to hear. "Look how he re-wrote the book of love. In blood. With a fuckin' carving knife."

"Then charbroiled her," said the tall one.

"Pay no attention to them," a furious Shine said. " 'Society everywhere is in conspiracy against the manhood of every one of its members.' "

"Emerson," Bobby said.

Shine smiled and said, "You actually read the Emerson I sent you?"

"Well, I sure had the time," Bobby said, washing down the food with some orange juice. "I read it at least three times. I agree with a lot of what old Ralph Waldo had to say. The stuff that's not outdated is right on. Some of it is transcendental bab-ble. But, look, getting back to Stone . . ."

"He was a Vietnam vet, and I never met one of them who didn't inhale," Shine said. "He liked broads back then. He's politically conservative. He's ambitious."

"Why would he single me out?" Bobby asked.

"Big case," Shine said. "High profile. Votes."

"There are other big cases," Bobby said. "Why would he have someone tailing me?"

The two cops at the bar were getting louder. "I hear his nick-name upstate was Officer Bobby Bunghole," said the tall cop and they both broke up laughing like a pair of cartoon magpies. Shine looked at Bobby across the butcher-block table and said, "You don't have to listen to this garbage in my place. I can still personally eighty-six two Cro-Magnons like them, bad back or not."

Bobby stopped Shine when he started to get up to deal with the drunken cops.

"I'm used to it, John," Bobby said. "And believe me, I've heard worse. Think what the church said about Emerson after his speech about every man's individual divinity at Harvard. He wasn't invited back for years."

Shine laughed and settled back in his seat, his face a twisted grimace from the four herniated back disks he'd suffered several years before, wrestling on a rooftop with a crack addict.

It didn't seem to bother him that the perp later walked and made half a million dollars in a title fight. Or that Shine had been in a back brace ever since. He'd done what he was paid to do, and the injury was part of the job.

Bobby had admired Shine, twelve years his senior, since the days he'd taught Bobby the ropes. Taught him how to win friends in the precinct streets by walking a beat with confidence rather than a swagger. How to finesse brass with a genuine inquiry about the welfare of his wife and kids. How to get a confession from a perp with a hero sandwich and a pack of smokes faster than a beating. How to maintain your dignity among the lying, cheating, corrupt cops by remembering you didn't take this job to become rich or to maim people.

"I've worked almost every detail on the job," Shine had said one day long ago when Bobby was a rookie, as they drove in a sector car through the violent and racially strained streets of the 71st Precinct in Crown Heights. It was a lecture on policing Bobby would never forget. About how Shine had worked everywhere from Harbor to Aviation to Vice, the U.N., Narcotics, Bunco, Organized Crime. "I pulled duty at City Hall under Beame and Koch and Dinkins, worked presidential motorcades, walked a beat, did community relations," Shine had said. "I learned in one of my first details, a post outside the United Nations, that you couldn't hit anyone without the possibility of causing an international incident. Treat everyone like they were a diplomat and you wouldn't get in trouble. From guarding mayors and presidents, you learn that the citizen should have just as much protection, because these guys work for the citizens. And as Emerson said, 'Pay every debt as if God wrote the bill.'"

Shine was a tall, elegant-looking man with the long, strong tapered body of a swimmer and the clear-thinking, focused, predatory mind of a hunter. He had wrinkles around his eyes from many years of sun, sea, and laughing. But in the two years Bobby had been away, pain had bitten even deeper lines in his face.

The NYPD brass hated him because he was a maverick, and women loved him for the same reason. But John Shine was rarely with the same woman twice. Ever since the death of his wife and kid early in his police career, whenever Bobby or anyone else asked him about remarrying, John Shine's response was always the same: "I've already had the one great love of my life."

Bobby knew that Shine's wife and kid had disappeared while sailing one stormy day off Montauk Point, and the cop had never forgiven himself for not stopping them from going out that day. A grieving sadness burdened the man. So it was good to see him active, Bobby thought, with a successful saloon partially filling the void in his life.

"I hear even the guards wouldn't take care of him up there," the big cop at the bar said, referring to Bobby. "Knew he was a guy who ratted on his own kind . . ."

Shine made another move toward the two obnoxious cops at the bar. Again, Bobby grabbed his hand, motioned with his eyes for him to sit back down in the booth.

"Not worth it," Bobby said.

"These bastards . . ."

"It's good I know where I stand," Bobby said softly. "Let them talk. Assholes might wind up saying something I need to know."

"I miss the action of the job, Bobby, but I don't miss the ignoramuses," Shine said.

"Relax, John," Bobby said.

Shine took a small white tablet from a pill box and washed it down with a drink of plain ice water, grimacing.

"You okay?" Bobby asked.

"This back of mine is like living with a Siamese twin who hates my guts," said Shine.

"What do the doctors say?"

" 'Get used to it.' " Shine chuckled dryly.

"Why didn't you ever put in for three-quarters?" Bobby asked. "If anyone ever deserved it, it's you."

Bobby already knew that Shine had too much pride for what he had always called the "police hero fund."

"Because it's for real heroes," Shine said. "Not for guys like me who get knocked around a little by a high-risk job. Especially not for dust mites like them. I hear them talking about getting on three-quarters all the time, like it was a lifelong ambition."

Shine again nodded to the two cops who were bent over their piece of the horseshoe-shaped bar, laughing uproariously now, as the bartender pulled them two fresh mugs of beer.

"Not for shitheads who abuse the system," Shine continued,

the rough street cop occasionally surfacing with the anger. "Three-quarters was designed for people who simply can't work anymore. Guys paralyzed by a bullet in the spine; men crippled and maimed. Me, I can still work. I don't need a cripple's pension so long as I can fend for myself."

The big cop belched in John Shine's general direction as he caught the tail end of his tirade.

"They're part of the Lou Barnicle crew?" Bobby asked, nodding toward the two giggling cops.

"Not yet," Shine said. "Farm team. But you don't need me to tell you how it works. Soon as they get three-quarters, they'll probably go to work for Barnicle. That's the routine. Work ten, twelve years on NYPD, take the first injury you get, put in their three-quarters papers. If they're lucky enough to get it, they go to work for Barnicle, and between the pension and the salary, and the SSI, if you work off the books, you're making more than a deputy inspector."

"I was half-looking into this racket when I was framed for Dorothea's murder," Bobby said. "I think she's still alive. . . ."

"You know what the chances of that are, Bobby. Slim and none."

"I'm not so sure," Bobby said. "But now, the day I get out of jail, a car from Stone's campaign starts tailing me. You don't think he's personally involved in this pension scam, do you?"

"That's a stretch," Shine said with a laugh. "But I can't name one retired member of NYPD brass I ever worked under who isn't collecting three-quarters. Almost every former deputy inspector. Going back to Chief Jackson, who worked a Rolling Stones concert at Shea Stadium and claimed he got too close to the massive speakers during 'Jumpin' Jack Flash' and it ruptured his eardrum. He was making a hundred and ten thousand a year when he put in his three-quarters papers. With special bonuses for every year over twenty years he served on the force, he was rubber-stamp approved for a one-hundred-and-seventeen-thousand-dollars-a-year pension, tax free, for life. All for being verbally assaulted by Mick Jagger."

"That's obscene," Bobby said.

"Yeah," Shine said. "But I'd say trying to link it to Gerald *Stone* is off the radar screen."

From the bar the big cop in the Giants jacket stopped laughing and roared: "The broad was some piece of fucking ass, though."

The fat little cop, dressed in a red jacket, white shirt, blue pants, who Bobby thought looked like a U.S. mailbox, nodded and said, "They say the broad was a foreigner, so I wonder what fuckin' lingo she pleaded for her life in."

Bobby couldn't stop Shine this time as he leaped from the booth to the bar, forgetting his pain, grabbing the big cop by his jacket, twisting him to a half-prone position, and yanking him across the floor of the bar toward the front door.

The customers froze at the outbreak of the commotion; the bartender was literally shaking, two glasses clinking together in his hands. Bobby quickly rose and glared at the short, fat cop, who was making a tentative move toward Shine's blind side. He took one look at Bobby Emmet and then made a quick dash out the back door, leaving his money on the bar and the fate of his drinking buddy in question.

A waitress opened the front door for Shine, and he hauled the big cop out onto the sidewalk like the evening trash. He fought for air as Shine lifted him to his feet and rammed his back into a parking meter. The other cop now circled over to help up his big pal.

"I ever see either one of you mutts in here again, I'll slap your dirty mouths," Shine said.

He turned from them, walked inside, smiled, and winked at Bobby. The patrons returned to their lunches, the bartender and the waitresses went back to work.

"You okay, John?" Bobby asked, half-amused. Shine didn't give a shit who you were; he feared no one.

"That's the smegma they let wear badges today," Shine said, as he groaned into his seat in the booth. "I'd rather pin a star on a fucking shoemaker."

"You haven't lost a step," Bobby said, smiling.

"My back is exploding," Shine whispered. "If that galoot had fought back, he would have killed me. Makes you wonder what the hell he's going to do when he's confronted by some ghetto kid who is fighting for his freedom and his life?"

"No wonder they want out on three-quarters," Bobby said.

"Perfect Lou Barnicle candidates," Shine said. "He'll morph them into square badges, rent-a-cops, guarding colleges and shopping malls while they also collect three-quarters. As a matter of fact, I wouldn't be surprised if that big ape parlays the bang I just gave him into a pension. End of tomorrow's tour, he claims he wrestled with a perp on duty, messed up his back, takes a sick-out, pays off some corrupt quack for a bogus report, and puts in his papers."

"What do you think of Barnicle?" Bobby asked.

"Unfortunately, he's my neighbor down in Windy Tip—bay-front houses about a hundred yards apart," Shine said. "The whole peninsula is balls deep in cops now. Retired, still on the job. See, it's in the city, so you get the dirt cheap property taxes. But it's got zero crime."

"And zero minorities," Bobby said.

"For god sakes, don't start with that racist-closed-community routine," Shine said. "Yeah, it's a white neighborhood. Like East Hampton and Southampton, where all the millionaire liberals flee in the summer. You don't see them going down Coney do you? Yeah, Windy is white; just like Harlem is black. But it isn't that sinister. Judges, politicians, businesspeople have summer homes there, too. Cops just happen to gravitate to it in flocks. I think it has to do with the sea. Cops like boats to get away from it all, to unwind from the job on the wild blue yonder. At least that's why I originally bought there. And to be near my wife and kid . . . the ocean is their grave."

He quietly ate another pain pill and washed it down with his drink.

"I have nothing against the place," Bobby said. "But there is a mind-set there, a xenophobia, a fear of outsiders. Security gates, private cops—they do everything but take a blood test to let a visitor in. The people there are afraid of anyone who doesn't wear blue for a living."

"There's some truth to that," Shine said. "Even the rookies spend summers there in rented bungalows, hanging out in a saloon Barnicle owns called Central Booking. Subtle, no? But Barnicle, as menacing as he tries to be, is really just a big windbag now. Full of himself. He had a rep on the job for being a bully, smashing guys' faces into walls, shoving perps' heads into toilets filled with shit and piss. Giving out crummy duty, passing good cops over for promotions. A fascist streak, unless you kissed his ass and licked his boots. He took a perverted delight in beating prisoners when they were handcuffed, and you already know my theory on cops who beat criminals . . .''

"Yeah," Bobby said. "They take petty criminals and turn them into cop killers. You taught me that the first week we worked together, John. But you let the Barnicle crew hang out here, too?"

"Yeah, they drink at the bar, mostly. But Barnicle eats here at least three times a week in the dining room. In fact, about an hour ago, his lady friend, Sandy, called for a seven o'clock reservation. Oddballs. She always arrives first. Then he arrives twenty minutes later with the two goons, like the pope. They pay cash money, usually behave themselves. Sometimes they fight. About that cute kid of theirs. But Barnicle's crew knows I don't tolerate locker-room antics in my place. I figure the best way to know what these assholes are up to is to have them around."

"Keep your enemies close," Bobby said, "as Michael Corleone said."

"Actually it was Machiavelli who said it first," Shine said. "But the guy you should talk to about Barnicle and your case is Tom Larkin. You know the cranky old house mouse from the seven deuce?"

"Yeah, I had him on my must-see list."

"Oh, yeah?" Shine said. "Well, I hear that Larkin greedily hordes certain critical information about your case that he's not putting out for general consumption. He knows something about everyone, old Tom does. He's a paranoid old bugger. Precisely what he knows about you, if anything, and who he's told it to, remains a mystery. But I hear rumors. I don't believe in rumors, but I do believe in checking them out. And I'm willing to bet he talks to you. He always liked you, always believed in your innocence. And I know they never meshed very well when Barnicle was his commanding officer. Talk to Larkin; probe him, oil him, see what he knows."

"I will," Bobby said. "Remember, John, I never had a chance to investigate my own case. I was inside the whole time without bail before trial. So, I intend to talk to everyone. That's another reason I'm here. I wanted you to be one of the first to know that I think Barnicle and his people are somehow involved in Dorothea's disappearance and my frame. If I have to get down and dirty with this prick, I don't want to put you in the middle. So if I avoid you, or seem aloof, it's only because I don't want to contaminate you with any of this. It's my problem. I'll deal with it.''

"You crazy?" Shine said, looking playfully offended. "You're my friend. 'The only way to have a friend is to be one.' ''

"Again with Emerson," Bobby said.

"He is my North Star," Shine said. "I want to help you, Bobby. I mean, running a restaurant is fine, distracting, a livelihood. But I miss the juice of the job, working a case, mixing it up. You need me, you call me. Or else I'm insulted. In fact, anytime you want, you should come down to my house on Windy Tip. Hang out, swim, get some sun on your jailhouse face. Bounce things off me. I'd appreciate being needed now and then. 'Make yourself necessary to someone.' ''

"Thanks," Bobby said, shaking Shine's hand good-bye. "I might take you up on that."

14

As Bobby approached his car, he saw a familiar, impatient black man leaning against the front fender, looking as if Bobby owed him money.

Bobby was no longer a member of NYPD, but years of fearing Internal Affairs cops had instilled a lingering paranoia in him. The uneasiness returned when he saw Forrest Morgan of IAB waiting for him, looking smug and cocky.

"Hello, Forrest," Bobby said.

Morgan grunted. He was a big man, and Bobby recalled the first time he ever saw him, across the ring in the NYPD heavyweight championship ten years earlier. Morgan had looked as if he were hammered together in a blacksmith's shop. His bald black head sat on top of an eighteen-inch neck, like a cannonball that wouldn't fit into the barrel. In the decade since they fought the last of four ring wars—two wins each, all decisions—Morgan had only added about ten pounds, which he wore on his chest like armor plating. His dark polyester suit was shining cheaply in the sun.

Bobby's fights with Morgan had made Bobby a much better fighter. Some said they'd pounded each other into departmental legend. After fighting him, Bobby was never intimidated by anyone else, ever again.

"We better talk," Morgan said.

"How'd you find me so soon?" Bobby asked.

"You're like a fucking homing pigeon," Morgan said. "I knew as soon as you were set free you'd fly home to your trainer."

"You always were a thinking cop," Bobby said.

"Half the dirty cops in Brooklyn flock to this place to spend their dirty money," Morgan said. "Why not you? I sit on this place at least once a month."

"Anything big?"

"Not as big as you," Morgan said. "Yet. I saw that little fracas with those two asshole cops. Daniels and Lebeche. Dirty as earthworms. That figures; you're out one day and already you're consorting with a couple felons waiting to happen."

"Jesus, Forrest, it's always so sweet to see you."

"It ain't nice to see you," Morgan said. "Never was. Never will be. Reason I'm here is I know you know something I wanna know."

"Like what?"

"Like when you went in the can, you were looking into a pension scam."

"Yeah?"

"Yeah," Morgan said. "I figure, now you're out, still insisting you're innocent, you'll be going right back to looking at this scam."

"And you want what I find," Bobby said.

"On a sesame-seed bun, extra pickle, special sauce," Morgan said.

"You had eighteen months to look where I left off."

"But, see, maybe it's because I'm the wrong flavor that I don't get assigned to big cases like this," Morgan said. "Instead they got me doing integrity tests on rookie brothers. Going after black beat cops taking skim from weed dealers."

"And you can't get any promotions doing that," Bobby said.

"That's right," Morgan said.

"And you need some promotions to hike your own pension when you retire," Bobby said.

"My bride, my kids, would appreciate that," Morgan said.

"And you'd like to sort of stumble into something big," Bobby said, nodding his head.

"Well, I wouldn't be a very honorable cop if I looked the other way, now would I?" Morgan said. "I also know that now that you're out of the job, you don't have the juice you need to investigate this sort of scam."

"And you're offering to help me if I help you," Bobby said.

"I do know that you have a tendency to attract mutts. Like those two that John Shine just eighty-sixed. But I know and you know, they're guppies. I want some big game fish, ones I can pose with for pictures. Front page, *News* and the *Post* type pictures. Hear what I'm saying?"

"You're looking out for you," Bobby said.

"Yes, I am," Morgan said. "Only way this face is getting promoted in my bureau is by posing with something big."

"Why should I help you?"

"Because if you don't, maybe I'll help the DA put you right back where you just came from," Morgan said.

"Still trash talking, Forrest? At your age?" Bobby turned away, smiling thinly, and noticed John Shine was watching their exchange through the front window of The Winning Ticket.

"Just making myself clear, Bobby."

"Well, your mouth didn't scare me when we fought, Forrest. It's not gonna scare me now. I didn't like the way IAB did business when I was on the job. With fear, entrapment, threatening to expose marital infidelities, intimidation. I like it even less now. So catch your own fucking fish, Forrest. You ain't using me for chum."

Bobby pulled open the driver's door and got into his Jeep.

"One way or the other," Forrest Morgan said. "I'm gonna know what you know. Just thought you should know it. I *will* see you around, Bobby."

"Not if I see you first," Bobby said.

15

The encounter with Forrest Morgan made Bobby ten minutes late for his rendezvous with Tom Larkin. The old cop had written Bobby in jail to tell him that if he ever got out on an appeal, he should come see him. Said he had some information he wouldn't dare put into a letter that would be screened by prison authorities. Bobby had regarded the letter as the ramblings of a well-meaning but out-of-touch old cop.

But now Johnnie Shine said he'd also heard on the tom-toms that Larkin knew something he was keeping close to the vest. Things were getting interesting.

After Bobby parked the Jeep on Forty-second Street in Brooklyn, outside Sunset Park, Bobby and Larkin shook hands and exchanged a few minutes of catch-up small talk. But Larkin soon noticed that Bobby was distracted, looking intensely at the passing traffic.

"What the hell are you looking for?" Larkin asked.

Bobby told Larkin about the tail. Larkin handed Bobby his blue uniform-hat, squatted, and began exploring under the bumpers and fenders of Bobby's Jeep.

"Let's have a look," Larkin said.

Larkin was sixty-one, a tall, lanky man who moved with a sturdy durable grace, as if he were made of bamboo. He looked a little like Abe Lincoln with a shave, all droopy, sad eyes and strong pronounced jaw. He rubbed his swollen jaw where his lower right molar was giving him hell. He'd already told Bobby he'd been at the dentist that morning and would have to go in for the second stage of a root canal the following Thursday. He dreaded it but was eager to have it finished. He felt foolish still getting major dental work done at his age, but there was finally a special lady friend in his life. Rose was a widow and Larkin's first girlfriend since Eleanor died five years ago, after twenty-eight years of marriage. Rose had urged him to start taking better care of himself because she wanted to keep him around.

"What're you looking for?" Bobby asked.

"A transmitter," Larkin said. "We used them all the time when I worked Intelligence. You could even track a gypsy cabdriver on a Saturday night with a good bug."

"I hear you might have some new information for me," Bobby said.

"Yeah," Larkin said, standing up and walking to the other side of the Jeep. "I think your lawyer, Gleason, even though he can be a colossal asshole, is onto something about them never really producing a body."

"Why's that, Tom?"

"You have to try to see a guy named Carlos Orosco at the crematorium in Evergreen Cemetery," Larkin said, flaking off rust and caked mud from the wheel guards of the Jeep as he searched. "I think you'll find what he has to say very interesting."

"Like what kind of interesting stuff?"

"Like maybe it wasn't Dorothea he found in the furnace that night," Larkin said.

"Oh, yeah?"

"He can explain it a lot better and with more convincing details than I can," he said. "He's a guy you gotta get on the stand."

"Will he testify?"

"I think so," Larkin said. "You have to reassure him. Work him. I don't have to tell you how to convince a witness to talk. I don't even know if his testimony will help this late in the game. But you should talk to him."

From inside the park Bobby could hear the splashing and shouting of children in the big public swimming pool. Most of the shouts were in Spanish. When he was a kid, it was all Irish and Italian. Bobby remembered learning to swim here, the chlorine-and-cement equivalent of Coney Island. A city kid's summer paradise.

"I got my first hunch something was wrong when they closed your case too soon for my liking," Larkin said. "Stopped investigating too fast. Like they were sealing a tomb instead of closing a case."

"Besides Carlos, you find out anything new that I should know?" Bobby asked, eager for information.

"Mostly hunches," Larkin said.

"What hunches, Tom?" Bobby asked. He'd been locked away from a normal flow of information for so long he felt disoriented and ignorant about his own case.

"Since they made me the house mouse, I've become pretty damned good with that PD computer. Surfing around, I've noticed some things about a few people that don't seem kosher. Things that give me *agita*. I search for the cure in the old case files."

"Things that have to do with my case?" Bobby asked.

"Maybe," Larkin said, still rummaging under the car, his hands getting dirty. "I tried to get Brooklyn homicide to look into a few things. But I might as well have been asking to open up the freaking Kennedy assassination. . . ."

"Such as?"

"Such as you say your girl was from the Ukraine?"

"Yeah," Bobby said.

Larkin just nodded. Then he shook his head, looked at the blue sky, and continued to search under the Jeep.

"Is that significant?" Bobby asked.

"It could be," Larkin said, crab-walking toward the back of the Jeep. "But I won't point fingers until I get more information. I need to see if my hunches pan out. Until they do, I refuse to speculate about something that might ruin someone's reputation. I'm sure you're sensitive to that."

"Big time," Bobby said. "But you'll let me know? I still gotta worry about my reputation."

"Of course," Larkin said.

As Larkin spoke, Bobby spotted a police patrol car creeping their way. It didn't seem to faze Larkin to be seen with him. In fact, Larkin had wanted to meet in the Kopper Kettle, the diner where all the cops from the 72nd Precinct ate, half-price or free. Larkin nicknamed it the Keystone Kopper Kettle. Bobby had nixed that idea. But Larkin defiantly insisted they meet here near Sunset Park.

Bobby always felt he could trust Larkin because he'd been a good friend of his father's, was there with him as a member of the Stakeout Squad on the day Bobby's father was killed in a shootout.

"Here it is," Larkin said, squatting in back of the Jeep, shaking his head and smiling. "The bastards!"

Bobby helped the older cop to his feet. Larkin was holding a small white microchip transmitter with magnetic backing. It was the size of a quarter.

"This is how they managed to follow you even after you ditched the tail," Larkin said. "Jesus Christ, but they're making these bugs smaller and smaller since I worked the Intelligence Unit. Here I am searching all over creation for it and the bastard has it in plain view, stuck to the bottom corner of your license plate."

The police patrol car pulled abreast, windows open, two young uniformed cops sitting in the front seats. The driver wore a name tag that read Caputo. The other cop's name tag read Dixon. Both obnoxiously chewing gum, they looked out at Larkin and Bobby.

"Hey, Larkin, they sent us up here looking for you; an emergency," Caputo said, mocking the older man. "When you mopped the interrogation room before, you missed a spot of yom blood. Sounds like a job for Mighty House Mouse."

Dixon broke up laughing. Bobby glared at the two young cops. Larkin glanced briefly at them and then turned back to Bobby, as if the young cops didn't exist.

"The PD today is a catch basin for assholes who don't know what else to do in life," Larkin said as Bobby handed him a rag from the glove compartment. Larkin wiped his hands as the cop car sat parked next to them, the young cops smiling, radio crackling.

"It's become a mere paycheck factory for duncecaps who can't do plumbing, carpentry, write a song, hit a ball out of the stadium, or pick a stock," Larkin said. "These assholes don't join NYPD to become *lawmen*. They only *protect* their own asses and *serve* only their own interests. Most of these clowns don't even live in the city. They only join for the holidays, unlimited sick days, medical and life insurance, and the credit line. They love the money and the authority of the blue uniform, the nightstick, the siren, and the cherry light. They wallow in the bully power of the gun and badge. But they *hate* being *cops*. So all they ever talk about is getting out of the job on the *pension.*"

"Hey, yo, pal," said the cop named Dixon. "Yo, yeah, you, you're fuckin' Bobby *Emmet,* ain't ya?"

"Yo, yo-yo, he's with me," Larkin said. "Put it on the bulletin board, over the radio if you want. But speak with proper respect when you wear that uniform while addressing a *citizen,* duncecap. He's paying your fucking mortgage."

Caputo, behind the wheel, leaned across the seat to get a look at Bobby and Larkin.

The young cops laughed as the radio crackled and blared a "1052." Bobby knew that meant a domestic dispute. "The non-Caucasians are doing their bit for population control again," said Dixon. Then the cherry light ignited on the roof of the car and the siren roared. Before they drove off, Bobby attached the electronic tracking device to the back of the police car.

"That's what the community sees as its first hand of government," Larkin said. "Immature, racist kids with guns and badges and a license to steal."

"Some of the older ones aren't much better," Bobby said. "The rookies learn it from someone."

Larkin took a small bottle of oil of cloves from his pants pocket and rubbed it on his back gums. "Jesus Christ, but this tooth is killing me," he said. "I can't wait for next Thursday when he finishes this goddamned root canal. I have to meet Rose at the cemetery that afternoon. . . ."

"The cemetery?" Bobby said.

"Well, I still visit Eleanor's grave, and Rose visits her dead husband's grave," Larkin said. "Same hill. It's where we met. And how I met Carlos. He used to tend the graves before he got promoted to the crematorium two years ago. Tell Carlos I sent you."

"I will," Bobby said.

"Meanwhile, I have my own hunches that I want to check out. And I gotta get back to work."

"Thanks, Tom," Bobby said, shaking the older man's long, firm hand.

"You're sure Dorothea said she was from the Ukraine?" Larkin said.

"Positive," Bobby said.

Tom Larkin shook his head and looked at the sky again.

"I hope my hunch is wrong," he said, and strode like an old-fashioned flatfoot through the streets of his precinct back toward the station house.

16

The late afternoon shadows fell over the gothic archways of Evergreen Cemetery. The uniformed security guard at the gate asked Bobby which grave he was going to see. Bobby was momentarily stumped and then said, "Larkin, Eleanor." The guard punched the name into a computer and waited about ten seconds before the name appeared on the screen. Bobby saw the small red eye of a security camera blinking above the guard.

"You know where it is?" the guard said.

"Yeah," Bobby lied.

The guard looked at his watch and said, "You got about twenty-two minutes till closing, mister. Between me and you, there's a fifteen-minute grace period till six-fifteen."

The guard then pointed Bobby to a parking area, and soon he was walking past the tablets of the dead, glancing at the graves of political-machine bosses, celebrated mobsters, and robber barons of Brooklyn's notorious past. All safe from the law at last. There wasn't a more appropriate place in all of Brooklyn to fake a murder, Bobby thought.

He followed an arrow marked CREMATORIUM and soon saw a small house of worship, a glass-and-marble columbarium where the remains urns were stored for eternity in polished-brass wall niches, and then the actual cremation building. The warm wind rustled the surrounding trees, and Bobby could hear soft, smothered sobs. Thin, white smoke rose from the hooded chimney as a group of grieving mourners gathered outside the house of worship near an urn garden, waiting for the remains of a loved one.

A young priest stood among the mourners, looking as if he were groping for words of comfort for his elders. Bobby studied the faces of the bereaved, a white clan in black clothes, most of them in their sixties or seventies, each probably wondering when his or her turn in the fire would come. Bobby imagined them wondering where their souls would go. For a long time only the Protestants that Bobby knew got cremated. Then in Vatican II the Catholic Church, while steadfastly opposing birth control and abortion, gave in to the problem of the population explosion by okaying cremation. Now even devout Catholics could pass through earthly fire on the way to the cool celestial plain.

Bobby watched the wispy smoke rise into the die-hard sun, saw birds fly through the white puffs of human soot, and wondered if he was wrong. Maybe all that was left of his Dorothea was ash and acrid gas scattered in the dirty city wind.

He walked around the back of the crematorium to the carport, where the hearses delivered the bodies. This was where the cops had found him parked and unconscious, covered in someone's blood. In the sunlight, the place looked a whole lot better than it had that rainy dawn.

Two caskets, one a gray-colored, pressed-wood box and another an expensive mahogany coffin, sat on biers on the loading platform. Bobby saw a tired-looking worker, a Hispanic man in overalls and work boots, sitting on the fender of a pickup, eating an apple. Bobby nodded and the man nodded back. From inside the stone building Bobby heard the low, hungry rumble of an intense fire and the whining of other machines, a gurgling water-filtration system and something that sounded like a sanding machine. All around them were the sounds of life. The cemetery was an urban bird sanctuary, a daily songfest of magpies, crows, geese, mockingbirds, sparrows, quail, seagulls, robins, cardinals, owls, and even parrots. Rabbits, raccoon, chipmunks, squirrels, field mice, scurried in the thick bush, the wind fanning over the hillocks and eternal meadows of the magnificently cared for necropolis.

"Carlos?" Bobby asked. "Carlos Orosco?"

The Hispanic man seemed surprised, took the next bite of the crisp apple slowly. "Who's asking?"

"Someone said you might be able to help me," Bobby said. "You're the head burner, right?"

"Called retort director," Carlos said. "Someone's dead, you gotta go to administration."

"Someone might not be dead," Bobby said quickly.

"Maybe you need a priest," Carlos said, chewing the apple, the juice rolling over his lip. "Or a head doctor . . ."

"Tom Larkin, he's a cop, he sent me," Bobby said.

"Yeah?" Carlos said, wary. "How you know him?"

"He's a friend," Bobby said.

Carlos stood and said, "Old Tom is a nice guy. Good Christmas tipper when I tended his wife's grave. I'm glad he finally found a girl. You be surprised how many people find companions in a cemetery. Widows and widowers, a regular Love Connection."

"He told me you're the one who found Dorothea Dubrow's remains," Bobby said.

"You're Bobby Emmet, right? Tom called and said you might come by," Carlos said.

Bobby knew from years as an investigator that the one thing people loved to talk about almost as much as their kids was their jobs. It was because it was always the one topic on which they were experts.

"What you wanna know?" Carlos asked, looking past Bobby at the empty path. "Ask fast. I can get in trouble from my boss for talking to you out here. Come inside where no one can see us."

Bobby followed Carlos into the hot crematorium building, where the rumbling sound of intense heat grew louder. Carlos walked directly to one of five ovens built into a brick wall.

"I found her remains right in here that morning," he said, pulling open the metal hatch cover, pointing inside the cremation chamber, where the rumbling sound now became a roar. "You were in the car outside. I called security. They called the cops."

The mouth of the oven was three-feet wide and ten-feet deep, and when Bobby peered inside, he was transfixed by the raging flames of thousands of gas jets eating away a pressed-board box. The giant glowing ember inside resembled a human log. Head and shoulders. Arms and legs. Protruding feet. All one blinding white-hot image. There was no odor as the smoke was quickly sucked up in a roaring draft through a water-filtered chimney.

"How long does it take a body to burn?" Bobby asked.

"With a casket, at sixteen hundred degrees, takes about two hours to burn a human being, maybe a little longer, depending on the body weight," Carlos said. "Fat guy, he can take three hours. Then it's supposed to cool for another two hours, to let the rest of the smoke go up. You know, it smolders, like a wet mattress. When the smoke cools, it falls as dust. Since eighty-seven percent of the human body is water, most of it goes back into the atmosphere as steam."

"Afterlife is a puff of steam?" Bobby asked.

"Well, the soul doesn't burn, unless you go to hell," said Carlos with a laugh. "Like teeth."

"Teeth don't burn?"

"Teeth and bone, they scorch," he said. "See, the big misunderstanding about cremation is that you wind up with a pile of ashes. Not true. What you wind up with is really bone dust. A lot of the bones, especially the skull, knee and elbow joints, don't burn so good. Come on the other side, and I'll show you."

He closed the oven hatch, and Bobby followed Carlos around to the far side of the ovens.

They passed the same open hearse port where the undertakers delivered the dead. From there, Carlos explained, the caskets were placed on biers, rolled to the mouth of the cremation chamber, and sent into the center of the oven on steel rollers. "Then I just light the fire," he said.

When Bobby and Carlos reached the other side of the ovens, only one was burning. Another body lay in oven number two, cooling.

Carlos opened a trapdoor beneath the oven, where dust from the cooled corpse had fallen the same way ash falls through a fireplace grate. He took a long backhoe and scraped the grainy beige dust into a metal pan. If they were flour, these human remains would have been about enough to make a loaf of bread. Carlos carried the dustpan, lumpy with knuckles, joints, and teeth and some odd-looking metallic objects, into an anteroom, where a machine not dissimilar to a meat grinder sat bolted to a worktable. Along a second wall were various kinds of urns and plain, plastic-lined cardboard boxes marked with the brand name Aftalife.

"You take this here dust, and you sift it to get rid of all the nonorganic material," Carlos said as he pulled on a pair of surgical gloves and sifted the remains through a screen into another pan. This process left behind bones and teeth and what looked like melted and deformed metal screws on the screen.

"Tooth fillings, metal pins and bolts that hold people together after injuries," Carlos said. "Mostly in older people. These days they use flammable plastic joints."

Bobby thought Carlos looked like a prospector panning for gold in the dust of the dead. Carlos lifted the gnarled metallic nuggets from the screen and dropped them into a large white plastic container that was half full with other melted and twisted metal objects. "And you dump what's left into this here hole in the top of the remains pulverizer," Carlos said as he poured the dust and bones through a funnel into the grinding machine. "The knuckles, elbows, knee joints, skull fragments, and the teeth go down to the pulverizer. Then I grind them down to a dust so fine that you could sprinkle her remains from a salt shaker."

"Salt of the earth," Bobby said.

"Yeah," Carlos said as the machine crunched and vibrated and ground the last vestiges of the dead stranger. "But that thing with you? I knew something was wrong when I saw it."

"What was wrong?"

"Well, to begin with, I scraped up the remains of the woman in the chamber that morning," he said. "But I never pulverized that dead woman's teeth. I came in and the body was already cremated. I scooped out the dust like the cops asked, but I didn't pulverize the teeth because I knew they would probably need them for an ID."

"Teeth?" Bobby said, growing excited. "What the hell happened to them? What happened to the teeth?"

"I put them aside in a plastic bag," Carlos said. "Then a guy from the medical examiner's office, he came, and I gave them to him. His name was Franz. He put them in an evidence bag, and he took them away."

"This is the first I ever heard of dental remains in my case," Bobby said.

"I followed the trial on Court TV," Carlos said, pointing to a TV mounted on a high shelf on the wall near the window. "You have some downtime while the body is burning or cooling. When I watched your trial, I figured someone would have called me. Prosecution. Defense. Nobody did. And no one ever mentioned her teeth. They just said she had no dental records anywhere."

Bobby remembered that there was no way to match the teeth of the corpse to Dorothea's dental records because there were no records. His excitement ebbed. That's why neither side introduced the teeth as evidence, he thought. You can't match something to nothing. Still, the actual teeth might tell him something. He would go see this Franz guy anyway.

"Thanks," Bobby said and reached out to shake Carlos's hand. But Carlos's hand was covered with a plastic glove and human dust. They smiled and did not shake. Bobby patted his shoulder.

"So maybe that's why they never used the teeth," Carlos said, walking Bobby toward the door to the anteroom. "But they never called me about the pacemaker either. So, who knows?"

Bobby stopped before he reached the door, looked at Carlos oddly.

"What do you mean, 'pacemaker'?"

Carlos pointed into the white plastic pail where the metal objects were gathered. "You get your bolts from people's backs, your pins from their broken bones, your tooth fillings, a lot of bullets, even a spoon or two, and rings that people swallow. Be surprised the shit you find in people's bodies that won't burn. Religious medals, coins, hearing aides, metal rosary beads. People get metal plates in their head, they go in the pail. . . ."

"You found a pacemaker in the body that was supposed to be Dorothea's?" Bobby asked excitedly.

"Of course," said Carlos. "She had a bad heart, a pacemaker, your girlfriend, no?"

Bobby's eyes widened, and he dried his palms on his jeans, "Did you throw that pacemaker into the pail?"

"No," Carlos said. "I thought it might be important, because it was a crime, so I put it aside."

"You gave this to the ME, this Franz guy, too?"

"No," Carlos said. "I gave that to the lady from the DA's office. The one who hung you . . . face like a tomahawk . . ."

Carlos snapped his fingers several times, trying to pop the name into his head.

"Tuzio?" Bobby asked.

"That's her," Carlos said. "So how come no one ever mentioned the teeth or the pacemaker in the trial?"

"That's a very good question," Bobby said.

One thing Bobby knew for sure: In order to have a pacemaker installed, Dorothea would have required surgery. Bobby knew every inch of Dorothea's flawless body. Even the smallest scar would have stood out. Especially around her heart. And he certainly would have felt the battery and small mechanism of a pace-maker above her lovely breast.

"You gotta do me a favor," Carlos said. "You can't tell my boss you was here or I get fired. Funny, huh, cremation director *fired?*"

"Hilarious," Bobby said.

"I'm thinking of doing a cookbook," Carlos said, laughing.

"I might have to subpoena you," Bobby said. "My lawyer will want to do a deposition."

"That's covered by the union," Carlos said. "Bringing you in here ain't."

Bobby was about to leave when he stopped to ask one last question. "I know you found the body in the morning," Bobby said.

"The remains," Carlos corrected. "It was already burned."

"How do you think they got the body in here the night before?" Bobby asked.

Carlos waved his hand and laughed. "That's easy, man," he said. "People think we have guard dogs and armed guards with shotguns. That's bullshit. We got the laziest rent-a-cops you ever saw. Mostly retired cops. All they ever do is sleep. Half-dead. They fit right in around here."

"What's the name of the security firm?" Bobby asked.

"Gibraltar Security."

17

At ten to seven Bobby returned to The Winning Ticket to meet Sandy Fraser. Although feeling the first wave of fatigue, he was fidgety with excitement over what he'd learned from Carlos. Dorothea was alive, he was certain. Now he needed to get some answers from Sandy.

The Winning Ticket was packed, two deep at the horseshoe-shaped bar, the maître d' occasionally walking in and paging diners with reservations, leading them past the smoked-glass divider into the crowded dining room that was a buzz of conversations, rattling silverware, occasional bursts of laughter.

At the end of the bar, John Shine seemed surprised to see Bobby back so soon.

"Did you get to see Tom Larkin?" Shine asked as Bobby wedged himself through the crowd of men and women.

"Yeah," Bobby said.

"He have anything for you?"

"Just hunches," Bobby said.

"What hunches?"

Bobby didn't feel like regurgitating what Larkin had said. And he wasn't going to tell anyone but Gleason about what he'd learned from Carlos. A good investigator always asked everything and offered nothing. He watched the front door as customers arrived in groups.

"Case files," Bobby said. "He wouldn't be specific until he had something positive."

"He's a cryptic old coot, all right," Shine said. "He might be able to help. Me, too. But in the end, you'll have to crack your case yourself. 'Trust thyself; every heart vibrates to that iron string.' "

"You have an Emerson quote for every occasion," Bobby said.

"That's because every occasion is about life," Shine said. "And Emerson decodes the mystery of existence. At least for me."

Shine offered to buy Bobby a drink, which he declined.

"The last time I had a drink, I wound up in the clink," Bobby said.

"Suit yourself," Shine said, and ordered himself a Stolichnaya vodka on the rocks with an orange rind. "But I'm always out of here by nine, the *latest,* so I can have *one.*"

"What time does Sandy show up?"

"Around now," Shine said. "Her first. Then Barnicle. He feels a need for a royal solo entrance with his court jesters."

Just then Bobby caught a glimpse of Sandy Fraser, in a tight white skirt suit and red high heels, wearing small oval sunglasses, entering the front door, her radiant beauty catching the eyes of the men at the bar.

"Here she is," Bobby said. "Mind if I play a little?" Bobby pointed to the kitchen, telling Shine what he'd like to do.

"Knock yourself out," Shine said. He laboriously pushed himself up from the barstool and escorted Bobby through the flapping doors that led from the bar area into the spacious commercial kitchen.

A tired-looking waitress was busy telling a busboy to set up Sandy's table. Bobby placed a starched linen napkin over his forearm, walked to the busboy, and gently took the basket of bread and glasses of water from him. The busboy was confused until Shine nodded his approval.

Bobby smiled at the nervous waitress and softly said, "For the record, it isn't true what they say about me."

The waitress looked him straight in the eye and managed a half-smile. Bobby carried the table setup through the flapping doors leading from the kitchen to the dining room and walked briskly to Sandy's table. Sandy paid little attention as he stood to her left, reaching past her to place the bread and water on the tabletop.

"The specials today are Oysters Barnicle and a very Sandy spinach salad, rather an odd combination, no?" Bobby said in an oily voice. Sandy looked up, startled. She swallowed hard as Bobby sat down at the table and took a sip from a glass of water. She checked her diamond-studded Rolex watch and then the front door, anxious.

"He'll go ape shit if he finds you sitting here," she said, and then smiled sweetly. "How *are* you, Bobby?"

"I need to talk to you," Bobby said. "I need your help."

"I can't," she said. "I have more to think about now than myself. The baby . . . you understand."

"How the hell did that happen, anyway?"

"It's too long a story," Sandy said. "Look, Bobby, I know you could never hurt a hair on Dorothea's head. And I wish I could help. But if I get involved, they'll take my baby, and . . ."

"No one's going to steal your baby," Bobby said, leaning across the table toward Sandy.

"What do you want?"

"Tell me what you know about Dorothea. She was your friend, Sandy, before she was mine. I have to know everything you know. . . ."

The menu in Sandy's hands began to quake, her fingers sliding up and down its glossy spine. Her long eyelashes batted like little black wings. She took a trembling sip of water, cleared her throat.

"Bobby," Sandy whispered. "I'm glad you're home. But please . . . please don't put me and my baby in deep shit. You simply have no idea. You can't even help yourself. How can you help me? My baby? These bastards have connections, money, power. Plans. Big freakin' plans. They are very, very dangerous, *capisce?*"

"I think maybe me and you should go somewhere and talk," Bobby said. "In a place you'll feel safe."

"He has friends *everywhere*," Sandy said. "You were probably safer inside than out here."

"You don't even *like* Barnicle, do you?" Bobby said. "I could tell this morning."

"You didn't like it when people rushed to judgment against you," Sandy said, angry and defensive now. "So don't you dare judge me, Bobby. I never did you wrong in my life."

"If you don't tell me what you know about Dorothea," Bobby said, "you are doing both me *and* her wrong."

"I'm doing what I gotta do for my kid," Sandy said, her eyes icy. "Fuck *you,* if you interfere with that."

Bobby considered her for a long moment. The expensive perfume. The invisible price tags on the clothes. The real jewelry. He searched her big, confused eyes. He studied her full, painted lips, wishing they would tell him what she knew about Dorothea. The lips remained pressed together. He felt like biting them open.

"You're better than this Barnicle, Sandy," Bobby said.

"Grow up," she said. "You have no idea . . ."

"I'm gonna find her, Sandy."

"I hope you do," Sandy said. "In fact, I'm sure you will. If you dig deep enough. But I'm not willing to do that, Bobby. If I start digging, it'll be my own freakin' grave. So please . . ."

"You think she's alive," Bobby whispered, leaning closer, "don't you, Sandy? You think Dorothea is alive, too."

She turned toward a small bustle at the front entrance, where Zeke held open the door for Lou Barnicle, who wore a light-colored summer suit, a straw hat, and white Italian mesh shoes with mahogany-colored leather heels. No socks. A parody of himself. To his right was Kuzak. With Bobby's back to them, they didn't notice Bobby.

"I'm gonna do this with or without your help," he said quickly. "I don't want to hurt *you* doing it."

"All I know is threats," Sandy said. "One more won't matter."

18

Someone was already on board.

It was his first night of freedom and of fighting goddamn traffic on the West Side Highway again; Bobby was exhausted and looking forward to collapsing into bed. But he had uninvited company.

He'd stopped on the rotunda above the boatyard before he drove down the incline to the parking lot. From up there he'd noticed that the boat was swaying differently from the other darkened vessels lolling in the night tide. Something moving, something *alive* was on board. He parked in the old indoor garage and carried The Club antitheft device with him as a weapon. The security shack was empty, which meant that Doug the dockmaster was probably on a break or doing his rounds. So Bobby walked cautiously along the wooden walkway toward *The Fifth Amendment*, moving quietly under a sky without stars.

Control. They are here to mess with you, but you must take control.

As he walked cautiously up the small gangplank, he heard muffled mumbling from inside the cabin. Then he saw a flashlight splaying across the floor, the light bleeding under the closed door. Whoever was inside was very close to the door. He jerked it open, cocking his Club like a cave dweller protecting his lair.

"Go ahead, crack my skull open; what's one more dead woman on your yellow sheet, Emmet," said the short-haired woman in the black pinstripe pants suit. Bobby reached for the wall switch and turned on the overhead light in the galley. Cis Tuzio might once have been pretty if there had ever been a pretty thought in that head. But to Bobby, her face resembled a bench warrant, with cold eyes like official government seals, a pug nose that might have been hammered flat by a judge's gavel, thin lips like a docket number. It was as if she had gotten the job and then fashioned a mask that smothered any ember of human warmth, even choosing funereal black pants suits to fit the caricature of a bloodless prosecutor.

"Dingdong, Attica calling," sang a man's voice from the saloon as he stepped through the door into the galley. Hanratty, one of Tuzio's Brooklyn DA cops, was now standing by her side. Bobby had worked with him on a few joint-county-jurisdictional cases during the five years Bobby was in the Manhattan DA's office. Hanratty had gotten the transfer from the NYPD Community Relations post to the Brooklyn DA's office for tireless work in the reelection campaign of Sol Diamond, Tuzio's boss. It was hard to imagine anyone taking Hanratty's advice on anything, but he had managed to deliver a good hunk of what was left of the Irish voting bloc from Bay Ridge. Bobby was convinced he was even a subordinate in Tuzio's bed.

"You're trespassing," Bobby said to Cis Tuzio, stepping out onto the deck, holding the door open for them to leave. "Unless you have a warrant, I suggest you leave the way you came. You're out of your jurisdiction in Manhattan, and you're on private property."

Tuzio had her hands in her pants pockets, trying to look like a tough guy as she stepped out of the galley into the cool night air of the deck. The boat swayed on what river people called a "snotty" tide. Every so often, all 3500 pounds slammed against the pier, the rubber bumpers bouncing her back on the roiled river. Tuzio took a few short awkward steps toward Bobby, pulling her hands from her pockets for balance. Bobby grabbed her by the arms to steady her and looked her deep in the empty eyes.

"Your attorney said I could find you here," Tuzio said. "That was tantamount to an invitation aboard. You're on bail. You're *shit,* and I'm in charge of shoveling you up."

"You got promoted to that, huh?" Bobby said with a grin.

"Fitting," she said as Hanratty helped ease her free of Bobby's firm grip. "You living on a boat owned by one of the biggest sleazebag lawyers in the city."

"Jeez, Cis, you sound jealous of old Izzy," Bobby said.

"I came in person, as a professional law-enforcement courtesy, because you once worked for the Manhattan district attorney's office," Tuzio said. "I think you're scum. But you did adequate work for the people once. So I'm here with a deal. Cop to manslaughter one, ten to fifteen, time served included. You would save the state the money of trying you all over again."

Bobby took a pack of peppermint Tic Tacs out of his jacket and shook the plastic box, popping one into his hand and offering the box to Tuzio. "Please, do me a *favor*, take one, will ya."

She was momentarily flustered, self-conscious of halitosis, and her right hand went involuntarily to her mouth. It was a gimmick Bobby had used when questioning seemingly unflappable white-collar suspects. A simple interruption in someone's prepared alibi often made a hole small enough for the truth to leak out like gas.

"I didn't mean to be rude," Bobby said. "But everything that comes out of your mouth smells bad."

"Careful," said Hanratty.

"Plus you got some nerve discussing a plea when my lawyer isn't present," Bobby said.

"I didn't hear a thing," Hanratty said.

"What's his feeding time?" Bobby asked Tuzio. "He looks restless."

"I'm here to see that you haven't left the jurisdiction," Tuzio said. "And to tell you that I am going to send your murdering ass right back to jail as soon as I can schedule a trial."

"Fess up, Hanratty," Bobby said, smiling, popping another Tic Tac. "You wrote that little speech for lovely Cissy here, didn't ya? With your little pocket dictionary next to you, you pecked it out on your typewriter one letter at a time."

"How about I peck out your eyes, Emmet," Hanratty said.

"Cis, wasn't that a threat? You're an officer of the court; quick, impanel a grand jury."

"You find this amusing now," Tuzio said. "It won't be after the trial. You'll be right back where you belong."

Bobby leaned closer to the austere woman and said, "You're right. This isn't amusing. So, why don't you and Columbo here *really* investigate this case. Find out if Dorothea is dead or alive and who actually was cremated and where all that blood came from . . ."

He was tempted to tell her what he knew about Carlos Orosco and the pacemaker he found in the cremation furnace. But he wanted to tell Gleason first.

"Same lame, tired alibi," Tuzio said. "We did investigate and it was you."

"No," Bobby said. "It wasn't me. But it was me you wanted."

"Twelve people agreed it was you," Tuzio said. "They will again."

"You don't really care whether Dorothea is alive or not, do you?" Bobby said. "All you want is me as a trophy conviction so you can continue to climb your political ladder. Well, that isn't gonna happen . . . bitch."

"You better watch your language," Hanratty said.

"Oh, sorry, Hanratty, you thought I was talking to *you*," Bobby said with a wink. "Wrong bitch."

Hanratty stepped past Cis Tuzio and threw a punch at Bobby. Bobby bent under the punch, and the boat rocked. Hanratty's forward motion sent him stumbling across the deck and lurching over the three-foot railing of the swaying boat. Dangling on the outside of the boat, the big cop grabbed desperately for the slippery railing. He tried to get his footing on the slimy hull, but his feet couldn't find traction. The boat was shifting back and forth, occasionally careening against the pier with the rough tide. When the next swell came, Hanratty would be in danger of being crushed between the heavy boat and the pier.

"Help me!" Hanratty shouted.

" 'I've fallen and I can't get up,' " Bobby mocked.

"Do something!" Tuzio demanded, looking alarmed.

As Hanratty hung on to the slick railing, Bobby popped another Tic Tac and offered one to Tuzio.

Bobby detected a scribble of human concern in her cold, antiseptic eyes. She ran to the edge of the boat, got on her hands and knees, and grabbed Hanratty's arm, but he was too heavy for her.

"Help me!" screamed Hanratty again.

"Jeez, Cis, he sounds like he wants to cop a plea," Bobby said.

"Help him," Tuzio said. "Please . . ."

The boat was ready to follow the rolling tide back against the pier again. Bobby casually reached down and grabbed Hanratty by his thick head of Irish red hair and lifted him straight up. Bobby's strength, from doing jailhouse push-ups, courtesy of Cis Tuzio, paid off. Hanratty howled in pain as his hair pulled from its scalp, contorting his eyelids into cartoony shapes.

Then as the tide lifted the boat to full crest, priming it to crash its rubber bumpers against the stone pier, Bobby grabbed Hanratty by the necktie, twisted it into a tight noose, and hauled him in one fluid motion up over the side and onto the deck. Hanratty landed in a wet, greasy, algae-covered splat, panting as he loosened his tie, coughing and heaving on the deck.

Cis Tuzio helped him to a sitting position and then finally onto his feet. Hanratty's hair stood up straight, making him look like a redheaded Don King.

"I owe you one," Hanratty panted, his expression belying his words. He was smoothing his hair, trying to brush off his suit but only spreading the grease and the algae.

"Nah," Bobby said. "I still owe *you* one."

"See you in court, Emmet," Tuzio said as she and Hanratty left the boat.

19
Friday

Bobby sat up straight in bed, his face dripping with sweat. He was looking directly into the smiling, squawking face of a seagull that was perched upside down, its feet clamped onto the frame of the open porthole window, eating a Devil Dog out of Gleason's hand. Gleason stood next to the bed, dropping crumbs onto Bobby's disbelieving face.

Gleason took a gulp of some awful-looking chocolate-colored concoction and offered the tall clear plastic cup to Bobby.

"What the hell is it?" Bobby asked, waving it away, squinting.

"I call it a Yoo-driver," Gleason said. "Yoo-Hoo and vodka. Easy on the Yoo."

Bobby sat up, mopped sleep from his face. "I know I owe you," he said. "But we gotta set some ground rules. If you're going to defend me, you gotta do it sober. I don't want you showing up *Yooed.*"

"I'm not drunk," Gleason said, a tinge of defensiveness in his voice.

"And I can't stand the smell of cigarettes," Bobby said. "Smoke slows me down, and I have no time to waste."

"So far you're trying to tell *me,* me, the guy who got you out of the joint, that I can't drink or smoke when you're around," Gleason said, smoothing his sharkskin suit jacket and straightening his red-and-blue silk tie. "Anything else before I give you my reply?"

"Yeah," Bobby said. "The candy-bar, potato-chip, sugar-jones routine. That has to stop. I'd rather you ate your face. I can't have a normal conversation with you when your teeth are glued together with a goddamned Milky Way."

"What you're asking me is to—"

"—to act fucking *normal,*" Bobby said, standing, taking a pair of clean underwear from his suitcase and walking into the small bathroom.

"I'll tell you what, Mr. Health Resort," Gleason shouted into the bathroom, taking another sip of the Yoo-driver and giving the heel end of the Devil Dog to the seagull, who flew off with it. "Find someone who can prove Dorothea is alive, or that someone else had reason to kill her, and I'll be in court, front and center, more sober than the fuckin' judge."

"I think I might have," Bobby said, and then told Gleason all about Carlos and the pacemaker he gave to Tuzio.

"Jesus Christ, that could be suppression of evidence," Gleason said. "I have to check the records to see if she logged it."

Bobby also told him about the teeth that Carlos gave to an assistant medical examiner named Franz.

"You gotta talk to him," Gleason said.

"I called, but the receptionist said he was out of town until next week," Bobby said. "I didn't want to leave my name, so I said I'd call back."

Bobby turned on the weak shower, soaping himself down, lathering shampoo into his hair, doing it all as quickly as he could, jailhouse style.

"Excellent," Gleason said. "You should be a cop."

"You're a real wit," Bobby said, rinsing off.

"I hope you didn't mention any of this to anyone," Gleason said.

As he turned off the shower, Bobby assured him he hadn't.

"Now, I need a quick rundown on who else you saw and where you went," Gleason said.

As he dried off, Bobby told Gleason about meeting his ex-wife and her new husband, Trevor Sawyer. About how his daughter Maggie traced the white Taurus to the Stone for Governor Campaign. About his lunch in John Shine's saloon, the incident with the two cops named Daniels and Lebeche, and then the encounter with Forrest Morgan. He told him about Larkin, who discovered the electronic bug on Gleason's Jeep, and his obscure questions about the Ukraine, and more details about Carlos at the crematorium and about his conversation with Sandy and the visit from Tuzio and Hanratty.

"Busy day," Gleason said.

"I had a lot of catching up to do on my social calendar," Bobby said.

"The bastards bugged *my* car?" Gleason said, indignantly. "I take that personally."

"Yeah, but they were following *me,*" Bobby said.

"I'll wait for you up on deck," Gleason said. "I got company. . . ."

Seven minutes later Bobby was on the deck, dressed in jeans, a plain white T-shirt, and his work boots. He shielded his eyes from the high morning sun and saw Gleason seated on a chaise lounge chair, with a young woman.

Bobby nodded hello, and so did the girl, who smiled, revealing three badly chipped front teeth, which looked as if someone had hit them with a tack hammer. Gleason flicked his cigarette butt into the river.

"Fish can choke on those filters," Bobby said.

"But if I put a hook on it, used it as bait, and then *ate* the bastard, that's okay, right?" he asked. "Personally, I like the spotted owl better . . . deep fried."

Bobby shook his head, waiting for an introduction that was not forthcoming, and finally said, "Hi, I'm Bobby."

"She's Alison," Gleason said. "She changed it from Zelda."

"Really," Bobby said, trying to be polite. "How come?"

"Alana, not Alison, and I'm not sure why," the woman said, and smiled, showing the jagged teeth. "I got tired always being at the end of the alphabet."

"Nice to meet you, *Alana,*" Bobby said, and looked to Gleason, deadpan, hoping for a further explanation. Gleason shrugged and passed the Yoo-driver to Alana. She took several small, deliberate swigs. Gleason patted his thigh, and Alana moved from the stiff-backed chair, slinked over, and plopped onto Gleason's lap. Alana was about thirty, with a hard, athletic body, and wore tight white pants, a dark halter top, and a white denim jacket. She wore heavy mascara and orange lipstick, which stained her chipped teeth. With some dental work and less makeup she'd be a very attractive woman, Bobby thought. Right up Gleason's alley. . . .

"I got your first assignment," Gleason said, handing the woman a slip of paper. Alana got up and gave the paper to Bobby with nail-bitten fingers before grinding her way back to Gleason's lap. "His name is Herbie Rabinowitz, and he's a little nuts," Gleason said over Alana's shoulder.

"If he's nuts by your standards, then I should bring a stun gun and a straitjacket," Bobby said.

"You gotta pick Herbie up at three at that address and bring him here and keep him out of trouble over the weekend," Gleason said.

"Here? You mean he sleeps *here?*"

"What, solitary made you unsociable?"

Bobby sighed.

"He's a payday," Gleason said. "You meet; we eat."

"I didn't know the boat was an underground railroad station for all Gleason clients," Bobby said. "I thought it was where I *lived.*"

"Three fuckin' days," Gleason said. "You could put up with Charles Manson for three days."

"Hey, Izzy, lady here . . ."

"See, didn't Papa Bear tell Goldilocks that Bobby was all

class?" Gleason said, in baby talk, to Alana, who was still sitting on his lap.

"I like that he doesn't curse in front of a lady," Alana said. "Culture."

"What happens to this client on Monday?" Bobby asked, exasperated.

"He has a pretrial hearing," Gleason said. "I promised the Queens DA I'd surrender him there."

"And who's after him?"

Gleason bent his nose with his left hand and pointed a finger behind Alana's head with the index finger of his right hand and pulled an imaginary trigger.

"We'll talk about that later," Gleason said. He pinched Alana on the backside, and she stood up. He pointed to a taxi waiting on the rotunda above the boat basin.

"Hey, Alice baby . . ."

"Alana," she corrected.

"Right," Gleason said. "Wait for me up in the cab, will ya, babe?"

Alana waved to Bobby, and he waved back.

"We have to talk fast before I go," Gleason said as Alana walked down the gangplank and along the walkway.

"About what?"

"Who you trust," Gleason said.

"I hope my daughter is on the list," Bobby said.

"She might be the only one," Gleason said. "Let's go through the list again quickly. Barnicle, we know he's a belly crawler and dirty, somehow. Your ex-lawyer, Farrell, unless she has more guts than brains, I'd say she's just an incompetent, but you just never know. She has political connections. Be careful of her. John Shine, he sounds too good a friend to be true. But he has his own money, so I don't know where his motives to fuck you would come from. Still, be careful what you say around him. Ditto this old Larkin fuck. He sounds like a cynical old prick."

"He's angry, not cynical," Bobby said.

"All these so-called hunches he talks about," Gleason said. "How do you know he isn't leading you down some blind alley? He's asking about the fucking Ukraine, while you're trying to stay out of Sing Sing. What better guy to run a bogus three-quarters pension scam than some anonymous, manipulative, old computer geek on the inside?''

"He was with my father when he died, for chrissakes, Iz,'' Bobby said.

"Hey, Son of Sam was with his victims when they died, too,'' Gleason said. "And this Trevor Sawyer. I'm sure he'd like nothing better than to have you in the joint to keep you away from your ex-wife and your kid. Or to have you whacked out here. He has enough money to frame God for laying down on the job on the seventh day. I also never, ever, since the Three Wise Men, trust ex-wives either. So be guarded around yours. And this Sandy Fraser broad, if she don't sound like a PhD in Advanced Bimbology, then Einstein didn't know his times tables. Behind every beautiful face there is a crime, believe me. As for Forrest Morgan, I don't give a rat's balls how many times you boxed him; any cop who works IAB is as weasely to me as an MP in the service, and I never trusted one of them since they clubbed me into the brig in the army. He already admitted he's looking for a cheap promotion. Don't let him get it by helping Tuzio put you back in the can. And your buddy Max Roth . . .''

"I haven't even met with him yet,'' Bobby said, looking at Gleason in astonishment.

"He'd french fry his own kids just for a greasy headline,'' Gleason said.

"You have so much faith in your fellow man it's heartwarming,'' Bobby said. "By your thinking, why the hell should I even trust you?''

"You shouldn't,'' Gleason said. "Because like the rest of them, I'm using you. But at least I'm up-front about it.''

"You're all heart, Izzy,'' Bobby said, "—heart of darkness.''

"I'm just trying to warn you not to trust any of these bindle stiffs,'' he said. "Every time they do or say something, you better think they mean or want the opposite. Your motherfucking *life* and my *reputation* are riding on what you believe and what you don't.''

This part sunk in. Bobby nodded.

"I gotta go,'' Gleason said.

"Who is this Herbie Rabinowitz?'' Bobby asked. "What did he do? The charge?''

"You'll like him,'' Gleason said. "He has CIA training. He'll give ya a fill on all the details. Just keep him out of trouble till Monday. He has a rich young brother who is a cash-paying customer. But Herbie don't know the brother is paying, because he hates him. Our kinda guy."

"Me and you, Gleason," Bobby said, following Gleason to the edge of the ramp, "we don't have any 'our kindas' in common."

"We'll grow on each other," Gleason said.

"Where the hell are you going?" Bobby asked as Gleason moved to join Alana up in the waiting taxi.

"I know a dentist, who, with a few grand worth of veneers, will make this babe smile like a Steinway keyboard," Gleason said.

"Where do you find these women?" Bobby asked. "What about Venus?"

"She'll be in the fat farm until she learns some English and fits into a size seven," he said. "Meanwhile, I'm still a practicing heterosexual."

Bobby watched Gleason hurry down the ramp and then looked down at the address for Herbie Rabinowitz. Working for Gleason wasn't going to be easy.

20

"I'll get whatever I can on Gibraltar and Barnicle," Max Roth said, biting into his spelt toast in a booth of the Earth First restaurant on Thirty-fourth Street and Tenth Avenue. "But ever since your case, a lot of my sources have dried up. Especially in Brooklyn."

"Because you went to bat for me," Bobby said, sipping his herb tea.

"That had a lot to do with it," Roth said. "But also because you were one of my best sources. I'd sometimes take stuff you gave me from the Manhattan DA's office that I wasn't going to use and swap it with someone else who'd stumbled across stuff they weren't using. That give-and-take is gone. But it's true the Brooklyn DA's office hates me for going to bat for you."

"And Gibraltar is located in Brooklyn. . . ."

"Everyone in Brooklyn is paranoid these days because Diamond and Tuzio are so involved in the Stone campaign," Roth said. "Which, as you already know, is directly hinged to your case. Anyone considered even remotely off agenda is given lie detector tests, fired, some of them smeared with press leaks."

"But doesn't Gibraltar, like all PI firms, come under the jurisdiction of the New York Department of State?" Bobby asked.

"Good point," Roth said, making a note in a reporters notebook. "That's Albany. I still have some sources I can check with up there."

"Those sources will dry up, too, if Stone gets elected."

"Yeah," Roth said, "but until then, I have a few markers I can call in."

"Is my case really that politically connected?" asked Bobby.

"So much has happened politically in your absence that it made sense that you were set up because you were in the way," Roth said. "Because you were sniffing in the right places about bad people at the wrong time."

"Starting with that cesspool they call the Brooklyn DA's office," Bobby said.

"Which looks like it might hold the key to the gubernatorial campaign," said Roth. "Governor Johnson is in trouble; everyone knows that. Even his fellow Democrats are disappointed in him because he hasn't done dick about the economy, the erosion of the manufacturing base in the state, the loss of major corporations to Jersey, his inability to get the money we deserve out of the Feds."

"His wife divorcing him over that bimbo scandal in office didn't help," Bobby said.

"No, it didn't," said Roth. "But it paved the way for a family-values Republican like Stone. Everyone agrees that a strong Republican candidate can beat Johnson in November. Democrats are even jumping on his bandwagon. Gerald Stone has a recognition problem, but he has that family-values platform and the war hero background. If he beats Jimmy Garfalo in the Republican primary a week from next Tuesday, he's a shoo-in come November."

"I'm a little out of touch, but as I remember, Garfalo is the state senate majority leader," Bobby said. "Lots of upstate support."

"Yeah, but oddly enough, this is one Republican primary where the city could be the key," said Roth. "And Sol Diamond, who's running Stone's city campaign, got a lot of mileage out of sending you away. Now that you're out, you're an embarrassment to Diamond's office. Which reflects on Stone and his law-and-order platform now that the campaign is in the stretch."

"The primary is only twelve days from now."

"Which means you could make these people desperate," Roth said. "In the meantime, my editors are breaking my balls about an exclusive with you."

"Gleason says I have to hold off for a few days," Bobby said.

"No more," Roth said.

"Please find out whatever you can about Gibraltar," Bobby said. "Their personnel files, their tax returns, a client list. I'm convinced this place is dirty."

"An exposé of a dirty private-eye firm staffed by ex-NYPD cops is a hell of a story, too," Roth said. "Especially if they're tied in to your case *and* the Stone for Governor Campaign. Just remember I get first exclusive on the story."

"Of course," Bobby said, leaving a ten-dollar bill for the seven-dollar tab as the two men walked out of the restaurant onto Tenth Avenue.

"By the way, I am convinced that your boy Gleason is certifiably insane," Roth said. "But there's no gainsaying his talent in front of a jury. Which sometimes makes me worry about the jury system. He's not one of my favorite people. You ever see the way he eats? No other known species on planet Earth survives on a diet quite like Izzy Gleason's. Still, if I were you, I'd rather have him than Moira Farrell, especially considering who she's working for now."

"Who?" Bobby said.

"Yesterday, you left a message asking me to get an intern to do a 'Where Are They Now?' computer search on all the principals of your trial," Roth said. "Well, I did it myself. Good call. I came across Farrell's name. Odd bit of info. There've been no press releases, stories, or fanfare about it. It's just one of those little political factoids that go unnoticed by most people unless they're trying to make a specific connection. I was doing a cross-reference to the principals of your trial with the Board of Elections database, and Moira Farrell's name popped up."

"Popped up where?" Bobby asked, furrowing his brow.

"Moira Farrell, your ex-defense attorney, once loyal Democratic-machine hack, is now a registered *Republican* and listed as the main Brooklyn fund-raiser for the Stone for Governor Campaign."

"Is that a fact?" Bobby said, thinking about the white Taurus.

21

The little old lady stood in the doorway of the tree-shaded one-family brick home in the Bay Terrace section of Bayside, Queens, a neighborhood with one of the lowest crime rates in the city and a large population of Irish, Germans, and Greeks. Lately there had been a great influx of Koreans. It was also once home to W.C. Fields and Gentlemen Jim Corbett, and now, for reasons no one understood, there were more nail manicure parlors on Bell Boulevard than on any other street in the city.

Bay Terrace was so quiet that Bobby had been afraid he'd wake up the whole neighborhood when he knocked on the door.

"Is Herbie here?" Bobby asked.

"What are you selling, sonny?" the woman asked.

"I'm not selling anything, ma'am," Bobby said. "I'm just looking for Herbie. Herbie Rabinowi . . ."

Before Bobby could finish the last name, pinwheels danced before his eyes, his brain swelled with sudden panic, and nothing happened when he tried to breathe. He lurched, bucked, attempted to wrestle his powerful attacker, who had come silently from behind and slammed a giant arm around his neck. Bobby's resistance only tightened the vise. Then he felt something cold screw into his right ear. He was starting to enter a world of shadows and silence. The more he resisted, the darker and quieter the world became.

Control, he thought with a last glimmer of consciousness. *Stop fighting the attacker.* He went limp in the big man's grasp and instantly felt the arm on his neck loosen a millimeter. He breathed in, feeling oxygen zigzag to his brain. The gun barrel remained pressed in his ear. *I can't believe it,* he thought. *Let down my guard. Guy obviously came up from the basement door leading to the areaway. Got behind me on the stoop. Stupid.* Bobby was angrier at himself than he was at the man who was a tricep flex away from crushing his windpipe.

"Who are you?" the man growled. "Talk fast. I'm in no fuckin' mood. If you're a wop or a cop, you're dead."

"Watch your language like that, Herbie," the little woman said. "And why do you have a gun in that man's ear? For what?"

"Izzy Gleason sent me," Bobby croaked.

"Lunch," the woman said. "Bring him in for lunch, Herbie. Izzy sent him."

"Go inside, Aunt Ruth," Herbie said, leading Bobby into the house. They stood in a foyer with a thick maroon-and-gold rug and sponge-painted walls. Overhead light came from a small imitation Tiffany fixture. The house smelled like cabbage.

Herbie Rabinowitz let go of Bobby's neck. Bobby straightened and turned around, half gasping. Herbie Rabinowitz, wearing a strapped T-shirt, was six foot six, with muscles flexing everywhere but his earlobes, a big angular face, and wide-set wild eyes. His hair was an explosion of coiled black springs on a head that would be a sniper's dream. On the top of his skull he wore a yarmulke, fastened with two large bobby pins. He switched his .44 caliber bulldog revolver from his left hand to his right and let it dangle at his side.

"I thought you were one of them," Herbie said.

" 'Them' who?" Bobby asked, rubbing his neck, trying to get blood and air back into all the appropriate pipelines.

"The wops or the cops," Herbie said.

"Not in this house with that language, Herbie," said Aunt Ruth.

"Go inside, Aunt Ruth," Herbie said. "Please. Or else I'll put you in a home."

Aunt Ruth hurried off into the kitchen, mumbling.

"I wouldn't really do that to the old doll," Herbie assured Bobby. "But a nursing home is the only thing in the world that woman is afraid of. She'd wrestle a skinhead in a phone booth."

"Izzy sent me to get you," Bobby said. "Pack a bag."

"My cousin Izzy is a great guy," Herbie said with a big goofy grin.

"He didn't tell me you were his *cousin*," Bobby said.

"His father and my mother were stepbrother and -sister or some shit like that," Herbie said. "Anyway, I knew he'd come through. I can't even go back to work at the dairy diner on Queens Boulevard. The wop leg-breakers came in yesterday. I was in the kitchen, cooking. I dropped ten grand on the Yankee–Red Sox game two nights before. I'm there, working, and they come in to collect, and right away they gotta get guinea-garlic tough on me. You know, one of them little broad-backed dagos, built like a jukebox, talking smartass with his big fuckin' mouth. I told him I'd have the money in a week."

"Which was a lie," Bobby said. "No?"

"Which was true. I went to the finance joint up the street; they were gonna front me fifteen large on the house. But this little, fat wop has to make with the mutz-a-rel dialogue, which I'm not real fond of. Especially when I'm working and he's putting the strong-arm on me. I was tolerant until this little greasy guido called me a deadbeat Jew bastard and that he'd put me in an *oven*. This little siggie-zip prick is gonna put me in an *oven*? So I picked him up by his balls and his collar and I ran him through the swingin' doors from the kitchen. The front door was blocked by two old ladies on walkers, so I heaved the dago bastard right through the fuckin' front window out onto Queens Boulevard. He body-surfed on the broken glass all the way to the gutter. Where he belonged. Like the pile of dog shit that he is."

"Oh," Bobby said.

"The second one with him, one of them elegant wops learns how to dress watching Scorsese movies, he fires a shot that misses. I grab ahold of him and I take the gun offa him, and I shoved the barrel so far down his friggin' throat he gagged and threw up and passed out choking on his own vomit. The gun was still sticking out of his mouth when he spread out on the floor. But the bullet he fired whizzed right past a uniformed cop who was eating a freeload meal. The cop jumps up and tells me I'm under arrest. These wops are in the place where I work trying to put the bull on me and I take care of them, and he wants to lock-me-the-fuck-up!''

"What'd you do?'' Bobby asked, impressed by Herbie's recollection of detail.

"I knocked him out cold as a mack'rel,'' Herbie said. "I took off my apron and left through the broken window. Now I got the cops and the wops after me. The bookies I can eventually work out a deal with because they're businessmen and they really do care more about the money than the bullshit respect they're always yappin' about in the movies. What respect? These bums don't even hold down a job and they talk about *respect*? Them, I can square root a deal with. But the cops, they make a habit of beating the shit out of me whenever they get me in cuffs. This was yesterday, and I know if I stick around, I'm not seeing a judge till Monday, and I ain't lettin' the cops beat the shit out of me for a whole weekend. Uh-uh. So I call Izzy, and he says I should lay lower than whale shit. Especially on Sabbath. There's something not too kosher about having the shit beat out of you by a bunch of ham-faced mick cops on the Sabbath. So I figure I'd hide till Monday. This is my aunt's house, but my mother left me half of it in the will. I don't live here, but they'll get around to looking for me here.''

"Has this happened to you before?'' Bobby asked.

"I'm on a losing streak,'' Herbie said. "Cold dice and slow horses, and the Yanks are in a slump. And I'm not big on cops. What can I say? It's not like I do drugs or anything. I'm actually a religious guy. But I gamble a little.''

"Look, my job is to keep you out of trouble until Monday when I surrender you for the pretrial hearing,'' Bobby said. "So get packed.''

Herbie jammed his .44 in his belt and said, "Packed.''

"Unpack,'' Bobby said. "I'm not going anywhere with you while you're packing a gun because I'm out on bail myself.''

"For what?''

"Murder,'' Bobby whispered dramatically.

"Who the fuck *are* you?''

Bobby told him, and Herbie shook his head and laughed a big belch of a laugh that sounded like a backed-up toilet. "Leave it to cousin Izzy to send a murder suspect to keep me out of trouble.''

"Izzy says you have CIA training," Bobby said, skeptically. "That true?"

"Cousin Iz told you that?" Herbie said with a blush of pride.

"Yeah," Bobby said.

"It's true," he said. "But I didn't think he'd remember."

No wonder the Cold War lasted so long, Bobby thought.

Herbie pulled on a zippered jacket and hid the .44 under a couch cushion, then went into the kitchen to kiss Aunt Ruth good-bye. She insisted they eat, and Bobby shrugged. He had a bowl of cold cabbage soup, a turkey-salad sandwich on seeded Jewish rye, a dill pickle, cole slaw, and a glass of Cel-Ray soda. Aunt Ruth was a traditionalist. Max Roth would have fainted.

Bobby thanked her, and then he and Herbie walked to the Jeep. Herbie climbed into the backseat and lay down on the floor. When Bobby climbed into the driver's seat, a blue Ford Explorer turned the corner and drove slowly past, as if someone was looking around through its black-tinted windows. He pulled away thinking maybe it was nothing, but nothing was nothing anymore in his life.

"I have to get indoors before sundown," Herbie said as Bobby drove the car over the Fifty-ninth Street Bridge. "Sabbath."

On the Manhattan side of the bridge, Bobby studied his rear-view mirror and there, five or six car lengths behind him, was the dark blue Ford Explorer. Bobby didn't mention it to Herbie, who remained on the floor in the back of the Jeep, grunting occasionally when the car hit a bump or a pothole.

Bobby drove downtown to Fifty-first Street and, without signaling, made a sudden right-hand turn. After the turn he saw that the Ford Explorer also made a right after about twenty seconds. Bobby made two more unsignaled rights. The Explorer followed the circle. Bobby then accelerated through the intersection at First Avenue, knowing he'd be on a dead-end street. He quickly swung a U-turn and pulled to the curb. Bobby put the Jeep into park.

"Stay down, Herbie," Bobby said, and slid out the side door.

As soon as the Ford Explorer made the left into the cul-de-sac, it came to a full stop, the driver obviously searching for the Jeep. Bobby reached the passenger door of the Explorer and yanked it open. Sandy Fraser screamed, "Bobby, it's me!"

Bobby climbed in next to her.

"Okay, Sandy, maybe you'd like to explain," Bobby said. "First, how'd you pick up my tail?"

Sandy pointed to a Wackenhut microwave-beeper surveillance computer mounted into the console between the bucket seats. Orange letters zippered across an illuminated grid on a bright green, nine-inch screen. A flashing blip pinpointed the beep from the bug on Bobby's Jeep, giving the exact location on a superimposed street map. Across the bottom of the screen the letters also spelled out the exact location: *Fifty-second Street East of First Avenue.*

"You think they put only *one* bug on your car?" Sandy asked with a smirk. "Barnicle runs a snoop shop! This is a company car. The computer tracks you and prints out where you are at all times on the screen. Even if you lose me. I picked you up first outside a health-food restaurant near the *Daily News.* . . ."

"Where's the second bug?" Bobby asked.

He'd never told her about the first bug that Tom Larkin discovered. First a car rented to the Stone for Governor Campaign, he thought, now Lou Barnicle was tailing him. They were obviously in cahoots. But how? Why?

"It's the letter *O* in 'Cherokee' on the side of your Jeep," Sandy said. "I hear Barnicle and his stooges talking . . ."

"Okay, Sandy. Thanks for the information. Now, why the hell are *you* following me?"

"I thought about what you said yesterday," Sandy said, still parked in the center of the dead-end street.

"About Dorothea?" Bobby said.

"Yeah," she said. "I feel bad because if it wasn't for me, you probably wouldn't have gotten involved with her. In all this."

"You sent me the anonymous letter about the three-quarters racket, didn't you?" Bobby asked.

"I was three months pregnant; I was scared; I wanted out," Sandy said. "I thought maybe you could have him arrested."

"Who, Barnicle?"

"Yeah."

"What was it you wanted to tell me?"

"It's more than I thought it was," she said. "It's more than a few bad cops. It's huge. Every Tuesday they collect hundreds of thousands of dollars. Sometimes over a million. And because of me, you started asking questions and that got you in trouble, and poor Dorothea . . .''

"What about her?" Bobby said, making a mental note of the Tuesday collection day at Gibraltar Security.

"She never told you the real truth about who she was, did she?"

"No, I don't think she did," Bobby said.

"Bobby, I'm afraid of these people," Sandy said. "You see, Lou Barnicle isn't the father of my baby. Just like Dorothea isn't some ordinary immigrant student . . ."

Bobby looked at her oddly, and then suddenly both doors of the Explorer were pulled open. Two uniformed cops, one standing on either side, stood facing them with guns drawn.

"Nobody fucking move," shouted the first cop.

"Or I'll blow your head off," shouted the second.

"What the hell is this?" Bobby demanded.

"This car is reported stolen," said the first cop. "There's an all-points bulletin out on a Sandra Fraser. . . ."

"I have the registration," Sandy said. "Can I show it to you without you making me a DOA, chrissakes?"

"Go ahead," shouted the first cop. Sandy searched in her bag for her wallet.

"Who the hell are you?" the other cop asked Bobby.

"Saint Christopher," Bobby said. "The woman was lost and I was giving her directions."

"Directions on what, wiseass?" the second cop asked. "How to suck your joint? How much she charge you?"

"You must have me mixed up with your wife," Sandy said, her nostrils flaring in anger.

The first cop looked at the registration and walked to the rear of the Explorer, where he and the other cop conferred. One cop spoke into a handheld radio.

"We need to talk some more, Sandy," Bobby whispered. He told her to leave a message on the answering machine at Izzy Gleason's office in Manhattan.

"Barnicle and his crew want you *dead*, Bobby," Sandy said. "I'll be next. Or my kid. These people make adults like Dorothea disappear. How hard do you think it'll be to hide a baby?"

The two cops returned, one on each side of the car.

"Ma'am," the first cop said. "I think there's just a mix-up. But we'd like you to come with us to the precinct. Your husband is looking for you. We have our orders to bring you in, and the captain will straighten all this out. You can ride with me, and my partner will drive your vehicle back to the station house."

She turned to Bobby and whispered, "See what I mean? He makes a few calls to people he knows on the PD, they put out an APB, and he finds me."

"Okay, buddy," the other cop said to Bobby from the other side of the car. "You can hit the road."

Bobby stepped out of the Explorer and watched Sandy walk to the patrol car with the first cop as the other cop climbed behind the wheel of the Explorer. Sandy looked at Bobby with a desperate longing.

Bobby walked back to the Jeep and bent to examine the raised "Cherokee" letters embedded into the side of the car. The letter *O* had been pried off and replaced with a magnetic, round bug, just like the one on the license plate. Bobby pulled it off, placed it under the heel of his boot, crushed it. He got back into the Jeep. Herbie hadn't moved from the floor of the backseat.

"The cops are closing in," Herbie said. "They wanna do their 'Let's-smack-the-shit-out-of-the-Hebe-on-Sabbath' routine with me. Beat me over the head with an Iranian phone book . . ."

"It was my problem, Herbie," Bobby said. "Not yours."

Barnicle and Stone, Bobby thought. *Barnicle and Stone . . .*

22

Saturday

"I'll say this for Herbie," Bobby said to his brother, Patrick, as they sat outdoors on the deck of *The Fifth Amendment* late the next night, slicing into a pair of perfectly broiled sirloins, nibbling pasta and salad on the side, "he can cook like a fireman and he sure isn't afraid of a little hard work."

"This is the best meal I've eaten since Dorothea . . ." Patrick began, and then caught himself in mid-sentence. "Sorry . . ."

"Don't worry," Bobby said. "She'll be with us again."

Bobby and Patrick ate in reflective silence for a moment, watching Herbie in the kitchen cooking and cleaning in a fog of smoke and steam. To thank Bobby for stashing him on board, after sundown, Herbie had spent three solid hours domesticizing *The Fifth Amendment.* He scrubbed the deck, polished the railings. Washed her portholes and swept and hand-shampooed the rugs. Herbie even fixed the shower so that it now sprayed like a hurricane.

Herbie had given Bobby a shopping list, and by the time Bobby returned from the twenty-four-hour supermarket, Herbie had the kitchen so sparkling clean it could have passed a health department inspection without a bribe.

Patrick had showed up a half hour later, after Herbie had prepared pasta shells with broccoli and cauliflower florets, wedges of plum tomatoes, garlic, and shredded carrots. He tossed together a tricolored salad of arugula, endive, and radicchio with virgin olive oil and balsamic vinegar, flavored with freshly minced garlic and lemon pepper. He served Bobby and Patrick a pair of sizzling medium-well steaks, all presented with the pride of a professional.

"Where the hell did you learn how to cook?" Bobby asked.

Herbie looked at him oddly and said, "You already know I have CIA training."

Bobby looked at him for a confused moment.

"Culinary Institute of America," Herbie said slowly. "Hyde Park, upstate New York. CIA is considered the best cooking school in the country. But they threw me out after eighteen months for selling school food cheap to local restaurants to cover bets."

"That CIA," Bobby had said, blinking. It now made sense that he and Gleason were somehow related. Nothing was as it seemed.

Herbie ate his own food standing up in the kitchen as he prepared a chicken soup from scratch for the next day. "Wait'll you see what great chum the chicken soup scum makes when I scoop it off after it sits overnight," Herbie said. "I'll bag us a couple of striped bass . . ."

When Patrick had arrived, the brothers had hugged, patting

each other's backs and looking into each other's eyes, smiling. The Emmets weren't big on tears. The old man had always said to save them for funerals. The last time they had cried was at his. Bobby had not yet wept for Dorothea because he refused to believe she was dead.

After embracing, Bobby had held his kid brother at arm's length. He saw his mother's soft blue eyes and his father's high, strong cheekbones, a short burst of dirty blond hair and a perpetual smile on his good-humored face. Patrick wore a PAL windbreaker that covered the .38 service revolver tucked into a pair of faded jeans.

To break the silence, Bobby thanked Patrick for getting Gleason to take his case.

"I just hope I didn't create a Frankenstein," Patrick said.

"The Gleason payback promises to be the longest bitch on record," Bobby said. "But it beats the shit out of time. Anyway, how's the job?"

"Fine," he said. "In the PAL, I'm around kids, troubled kids with real-life problems most of the time. I have a badge and a gun, but I don't chase bad guys across rooftops."

"Anyone breaking your balls about me?"

"Some," Patrick said. "I won't lie to you. Enough people have done that to you. But nothing I can't handle. Heard you already rattled Barnicle's cage. True?"

Bobby told him about his visit to Gibraltar Security.

"I heard about most of it already," Patrick said. "It's on the tom-toms that you're out looking to settle a score, blaming him. Careful, he still has a *lot* of friends on the job."

"Yeah, waiting to get out on three-quarters to work for him."

"I'd love to catch Barnicle at whatever his game is," Patrick said. "Let me work with you on this in my time off, Bobby."

"No," Bobby said. "I can't let you risk going down with me if this doesn't work out. Mom would never forgive me."

"I'll never forgive you if you don't. I'm no trained investigator. But I still have a legal badge and gun. And the old man would have wanted it that way, too. Family sticking together was one of his biggest Irish cornball mottoes."

Bobby said, "His actual quote was, 'A family has to stick together like shit to a blanket.' "

"It might be crude, but I happen to agree with him. I'm your goddamned brother, Bobby. I'm not the little squirt you helped with his English homework and had to babysit for on Saturday nights when you'd rather have been out with the chicks. I'm a grown man, a cop, your blood. I'd die for you, like you would for me. Who else can you trust as much as me?"

Bobby looked Patrick deep in the eyes and nodded. Family was a very small army that stood between you and the rest of the world, and when you were at war, you enlisted the troops. Unlike hired help, they took the battle personally. There was no other adult on earth Bobby could trust more. "Okay," Bobby said. "You can start by finding out some stuff for me."

"Name it," Patrick said with a smile.

"There's an assistant medical examiner named Franz in Brooklyn," Bobby said. "He's out of town until next week sometime. Find out when. Also what his hours are. What time he takes lunch. He's a weird little guy, as I remember from my Brooklyn South days. Find out if he's a Tuzio flunky. Is he a registered Democrat or Republican? Get some background on him."

"Okay, Charlie, I gotta get to work," Patrick Pearse Emmet said. "But you need Number One Brother, you can beep me, or leave a short message. They relay it to me, and I'm there like the wind. Call yourself Charlie, for Charlie Chan, on any messages. I'll use the name Sonny, for Number One Son. We don't know who'll be listening or intercepting."

"Okay," Bobby said, impressed with Patrick's savvy.

"One more thing," Patrick said as he rose to leave. "I'm not letting you go back to jail."

His kid brother was no kid anymore.

That night, Herbie snored like a buffalo with a deviated septum. Bobby let him sleep in the big bed in the cabin, while he camped on the deck of the boat, in a large rubber dinghy, pulling a dark comforter over himself and staring up at the stars for the first time in a long while. The immensity of the night sky made his own problems seem smaller. He firmly believed that each individual, no matter what galaxy, what life-form, was responsible for its own destiny, its own private universe. He wasn't as swayed as John Shine was by Emerson's theories of the Oversoul and individual divinity. But he did believe each man was responsible for his own words and deeds.

After a few minutes, he drifted into deep, bottomless sleep.

Then somewhere in the black hole of the night, Bobby heard a tinkle of steel and feet squeaking on the polished deck.

Bobby's heart beat quickly as he lifted his head up slightly to see a hooded figure slinking across the deck. Then the flash of a straight razor zipping open and the glint of the summer moon reflecting in its blade. He saw the figure hurry like an apparition toward the cabin from which came Herbie's snoring.

"HERBIE! YOU JEW BASTARD!" Bobby shouted as loud as he could, hoping to get the reaction that would save Herbie's life.

Herbie came to life like a rocket booster, fire and fury erupting, arms and legs exploding in a swinging, kicking fit. "Motheeeeerfuuuuuucker!" Herbie shouted, grabbing the attacker by the wrist and bending the arm sideways until cartilage popped and the razor fell to the floor. Clutching the attacker by the back of the hood, he smashed his right fist into the face like someone pounding a catcher's mitt.

Now Bobby caught a glimpse of a second hooded attacker in time to partly deflect a swinging oar. Bobby bent and crunched a left hook into the attacker's rib cage and heard him groan so loudly it didn't sound quite human. The guy collapsed to his knees, and Bobby bent to lift him to his feet and hit him again. But as he did, Herbie came charging, holding the first attacker like a battering ram, heading right for the door. Bobby jumped out of the way, allowing one goon to escape.

"Hold on to that fuck!" Bobby shouted. But Herbie was driven now by white-hot rage as he lifted the first attacker high above his head like a sack of coffee. He whirled in a demented circle while the second attacker abandoned his buddy and raced down the gangplank and dove into the water.

"Hold on to him, Herbie!"

But instead he flung the hooded man a good seven feet from the boat.

"Shit," Bobby said, turning to the opposite direction in time to see the other attacker scaling the ten-foot fence. He looked back out into the swift moonlit river, but there was no sign of the first thug.

"They found me," Herbie said. "Nowhere is safe from the wops and cops."

"They were after me," Bobby said.

"*Me*," Herbie insisted.

Bobby's father had a saying, "Sometimes, to argue with them is to educate them." Bobby knew the hit was intended for him. But if Herbie believed he was the target, it would keep him as alert as a human rottweiler.

"Maybe you're right, Herbie. I better find you a new place to stay come morning."

But Bobby was feeling exhilarated; he was now controlling the situation. He had sent a shiver through the nervous ranks of his enemies. *They have come looking for you,* he thought. *You have smoked them out. They are certain to make mistakes. Control the situation. Force them to make mistakes. Make them lead you to Dorothea.*

23

Sunday

As he drove crosstown, the clock on the Jeep dashboard flashed 9:45 AM. Bobby checked in with Maggie on the cell phone, but Connie answered, "You get laid yet?"

"Mom, you're on my line," came Maggie's voice.

"Oh, Jesus," said Connie, clearly embarrassed.

"Way to go, Con," Bobby said. He heard Connie hang up and Maggie laughing.

"You didn't hear that," Bobby said, and laughed as he drove from the Seventy-ninth Street Boat Basin through the empty streets of Manhattan. Herbie Rabinowitz was on the floor in the back of the Jeep.

"Hi, Dad," Maggie said. "I miss you."

"Same here," Bobby said, and he gave his daughter a vague update, telling her he'd learned some encouraging news about Dorothea that made him believe she was alive.

"I'm looking forward to our trip to Coney Island," she said.

"Maybe next weekend," Bobby said as he approached the underground garage of the Empire State Building, checking his rearview mirror to be sure no one was tailing him. The street behind him was Sunday-morning empty. "This is going to cut off in a minute because I'm going underground. I just wanted to tell you I love you and I was thinking about you."

"Real quick, Dad," Maggie said. "I was going through the press-clips file I have on your case last night, like you asked. There was a story in the *New York Times* back at the time of the trial, about that awful woman named Cis Tuzio? Like a biography . . ."

" 'Woman in the News'?" Bobby said, vaguely remembering reading it.

"Yeah," Maggie said. "In the middle of the story it says that she graduated from Brooklyn Law School in 1982."

"Yeah?" Bobby said. "And . . ."

"Well, then I read another story in *Brooklyn Bridge* magazine about your old lawyer, Moira Farrell," Maggie said.

"Yeah," Bobby said.

"She graduated from the same school, the same year," Maggie said.

"You sure? I never made that connection."

"Coincidence, huh?"

Bobby was impressed that his kid had put this together.

"Maybe not," Bobby said. "Maybe they knew each other. . . ."

"Cis Tuzio was born and raised in Scranton, Pennsylvania," Maggie said. "It doesn't say where Moira Farrell was born."

"Try to get a yearbook from the school," Bobby said.

"I already E-mailed the school with Mom's FedEx number asking them to send it ASAP," Maggie said. "It costs twenty dollars for a back issue."

The phone began scratching madly as the Jeep entered the underground garage. "This is breaking up, gotta go, Mag. I love ya."

"Love ya, too, Dad."

"No self-respecting hit man would be caught dead looking for you in Gleason's office," Bobby assured Herbie. The big man walked directly to the TV, turned it on, took a beer from the fridge, and plopped into the recliner. A Stone for Governor Campaign commercial came on on New York 1.

"You got a shower," Bobby said. "You can sleep in the recliner;

just keep the door locked and the snoring down to a lion's roar, and you'll be okay till Monday."

"Family values are the answer to a whole host of our society's ills," said Stone in the commercial, addressing a group of senior citizens. "If we return to the values that your generation believed in, we will see a reduction in crime, drug addiction, teen pregnancy, soaring high school dropout rates, welfare families, and therefore taxes. We won't have to cut Medicaid or Social Security if a return to family values takes care of most of the problems of our youth." There was wild applause from the seniors on the soundtrack and then the deep resounding voice-over of a narrator: "Join the family; join Stone for Governor."

"You see," Herbie said. "Politics is just organized crime with campaign buttons."

There were two calls on the answering machine. The first one was from Moira Farrell, asking Gleason to congratulate Bobby on his release. "Bobby, if you hear this, don't be a stranger, darling," Moira Farrell said in her sexy, purring voice. "Drop up to the office sometime for a drink. I'd like to personally welcome you home. Bye for now. You know the number."

Eventually he would take her up on the invitation.

The second message was from Tom Larkin, asking Bobby to call, which he did pronto.

"I don't like talking on a PD phone," Larkin said after they exchanged hellos. "But I wanted to tell you I'm looking into an old kidnapping case that I think could be related to your girl Dorothea's disappearance. It happened too long ago for it to be on computer, so I'll have to go to the main file room, search the archives. Could take a while. Be patient."

"I appreciate it, Tom," Bobby said. Since Larkin had steered him there, Bobby told him about Carlos and the pacemaker in the crematorium.

"Carlos told me about the teeth but not the pacemaker," Larkin said.

"He didn't think it was significant," Bobby said. "It was an afterthought."

"Jesus," Larkin said in a hushed whisper. "This is getting good, juicy. I might be able to answer some questions with that piece of information. I gotta go. One more thing. I know I asked you this a couple of times. But you're positive it was the Ukraine, Dorothea said she was from?"

"Certain," Bobby said.

"Not Romania, Georgia, Bulgaria, Russia, or . . . ?"

"Dorothea Dubrow said she was from the Ukraine, Tom," Bobby said, a tinge of annoyance in his voice. "Tell me why that's so important?"

"God bless," Larkin said and hung up abruptly. The old cop came from a time when people actually wished God's good graces on one another. Bobby felt bad for getting annoyed with him.

Bobby shook his head again and then left Herbie in the office with a tub of the chicken soup he'd made the day before. "I'll be back for you in the morning," Bobby said. "Don't you leave here. Don't answer phones. You have food, sodas, whatever you need. Just lie low."

"Enjoy your day," Herbie said. "Thank you for all your kindness. Shalom."

"Shalom," Bobby said and double-locked the door behind him.

24

An hour later, Bobby stood on the fly deck of *The Fifth Amendment,* put the key in the ignition, pushed in the buttons of the two parallel start switches, which brought the twin diesel engines to life. Because they hadn't been used in so long, he let them warm up for a good fifteen minutes, while he watched the gulls wheel and surveyed the quiet boat basin. As he grabbed the dual-lever engine and throttle controls, he saw three women wearing large sunglasses and minuscule string bikinis emerge from inside a Chinese junk moored in the neighboring slip about twenty feet from *The Fifth Amendment.* They each sat dramatically on deck chairs draped with thick towels, as if they were auditioning for a part in a movie.

Gleason had told Bobby that a junk-bond dealer with a sense of humor had bought that boat at the height of the greedy eighties and named it *Armage*. The women were young, gym-muscled, parlor-tanned, and blond-dyed. They looked over at a bare-chested Bobby in his cutoff jeans, whispered among themselves as he unhooked the stern line from the dock cleat and then untied the bow line. They waved to him and smiled, and three sets of white teeth beamed against their chestnut tans. Bobby smiled and waved back. His libido was alive and well. The junk-bond dealer, mid-fifties, nut brown, good shape, the hair on his chest a whiter gray than the silver mane on his head, walked up from below and handed out flutes of champagne. He winked at Bobby and shrugged. Bobby nodded.

"Drop in some time when you're feeling bored," said the man.

"Anytime," said the woman wearing the white bikini that didn't consist of enough fabric to wipe her full, pouted lips.

"Yeah," shouted the other two as they raised their glasses.

"Love to," Bobby said. "But I'm working today."

"Too bad."

"It certainly is," Bobby said.

The Fifth Amendment bobbed in the water as Bobby climbed up into the cabin. He took the helm and backed out of the dock into the river and pointed south on the Hudson. The junk-bond dealer and the three women waved good-bye. Bobby waved back. Maybe if things were different, he could think of mindlessly flirting with lovely women.

In fifteen minutes he was passing a fully dressed Statue of Liberty and the Red Hook docks of Brooklyn; he slid past the Sixty-ninth Street pier and Shore Road, glided under the Verrazano Bridge into the Narrows, and swung east past the man-made Hoffman and Swinburne Islands, formed from the accumulated bedrock unearthed to make way for the awesome skyscrapers of the Manhattan skyline. At one time these isolated islands had been used as quarantine centers for victims of tuberculosis and other communicable diseases. But Bobby remembered them from his Harbor Unit days as a place where on-duty water cops took babes, whom they had picked up from the decks of pleasure craft, for barbecues and bare-ass romps. Bobby had been invited along a few times, but had declined. Not that he wasn't tempted. But he would never risk his job, his gun, badge, reputation, integrity, and especially his marriage for an afternoon fling. Besides, it was just wrong. He'd never have been able to live with himself if some citizen drowned while he was muff-diving.

Beyond the Narrows, he cruised the Coney Island Flats, passing the lighthouse at Norton's Point at the tip of Coney Island. He chugged by Sea Gate, a once thriving private Jewish community now in sad decline, rounded the mythical Steeplechase Pier and the Cyclone and Wonder Wheel of the Coney Island amusement parks. He continued three miles east beyond Brighton Beach, the Little Odessa of Brooklyn, and Manhattan Beach and Kingsborough Community College before taking dead aim at the peninsula of Windy Tip, a secluded dot on the tip of the nose of Brooklyn. He cut the engines and drifted to about one hundred and fifty feet offshore, dropped anchor, and tied up to a white plastic mooring bubble.

Bobby had come to Windy Tip because he wanted to see where Lou Barnicle lived, where Sandy was raising her baby with his dirty money. He wanted to get the lay of the land of this private community where most of Barnicle's ex-cop employee goons lived and hung out, and wanted to bounce a few things he'd learned off John Shine.

Bobby used a pair of binoculars to locate John Shine's brand-new luxury two-story beach house with attic. *If you win the lottery, you might as well spend some dough,* he thought. He watched a cat chase a squirrel across the rooftop and into an attic window in a hunt Charles Darwin would have understood.

Bobby dove right into the thirty feet of water, in cutoff shorts and sleeveless T-shirt, and swam to shore in the tame, warm waters of Jamaica Bay.

He mopped his face, wrung the excess water from his hair. He walked through the warm, shell-studded sand toward Shine's house, scanning the brilliant beachfront. A few kids dug in the sand with plastic shovels and pails. Plump women sunbathed on large beach towels emblazoned with the names of Caribbean hotels. Three guys wearing NYPD T-shirts held beer bottles and tossed a Frisbee in a lazy, hazy triangle. In the distance he saw a group of guys and girls playing a game of volleyball in front of a squat cinderblock building, the local cop hangout called The Central Booking Saloon, owned by Lou Barnicle.

He was still walking toward Shine's house when he saw a familiar-looking blue Ford Explorer next to a BMW in a driveway a hundred feet down the common beach. Then he saw Sandy Fraser step out onto a sundeck of the second floor of the house above the driveway, in a yellow bikini, not looking as though she'd recently given birth. She had obviously seen Bobby from the window and now stepped out onto the deck, with her arms folded across her breasts, staring at him as if for salvation.

A toddler ran out onto the deck and grabbed at Sandy's leg. Bobby understood Sandy's fear—when you become a parent, fear for your own life takes a backseat to that for your child's.

"Bobby!" The man's voice from his right was unmistakable, and Bobby turned to John Shine, who was standing on his large back deck, wearing a faded NYPD T-shirt, beat-up tennis shoes, and a pair of baggy khaki shorts. Under the T-shirt his corsetlike back brace was visible. He grimaced only slightly when he walked down from his deck and along the beach to greet Bobby.

Sandy troubled him. Bobby needed to talk to her again, needed to find out what else she knew about Dorothea. Needed to help her before something bad happened to her and her baby. But he took John Shine's hand in his, shook it firmly, and Shine threw an arm over his shoulder and led him toward his house. Bobby looked back and saw Lou Barnicle step out onto the deck, dressed in shorts and a sleeveless T-shirt, wearing aviator glasses and gold chains around his hairy neck. Barnicle animatedly pointed to his watch and then pointed into the house, as if Sandy was late for something.

"Forget him," Shine said. "The man has fearful followers but no true friends."

"That another Emerson quote?" Bobby asked.

"No," Shine said, laughing as he led Bobby up the wooden stairs from the beach to his deck. "But Emerson did say, 'The only reward of virtue is virtue; the only way to have a friend is to be one.' Barnicle wouldn't understand that if it bit him on the ass, and even if he did, he'd ignore it. But if you want to be my friend, be one by coming inside. Like most white trash made good, I'm dying to show off."

"How's he treat Sandy?" Bobby asked.

"She reminds me of Rapunzel trapped in the tower," Shine said. "But I see her come and go on her own. She wears the best of clothes. Drives a new Explorer. Does busywork at the Gibraltar office a couple of days a week, where he can keep an eye on her. She swims, sunbathes, eats with him in the best restaurants. I never see any black eyes. The ambulance never shows up at the door. I've never heard a single domestic argument. You see any bruises?"

"She ever leave with the kid?" Bobby couldn't let go.

Shine pondered for a moment. "I've never thought about it. She has a nanny slash housekeeper who helps her with the kid. Looks like Ma Barker, for Christ sakes."

"You think Sandy can come and go as she pleases with the kid?" Bobby asked.

"Christ," Shine said. "If she was being held against her will, she could call the cops, Bobby."

"On Barnicle? Which cop?"

"Well, she could get an attorney, no?"

"With what money? I'd bet she lives on an allowance. Maybe her jewelry is fake."

"She could go to the DA."

Bobby just stared Shine in the eye. "Diamond? Tuzio? This is still technically Brooklyn."

"I think you're a little too paranoid," Shine said. "Come on in; I'll show you around."

Bobby looked again at the balcony, but it was empty, except for Barnicle, staring through the aviator glasses in Bobby's general direction, smiling.

Shine led Bobby up onto the deck, where he unlocked two Medeco locks on the sliding glass door. He opened the door and a mechanical barking dog exploded to life and a two-tone horn alarm blared before he turned the system off.

Bobby followed Shine into a large kitchen with butcher-block counters and hanging copper-bottomed pots. Copper-colored kitchen appliances blended into a rustic motif. Blue delft was racked on a teakwood hutch that matched a big, round teakwood dining table. A real Tiffany lamp hung over the center of the table, where a bowl of fresh fruit sat next to a cordless phone and a pair of ledger books.

"I only eat here when I have houseguests," he said. "And that's only if she knows how to cook."

"Still looking for love, eh, John?"

"Anyone can get laid," Shine said. "Falling in love with the right woman takes more luck than the lottery. The odds are higher. I date, but I don't look for love. I've already had the one great love of my life. I firmly believe you get only one. Even if I'm wrong about that, I'd never set myself up for the pain of losing another one. It's just too overbearing."

"Maybe your standards are too high," Bobby said.

"I don't think anyone's standards or goals can be too high," Shine said. "Setting them lower is to aspire to mediocrity. Come on, I'll show you around."

He led Bobby into an immense living room with twelve-foot, oak-beamed ceilings and hanging fisherman's nets, rope ladders, and seascape prints.

The nautical motif included a coffee table and end tables set made from the hatches of old ships and a huge rusted anchor that leaned against a big, black potbellied stove. The floor was wide-plank oak with expensive Iranian area rugs spread around haphazardly. The deep, soft couches were scattered with throw pillows. A twenty-five-foot bay-front window looked out onto Jamaica Bay and the city beyond. One whole wall was lined with books, a special section dedicated just to different editions of Emerson's books and biographies and appreciations of his work.

Tony Bennett sang "I've Got the World on a String" from an elaborate stereo system. Bobby couldn't see the speakers, which meant they were probably buried in the ceilings and the walls.

They toured the handsomely decorated upstairs bedrooms, where four-poster beds, deep carpets, and heavy teak furniture promoted a sense of timelessness. Bobby heard mad scratching from the attic above.

"Squirrels," Shine said. "I keep the small attic roof window open a crack to prevent spontaneous combustion, and they get in. I keep meaning to call an exterminator, but I hate killing the poor critters. And I have no time for the relocation traps. Eventually . . ."

Shine's office was more space age, replete with computer, fax and photocopy machines, and a multipaneled telephone system. The retired cop was enjoying showing off his house. Bobby had never known Shine to be materialistic, but in middle age, men with no children tend to take great pride in their possessions. The place was magnificent, Bobby thought.

Withdrawn, paranoid, laconic, Bobby wasn't being such a great friend to a guy who was showing him some genuine human hospitality. Bobby was out of jail, but jail wasn't out of him yet.

"You okay?" Shine asked.

"Sorry," Bobby said. "I'm still decompressing. Your house is wonderful."

"At the risk of being politically incorrect—house tours are for women. The only thing I wish I had was a finished basement. No one in Windy Tip has basements, because of the sand, so I can't take you downstairs to the bar for a beer and game of pool."

"Then take me to the bar down the beach," Bobby said.

"The Central Booking?" Shine said. "That's owned by Barnicle. His guys hang out there. In fact, there's a christening party going on there today. But the bar section is still open to the public."

"Even better," Bobby said.

"It'll drive Barnicle nuts to see you walk in his joint," Shine said with a salty grin.

"Good. Then by all means let's go."

On the way they passed Lou Barnicle's house again, but Sandy was nowhere to be seen. Her blue Explorer was still parked in the driveway, a plastic tricycle nearby.

"What do you know about Cis Tuzio's past?" Bobby asked.

"Not much," Shine said. "Came up the political ranks. Good lawyer."

"She friendly with Moira Farrell?"

"They obviously know each other," Shine said. "But you could fit most of Brooklyn's Court Street lawyers at one bar mitzvah. In fact, they probably have on a few occasions."

Bobby could hear the roar from inside the barnlike saloon from twenty feet away. Dark green screens covered the bay-front windows, and the alcohol-inflated blare of a party in progress poured out of Central Booking, which was a concrete-block-and-stucco affair with a sloping clay-tiled roof. Bobby and John Shine walked in through the screen door from the bright sun to the dark, cool barroom.

Bobby recognized at least two-dozen cops—both retired and on the job—wives or girlfriends, their kids, all celebrating a christening. A Catholic priest jovially worked the crowd. Many of these people had been at the Christmas party where Bobby had met

Dorothea. He recognized Kuzak, Zeke, and two very young faces in the room, guys in their twenties, and tried to place them. Then he realized that it was the absence of police uniforms that kept him from immediately putting names to the cherubic faces: Caputo and Dixon, the two cops he'd encountered with Tom Larkin.

In the far corner of the room Bobby noticed men in business suits at a round table. A small, balding older man surrounded by large young men who Bobby was certain were cops.

"Come on, I'll buy you a drink," Shine said.

Bobby followed Shine toward the bar, his eyes still on the rear round table. Shine put his arm around Bobby's shoulder and eased him up to the bar. The bartender dried his hands on a bar towel and shook Shine's hand; then he turned to Bobby and froze. Bobby recognized O'Brien right away. He was the cop whom Zeke and Kuzak had propositioned in the men's room about three-quarters at that long-ago Christmas party. The same O'Brien who ran out of the men's room after Bobby stepped out of the stall. The same O'Brien who put a quarter in the phone at The Anchor in Gerritsen Beach the night Bobby was drugged and charged with Dorothea's murder.

"Hey, O'Brien," Bobby said.

O'Brien nodded and said, "Emmet."

This brought a halt to the conversation nearest them, and then the rest of the afternoon bar crowd began to quiet down, as they turned to look at Bobby Emmet. The only sounds came from the party room, where the band played "All My Exes Live in Texas."

"Long time no see," Bobby said.

"Yeah," O'Brien said, and nodded to a patron and then at the party room. Bobby knew O'Brien was calling for backup.

"Fact, you said you didn't even remember seeing me in The Anchor that night. . . ."

"I don't know what you're talking about," O'Brien said.

"How's the job, O'Brien?" Bobby asked, staring him dead in the fidgety eyes.

O'Brien looked around, and now slowly, one by one, Kuzak, Zeke, Lebeche, Daniels, Flynn, Levin, Caputo, and Dixon started drifting from the party room into the barroom. They stood in a loose, wordless semicircle behind Bobby and Shine.

"Retired," O'Brien said offhandedly. "What're you having?"

"Get out on three-quarters?" Bobby asked.

"I got hurt. I'm not a well man."

"No, no, you're not *well*," Bobby said. "The *man* part you never were."

"I don't have to take this shit," O'Brien said, throwing down the bar towel, shaking, his eyes skittering around to the faces of the other off-duty cops. Many of them wore their guns in plain view. "I don't have to serve you. . . ."

"If I'm buying, you will," Shine said in a low, firm voice that dripped with authority.

"Make it a roofies cocktail," Bobby said. "Your special."

O'Brien swallowed, blinked, his face a tangle of tics. He said, "I don't know what you're talking about."

Bobby turned and saw the other cops staring with smoldering eyes. Nobody moved.

Then at the round corner table at the rear of the dining room, Bobby noticed Hanratty and another cop from the Brooklyn DA's office stand and abruptly escort the small, balding older man out a side door into a blinding rectangle of sunlight. Bobby thought the man looked like Sol Diamond, Brooklyn district attorney.

"Wasn't that . . . ?" Bobby began to ask Shine.

"Yep," Shine said.

"Give Bobby Emmet whatever he's drinking," came a deep voice from the front door. Lou Barnicle walked into his saloon, wearing the aviator glasses he'd had on earlier, a pistachio-colored suit, and white shoes. Sandy was holding her bright-eyed son by one hand, the other hand holding a large gift-wrapped box.

"Nice place, Lou," Bobby said. "I saw your fine house down the beach. BMW and an Explorer in the driveway. Beautiful lady. Little boy in blue. Luckily he looks more like the mother than you. . . ."

Barnicle turned to Sandy. "Go sit down."

"What's my name?" Sandy said. *"Lassie?"*

"I'm talking men's talk here," Barnicle said.

"Then act like a man," she said. "For a change."

Sandy looked at Bobby and led her son toward the party room.

"Have a nice quiet drink, Bobby," Lou Barnicle said softly. "I'll see no one bothers you."

"I guess my future is looking up," Bobby said. "Ex-cops live like ex-presidents these days."

"All hard-earned, Bobby. Every dime."

The men at the bar focused on Barnicle and Bobby. Shine had a crooked smile on his face, enjoying the exchange.

"Let me ask you a question, Lou," Bobby said.

"Shoot," Barnicle said.

"When that little boy of yours grows up, you ever gonna tell him the truth about where his daddy the civil servant police officer got all his money?"

Sandy had said that the kid wasn't even his, and Bobby knew this would make Barnicle all the more sensitive. He would have to fake a father's indignant pride. Everything about him was a lie.

Barnicle removed the sunglasses and stared at Bobby with cold cobalt eyes.

"Maybe you should skip the drink and go for a nice quiet walk," Barnicle said, no trace of emotion in his voice.

"Are you gonna tell him you want him to grow up to be just like dear old *Dad?*" Bobby asked. "Follow your flatfoot footsteps on the bagman route?"

Bobby stepped closer, mimicking Barnicle.

" 'Okay, Junior,' " Bobby mocked, " 'you put on your shiny policeman's badge, and now you go get the gambling skim from that nice gangster with the flat nose over there.' Or, 'Go tell that nice drug dealer with the machine gun over there that you want a piece of his action so you will turn your eyes and your badge the opposite way.' "

"You're out of line," Barnicle said. "Shine, maybe you should go read Bobby here some of your poetry. Teach him some manners."

Shine smiled and said, "I'm rather enjoying his recital."

Bobby stepped closer to Barnicle. Kuzak and Zeke made a move toward him, but Barnicle held up a hand to stop them.

"Or 'Okay, Junior, now go rig a three-quarters medical pension for that phony able-bodied cop over there so he can collect taxpayers' money for life.' "

"You better leave while you still got a *life,*" said Flynn, the Gibraltar goon who looked like a marine poster.

The priest walked into the bar area with a smile on his face and a beer in his hand. "Is everything all right here, boys? It looks like Judas is ready to kiss Jesus in the garden."

"Everything is fine, padre," Barnicle said, leading the priest to the side, handing him an envelope.

The other cops stared at Bobby, ready for Barnicle to give the signal to tear him apart. Shine put a hand on Bobby's shoulder.

"The odds stink," Shine said, nodding toward the others. *"They* don't stand a chance. Let's go."

Bobby smiled and followed Shine out the door.

25

Monday

"Tell me, Officer Grabowski, how often do you eat in Kirsch's Kosher Dairy Deli?" Gleason asked as he paced in front of the young uniformed cop on the witness stand at the pretrial hearing in Queens County Courthouse. It was Monday, 10:30 AM. Bobby had given Gleason one simple usable fact that he had gleaned from his time with Herbie, and Gleason spun a defense out of it.

"I eat there almost every day at meal," Officer Grabowski said, looking at Gleason, who jingled some coins in the pants pocket of his beige Armani suit, winking at Alana, who sat next to Bobby in the third row of the courtroom. Alana smiled at Gleason, and for the first time Bobby noticed her newly capped teeth.

"So, Officer Grabowski, we're talking about five times a week, that you eat there," Gleason said, walking to the defense table, where Herbie Rabinowitz sat in a dark suit, cleanly shaved, wearing his yarmulke, looking as innocent as a baby's rattle.

"That would be correct, Counselor," Grabowski said.

Gleason picked up what appeared to be a menu from the defense table and held it in his hands, behind his back.

"And what do you usually order?" Gleason asked, his voice booming, as he began to thumb through the menu of Kirsch's Kosher Dairy Deli.

"Objection," a petite female assistant district attorney said. "Relevance. His tone badgering, Your Honor."

Gleason looked up at the judge. His name was Popadopolous, and he had a face like a basset hound's, with droopy eyes and baggy jowls.

"Is this going somewhere besides a calorie count, Gleason?"

"You betcha, Judge," Gleason said.

"Cut to the entrée, then," Popadopolous said, turning to the ADA. "And, Counsel, he isn't badgering. Gleason talks in that tone to pet parakeets. Overruled. Answer the question, Officer Grabowski."

"It depends on the shift," Grabowski said. "If I'm working nights, I always get a turkey sandwich platter and a Coke. Mornings, lox and bagels and a coffee."

"You're positive about that?"

"Positive," Grabowski said with a confident sneer. "I know what I eat."

"Nothing wrong with your memory, then?"

"No, my memory is perfect."

"Okay," Gleason said as he approached Grabowski and looked him dead in the eye, this time lowering his voice to a near whisper.

"How much does a turkey sandwich platter cost in Kirsch's Kosher Dairy Deli, Officer Grabowski?"

The cop looked at Gleason and his pink face quickly blanched.

"I'm not sure. . . ."

"How about lox and bagels?"

"Relevance!" shouted the ADA as she rose to her feet.

"Goes to memory, Judge," Gleason said, turning, winking at Alana again. Bobby sat impressed and amused. He looked at Alana, who kept grinning, showing off her new teeth. It was quickly becoming a gold-star morning for Izzy Gleason.

"Overruled," Popadopolous said. "Answer the question."

"I'm not sure," the nervous, sweaty cop said.

"What about coffee?" Gleason asked. "You eat in this place for the past three years, five times a week, surely you must know how much a cup of coffee costs."

"I dunno," Grabowski said. "A half a buck. A dollar . . ."

"What about a soda, Officer Grabowski?"

"No idea."

"You know you are under oath, Officer Grabowski, don't you?"

"Yes, I do."

"And that if you lie here, you can be charged with perjury? Lose the job and the pension?"

"Yeah," Grabowski said, shifting in his seat, clearing his throat.

"So I am going to ask you to answer the next question honestly because there are many witnesses who can attest to the truth."

There was a long silence as Gleason turned his back on Grabowski, took a sip of water, ignoring Alana this time, his eyes as glazed as those of a shark heading for meat, and then turned and strode directly to Grabowski until his face was inches from the young cop's nose. He shouted, "Have you ever, in three years, five days a week, *ever* paid for a *single* meal in Kirsch's Kosher Dairy Deli, Police Officer Grabowski?!"

"Ob-jec-tion!" the ADA shouted, launching to her feet.

"Goes to memory, credibility, and moral turpitude, Judge."

"O-ver-ruled!" snapped Popadopolous.

The cop wet his dry, trembling lips. He looked as if he were gagging on his Adam's apple. He squirmed in his seat, looked at the judge, who glared down at him. When he finally answered, his voice rose steadily to a soprano, "What's that, you know, like, I dunno, got to do with that big ape hitting me?"

"Nonresponsive, Your Honor," Gleason said.

"Duly stricken," the judge said, and glowered at the composting cop. "Answer the question, Officer."

"I can't remember," Grabowski said.

"Have you ever written a parking ticket for any customer who double-parked outside Kirsch's Kosher Dairy Deli? Or do you look the other way in return for the free nose bag?"

"I can't remember," Grabowski said again.

"In three years you can't remember whether or not you ever paid for a meal or wrote a ticket at Kirsch's Kosher Dairy Deli?" Gleason asked.

"That's right," Grabowski said. "I can't, whomyacallit, remember for sure . . . too clear . . . I guess my memory isn't as great as I said . . . sometimes."

Grabowski took a deep slug from his water with a trembling hand. Bobby knew the cop couldn't answer either way. If Grabowski said he did pay his meal tabs and Gleason had witnesses that would say he never paid, he could be fired and charged with perjury. If he said he took free meals, he would be fired anyway. All he could do was claim he couldn't remember. If he couldn't remember paying a meal tab in three years, how the hell could he remember what happened in a melee in which he was cold-cocked? The prosecution's case was going down in flames.

"Your Honor," Gleason screeched in his high-pitched voice, "I ask that these charges be dismissed for lack of credible evidence. This witness is a bad joke!"

Popadopolous nodded to the ADA. She just sagged and waved her hand. The judge banged the gavel and looked at Grabowski.

"Son," Popadopolous said, "I was you, I'd get me some Maalox for the indigestion you got coming when I contact your superiors. Case dismissed."

He banged his gavel, and Grabowski raced out of the courtroom, holding his hat over his crotch, looking as if he needed to find a men's room.

Bobby had seen Gleason in action before, but his performance this morning assured him that the lawyer was well on his way to a brilliant comeback.

"Am I an alchemist or what?" Gleason said to Bobby, pointing to Alana's dazzling smile. "In return, I'm handling the dentist's divorce. Eventually, I might need you to follow his wife around."

Herbie walked over to Bobby and shook his hand and hugged him.

"I can't thank you enough, Bobby," he said. "Now that I don't have to worry about the cops, all I have to deal with is the . . . Italian fellows."

That morning, while Bobby watched Gleason's performance in Queens, the two uniformed housing-unit cops named Lebeche and Daniels sat in their radio car on West Twenty-first Street off Surf Avenue outside the Coney Island projects. Slumping in the backseat was a black snitch named Rollo.

"Dealer's name is Martinez," Rollo said, a hoodie pulled up over his head, dark shades shielding his eyes. Rollo was being cautious, although he knew that no one even remotely connected to the Coney Island drug trade would be awake before noon.

"Which apartment?" asked Daniels.

" 'Partment Four-E. He got enough product to keep alla Coney high till day afta Christmas. I don't know where he keep his cash, but he stash his product under the box where his pit bull keep her puppies. Anybody but Martinez go near the fuckin' puppies, they lunch. Now, what you gots to do is, you knock twice. Wait a few second. Knock two time again more. He always send his wife to answer the door. That her job. She ask in Spanish who it is. You gotta say one word—'Boardwalkbrown.' "

"That's two words," said Daniels.

"Say it like that fast, spic fast, like," he said. "Like 'Boardwalkbrown.' That his nickname for his shit. Mexican brown heroin. Good, too. I could unload it fass. Niggas be comin' from all over Brooklyn for Boardwalkbrown."

Lebeche handed Rollo a fifty-dollar bill and said, " 'Boardwalkbrown'?"

"Thass it." Rollo put the snitch fifty in his hoodie pocket.

"Meet us in the parking-meter lot next to Nathan's in twenny minutes," Daniels said. "Don't keep us waiting or I'll shoot you through the face."

"You got it," Rollo said, and climbed out of the car and walked east along Surf Avenue toward Nathan's Famous, which made the best hot dog on planet earth. From the distance the strains of hurdy-gurdy music floated on the sea air, past the amusement parks of Coney Island, down here to the man-made palisades of poverty known as the projects.

"Frogs' legs, a dog, and fries?" Lebeche said, snapping a twenty-dollar bill as a wager on what Rollo would eat for lunch at Nathan's. "What you say?"

"I say he can't help but go for the chicken in a basket and a grape soda," said Daniels, throwing his twenty-dollar bill on top of Lebeche's. "Only spades drink grape soda. I lie awake nights sometimes wondering why."

When they met Rollo in twenty minutes, they'd ask what he ate and the winner would take all.

"What a sewer this fuckin' city is," Lebeche said as they sat for another minute until Rollo was safely out of sight. "Welfare yoms, spics, imports, the dregs of the universe are all here in New York."

"The only civilized place left in this city is Windy Tip," said Daniels. "Tellin' ya, your old lady's right, ya gotta buy down Windy. I can't wait every night to get home to Windy, climb in the shower, wash scum-city down the fuckin' drain. I go outside for a walk—it's whiter than a Bing Crosby Christmas. Only place left in the city, where the property taxes are low, to raise a kid right.''

"Everything goes right here," Lebeche said, "we'll have the hundred grand we need so we won't have to do this shit job no more. Once I get three-quarters, I'm buyin' down Windy. No more risking my life to protect nigs from jigs. I mean, that's not how I wanna go. Too bad it's come down to *this,* but it ain't like we're robbing a citizen. This is a piece of shit we're taking off. He poisons his own.''

"Come on," Daniels said, getting out of the car. "Let's do it. It's now or never.''

"What if he asks for a search warrant?" Lebeche asked, laughing, as they walked through the small lobby of the projects building and into the graffiti-covered stairwell.

"We don't need no stinking warrants in Planet Projects," Daniels said.

On the second-floor landing Lebeche and Daniels encountered a young black couple making out. The two teenagers broke apart when they saw the cops approaching. The young man, about nineteen, was tall, with the rippling muscles of a natural athlete. He wore a sleeveless Lincoln High basketball shirt with his last name, WALTERS, emblazoned on the back. He stood protectively in front of his pretty girlfriend, who had her hair in neat jherri curls.

Daniels bopped Walters on the forehead with his two-pound, foot-long flashlight. "You dumb fornicating coon," Daniels said. "Atta the way, lemme get a gander at your ho. Bet she could serve mint juleps on her shitter.''

"My lady isn't no ho," Walters said, his muscles tensing, eyes skipping back and forth.

"You callin' my partner a liar?" Lebeche said, grabbing Walters by his shirtfront and tossing him sideways down a half-flight of stairs.

"We weren't botherin' anyone," Walters said, seething, humiliated in front of his frightened girlfriend.

"Dickin' this ho in a public-housing stairwell is a crime, shineboy," Daniels said. "We saw you with our own four eyes, both of you with your pants down, banging her doggie style against the banister railing. Paying her. We could put you both in cuffs. A pros rap'd look sweet on her yellow sheet when she grown up to become a NYNEX operator.''

"Leave us alone," said the girl, whose eyes were brimming with rage and tears.

Lebeche grabbed Walters and spread-eagled him against the wall and started going through his pockets. "I better not get stuck with no needles, asshole, or I'll bury it in your ho's eye. Hear me?''

"She ain't no ho," Walters said. "And I ain't no junkie. I play for Lincoln . . .''

"You play with your licorice stick," said Lebeche, pulling a neatly folded batch of cash from Walters's pocket. "And she helps ya. Lincoln fuckin' High, huh? Well, if old Honest Abe knew he was freein' the likes of you two, he woulda whistled Dixie.''

"She musta been out trickin' all night for ya," Lebeche said, counting the money. Walters looked over at his girlfriend with eyes that said he was ready to snap. She shook her head no, telling him not to react and strike out at the cops. Walters did his best to control his mounting fury.

"How else you come up with a hundred and eighty American cash dollars, shineboy?'' Lebeche said. "Unless your ho is bringin' it home with scabs on her knees?''

"I work in Mickey D's," Walters said, referring to his after-school job at McDonald's. "I saved that money to buy a present for my father's birthday.''

The two cops laughed hysterically. "Father's birthday!'' Lebeche scoffed. "Did I hear this boy say 'father's birthday'?''

"That's what the boy said," Daniels said, chuckling.

"This is wrong," the girl said, drooling tears. "Stop doing this. It ain't right!''

"If there's one thing I hate," Lebeche said, ignoring the girl, "it's a liar. Now, I know and you know that this money couldn't possibly be for your father's birthday. I know that for a fact, Buckwheat, because there is no such fuckin' thing as a father's birthday in the *ghet-to* because there ain't no fathers in the ghetto. Just motherfuckers who drop their load and hit the road. Maybe, your father should have shot his load on a rock.''

Daniels broke up laughing as Lebeche shoved Walters halfway down another flight of stairs. "Take a hike or take a bust,'' Lebeche said, pushing the cash into his own pocket. Walters looked up at Lebeche and Daniels with a stare that would last a lifetime. He held out his hand for his girlfriend, who trotted past the two cops. She took Walters's hand and led him down the stairs. Walters looked back once.

Lebeche handed Daniels $90, half of the $180.

"Even if this spic don't pan out," Lebeche said, "this covers Rollo's half a yard."

"Plus some," said Daniels. "Let's hope this is the last chump change we ever have to scrounge."

The two cops climbed two more flights of stairs to the fourth floor. As they approached apartment 4-E, they took their Glock 9 mm automatics from their holsters, adjusted their bulletproof vests under their pale blue NYPD summer shirts. Lebeche knocked twice, waited, knocked twice again. A woman's voice from inside said, *"Quienes?"*

"Boardwalkbrown," Lebeche said.

Then he heard the sound of locks being unfastened, and the door opened to a chain lock. A dog was barking from inside, and Lebeche stepped out of the way as Daniels came barreling from across the hall, slamming right into the door. The chain snapped off its screws, and Daniels hit the ground inside the long apartment hallway with the gun out. Lebeche held his gun over him, aiming inside the apartment. Children began to scream, and a pit bull came roaring down the long apartment hallway, teeth bared, barking violently. Daniels fired a single bullet into the dog's mouth, and it did a blood-whipping 360 degree flip in midair and landed in a silent crimson heap.

"He does good tricks," Daniels said, and the two cops moved deeper into the apartment, shutting the door behind them, locking it. The woman held an infant in her arms and stamped her feet as she screamed. Lebeche forced her along the hallway of the apartment, using her and the baby as human shields. When they reached the kitchen, Lebeche shoved her down into a kitchen chair. Two more hysterical children ran down the hallway from a bedroom. The little girl clutched at the mother's legs and buried her face in her lap. Her slightly older brother scrambled to the dog and tried to cradle it, starting to wail. The mother shouted at him in Spanish, and the boy walked quickly to the mother, covered in the dog's blood. The boy looked at the cops with astonished, wet eyes.

"If you move, I'll kill your kids," Lebeche said to the mother. "Compre-hendo?"

She nodded as she gathered her kids closer to her. *"Silencio, m'hijos, silencio, todos,"* she mumbled. *"Dios."*

Both cops moved further into the apartment, guns drawn, checking each room. The bathroom and a small bedroom off the hallway were empty. They heard a sound from the far end of the apartment and rushed to the master bedroom. The door was closed and locked. Daniels kicked it open, and they saw a tall, thin bare-chested Hispanic man, Martinez the dealer, trying to lower himself from his oceanfront balcony to the balcony below him. He would have failed freshman gym.

Daniels and Lebeche rushed to Martinez and managed to drag him back into the bedroom. Lebeche whacked the side of his gun off Martinez's left ear. Martinez made a whimper that wasn't much different from the ones being made by four adorable pit-bull puppies penned in a large doggie bed in the corner of the room. Martinez had a tattoo of his wife's face on one pectoral, Jesus Christ on the other. He had the tattooed faces of each of his kids on either shoulder.

"Where's the money?" Lebeche demanded.

"I want a lawyer," said Martinez. "Read me my rights."

"You don't up with the fuckin' loot and the dope, you'll get rights all right, *last* rites," Daniels said.

"You wanna make a deal," Martinez said with a half smile. "That's what I do. I *deal.*"

Lebeche smacked him on the other ear with the gun. Martinez clasped both ears and crawled across the floor to a wall closet. The bottom of the closet was covered in shoes, sneakers, high heels, Rollerblades, two baseball gloves, an umbrella. He pushed aside a suitcase and then lifted the corner of the rug that lay on the floor of the closet. From the foot-deep hole under the floorboards of the closet, he took out a small gym bag. He opened it. It was filled with cash—tens, twenties, fifties—all bound in rubber bands.

"Eighty-five grand, man," said Martinez.

"Where's the fuckin' dope?" Daniels demanded.

"Tapped out, man," Martinez said.

Lebeche walked to the doggie bed and lifted it. Underneath were two large Baggies filled with what resembled brown wheat flour. He also lifted three pistols, a .25, a MAC-10, and a 9 mm Glock.

"Boardwalkbrown," Lebeche said.

"You good," said Martinez. "Finders keepers."

Lebeche tossed one of the Baggies to Daniels, and they each put one inside their bulletproof vests. Lebeche shoved the guns into his belt and one in each sock.

"You want a puppy for your nephew?" Daniels asked Lebeche.

"Sure," said Lebeche.

Then Daniels noticed a brand-new Martin acoustical guitar leaning in a corner of the room.

"My eight-year-old has been bugging me to buy him a guitar," said Daniels as he lifted the guitar.

"Name that tune," said Martinez.

Downstairs the two cops left the building carrying a puppy each. Daniels carried the Martin guitar. They passed tenants who were wheeling home groceries in shopping carts or pushing babies in strollers. The two cops nonchalantly walked with their swag of dope, guns, drug money, puppies, and a guitar to their radio car and climbed in.

"Supermarket perp-sweep," Daniels laughed as he put the car in gear.

"By the time Rollo sells these guns and the rest of the dope, we'll have the hundred grand we need to get the fuck outta this thankless job," Lebeche said. "Away from these fuckin' animals."

As Daniels drove toward the parking-meter lot next to Nathan's, they passed Walters, who stood with his girlfriend on the corner. Lebeche, Daniels, and Walters exchanged a long last stare before the police cruiser headed along Surf Avenue toward Nathan's.

"All right," Lebeche said to Rollo after he gave him the guns and the Boardwalkbrown heroin to sell that night. "What the fuck did you have for lunch?"

"Clams on the half-shell," said Rollo. "And a diet Coke."

"Bet's a push," Daniels told Lebeche.

26

Tuesday

Bobby had told Patrick to make himself available for a little bit of surveillance of the goons from Gibraltar Security on Tuesday, the day Barnicle's guys collected the money in the three-quarters pension racket. Bobby wanted to see for himself.

Using a divorce client's credit card, Gleason rented Bobby a new Mustang. If any of Barnicle's crew ran the plates, they'd be traced to a dentist from Queens.

Bobby had the disguise he'd bought in the costume store in a plastic bag with him. In Brooklyn he'd also stopped at an Army and Navy store and bought a floppy-brimmed Irish walking hat, a Yankee hat, a hooded sweatshirt, some dark sunglasses, a reversible zippered jacket that was navy blue on one side and tan on the other, and a pair of binoculars. He called Patrick and told him to dress in a sports jacket, white shirt, chinos, and loafers.

Of the original $500 Izzy Gleason advance, Bobby had $128 left. At the newsstand on Ninth Street he bought a copy of the upscale *New York Times,* the working-class-based *Daily News,* the right-wing and sports-oriented *New York Post,* and an *Irish Voice.* In a multiethnic, economically tiered city, people often identified you by what you read.

Bobby picked up Patrick in the Mustang and drove directly out to Gibraltar Security.

"Remember that assistant medical examiner you asked me about?" Patrick said.

"Franz?"

"Yeah," Patrick said. "He gets back Thursday. He works nights. Four to Twelves."

"Good," Bobby said. "I need to talk to him about the teeth in the crematorium furnace."

Parking a hundred yards up the block from Gibraltar, the

brothers watched the front door using the binoculars, listening to an all-news station and waiting. Watching. Waiting.

"I'm going down to see Mom in Miami for Thanksgiving and her birthday," Patrick said. "She'll be sixty-eight. Imagine that? I sure wish you would come."

"If this business is finished, I will," Bobby said. "I don't want to see her until I'm completely exonerated. Then I want to bring Maggie, too. Shit, maybe we'll take the boat down. Stay awhile."

"She never really got over Dad," Patrick said.

"No, she didn't," Bobby said. "She begged me not to go on the job, too."

"She actually moved down there because *I* joined," Patrick said. "She said she didn't want to live in the city that killed her husband and now was going to kill her sons. Then when you went into jail . . ."

"I'm surprised it didn't kill her."

"Let me ask you something," Patrick said. "You knew him better than I did, so what would the old man do in a situation like this one we're involved in?"

"You mean *I'm* involved in," Bobby said.

"If you're involved, so am I," Patrick said.

"He'd do what we're doing," Bobby said, smiling at his kid brother. "He'd study the enemy and use information to attack their weakest points."

"He'd kick ass and take names?"

"He would have done that *after* they were dead," Bobby said.

"I'm glad he was my father," Patrick said, laughing.

"Why?"

"Because he gave me a terrific big brother."

Bobby looked at him and felt a wave of emotion rush over him. But he remembered what the old man had said about saving tears for funerals. Which reminded him of what had led up to their father's.

Patrick had been about eight when it happened. The check-cashing joint on Nostrand Avenue had been stuck up on the first of the month for the previous five months. Tom Larkin and Bobby's father, Sean Emmet, were part of the notorious "Stakeout Squad" of the late seventies and early eighties that had later been branded as a hit squad by the press and civil libertarians. That sweltering August afternoon, Sean Emmet, Larkin, and another cop named McCarthy had taken their positions behind a newly installed two-way mirror in the check-cashing joint, waiting for the same defiant, brazen stickup artist to appear. Larkin and Sean nudged each other when they finally saw the perp, but McCarthy didn't see that the woman in a flowing dress and sunglasses who'd entered had an Adam's apple bigger than his own. McCarthy lit a cigarette in boredom before Larkin and Emmet could alert him. The flame became visible through the two-way mirror and the "woman" lifted a sawed off shotgun from under the dress and blew a hole through the mirror before even announcing the stickup. McCarthy never got to blow out his match. He died instantly.

As Larkin fired through the shattered mirror, Sean Emmet kicked open the door leading to the store and came out firing. The perp in woman's clothes also had a .45 automatic and shot a fusillade of bullets at Emmet, one catching him in the right thigh. From the floor, Emmet returned fire with a pump-action twelve-gauge shotgun, blowing the perp into eternity. As they waited for the ambulance, the damage from the .45 Teflon slug that had dum-dummed up Emmet's thigh, severing his femoral artery, swiftly drained his life. Sean Emmet bled to death before he reached Kings County Hospital.

Bobby's mother begged him never to join the police force. He'd never had any intention of being a cop until that day, when, at the age of seventeen, "the job" took his father from him. Somehow he thought he could get his father back by joining Sean Emmet's beloved NYPD that had given an immigrant and his children the dream of America. Bobby put his name on the NYPD waiting list a week after the Emerald Society Bagpipers followed his father's coffin out of Holy Name Church in Windsor Terrace. He was called up three years later.

"This them?" Patrick asked, looking through the binoculars and handing them to his brother.

"Yeah," Bobby said as he saw Kuzak and Zeke walk out the door of Gibraltar Security. "You ever meet either of these two guys?"

Patrick took the binoculars and studied Zeke and Kuzak as they moved along the sidewalk to the parking lot next to Gibraltar.

"You asked me to stay away from the trial," his brother said, looking through the glasses. "I did. I'm as low profile on the job as you can get. Only the people in PAL know me. I don't hang out in cop bars. I don't play on cop teams. I don't belong to any of the ethnic societies. So, I'm happy to say, I've never met either of those two stooges."

"Perfect," Bobby said.

"These the bagmen?" Patrick asked. "The guys who collect the three-quarters money?"

"Let's find out."

Zeke and Kuzak eased into a brand-new cream-colored Oldsmobile 98. Zeke got behind the wheel and slid out into light traffic. Bobby gave the Oldsmobile a good one-block lead, allowing three other cars to fill the space between them, and then began to tail. After the Olds made two rights Bobby knew that Zeke, the driver, was doing the "four-rights-to-spot-a-tail" routine. The same routine he'd used on Sandy. In counterpoint, after the Olds made the second right, Bobby made a U-turn and drove in the opposite direction until he came to the intersection where the Oldsmobile would wind up after the four predictable right turns. He waited at a hydrant until the Oldsmobile appeared. Thirty seconds later it went by. Bobby gave it another one-block lead and began the tail again.

This time a confident and complacent Zeke didn't even change lanes as he drove the Olds on the Brooklyn streets.

Bobby stayed at a comfortable, unnoticeable distance on the tail until the Oldsmobile came to a stop outside a bar on Flatbush Avenue called The Gold Shield, a well-known cop haunt. Bobby knew from an old police-cocaine corruption scandal that groups of cops from The Gold Shield would rent "goom pads" about a mile away by the shore of Brighton Beach, where four cops would throw in one-fourth share of the monthly rent of an apartment. This entitled each cop to one or two nights a week in the pad with a "goomatta," or "goom," the Mafioso name for *mistress*. The cops furnished the apartments by flashing their badges, "tinning" furniture, dry goods, and appliance stores for freebies or major discounts in exchange for extra protection for their stores or looking the other way when the store owners fenced and sold hot property.

The amount of money the married cops kicked in for rent and utilities was so small that their wives, at home with the kids in Long Island or in upstate Orange County, rarely caught on that they were having affairs. Some cops moved to the suburbs simply to relocate their wives a hundred miles away from their mistresses and their goom pads in the city. With an apartment, usually rented in a rookie bachelor's name, there was no paper trail, hotel receipts, credit cards, or nosy clerks to expose them. Plus the chances of a wife driving two hundred miles round trip on a jealous hunch were slim.

So, once a week, each married cop would tell the suburban wife he had to work a night shift and he'd go directly to The Gold Shield, where he'd meet his "goom" or pick up a cop groupie and go for a roll in the hay.

"I'll be across the street, a few car-lengths up the block," Bobby told Patrick as he dropped him at a bus stop a half-block from The Gold Shield. He pointed to a hydrant diagonally across from the saloon where he would park the Mustang. "Put this on."

Bobby tossed him the reversible jacket, turned to the blue side. Patrick took off his sports jacket and tie. When he was done, Bobby put a Yankees hat on Patrick's head and handed him a copy of the *News*.

"Just observe, have a beer, listen," Bobby said. "Don't look too much. Read the *News*. Casual."

Patrick took a seat at the foot of a half-full, L-shaped bar, near the front window of The Gold Shield. The saloon was something out of the past: polished oak-wood trim, high tin ceilings, mirrors with peeling silvering. Sawdust was scattered on the floors, and the window was decorated with shamrocks and Irish tricolored flags. Mounted behind the bar were framed *Daily News* front pages of great police busts from yesteryear. There were also mounted plaques from the NYPD thanking the bar for running Police Widows and Orphans Fund benefits and donating beer for PBA picnics.

Zeke and Kuzak were perusing the opposite wall, which was like a Police Hall of Fame, displaying old nightsticks decorated with brass nameplates of infamous old flatfoots and hundreds of gleaming facsimiles of gold shields of retired detectives. All were mounted in neat rows in handsome glass display cases. Zeke was pointing out some of the nameplates.

Patrick ordered a mug of Bud from a reed-thin bartender with an NYPD ring and opened the *Daily News* from the back to the sports section, thumbing to Vic Ziegel's column about the Yankees. He looked at the badge-shaped clock above the back bar and saw it was 12:12 PM. The bartender brought Patrick his foamy beer and took a five-dollar bill, rang up three dollars, and brought him back two singles change.

Zeke and Kuzak walked from the wall display to the bar. Patrick noticed each man place three singles on the bar. The act was deliberate and almost ritualistic. Each ordered a mug of Bud. The skinny barkeep pulled the mugs of beer, placed them in front of Zeke and Kuzak. He grabbed the six singles, rang up $2.25 twice, and came back and placed a small stack of three quarters in front of each man.

"Them Mets need relief pitching something terrible, don't they?" the bartender said to Kuzak and Zeke.

"The bullpen is like a paraplegic ward," said Kuzak.

Hanging behind the bar was a big brass nautical bell, salvaged from an old police boat and imprinted with the NYPD insignia. The bartender grabbed the rope on the clapper and rang it loudly three times. He paused, his hand still on the bell clapper for a moment, then rang it again four more times.

Odd, Patrick thought. Same beer, different prices. Two sets of three quarters. Three rings of the bell and then four. After the bells, Lebeche and Daniels, the two cops who had robbed Martinez the drug dealer in Coney Island earlier in the morning, now off-duty and in civilian clothes, walked from the end of the bar and took positions on either side of Zeke and Kuzak. Patrick glanced over the *News* and saw Lebeche and Daniels in another precise, deliberate ritual; each lifted the small stack of three quarters from in front of Zeke and Kuzak and replaced the coins with dollar bills.

Zeke and Kuzak didn't flinch.

"If the Mets don't get some arms, they're out of the race," Zeke said to the bartender as if nothing else had transpired.

"I think the race is already over," the bartender said.

Kuzak looked around the bar, glancing at Patrick, buried in Ziegel's column. Patrick noticed peripherally as Lebeche and Daniels left through the back door, now each carrying two envelopes, one manila, one white.

After a minute, Zeke and Kuzak left through the front door

and walked out to the Oldsmobile. Through the window Patrick saw Daniels and Lebeche climb into the backseat of the Oldsmobile, while Zeke and Kuzak sat up front.

Across the street, Bobby watched it all through the binoculars. Lebeche and Daniels, he thought. No surprise. He remembered them from The Winning Ticket and The Central Booking Saloon. Through the glasses, he watched them hand the letter-sized white envelopes to Zeke and the large manila envelopes over the seat to Kuzak.

Patrick stepped out of The Gold Shield and jaywalked between the Oldsmobile and the car parked in front of it. He waited as a car passed on the street, pausing long enough to see Kuzak in the passenger seat ruffle through a stack of cash. Zeke sat in the driver's seat, examining a sheaf of white forms. Patrick crossed the street and walked very casually to the corner and crossed the avenue and climbed back into the Mustang.

"What's in those big manila envelopes?" Bobby asked immediately.

"Cash," Patrick said, and then told Bobby about the difference in the price of beers, the rings of the bell, the two stacks of three quarters, how the two guys he made for off-duty cops picked up each little stack of three twenty-five-cent pieces.

"Three quarters," Bobby said, nodding his head. "You said they also had forms in the envelopes?"

"Yeah," Patrick said. "From what I could see."

"Medical disability retirement forms," Bobby said.

Bobby gave him a quick scenario: The Gold Shield was a transfer station, a neighborhood saloon owned, run, staffed by ex-cops on three-quarters where three-quarters pensions were for sale. From there those who wanted to buy their way onto the rolls for a price could pass their money and forms to Zeke and Kuzak. They would take them to Barnicle, who must have an in at the police medical office. Barnicle was too smart to allow such a transaction to take place in The Central Booking, which he owned.

"Jesus Christ," Patrick said. "No wonder they set you up. Major money. And they knew you were on their ass."

The brothers watched as Daniels and Lebeche stepped out of the back of the Oldsmobile and did a high five.

"They look like they just won the lottery," Patrick said.

"They did," said Bobby.

As the Oldsmobile pulled away, Bobby eased out onto the tail. In the next hour and a half Bobby and Patrick observed Kuzak and Zeke as they stopped into a bar named Komar's on Sixth Avenue in Park Slope, another named LuLu's in Marine Park, and the Blue Diamond Inn in Bay Ridge. In each case Kuzak and Zeke collected the white and manila envelopes from men who Bobby was certain were off-duty cops, because they all wore summer shirts outside their pants to conceal their service weapons.

By 2:35 PM, Bobby had tailed them back to Gibraltar Security. Bobby and Patrick watched Kuzak carry the manila envelopes with the money into the windowless building, while Zeke carried in the six plain white business envelopes.

"What do you figure they pay to get three-quarters?" Patrick asked his older brother.

"The scuttlebutt has always been about fifty grand," Bobby said.

"About what a seasoned cop'll get a year on three-quarters," Patrick said.

"You pay one year up front to get a lifetime payback," Bobby said.

"How much money you think is involved?"

"If my math is right, they just collected about four hundred grand in an afternoon. Times that by fifty-two pickups a year and you're talking millions."

"More than enough to kill someone for," Patrick said.

27

Bobby and Patrick staked out Gibraltar Security for almost half an hour to see the next phase of the scam.

Bobby's cell phone rang; it was Maggie, with news about the *1982 Brooklyn Law School Yearbook* arriving in the overnight mail.

"Anything I should know?"

"Moira Farrell and Cis Tuzio not only knew each other in school," Maggie said. "They were *both* from Scranton, Pennsylvania. They became *roommates* at the same Brooklyn Law residence hall. Belonged to the same sorority. There's a picture of the both of them at a party with their arms around each other, with the caption, 'Best Friends Till the End.'"

"You sure it's them?" Bobby asked.

"It has their names, Dad," Maggie said. "Same names. Isn't there something wrong with this picture, Dad?"

"There sure is, kiddo," Bobby said.

Then Bobby saw Lou Barnicle emerge from his fortified headquarters with a briefcase handcuffed to his wrist, like a jeweler making a delivery.

"Great work, Mag," Bobby said. "Hold on to that book. I'll call you later."

Bobby watched Barnicle climb into the back of the Oldsmobile 98. Zeke again drove, with Kuzak riding shotgun. Bobby tailed them as they moved north on Flatbush Avenue, the spine of Brooklyn that ran from the blue Atlantic sea to the cesspool of downtown Brooklyn.

Downtown Brooklyn bore no resemblance to downtown Manhattan. It was an incubator of political corruption sandwiched between the million-dollar brownstones of Brooklyn Heights and a sprawling, street-crime-plagued shopping center known as Fulton Mall. But it was the white-collar crime in the patronage-staffed courts and politically stocked municipal buildings of the bureaucracy that handsomely fed the infamous "Court Street Lawyers" of Brooklyn. In those anonymous law offices of Court Street, corrupt cash passed hands much as it did in the counting rooms of the Atlantic City casinos.

The beige Oldsmobile pulled into a spot on Montague Street, the restaurant row of downtown Brooklyn, in front of an eatery called The Broken Land. It's what the word "Brooklyn," or "Breukelen," means when translated from the Dutch of those who first settled here. *It could describe the place where I live now,* Bobby thought. *Bobby Emmet in the broken land.*

Bobby parked the rented Mustang up the block behind a Con Edison truck. A panhandler walked from the front of a bank, where he was mooching from ATM customers, to Bobby's open car window.

"Yo, man, spare a quarter?" asked the rummy, shaking his cup.

"What for?"

"Wine," said the bum.

Bobby laughed and gave him a dollar. "You're probably the only honest man left around here."

"Thanks, brother," said the rummy, and then he chased after another bank customer, rattling his change cup.

Bobby watched as Lou Barnicle, with Zeke and Kuzak flanking him, stepped out of the Olds. Barnicle walked directly to the attractive woman with the trademark red hair and tight white skirt.

"Jesus Christ," Patrick said, "isn't that redhead your . . ."

"That's her," Bobby said. "It's all starting to make sense now."

Moira Farrell, wearing red high heels, greeted Barnicle with a hug and a kiss on the cheek. Bobby's stomach flopped. A tall, broad-shouldered man, in his mid-twenties and athletically built, stood at Moira Farrell's side like a sentry, looking both ways.

Bobby had hired Moira Farrell to defend him in his murder trial because she had a reputation for being one of the best-connected Court Street lawyers in Brooklyn, the epitome of the saying: "It's better to know the judge than to know the law." In practice, her defense was uninspired, lifeless, miscalculated. In her jury-selection voir dire, she had approved too many elderly and middle-aged female jurors, which was prejudicial to Bobby because he was accused of carving up his female fiancée. Bobby wasn't helped by Moira Farrell's provocative attire, the high heels and tight skirts that made plump housewives envious. Her Wonderbra and curvy ass might have won over a horny male jury, but many pundits in the press and on Court TV said she had probably offended the female jurors.

"Jesus Christ," Patrick said, "this dame is working with the enemy now."

"Maybe she was working with him all along," Bobby said as he watched his former lawyer hook her hand through the free arm of Lou Barnicle, the man he was convinced had framed him for the murder of Dorothea Dubrow. Barnicle led Moira Farrell down a short flight of steps into The Broken Land, dismissing Kuzak and Zeke with a nudge of his shoulder. They both unbuttoned their sports jackets and got into the Oldsmobile to wait.

Moira Farrell's muscular male assistant went into The Broken Land behind his boss and Barnicle.

"Quick, put on the white shirt, tie, and sports jacket," Bobby said.

As Patrick changed clothes, Bobby summoned over the panhandler. "Listen, my man, I'll give you ten bucks if you go over and rattle that cup in the faces of those two guys in the parked Oldsmobile for a full minute. Just don't point me out."

"I'll do a soft-shoe if you want," said the panhandler, who sauntered across the street and walked directly up to Kuzak in the driver's seat, shaking his cup, and proceeded to do a soft-shoe. Kuzak and Zeke laughed, gave the bum change, as Patrick got out of the Mustang carrying the *New York Times*. He walked with a bounce to The Broken Land and hurried down the stairs and into the restaurant as Kuzak and Zeke were distracted.

Patrick took a seat at the bar, where three other patrons sat spaced apart, watching baseball on ESPN. The restaurant was going through a post-lunch cleanup, and only two tables by the front window were occupied with diners. Patrick ordered a beer and watched Moira Farrell and Lou Barnicle at a small corner table in the rear. The restaurant was an ode to the long history of Brooklyn, the walls covered with old lithographs and photographs of the Fulton Ferry, the Brooklyn Bridge, Coney Island, Prospect Park, Ebbets Field, Park Slope, the docks, and the navy yard. A waiter brought Barnicle and Farrell their drinks.

Moira Farrell's assistant sat alone two tables away.

Patrick saw Barnicle unfasten the handcuff from his wrist and place the briefcase on the leather banquette between him and Moira Farrell. She looked down, widened her eyes, and punched numbers into a cellular phone. She checked her watch as she spoke, nodded, and hung up.

Patrick could see that Barnicle's hands were now free, and he looked as though he was opening the combination lock on the briefcase, moving his lips as if reciting the combination numbers. Moira Farrell wrote down what he said in a small notebook she had taken from her purse. Patrick saw the lid of the briefcase swing into view. Moira Farrell reached down and removed a stack of white envelopes, counted them, and summoned over her assistant. He picked up the envelopes, as if this was a common practice, and stuffed them in an inside jacket pocket, then silently returned to his table.

Now Patrick saw Farrell pick through the many large manila envelopes, choosing one from the middle as a sample. She opened it and looked inside, pulling her head back as if something might leap out and bite her. She finally smiled, with impressed approval. She lifted her cocktail glass, and so did Barnicle, and they toasted their continued success.

Barnicle and Moira Farrell drank and talked for another four or five minutes as Patrick scanned the pages of the *Times,* his eyes resting on a three-paragraph story in the Metro section: "No Date Yet Scheduled in New Robert Emmet Murder Trial." Patrick glanced from the small headline back to Moira Farrell. She looked at her watch again, clearly waiting for someone. Then a large man in an olive-colored summer suit came down the steps into the restaurant, shuddered in the air-conditioning, and walked past Patrick, directly to the table in the rear. Patrick thought he recognized him, but he couldn't be sure. The man took a seat at the table and put one hand out, as if for inspection.

Moira Farrell snapped the briefcase handcuff to the man's wrist. She looked him dreamily in the eye, as if she wished the briefcase were a bedpost. Barnicle handed the man the handcuff keys and took out a wad of cash, peeled off a twenty-dollar bill for the waiter, and dropped it on the table.

Patrick headed out the door. He paused in the sudden heat, faked a yawn, glanced at Zeke and Kuzak, sitting in the Oldsmobile, the engine running to push the air-conditioning, and walked casually up to the Mustang. When he got in, Bobby was wearing the mustache and beard, floppy Irish walking hat, and a pair of dark wraparound sunglasses. Patrick laughed at Bobby's disguise.

"You look like the fuckin' Unabomber," Patrick said.

"Up yours," Bobby said, laughing.

"Who was the last guy that walked in?"

"His name is Hanratty," Bobby said as he watched the man walk out carrying the briefcase, alongside Barnicle and Moira Farrell and her dutiful assistant. "He works for Cis Tuzio at the Brooklyn DA's office. He almost crushed himself to death on the boat the other night."

"He's a DA cop?"

"Yep."

"So all the bastards are involved," Patrick said. "Barnicle, your old lawyer, the DA. . . ."

"What Dad would have called, 'The whole shower of bastards,' " Bobby said. "And I know there's gotta be even bigger bastards."

"The money is in the briefcase," Patrick said. "Maybe ten manila envelopes."

"Nothing stops the arrogance. My guess is there's a half a mil walking down the street there."

"The other guy," Patrick said, pointing to the broad-shouldered guy walking away from the group. "Farrell's flunky? He has the white envelopes."

"You follow him," Bobby said. "Call me on the cell phone when you see where he brings those white envelopes. I'll follow the money."

Bobby stepped out of the Mustang in plain sight of Moira Farrell and Hanratty and browsed in a bookstore window three storefronts from The Broken Land. They didn't recognize him and paid him no mind.

Patrick had slid over to the driver's seat of the Mustang and watched Farrell's muscular male assistant walk to a white Ford Taurus, parked in a painted curb area reserved for the Brooklyn district attorney's office's vehicles. When he pulled out, Patrick followed.

Bobby tailed Moira Farrell and Hanratty up to Court Street, a busy commercial street of lawyers and their clients, lined with a Casbah of street merchants selling wallets, perfume, socks, incense, and books. Moira Farrell and Hanratty entered her office building, taking the elevator first to the thirteenth floor and then to her penthouse office.

Bobby remembered this was the address that Maggie had uncovered in her DMV search on the white Ford Taurus.

"Where's Stone for Governor," Bobby asked the lobby attendant of the Court Street building.

"Thirteen," the guard said.

Bobby sat on a bench in Borough Hall Park watching the front door of the office building. Seventeen minutes later he saw Hanratty leave and walk across the street to the Brooklyn Municipal Building, where the Brooklyn district attorney's office was located, where Cis Tuzio and Sol Diamond were preparing their new murder trial against him and simultaneously orchestrating the Stone for Governor Campaign.

After a half hour, Bobby's cell phone rang.

"The guy drove a white Ford Taurus directly to the police medical board in Rego Park, Queens," Patrick said.

Bobby gave him the plate number of the Ford Taurus that had followed him from the upstate prison.

"Is it the same car?" Bobby asked.

"The very same," Patrick said. "Who's it registered to?"

"Stone for Governor," Bobby said.

Before Dr. Hector Perez was finished for the day, a new stack of medical disability retirement forms with the coded 91s at the upper right-hand corner were plopped on his desk by an indifferent Ms. Burns. Dr. Perez looked down at the forms in dread. At the morning meeting of the police medical board, the panel of three doctors had reviewed the three-quarters pensions that had been approved. Perez verbally gave credence to the signatures he had written on those extorted, bogus claim forms. As he did, he'd stared at Dr. Benjamin Abrams, who'd looked as cool as a lemon ice.

The story about the dead hooker had disappeared from the news already. Homicide detectives had made a cursory call to ask Deputy Inspector Hector Perez if he remembered seeing the woman at the hotel on the night of the convention. He told them he had never laid eyes on her.

But all through the meeting, Dr. Perez felt the perspiration drip from his armpits down his rib cage. He thought of poor Karen Anders and her severed throat and the horrors of what her family must be going through as these corrupt cops popped champagne corks to celebrate their lifelong, tax-free pensions, partly paid for with her blood.

And now, before he was to leave for the day, another batch of fraudulent pension forms fell upon his desk for his signature, engaging him in massive fraud to save his own ass. He looked down at the forms and saw the strong, bold signature of Dr. Benjamin Abrams. How was he able to live with himself? Perez wondered. How could Abrams adorn these forms with a once-proud signature? Dr. Perez realized that every time he signed one of these forms, his own signature became smaller and smaller, like a handwritten whisper. If this kept up, he thought, they'd need a magnifying glass to read his name.

He picked up the two top forms. Lebeche. Daniels. Caucasian, males, early thirties. But of course! Not one of the "91s" he'd signed was for a Hispanic or a black man. None of them were for women. This was a young white guy's club, he thought.

There must be plenty of blacks and Hispanics and women trying to get on three-quarters with trumped-up injuries, he thought. Like that policewoman from the Queens property office who had intentionally slammed a police car door on her trigger finger but claimed a perp did it in a struggle for her gun during an attempted arrest. She could have worked light duty until retirement. But she got greedy and tried to parlay the self-inflicted wound into a three-quarters pension. She had almost pulled it off, too. She had even gone out and bought herself a five-bedroom country house she couldn't afford in anticipation of the pension's being approved. Then she got caught on an IAB wiretap of another policewoman, who was being investigated for cocaine trafficking, bragging that she had falsified her injury. IAB had busted two dirty cops with one wiretap. She was fired, arrested, convicted, and given five years of probation on the felony fraud conviction. She also lost her pension.

But none of those minority applications, not even that greedy Latina's, had ever arrived on his desk with the all-powerful 91 code, Perez thought. If anything, with all those "91s" going through, he'd have to start rejecting some of the legitimate claims, just to balance it out. Or else the controller, city corporation counsel, and the mayor would be asking why they were handing out so many approvals. So, all over the city, there'd be cops with legitimate claims hobbling through life with no assistance.

"How's the missus?" asked Dr. Benjamin Abrams as he appeared in Dr. Hector Perez's doorway, trying to act normal. Perez looked up, pen in hand above the pension forms.

"Due any time now," Perez said.

"Take a little free medical advice from this old sawbones," Abrams said. "Don't do anything that could upset her. It wouldn't be fair to her or your child. Or yourself. Understand?"

Dr. Perez nodded and signed his name in the approval box on Lebeche's form. Then he did the same on Daniels's form. One at a time, he signed all the others, each signature growing smaller and smaller until he could barely recognize his own name.

28

Gleason said, "If you go to your buddy Roth with this story about all these people in cahoots—dirty money, pensions, and elections for sale—and he goes to press with it, you better get ready for jail food again."

"You smell a sting operation?" Bobby asked.

"Yeah," Gleason said. "It could be a federal one or a state attorney general sting on Barnicle and Farrell."

Gleason snatched up the ringing phone and said, "Yeah?" Then his face grew ashen, and he covered the mouthpiece and spoke in a whisper. "Venus? You-o not-o supposed to call-o me-o here-o. Clients only-o. I told you to leave messages on the machine! Can't you understand fuckin' English? . . . Oh, you can?" He cupped the phone and whispered to Bobby, "She's a fast fuckin' learner." Then he whispered back into the phone, "So, babe? How much-o weight-o you lose-o?"

Gleason looked across the living room of the small suite to be sure Alana wasn't coming through the door from the bedroom. Bobby shook his head, gazing around the living room. Gleason's apartment in the Chelsea Hotel was so clean and neat that Bobby found it hard to believe it was inhabited by the same slob with the office in the Empire State Building.

"I'll call you later, babe," Gleason said, and clicked off the phone and turned to Bobby. "Where was I?" he said. "Oh, yeah, a sting. Never believe your first impression of anything."

"I thought of that, too," Bobby said. "Or that it could be a political dirty tricks setup of Stone. A new version of Abscam. Both are possible, Iz. But I don't think that's what this is. I think these people are all involved in extorting money from the police medical pension fund and siphoning it into the Stone for Governor Campaign."

Gleason pulled on a crisp starched white shirt and began buttoning it.

"In exchange for what?" Gleason asked. "What's the quid pro quo?" He walked to the window, where he lit a cigarette and blew the smoke out into the wind, which swept it right back into the room.

"Judgeships, access, patronage," Bobby said. "Power. The man is the executive in charge of the most powerful state government in the union. Major league juice."

"Good story if you can prove it," Gleason said, puffing frantically on his cigarette. "Can you believe this broad won't let me smoke in my own fuckin' room? I get her a new set of choppers, and all of a sudden this sweet little chick starts making rules."

"She's smart," Bobby said. "She subscribes to civilization. Hold on to her. But I sort of liked Venus, too. Let's backtrack to the real deal here."

"The real deal is that if you blow a legit undercover operation, you'll be arrested for interfering with governmental procedure," Gleason said. "I don't need the jury pool out there to read about you doing that in the *Daily News*. Forget for a moment what they're doing to the city, and focus on your case."

Gleason took another puff of the cigarette and buttoned his cuffs. Traffic noise filtered through the open window.

"Sure, we could go and report Tuzio and Hanratty to the attorney general's office and Farrell to the bar association ethics board and Barnicle to the PI licensing bureau at the New York Department of State," Gleason said, the cigarette bobbing in his lips. "But where's your proof? You seen guys hand other guys envelopes. How do you know they weren't birthday cards?"

Bobby heard the shower hiss stop in the bedroom, and Gleason fanned the smoke out the window.

" 'Cause your brother says he saw cash?" Gleason asked. "So since when is cash illegal? Did he see drugs pass hands? State secrets? You saw a third guy hand a lawyer a briefcase. The briefcase also had envelopes in it. And Snickers has peanuts. So what? The briefcase went on an elevator. So what? The elevator stopped on the same floor as Stone for Governor headquarters. So, they stopped to have a piss, all you know. This is a nice story, but it's bupkis. I don't think Roth could fly it past his copy desk, never mind us trying to fly it past a grand jury. You got Ivory Snow, ninety-nine and forty-four one hundredths percent soap suds. But no dirty laundry. Even if you had a wiretap and videotape and money passing hands, none of that would help you find out what the hell happened to Dorothea Dubrow. You're not going on trial for a goddamned pension plan. You're going on trial for murder. Find out what happened to Dorothea, an acquittal is a sure thing."

Bobby took a deep breath, exhaled, nodded again.

"I just wanted you to know I'm on the right track," he said. "There had to be a motive for the frame."

"Yeah," Gleason said. "Fuck the big picture; find the small details, the ones that concern Bobby Emmet and Dorothea."

Bobby could hear Alana humming "YMCA" now as she moved around the bedroom. Gleason took a last desperate drag on his smoke and flicked the butt out into the breeze.

"What if that lands in a baby carriage?" Bobby said, annoyed.

"Then the parents should be locked up for neglect," Gleason said, shrugging. "Anyone walks a baby in an open stroller in New York is guilty of child abuse. Don't blame me."

He tried to fan the last of the smoke out the window, but it swirled in the room. He quickly unwrapped a pack of Life Savers and put half the pack into his mouth. Alana stepped into the living room with a terry-cloth robe pulled around her and a towel turban wrapped around her head.

"I smell smoke, Izzy," she said in a singsongy whine.

"It must be from the fat fuckin' mick poet next door, babe," Gleason said. "Or the douche-bag rasta painter downstairs."

"You promised to watch your language around a lady," she said.

"I think I better go," Bobby said.

"Wait," Gleason said as Bobby reached the door. Gleason pulled on his pants, reached into the front right-hand pocket, and produced a wad of cash. He started counting hundred-dollar bills until he reached fifty. He folded them and backhanded them to Bobby the way dope dealers passed cash. Bobby figured it was the way Gleason usually got paid. Bobby hesitated and then took the money and looked oddly at Gleason.

"What the hell is this for?"

"Herbie's brother paid me fifty grand," Gleason said.

"For a day's work?"

"I said I'd get him off for a fifty-grand flat fee, whether it went to trial or I got it thrown out at a pretrial hearing," Gleason said. "I did. You told me about the freeloading cop. That made my case. So that five grand is your ten percent. We made a deal; you get a dime on every dollar of every case you work on."

Bobby felt as sleazy as Izzy as he put the money in his pocket.

"I want a ten-ninety-nine at the end of the year," Bobby said. "I don't want to beat a murder rap and go away on an IRS beef involving you."

"You just find out what happened to Dorothea," Gleason said. "The best thing to do is to continue to confront Barnicle directly. Stay in his face. Make him sweat. Sweat leads to panic. Panic leads to mistakes. Mistakes lead to the truth—the truth about Dorothea."

29

Wednesday

In the brisk morning, Bobby tried to keep pace with the smaller but fleeter Max Roth as they circled the Central Park reservoir.

". . . So: Moira Farrell, your former lawyer, is now lunching with Mr. Barnicle, who you think framed you," Roth said, still breathing easily enough to hold a conversation. Bobby was holding his own, but it would take time to get his wind back. "I'm not one bit surprised. . . ."

"You're not?" Bobby asked.

"Or that she's transporting swag with a bagman from Tuzio's office, which prosecuted you," Roth continued. "There really is no such thing as a free lunch, Bobby."

"Yeah, but Moira Farrell was always this big liberal idealist," Bobby said. "How does she wind up in cahoots with a law-and-order, family-values conservative like Stone?"

"Money," Roth said.

"What do you mean?"

"After we met, I kept digging, like you asked," Roth said, turning to run backward for twenty yards, facing Bobby, who was beginning to get his wind back. "I checked with Albany, the New York Department of State. Moira Farrell is now the lawyer of record for Gibraltar Security."

"You're kidding me," Bobby said. "Since when?"

"Since right after you went into the can. A few months later, Gibraltar got a contract to do security work for the Stone for Governor Campaign."

"Then she became the chief Brooklyn fund-raiser?"

"Yeah," Roth said. "You go to jail. She gets a big client. Then a major political job. Who knows what patronage job she'll get if Stone gets elected. Moira Farrell might be beautiful, but she isn't getting any younger. She's had plenty of bedfellows, but none as secure as politics."

"You can smash these bastards with this whole three-quarters scam, right?" Bobby asked.

"Wrong. I hate to say it," Roth said, "but I think Gleason is right. I can't touch this story without absolute proof. It could backfire on both of us. I'll find out on my end what I can. You still have some doors to knock on."

When Bobby got back to his Jeep, he checked the answering machine in Gleason's office. Patrick had called to say that he had learned Franz, the assistant medical examiner, was a registered Democrat. That he'd clashed in the past with Cis Tuzio's office. She once even labeled him a hostile witness. Perhaps this was why Tuzio never called Franz to the stand, Bobby thought. It didn't explain why Moira Farrell never called him, or did it?

The next message was from Maggie, saying she'd searched the DMV database as he'd asked and found out that both Cis Tuzio and Moira Farrell lived in different apartments in the same Brooklyn Heights condo brownstone. The former college roommates from the same hometown were still very close neighbors.

Tom Larkin had left a message saying, "Bobby I've discovered something very disturbing in the police archives about a seventeen-year-old kidnapping case involving a young woman named Kate Clementine. I need to check out another piece of information in the current missing-persons files about an architect who vanished. I'll get back to you later about getting together to discuss it. I'll explain about how your girlfriend being Ukrainian fits into all this."

John Shine had also left a message, saying he needed to see him about some ugly rumors he'd picked up in The Winning Ticket.

Finally, Connie had left a message saying she needed to see him ASAP about Maggie. She wanted to take him to lunch, somewhere private. They arranged to meet at the boat basin.

A few minutes before eleven, Connie climbed out of a yellow taxi, dressed in snug jeans and sneakers and a white tank top, her hair piled high, her face shielded behind a pair of big dark sunglasses.

"I'm glad you called," Connie said, attempting to kiss Bobby on the lips. He turned his face and caught the kiss on his cheek as her braless left breast pressed against his right arm. It sent a shock to the center of his body.

"I'm glad you came," Bobby said.

"You sure don't act it," Connie said, wiping lipstick from his cheek.

Under overcast skies, Connie climbed on board *The Fifth Amendment,* and Bobby took her over to Arthur's Landing, a waterside bar-restaurant in Weehawken, New Jersey, where he tied up, telling the kid at the fuel dock to fill the tank. Gas for boats was thirty-cents-a-gallon cheaper one mile across the Hudson River than it was in Manhattan.

"You always took me to the hippest places," Connie said with disdain. "Brooklyn. Jersey. S'matter, couldn't you get a reservation in the Bronx?"

"Screw you," Bobby said.

"I wish . . ."

"Don't get angry," Connie said after ordering drinks from a college-aged waitress. "As soon as summer school ends next week, I'm taking Maggie away until this is over. You can see her this weekend, and that's it until after the trial."

"Please, Con . . ."

"I've had the tabloid press outside my goddamn building for the last week," Connie said. "I'm afraid some sicko will try swiping Maggie for ransom. I don't want her exposed to questions like the one the great intellect from *Front Page TV* asked last night: 'Are you ever afraid your daddy will cut your throat, Maggie?' ''

"Oh, Jesus," Bobby said.

"I want her to see you, Bobby," she said, putting her hand on top of his, her ring finger displaying the big stone Trevor Sawyer had given to her. She quickly changed hands, putting the ringed one under the table.

"Where are you planning to go?" Bobby asked, his eyes drifting to a Japanese tourist with a video camera shooting tape of the Manhattan cityscape. The tourist turned, and his camera panned amateurishly around the restaurant.

"Southampton," Connie said. "Where we have electrified fences and German shepherds who can eat tabloid TV reporters like Gravy Train." She saw the disappointment in his face. "You can visit Maggie there. I've told Trevor. He said it was fine for you to stay in our guesthouse."

"Very nineties of him," Bobby said, then sighed. "I'm sorry. Tell him I said thanks, but if I do visit, I'll come on the boat and sleep on board."

Connie looked him in the eyes. "Trevor has to go to London next week," she said softly, stroking his hand. "I'll be there alone with Maggie. Maybe we could have dinner together . . ."

"Send the servants home for the night and all that?"

"Up yours," Connie said, squeezing his callused hand as hard as she could to hurt him. "I was trying to be nice."

Bobby noticed the Japanese with the video camera taking a seat and ordering a Coke and resting his camera on its side on the tabletop. The red light on his camera was on. Bobby made him for a dunce. But there was always the possibility he was working for Tuzio or Barnicle. Or tabloid TV. Paranoia was rampant in him. He looked around the restaurant, checking out the other customers. Three different couples sat at window tables looking out at the river.

Connie wove her fingers through his now, looking to make deeper contact. "Sometimes I do regret breaking up with you, Bobby," Connie said.

"It wasn't a breakup," he said. "It was a divorce, and it's still painful. At least Maggie seems to be getting over it."

Connie looked off at the skyline of New York, and Bobby followed her eyes, realizing again that the best part of living in

Jersey was the view of Manhattan. The Japanese tourist with the camera wasn't so dumb after all. But why was he taking footage of the restaurant? Looking to buy?

"I've been totally faithful to Trevor," she said, toying with Bobby's thumb and then kneading his palm and tracing all his finger joints and the gullies between the fingers. Connie's hands were soft and smooth and skilled and familiar, and Bobby could feel himself getting hard. "As I was faithful to you. But I don't know what he does on these business trips."

"I'm sure he takes care of business," Bobby said, feeling his penis growing along his thigh.

"All kinds of business," she said. "A man with his wealth attracts babes like flies to sugar. I've watched how some women look at men with money. Like hunters, killers."

"He adores you," Bobby said.

"And I'm free all afternoon," Connie said. "Maybe you could show me the harbor. Looks like a storm's coming. I've never been on a boat in a storm with you, Bobby. Alone . . ."

He was hard as an oar handle now and staring at her lips, at the cleavage exposed when she leaned closer. The air-conditioning in the restaurant had hardened her bra-free nipples, and they pushed against the white tank top. Bobby squirmed in his chair, remembering her small, firm breasts, the flat belly, tight, soft behind, the smell of her hot sweaty skin when she was aroused. He had once loved this woman completely. John Shine was wrong. You could have more than one great love in your life. Just not at the same time.

"Did anyone get it yet?" she whispered.

"Get what?"

"That first post-jailhouse tumble?"

Her smile always made his heart leap, the perfect teeth, the moist full lips. "Just a couple of guys who came on board in an unfriendly kind of way."

"No man has ever known how to take care of me the way you did," she whispered. "And I know how to take care of you."

Suddenly, after those eighteen months, looking at Connie made him very uneasy.

"You always did," Bobby said, his groin throbbing.

"Then to hell with lunch," she said. "Let's set sail."

Bobby took a sip of his coffee and cleared his throat, shifting in his seat as guilt melted his boner.

"I'm sorry," he said. "I . . . I just can't, Con."

"Because of Dorothea?" Connie asked.

He faked a cough, looked away, then met her eyes again.

"Maggie," Bobby said.

"Maggie!" Other patrons glanced over.

"You look too much like Maggie now for me to make love to you, Con," he said.

Connie withdrew her hand from his, her mouth open, her eyes narrowed. Aghast.

"You are one *sick* fuck, Robert Emmet," she said.

The waitress came over to ask if they were going to eat.

"I think we'll skip lunch," Connie said, and the disappointed waitress walked away.

Connie shook her head, took a sip of her soda. They sat in silence for another minute.

"I want you to see our daughter," she finally said, after composing herself. "I just won't let you expose her to the media madness. Understood?"

"Understood," Bobby said. "We better get going before the storm hits."

Connie tried to pay the bill, but Bobby insisted, saying, "I owe a lot of back child support." As they went down to the dock and climbed aboard *The Fifth Amendment,* Bobby noticed the Japanese guy with the video camera taking pictures of Manhattan again. Then he swung the camera down at them and waved. Bobby still didn't trust the man and cast off quickly from the restaurant dock.

"I guess I made a fool of myself," Connie said as they moved across the river through snarling whitecaps.

"I'm the fool for saying no," Bobby said.

"You don't think I'm slutty?"

"I think you're one of the classiest women I've ever known," he said as he worked the helm, guiding the boat through the angry swells that were not much different from his short-circuited emotions.

"Do me a favor, will ya?" she said as Bobby docked at his slip in the boat basin less than ten minutes later.

"Sure," he said.

"Go and get this nasty murder business over with," she said. "Maggie needs you back in her life in a normal situation. If I can do anything, let me know. Be careful. Be smart. But close the deal, Bobby."

Through binoculars, Trevor Sawyer watched his wife, Constance, kiss Bobby Emmet good-bye. He had watched them both since her arrival at the boat basin almost two hours earlier. He had watched the Japanese man pull away in the other boat, the one he'd hired to follow them. He dialed a cell phone, and after a brief pause he said, "Hello, is Mr. Gleason there please?" He paused a moment, watching Connie walk down from *The Fifth Amendment*. Then he spoke back into the phone: "Hello, Izzy? It's Trevor. We need to talk. . . ."

30

As the rain fell hard, Bobby parked the Jeep in the gravel parking lot and stepped into The Central Booking Saloon through an aluminum-clad side door. The bar was loud, smoky, dark, and crowded. A Yankees game blared from the TV, and Waylon Jennings howled from the juke, and the rain drummed on the tile roof. The neon of the jukebox, computer games, and the beer signs blinked on and off.

Bobby saw at least six three-quarters cops at the bar and one behind it: Kuzak, Zeke, Lebeche, Daniels, Flynn, and Levin. O'Brien was behind the stick, pulling foamy Bud into frosted mugs. Funny, Bobby thought, how O'Brien's bad back never seemed to bother him when he stooped to the back-bar refrigerator for freshly frosted mugs.

Lou Barnicle was seated at a cocktail table near the front door, with two drinks on the table in front of him. Bobby walked directly to Barnicle, who looked up at him, his arms folded across a black-and-red shirtfront that was silk-screened with a map of all the Hawaiian Islands. Neither said a word. The rain pounded. Now the other cops noticed Bobby, and they moved slowly from the bar toward the table.

"Jesus, Lou, look at all these invalids," Bobby said as he looked from the three-quarters cops to Barnicle. "Real walking wounded. Here for the physical therapy, boys?" Bobby smiled. "But, Lou, how come they move like the Giants backfield all the way to the bank with the three-quarters checks the first of every month?"

Flynn started taking off his jacket with a saloon brawler's flourish, as if looking for the chance he never got in the Gibraltar Security office the day he and Bobby first met.

"Easy, guppy, I'm here to see the kingfish," Bobby said to him.

"Come on," said Flynn. "One on one. Just you and me."

"I really don't feel like hurting my hands," Bobby said. "And now that I'm out of the job, I can't even get three-quarters."

Flynn bull-charged Bobby, who very calmly stepped to the side, like a matador. Flynn stumbled past, and as he did Bobby blasted a right hand into his lower spine, certain he heard a couple of discs crunch. The big kid dropped to all fours.

"*Eyyyaaaaaghhhhh!*" Flynn screamed and tried to straighten but couldn't.

"S'matter?" Bobby said, circling to the front of him. "Having trouble? Back problem?"

Flynn writhed on the wooden plank floor, screaming in pain.

"Geez, I think he might really qualify for three-quarters now," Bobby said. "That's if he was on duty for NYPD. But since he was on duty for a bag of shit named Barnicle, I'm not so sure they'd be so sympathetic."

Kuzak and Zeke now lurched toward Bobby. Lebeche and Daniels pulled out their Glock 9 mm pistols. Barnicle stood, raising his right hand, freezing them. Bobby cleared his throat and said, "I know your game, Lou. I know how low it starts and how far up it goes. It's a great racket. But I'm telling you, Lou, these morons you have working for you are going to be your downfall. Like those two Nobel Prize candidates."

He pointed at Lebeche and Daniels, who still held their pistols on Bobby. "They couldn't find a hot dog in Coney Island, and yet they find, what, fifty large apiece, give it to Kuzak and Zeke here to buy a three-quarters pension?" He turned to them. "What did you do, boys? Rob a drug dealer?"

Lou Barnicle appeared concerned for the first time since Bobby started his spiel. But Bobby was careful not to tell him how much he actually knew.

"Lou," Kuzak said. "Just give me the word, and he disappears."

"Heel," Bobby said, snapping his fingers twice, without looking at Kuzak. He was aware that every eye in the place was on him and that for every set of eyes, there was a gun. But he had to humiliate these guys in front of each other to make them over-react. To do this he knew he had to stand erect, cool, jitter free, in *control*.

"I have it all planned out how I'm gonna take you apart," Kuzak said.

"You'd need instructions to eat soup," Bobby said. He kept looking Barnicle deep in the eye, leaned closer, exploring the iris for flaws. He found a few, like little signs of mounting fury.

"I don't know who gets all the money," Bobby said. "Yet. But I'll find out. . . ."

Bobby didn't mention Moira Farrell.

"Why don't you take a hike, Bobby. There's no priest or John Shine around this time. . . ."

Barnicle was distracted by the tap, tap, tap of high heels on hard wood. Sandy Fraser walked from the ladies' room to the table with a hip-swinging stride as Barnicle ordered her to keep walking out the front door.

"Something I did or said?" Sandy asked.

"Yeah," Bobby said. "Excuse my language, but you have too many balls for this crew."

Sandy paused, smiled, assessed the strained situation. One of the Yankees hit a home run, and from the TV Bobby could hear the crowd at the stadium cheering wildly. Sandy picked up an oversized umbrella, then stepped out into the storm.

"No way to treat a lady," Bobby said to Barnicle. In back of him, Flynn made little yelping sounds as Levin helped him to a chair.

"I think you better leave, too," Barnicle said.

"Don't you want to hear the end of the story?" Bobby asked. "About how I'm gonna make the bad guys lose in the end?"

Barnicle glared at him.

"Look around you, Lou," Bobby said, his voice now very cold. "Then look at yourself. You were a real cop once. You had a reputation once for being brave, ballsy, by the book, honorable. Now you wind up with these pathetic scum. Where did you go wrong, Lou?"

Barnicle just stared at him, his lower lip trembling.

"Go, while the getting is good," Barnicle said.

"When I'm ready," Bobby said, walking closer to Barnicle, eye to eye now. "But let me ask you something. When it was still good, when 'The Job' was still *The Job*, the greatest show on earth, the noblest way to earn an honest dollar and still count for something in your lifetime, when you were actually catching bad guys and protecting the citizens, doing God's work, when you were the legendary cop you truly once were, would you have ever let any one of these pukes take your back? Would you have run into an alley or across a rooftop with Kuzak or Zeke, these two mama's boys? With any of these guys who have balls like Raisinets?"

Barnicle remained mute as Bobby pointed to Lebeche and Daniels and shook his head.

"If some skells had broken into your house and were after your sister or your old, gray mother," Bobby asked, "and they called nine-one-one, would you want these blue mice to be the first line of defense? These guys would show up after the dirty deed was done and steal the goddamned silverware, Lou." O'Brien shut off the TV and the jukebox went mute. The rain continued to hammer the roof tiles. "These aren't cops. These are *skells*. These are the *bad* guys, the mutts we joined the force to put away. No different than the bastard who killed my own father." Bobby's voice dropped to a whisper. "Jesus Christ, Lou, what was it that happened to you to make you become one of *them?*"

There was a fragile moment of silence as the rain pelted the tile roof when Bobby thought he detected a scribble of shame in Barnicle's eyes.

"Go," Barnicle said softly.

Flynn continued to moan in agony.

"I'm leaving here," Bobby said. "But I'm back to stay. And I'm gonna bring you all down."

*　　*　　*

Bobby now knew that Barnicle would have to act.

He drove along the coast road of Rockaway, past the wild reeds and the lumpy dunes where you could still see the abandoned, half-buried nuclear-missile silos of the paranoid fifties peeking through the dirty wet sand. To his right, five hundred feet up the beach, was a wooden walkway leading to the main road. The windshield wipers slapped in the pounding rain, and he could not see very far ahead of him in the gray wash that blew in off the Atlantic.

He hoped that if any of Barnicle's goons pursued him, they'd look for him on the highway, while he took this back road off of the peninsula. If they were going to come after him, he wasn't going to let them turn him into a simple highway accident.

No, if they were going to try to whack him, they'd have to do it up close and personal. It could be nothing but murder.

He thought he had some time. He was fairly certain that Barnicle wouldn't risk going after him so close to Windy Tip. If Bobby was miles away when it happened, Barnicle would have a perfect alibi. Watching a Yankee game. With a priest and fifteen other witnesses. But the goons would come. It might take as long as a day or a week, Bobby thought.

He was wrong.

Suddenly out of the gray blank of the storm, a white van appeared in front of him in a wild wet skid, lashing a spray of sand across Bobby's windshield. His wipers scraped at the clumps of gritty sand as Bobby hit his own brakes and spun the wheel of the Jeep to the right to avoid hitting the van. Adrenaline sizzled in his veins and his chest swelled and his heart began to pound. Bobby floored the gas pedal and mounted a small dune to avoid the white van. But the going was slow in the four-wheel gear, the tires chewing at the softer sand under the wet, hard-packed top layer. He picked up momentum as the Jeep rumbled downhill from a higher dune-covered silo, sending an explosion of seagulls into panicked flight. Because of the rain and the sand and the birds, he could see nothing. But he kept the accelerator floored.

He peered into his rearview mirror and could make out the white monster of a van in pursuit. When the gulls finally dispersed, he looked ahead again, and another white van was ominously there in front of him, like a portable prison wall. Bobby swung the wheel left this time, toward the surf, hoping to get to full speed on the hard-packed sand of the shore. The second van raced toward him, and even in the wet, windy haze Bobby could see that the license plate had been obscured by a black plastic bag.

Racing for the shoreline, Bobby realized he was now sandwiched between the two huge vans and could not swerve left or right. The only place to go was straight into the riotous sea. He slammed the brakes, the car lurching to a halt in the wet sand. The vans also braked. Bobby quickly shifted into reverse and heard the metallic grinding of sand trapped between the gears. The Jeep strained to climb the incline in reverse, and then he found himself hopelessly mired, the wheels spinning like those of a stationary bicycle.

The two white vans had him penned in on either side, making it impossible for him to open the side doors. Bobby saw men with black ski masks and zippered NYPD jackets, who had exited the far doors of the white vans, now circle around to the front of his Jeep. The men were animated with boozy machismo. He leaped over the backseat of his Jeep, into the hatchback area, braced himself against the seat, and kicked out the back window with both boots. He heard the roar of the wind and felt the rain on his face as he dove out the back window, hitting the ground in a roll.

He was on his feet in seconds and instantly confronted by a hooded, masked man who swung a blackjack at his head. Bobby ducked under the sap and dropped the man with a punch to the solar plexus.

Bobby began running, racing as fast as he could in the wet sand toward the walkway five hundred feet up ahead. He waited for a bullet to end his run. It didn't come. Instead, a hand grabbed him from behind and Bobby spun. He saw a black wool ski mask, and he punched at it with a right hand where the nose protruded. He felt bone and cartilage flatten under his knuckles. The man fell in a legless twirl. Now a second ski-masked goon grabbed him from the left, and Bobby threw a punch at this attacker, and he went down on his back with a soft thud. The third and fourth goons approached him from the sides, one hitting Bobby with a police nightstick across the backs of his knees, buckling him and forcing him to a kneeling position. The second one hit him with a blackjack across the right ear. Bobby looked up as his head spun, and he saw six masked faces looming down at him. Rain fell in his eyes from a funereal sky.

He imagined Maggie standing at his funeral. . . .

He could see the entire huddle of men over him, wearing NYPD jackets, NYPD rings, NYPD T-shirts, whacking him with blackjacks, kicking him, punching him. The pain jolted through him, as he instinctively tried to protect his face, then his balls, his back, as he was attacked from every angle. He tried to get up. He was stomped back down.

Then he heard the slide of an automatic pistol being cocked. Some sounds came with an edifying echo, telling you that although the ending was wrong, you had come to it the right way. *You are just out of moves,* he thought. *Out of control.* He was almost at peace, held his head high to the falling rain, awaited the bullet and wherever it would deliver him.

"Wait," shouted one mask-muffled voice. "I want the last thing he remembers before he dies to be me pissing in his face."

Through a prism of rain and blood, Bobby looked up and knew the voice. Kuzak. He could see the big man taking out his big fleshy dick as the others started to laugh. Guys who liked to publicly wave dicks always had small metaphysical balls and even smaller brains, Bobby thought. He saw Kuzak wave his dick in preparation to urinate, and with one last burst of rage, Bobby grasped Kuzak's dick in his big sandy hand and yanked it like an emergency cord, pulling it down over the iron teeth of the zipper of Kuzak's jeans. He rotated it like he was coring an apple. Bobby thought that at the very least, Kuzak's ferocious scream would drown out the report of the gunshot that would be coming right behind it. He felt warm blood gushing out over his clenched fist, mixing with the colder rain. He felt Kuzak pounding on him, his knuckles beating his head.

"Shoot him!" Kuzak screamed, hyperventilating. He beat Bobby on top of the skull, but couldn't shake his grip. "Hurry . . . fucking . . . shoot . . . him!"

Bobby heard the slides of several pistols, and he twisted and wrenched harder, determined to pull Kuzak with him through the jagged doorway into the next dimension. Then he heard a single shot cracking in the gale wind. And didn't feel a thing.

Then he heard startled gasps come from the masked cops.

"Put those fucking guns down," Bobby heard John Shine

scream above the howl of the storm. "And get outta here while you can still fuckin' walk."

The hooded men dropped their pistols to their sides as Bobby saw John Shine step out of the tempest, dressed in a green, hooded slicker, his gun outstretched. His red Land Rover was parked behind him, with the motor running.

Bobby still held on to Kuzak's mangled penis, yanking it as the big cop screamed and sagged toward his knees. Bobby pulled down harder, leveraging himself to his feet as Kuzak sank in direct counterweight.

"Please . . . I . . . beg . . . you . . . please," Kuzak screamed, unable to fall completely so long as Bobby held on to him.

Bobby saw that several of the hooded men were flanking John Shine, their guns once again outstretched. A standoff.

"Let go of him, Bobby," Shine said.

Bobby finally let go of Kuzak, who dropped to the ground in a blubbering fetal ball, his hands clutching his bloodied penis. While two masked cops aimed their guns in the standoff with Shine, two others lifted Kuzak under the arms and dragged him across the sand to one of the white vans. The guys with the guns followed the others, walking backward in the rain. Four of the men climbed into the first van, the white doors closed, and it quickly spun away into the tireless rain. The two men with the outstretched pistols got into the second white van and followed the first van.

Shine lowered his gun and looked at Bobby.

Bobby brushed himself off as John Shine pushed his pistol into his waistband with a pained grimace. The two old friends stood in the pouring rain. Angry waves crashed onto the shore.

"Thanks," Bobby said, unable to summon any other words.

"They would have killed you, ya know," Shine said, the rain popping on his rubber rain slicker.

"I know," Bobby said, moving toward his Jeep.

"Come back to the house," Shine said. "I'll get you cleaned up, dry clothes, a whiskey."

"No," Bobby said, as he reached the Jeep. "I gotta go. Things to do."

"You're fucking with an army, Bobby," Shine said as the rain beat down on him. They both climbed into the front seat of the

Jeep. Bobby searched in the glove compartment and found his cellular phone.

"You're messing with a militia of renegade ex-cops," Shine said, watching Bobby dial a number. "You're also being an asshole, challenging them by yourself. Good thing I got a call from Sandy telling me about your confrontation in the bar. Alone. *Dumb.*"

"I gotta find her, John," Bobby said. "I think Barnicle knows what happened to Dorothea. I gotta find out, or I go back to the can."

Bobby punched in the remote code to Gleason's answering machine.

"It's one thing to want a throwdown with Barnicle," Shine said. "But you're a threat to *all* these guys, to their families, their homes, car payments, kids' tuition, their boats, their second homes in the Poconos, their old-age security. Their very futures. You are their grim reaper. That makes you well worth killing, Bobby."

"You don't know the half of it," Bobby said, holding up a finger as he listened to a message from Tom Larkin on the answering machine. "TL on the qt here," Larkin said. "Learned something very important that connects that old kidnap case and the missing architect to the Ukraine business. See me tomorrow after the eight-to-four shift at the Kopper Kettle diner. Ten four."

Bobby's eyes brightened.

"Maybe you better tell me what you know," Shine said.

"You're better off not knowing, John," Bobby said. "It's just Larkin rooting around in some kidnapping case seventeen years ago. Some current missing-persons case involving an architect. Something to do with the Ukraine. I dunno if it's anything. . . ."

"You're chasing *ghosts*, Bobby," Shine said, annoyed, handing him a clean hankie to hold to the gash on his ear. "I tried calling you this morning to warn you that these guys were going to come after you big time. I admire your self-reliance. But you need a *real* ally. Larkin was a good cop. A great one. In his day. But he's from another age. Today he's like a paleontologist digging up old bones that the family dog wouldn't bring home. Forget Larkin's wild theories. Let *me* help you, Bobby."

"I don't want anyone else hurt, John," Bobby said as he started the Jeep. "But you can give me a hand getting this heap out of the sand."

31

Moira Farrell lit her second cigarette in ten minutes and said, "I tried everything to win you an appeal, Bobby."

"Except a declaration of your own incompetence," Bobby said, still touching a handkerchief to the small gash on his right ear. His clothes were soaked, and he still felt grimy with sand. There was swelling around both eyes, but he had covered his face pretty well during the beating, taking most of the shots to the body and top of the head. Both of which pounded with pain.

"That's not very nice," Farrell said, taking a puff of a new cigarette while her last one smoldered in a large Waterford crystal ashtray. "We just pulled a tough jury, Bobby. It happens."

"How much did they pay you to go in the tank on me, Moira?" Bobby asked, guessing that the white pearls that studded the black velvet choker around her long elegant neck were real.

He was tempted to tell her at once everything he knew about her past but was afraid it would make her retreat into a cocoon. He didn't want to frighten her into silence. He wanted to taunt her into spilling more information.

Moira Farrell wore a clinging, sleeveless, black minidress that was fastened by two straps and a single gold clasp at the nape of her neck. She walked from her large teak desk toward Bobby, who stood at her bay window looking at the three downtown bridges. The Manhattan skyline was ghostly with rain, low clouds sitting on the docks and foghorns playing on the sad soundtrack of the city.

Bobby watched Moira Farrell prancing his way, the dress dead tight around the girlie hips and round behind. Her legs were bare, tanned, and toned, with bunching calves, and she wore expensive black high heels.

"That's dangerous talk," Moira Farrell said, pulling the cigarette from her lips, the filter covered in red lipstick.

"Danger?" Bobby said, and laughed. "What the hell's left for me to be afraid of?"

"Being alone with me," she said with a coy smile as she walked toward him, past bookcases that lined the burnished teak walls, filled with volumes of law books. Bobby was sure she read *Vogue* and *Cosmo* more often than the *Law Journal,* but she hadn't come to afford all this because of her tight skirts and loose morals alone. Overall she was a much better lawyer than she had been in front of his jury, that's for sure.

"I've had worse odds today," Bobby said.

She stubbed out the cigarette and walked closer to Bobby, her hair thick and red and glossy, her eyes shimmering blue, her full painted mouth parting, her tongue moistening the lips. She touched the bruises on Bobby's face with the fingers of her right hand.

"You really should be more careful, Bobby," she said, her voice a low purr.

"Glad at least one of us is looking good," Bobby said.

She smiled.

"I'm so glad you're here," she said. "Really I am. I have a confession to make."

"A little late, no?"

"I always found you *so* attractive," Moira Farrell said. "But you were a client, and it would have been unethical. But you're not my client anymore. . . ."

She quickly looped her arms around Bobby's neck and lifted herself up on her toes. He let her press her mouth against his, and then she pushed her tongue into his mouth. It tasted of cigarettes. His hands found their way to her behind, and he grabbed her by the cheeks and she made a low moan. She wore no panties. She felt wonderful and smelled even better. She ground herself against him, and her right hand slid down from his shoulder, over his hard chest, and then searched lower between his legs, where she kneaded him and rubbed him and traced circular patterns with her long coral-painted nails.

She stepped back and unhooked the neck straps of her dress and let it fall down over her bare breasts, fleshy, firm, and natural. She bucked her hips from side to side as she slithered the rest of the dress over her thighs and let it slink to the floor. She was still wearing her high heels, the pearl-studded choker, a pair of pearl earrings, and a little bit of perfume. She grabbed Bobby by the belt buckle and led him toward one of two dark suede couches that faced each other. She reclined down, naked and ready.

"Get out of those wet clothes and slip into something more comfortable," she said with parted legs. "Like me . . ."

He leaned over her, grabbed a handful of her hair, and pulled her face toward him.

Go ahead, he thought. *Give her a savage fuck. A vengeance fuck. Turn her around, make her face China. Fuck her so hard she'll need a walker and orthopedic shoes. Fuck being noble. I already said no to Connie. But that was because I cared about her. But this evil bitch helped put me in a fucking cage. Separated me from my daughter. Was part of the crew that snatched Dorothea. Bang the ass off this treacherous cunt, and then after I take her body, slap the shit out of her until she tells me everything else she knows. . . .*

He stopped himself.

Control, he thought.

"Tell me about your new client," Bobby said, peering into her eyes, still grasping her by the hair. She pulled at his belt with eager fingers.

"Who might that be?" Moira Farrell said, pulling the strap to unbuckle him, kissing and mock-biting the outline of his erection through his snug, damp jeans. *Control,* he thought again. He wanted her, wanted to hurt her.

"Gibraltar Security," Bobby said.

She paused, only momentarily startled.

"Nothing underhanded, Bobby," she said, her hand on his pants' top button, looking suddenly vulnerable in her nakedness. "Sometimes I represent hero cops hurt in the line of duty. Gibraltar helps me build a case to get their medical pensions."

"You mean Lou Barnicle," Bobby said.

"It's business, Bobby," she said, looking up, kissing him again where it almost made him surrender.

"He knows how to cut through red tape."

"That's not all he knows how to cut through."

Moira Farrell now coaxed Bobby down to her, a determined woman who insisted on having her way. She kissed his mouth again. Then Bobby pulled away, sat on the arm of the couch looking at her face. She writhed naked down his body, kissing his chest, his belly, finally kneeling on the carpeted floor in front of him. She unzipped him with the coral-painted fingers, reached inside his pants, and grabbed him. He jumped. Swallowed hard. She kissed him through his wet underpants, leaving lipstick prints on the wet white cotton.

"So, Moira, is this how you do most of your fund-raising?" Bobby asked.

She looked up at him, startled.

"What the hell are you talking about?" Moira Farrell said, her grip loosening on Bobby's erect penis.

"You are Stone's main Brooklyn fund-raiser," Bobby said. Which means you're working with your old college roommate, Cis Tuzio. Who just happens to live downstairs from you in the same brownstone. The same way you guys were neighbors back in Scranton. The way you were both such good buddies in the courtroom at my trial. Where neither one of you ever called a certain Carlos Orosco to the stand."

"You're paranoid, Bobby," Moira said. "Plenty of defense lawyers and prosecutors are friends outside of court. Relax. Let me take care of you. Help you relax. I'll do all the work. . . ."

"I think that's what you told Cis Tuzio about my defense," Bobby said. "You told your childhood friend you'd let her get a big win at my expense. What's the payback, Moira? For dumping *my* case."

"Fuck you, Bobby," Farrell snapped.

"I think you already did, Moira," Bobby said, standing, zipping his pants, looking down at her in the kneeling position. "You fucked me like I was never fucked before."

"Get the hell out of here!" she screamed, getting to her feet and strutting across the office. She grabbed her dress, which she held in front of her like a tiny shield, abruptly looking foolish and pathetic and not very attractive at all.

"So where does all that cash Barnicle brings you go, Moira?" Bobby taunted as he buckled his belt. "The cash in the manila envelopes?"

"I asked you nicely to go," Farrell said.

"A minute ago you wanted me to come," Bobby said.

"I could easily scream rape," she said. " 'Disgruntled ex-client gets revenge.' "

Bobby finished buckling his pants.

"Save that last thought," he said, and left.

32

Bobby left the Court Street office building in downtown Brooklyn through a side door. In the past he had met many attorneys there when they wished to surrender a client to the DA's office without marching him through the gauntlet of the press. The secret fire exit was behind the newspaper stand, and it let Bobby out on Montague Street, fifty feet down from Court Street. A soft rain continued to fall. Bobby was anxious about leaving through the main doors onto Court Street. His Jeep was parked there. Someone from the Barnicle crew might be watching it.

He crossed Montague Street, moving carefully back toward Court Street, stopping to gaze in windows of shops. He slipped into the shelter of a pay phone bubble next to the entrance of the subway. He pretended to dial a number. Through the side panel he could see a man inspecting the smashed back window of the illegally parked Jeep. The man was Lebeche. He pushed his head inside the Jeep, then took his head out, walked across the street, and climbed into the passenger door of a Buick. Behind the steering wheel was Daniels. They both looked over at the Jeep. Stakeout.

Bobby decided to leave the Jeep where it was; at least he'd be free of Lebeche and Daniels for a while. Bobby checked his watch. It was 6:58 PM. The Jeep would be towed in the morning rush hour, and he would pick it up in broad daylight in the safety of the car pound.

He hurried down the subway stairs, bought a token from a drowsy attendant, bounded down another flight of stairs to get the N train to Thirty-fourth Street in Manhattan. A blind black man sang "I Only Have Eyes for You," with his eyes closed, a Seeing Eye dog and shoe box for change at his feet. Bobby dropped in a dollar and leaned against a pillar and listened to the old song.

He hadn't been in the subway for so long it felt exciting to hear the echoing voice of someone singing for his supper, mixed in with far-off trains and the commotion of citizens eager to get home.

After a short wait, he boarded the N train that carried him into the safety of the black tunnel. He took a seat in the half-empty car and found himself intrigued by the advertisements about AIDS, child abuse, Preparation H, high-school-equivalency diplomas, when the door leading from the next car clanked open. It sounded like a cell.

For the first time he could ever remember, the sight of a police uniform filled him with dread. The uniformed cop moved through the car with a rattle of keys, his radio crackling. *He's walking directly toward me,* Bobby thought, and closed his eyes, pretending to sleep, unwilling to look the cop in the eye. He saw again the hooded men in NYPD jackets and shirts, punching him with NYPD rings, kicking him, flailing with police batons and police blackjacks.

"Hey, buddy," the cop said, shaking Bobby.

Bobby opened his eyes, looked up into the young cop's face that was the color of bubble gum.

"Careful sleeping on the train, huh? Could wake up dead."

Bobby gave him a false smile, feeling edgy, needing sleep.

He reached Thirty-fourth Street in less than twenty-five minutes and hurried through the night-shift subway crowd to the street. As night began to fall, he walked to the Empire State Building, signing in at a security desk where a night guard sat passively, and took the stairs down to Gleason's office. There was something important he needed to collect there.

Before he unlocked the office door, he could hear someone's voice playing on the answering machine. He quickly opened the door and heard Tom Larkin's message about meeting him in the Kopper Kettle tomorrow at four being replayed. Gleason was obviously checking the machine with the remote code. Bobby wanted to talk to him. He switched on the light and moved quickly to the desk. As a message from his daughter Maggie began to play, he snatched up the phone to interrupt the playback. "Hello, Izzy?"

The playback stopped, and Bobby heard a short silence and then a click from the other end of the phone. Gleason had hung up. Bobby sat back on the swivel chair and called the Chelsea Hotel and asked for Gleason. The operator said he was out. He must have been checking the messages from a pay phone.

Bobby hit the message replay and listened to Larkin's message again and the next one from his daughter Maggie. "I love ya, miss ya, and you can meet me tomorrow at noon near the Delacorte Clock in Central Park. Important. Bye."

Bobby smiled. He'd be there. He sat silently, his muscles sore, his brain numb, his nerve endings scorched. He needed food and sleep. Maybe Gleason could make sense of Larkin's cryptic message, he thought. He certainly couldn't. Bobby pulled open the deep filing drawer of the desk. Gleason's bottle of vodka rocked back and forth inside the drawer like a striptease dancer. He reached into the drawer, past the alluring bottle, and took out a box of shells and the .38 Smith and Wesson.

He left the holster where it was. He had always carried his gun in the right-hand pants pocket, where, oddly enough, it was usually undetectable. Even when someone patted you down for a gun, they usually only checked for holsters around the belt line, under the arms, or at the ankles. Very few people thought of looking in your front pants pocket.

Bobby patted the pound and a half of precision steel resting against his muscular right thigh. He knew it was trouble waiting to happen.

33

Bobby had rigged the chain across the entrance to the deck of *The Fifth Amendment* so that when the clasp of the D-clamp was pulled backward, a tiny square of aluminum foil would fall out.

It had.

Which meant someone had unclasped it and walked on board in his absence.

Bobby took the .38 out of his pants pocket.

Before stepping on board, he paused to listen for sounds beneath the whine of the night wind, the slapping waves, and the nostalgic music of a houseboat party where yesterday's hippies, who were today's millionaire boat bums, were listening to Bob Dylan singing "Mr. Tambourine Man." The times they really weren't achangin' that much, he thought.

He rechecked his steps. He'd stopped at the security desk to ask Doug the dockmaster if anyone had entered looking for him; no one had, but there was a party on one of the houseboats tonight and Doug hadn't kept tabs on everybody who came through the security gate. "Someone might have slipped in with the party people," Doug had said.

Bobby climbed to the stanchion above the cabin door, holding on to an upper railing, his boots planted on the top of the doorframe. He dangled his gun hand and gently tapped on the cabin door with the barrel. He waited for an anxious moment. Then the cabin door swung open and someone wearing a baseball cap stepped out. Bobby dropped from his overhead perch, his two hundred plus pounds thudding onto the deck, and threw his left arm around the intruder's neck, sending the hat flying off and a coffee mug falling to the floor, spilling ice cubes and a pink drink. He placed the pistol to the back of the intruder's long-haired skull.

"Move and it'll be the last time you ever do," Bobby whispered, and then he felt the round firm butt against his crotch. Heard a startled feminine yelp. Smelled perfume on the night air. Felt two soft warm hands prying at his left arm, trying to dislodge it from the throat. Bobby loosened his grip, and his left hand glided down from the thin long neck over female breasts.

Sandy Fraser turned to Bobby, clutching her throat.

"Jesus Christ, Bobby," Sandy said in a choking voice that was also slightly slurry with booze. "I dropped by to pick up my cup. Some greeting."

Sandy bent and picked up her name-stenciled coffee mug that Bobby had taken with him when he left Gibraltar Security the day he got out of jail. Bobby could smell vodka, cranberry juice, and lime. And clean hair and a fragrant scent and all the other special odors of a woman. In the moonlight he could see that

Sandy was wearing tight blue jeans, a dark blue polo shirt, and expensive running shoes.

"Sandy," Bobby said, stepping back, jamming the pistol back into his pants pocket. "How the hell did you get in here?"

"I put my arm through some guy's arm and walked right through the security gate," she said, her eyes a little glazed with liquor. "When he turned right, I turned left. I knew the name of your boat, so I checked with a secretary I know at Harbor Patrol, and she told me where the boat was docked. It's listed in your attorney's name."

"Clever," Bobby said, but knowing she was lying, because the boat was still in Izzy's dead father's corporation's name. Which meant she probably got the name of the boat and its location from Barnicle, who probably got it from Cis Tuzio. Gleason was right: trust no one. Not Gleason; not Barnicle; not Sandy.

"I was staring to worry I'd have to spend the night alone here," Sandy said, smiling, dangling the coffee cup with one finger. "Make a girl a drink?"

"How many you have already?"

"Enough to know I need more. Coming here wasn't easy. . . ."

Bobby looked past her into the cabin, put her in front of himself as a human shield, and stepped inside in a half-combat stance with his gun outstretched.

"You don't trust me, do you?" Sandy said. Bobby reached inside the door and switched on the galley light. She looked offended. Without high heels she was shorter than he had thought she was.

"No," Bobby said. "I don't trust you, Sandy. You live with Lou Barnicle."

"You used to be a nice guy," Sandy said, disappointed, as she walked to the refrigerator, took out more ice, and mixed herself another drink, loudly and sloppily, dropping cubes, spilling booze.

"You used to be a sweetheart," Bobby said. "Now you're Barnicle's bimbo."

She whirled, swinging a punch at his face. He grabbed her wrist and pulled her closer to him.

"He sent you to pick my brains, didn't he?"

"That's a lie."

"Why are you here, then? Feel sorry for the ex-con? Kiss me where it hurts. Never mind: you couldn't find where it hurts."

"I'm here because I'm scared," she said, a single tear bulging from her left eye.

Bobby looked at her, wanted to believe her, but couldn't. He handed her the coffee mug and led her from the galley area into the bedroom of the cabin. She took a deep gulp of the vodka concoction. Bobby locked the door.

He half covered the porthole with a black curtain and turned on the bedside lamp. Sandy sat on the bed. Invitingly. She gave Bobby a longing he didn't want. He was devoted to Dorothea. He'd waited this long for her; he could wait some more. But jail could do strange things to a man. Still, he knew he couldn't let the time he'd spent in jail influence his mission on the outside. No matter how strong the temptation.

"Where's your baby?" Bobby asked. "Home with Dada?"

"He likes to say he's the father of my baby," Sandy said, raising the cup to her mouth with two hands and taking a sip. "But I already told you: he's not. And he'd kill me for saying that."

Bobby's eyes narrowed. "Then why continue with the charade? You sleep with him, right? Why? Status? Money? Security? Or is it his amazing personality?"

Her eyes drifted to the door.

"Why don't you stop judging me and listen to me?"

She was right, he thought. He was judging her the way everybody else was judging him. "Okay," Bobby said. "I'm listening."

"I was being set up for a crime I didn't commit," she said. "At the police medical board. Major pension fraud. Then I was introduced to a woman at a party, who told me I could make my problems go away by being . . . *nice* to a certain gentleman who found me attractive."

"What guy?"

"*That,* I can't tell you," Sandy said. "Not yet. Not until I'm sure I can get my kid somewhere safe."

"All right, so what happened?" Bobby said.

"He was married. I was lonely. I slept with him. I got pregnant. On purpose. He didn't know it. The woman told me that was part of the deal. Plus, I'm not getting any younger and I wanted that baby. I would never have made trouble for the guy. I might have never told him. Anyway, I intended to raise my baby on my own. Then the father found out about the baby."

"What did he do?" Bobby asked.

"He panicked, wanted me to give him up for adoption when he was born," Sandy said. "He offered me money. But the woman who set all this up threw the frame-up at work in my face again. I was being blamed for arranging approval signatures on three-quarters medical pensions. They made it look like I was the middleman between the crooked cops and the corrupt doctors. It was bullshit, but they had me nailed pretty good on paper. My initials and fingerprints were on all the forms. They had phone records of me talking to some of these cops, who I went on innocent dates with. Some not so innocent. They had me so good they said I would give birth in jail."

"Was the woman who played matchmaker Moira Farrell?"

"Yes."

"Where did Barnicle come into it?" Bobby asked.

"Barnicle came to me and said that the DA could send me away, that I'd lose my baby, but that he could straighten it out if I did what he said," Sandy murmured. "The first thing I'd have to do was move in with him. Have the baby, pretend it was his, let him sign the birth certificate."

"This didn't seem strange to you?" Bobby said. "I mean every day thousands of deadbeat fathers run away from their kids. And Lou Barnicle wanted to put his name on one that *wasn't* his?"

"I was scared to death," Sandy said. "He was offering me protection. I was facing jail time, the best years of my life. I had no money for a good lawyer. I have no real family, just an aunt in Jersey. Without my job and medical benefits, I was looking at welfare or the joint. The alternative was to live in a beachhouse with a new car and a nanny and an allowance and fancy meals. What the hell was I supposed to do? I went along with it, sure. And sure, it made me sick. It did make me feel like a bimbo. Still does. That's why I sent you the letter about the three-quarters pension scam they were running."

"Why *me?*"

"Because I knew the kind of cop you were," Sandy said. "Once I got involved with Barnicle, all the cops I met through him were crooked. Every goddamned one of them. I started to believe the whole PD was rigged. Bobby, this is a big operation. The one cop I knew who was straight and in a position to do something about this racket was you. I was hoping that if you blew it open, I could get out from under these people."

Bobby considered what she was saying. It fit Barnicle's modus operandi. Frame someone to neutralize a threat. He'd done it to Bobby. In this case they framed a beautiful, vulnerable woman. But for what? Sex? Barnicle could afford all the bimbos on the make or prostitutes he wanted with the money from the three-quarters scam.

"What did you have to do in exchange for Barnicle's deal?" Bobby asked.

"Just move in with him and go to work for him," Sandy said. "Promise that I wouldn't reveal the real father's identity unless Barnicle told me to. So I moved in, pretended it was his kid, even let him sign his name to my son's birth certificate. I didn't have a choice, Bobby."

"Do you sleep with him?"

"When he's interested," she said, dropping her eyes to the floor. "Which is rare. I'm sure he has other women. I'm his public woman. His prop. I'm not proud of it. But I do what I have to do to stay out of jail and keep my kid safe."

"How long is the statute of limitations on the pension scam?"

"Seven years," she said, looking up again, her eyes a mascara mess. "I've put in over a year as Barnicle's woman. I don't know if I can do it any longer. He thinks he owns me. If I cross him, he can have me indicted, and he'll go into court and win custody of the baby because he's the father of record."

"He can't do any of that if you help me put him in the joint," Bobby said.

She took a small sip of her drink and looked at Bobby. Either she was telling a terribly sad and diabolical story or she was a terrific actress. Bobby didn't dismiss the thespian theory.

"Who is the real father of the baby?" Bobby asked.

"That I can't say," she said, gulping more booze.

"Why not?"

"They'd kill me if it got out right now," Sandy said. "Worse, it was suggested that maybe they'd kill the baby and let me live. Blame it on me. I couldn't handle that. I'm not that heroic. You and me know that these people have ways of making people disappear and how to frame someone else. . . ."

"Yes, they do," Bobby said. "And the three-quarters scam goes higher than Barnicle, doesn't it?"

"Yes," Sandy said. "He gets phone calls from his boss all the time. He calls him The Fixer. I don't think he even knows who's really running it. I know this: He's afraid of the top banana."

She finished her drink. "Can I make another one?"

Bobby grabbed the cup, unlocked the door, walked into the galley, packed it with ice, poured in a shot and a half of Absolut, and splashed it with cranberry juice. He knew Sandy didn't need it but figured it would keep her talking. He brought it back to her. Sandy took another sip right away.

"Tell me about Dorothea," Bobby said, sitting closer to her, looking her deep in the eyes, trying to find the sweet dame from the medical office who always treated every cop like her brother or a boyfriend. "Tell me everything you know about her."

"I love Dorothea," Sandy said.

"That's not telling me a goddamned thing. I love her, too."

"She's one of the best women I ever met," Sandy said. "I . . . oh, goddamnit . . ." She took another big gulp of the booze. "The truth? I was envious; shit, I was jealous of Dorothea for making you fall in love with her. No man ever fell for me the way you did for her."

"But who was . . . is she, Sandy? I realized when I was in jail that I knew next to nothing about her except that I loved her and that I was charged with killing her."

"What do you want to know?"

"Who did she come to New York to see?"

"There was another man," Sandy said.

Bobby's heart sank and jealousy wormed through him.

"Who?"

"She wouldn't tell me," Sandy said. "But he wasn't a lover. He was like a sugar daddy without having to be too sweet."

"A relative?"

"I don't know," Sandy said. "But I know she got her money from him. The only relative she ever talked about was her mother, who died in disgrace back in Russia . . ."

"Ukraine," Bobby said.

"That's right," Sandy said. "Dorothea always made her share of the rent until she moved in with you. Then Barnicle came into my life. Dorothea is missing, and here I am . . ."

She sat there waiting to be taken. Bobby had never liked the idea of taking advantage of liquored-up, emotionally ravaged women. But there were no rules left. He couldn't trust Sandy. He still thought she might be a plant, sent here by Barnicle to fuck information out of him. Barnicle was probably low enough to order his own woman to use sex to learn what she could from Bobby. The racket must come first.

"Bobby, I don't want what happened to Dorothea to happen to me and my baby," Sandy said. She hung her head and softly began to sob. Bobby put the .38 in his pants pocket and lifted Sandy's chin. Her face was runny with tears. He wanted them to be real.

"No one has really held me in so long I feel like I'm drowning," Sandy said. "Hold me, Bobby, okay? Just hold me. . . ."

Bobby opened his big arms, and Sandy fell against his chest. He could feel the pressure of her firm breasts. She put her hands around him and hugged him. His hands almost drifted to her buttocks. He stopped himself. She was firm and warm and ready. He lifted her from her feet and laid her on the bed. She lay there, vulnerable. Through a corner of the curtain peeled away from the porthole window, Bobby saw the red tinge of the spire light of the Empire State Building blinking through the rainy city sky.

This was getting harder and harder to do, he thought. He looked down at Sandy and gently pulled the top sheet over her.

"Dorothea doesn't know how lucky she is," Sandy said.

"Get some sleep," Bobby said. "I'll be out on the sofa."

"Bobby, promise me that if anything happens to me that my son winds up with my aunt in New Jersey," Sandy said. "Not with Lou Barnicle . . . please, Bobby. . . ."

"Nothing is going to happen to you or your baby, Sandy. Get some sleep."

Lou Barnicle sat alone in his brand-new BMW, parked on the rotunda above the Seventy-ninth Street Boat Basin. He lit a Cuban cigar with a gold Tiffany lighter and looked down at the white-and-blue Silverton rocking slightly in slip 99-A. Through the Seco Ni-Tec starlight nightscope, which he gave most of his surveillance operatives, he'd seen the ghostly green image of Sandy Fraser appear on the deck of the boat. He knew that inside the boat she was busy with his enemy.

When she is finished with him, Barnicle thought, *I'll find out what she's learned and whatever she's told him.*

This Sandy Fraser fell into my life like a gift, he thought. *When she stumbled into our three-quarters pension operation at the medical board, the lady lawyer sent her to me for explanations and protection. And eventually I'll turn the fucking tables on the lawyer, too.*

Only one other person has more power in this operation than me. Only The Fixer, that anonymous, obnoxious voice on the phone. Eventually I'll turn the tables on that pompous prick, too, and run the whole fucking operation. But in the meantime I'll work for him because he holds the cards. And the money. If I stick to his scam for now, I'll get more money, status, and power than I ever dreamed possible. Who the fuck could have imagined all this on the day I left the academy thirty years ago with a little tin badge?

Eventually, what I can't accomplish with the badge, I'll do with balls and brains on the other side of the badge, Barnicle thought. *Because I understand power. These assholes think I'm working for them. But they've sat in fucking offices too long, on flat asses, like bean counters, tallying money and not realizing what and who it can buy. I know the miserable fucking streets and the flunkies who are willing to die on them in the name of blind loyalty. The flat asses in the suits just don't get it—when I work for them, they are really working for me. Me, Lou Barnicle, self-made man, who made his money the old-fashioned way: I stole it. But even beyond the law, these pricks like The Fixer and the lady lawyer think there are rules. Gullible assholes. The law has an Out-of-Order sign hanging off it. The law is out of order.*

The only one who could really ruin it all, who can hurt me, stop me, is Bobby Emmet. Only he knows that both sides of the fence are filthy. If I let him stick around, eventually he'll figure it all out. He survived again this afternoon. Got more lives than a fucking cat with horseshoes up its ass. But maybe it's for the better. I have to learn to control my temper, submerge my fucking ego. As long as I know what he knows, while he learns it, then Bobby Emmet is working for me, too, without even knowing it.

And Bobby Emmet is a brilliant fucking investigator. More resourceful and more ballsy than any cop I've ever met. If I use him right, manipulate him, then whatever he learns about the other scumbags in the scam, about The Fixer and the lawyer and everyone else, I also learn. That's called leadership. There are just a few more links to connect before I own the whole fucking chain.

Let Bobby Emmet find those missing links, and when he does, he won't even know he's been working for me. Me, Lou Barnicle.

I'll hear from The Fixer in the morning, and I'll tell him this latest piece of news, Barnicle thought. *The Fixer will tell me how to proceed.*

But tonight, sweet Sandy, be good to Bobby Emmet. While he's fucking you, I'm really fucking him.

34

Thursday

Bobby spent almost two hours of the next morning on line getting the Jeep out of the tow pound on West Street. He paid the $185 tow fine, $50 for illegal parking, and another $645 that Gleason owed in unpaid tickets. He was glad to have the Jeep back. He drove out of the pound to an auto glass shop on Eleventh Avenue and had the rear window replaced for another $150. Another hour of his life, wasted.

At high noon Maggie Emmet stood under the Delacorte Clock dressed in Guess jeans, a Michael Jordan T-shirt, and a pair of white Air Jordans.

"Nothing like rooting for the home team," Bobby said.

"Michael plays on everyone's home team," Maggie said, taking him by the hand and walking south from the clock into the park, readjusting the omnipresent JanSport backpack. "He is 'The Man.' Speaking of which, I have a man who wants to meet you. He's in the parking lot of Tavern on the Green."

"Who we meeting?"

"Mr. X," she whispered with histrionic flair, cupping her hands and looking both ways.

He'd learned a long time ago not to probe too deeply with Maggie, who as a preteen kid lived in a fantasy world of intrigue, derring-do, and secret agents. Her mother once dragged the child to a psychologist to find out why she was always talking to herself, sometimes taking a soda bottle into the bathroom and talking to it for hours. Connie was convinced Maggie was disturbed because Bobby was an undercover cop. He was so involved in deception and melodrama that it was affecting their daughter. The shrink told Connie to calm down; Maggie's behavior was perfectly normal. She just had a fertile fantasy life, and someday she might write fiction or be an actress or something else that required imagination.

Connie was relieved. In her circles the word of a shrink was as infallible as the pope's.

Bobby followed Maggie through the park, past joggers and dog walkers and young lovers strolling hand in hand.

"You're doing things you're not telling me about," Maggie said. "I'm not a little kid anymore, Dad."

"No, you certainly aren't kiddo," he said.

"When I was a little kid, you used to tuck me in and tell me stories about all the bad guys you used to lock up and help send away," Maggie said. "I know half of the stories must have been bull, but now I think a few of them were the real deal."

Bobby laughed and pushed her. She pushed him back.

"Which parts do you think I, uh, embellished?"

"The parts about the super police dog named Sticky who could actually smell a lie," Maggie said. "Miniature polygraph in his nose. Could smell it on the saliva when a suspect was lying."

"I think you were born with a polygraph in your nose."

"Mom calls it—and I'm quoting her—my bullshit detector," Maggie said. "And my bullshit detector tells me that you're not telling me the whole truth, Dad. I know we can't spend a lot of time together while you're trying to clear your name. I've lived without you long enough to handle that a while longer. But I want you to be honest about what's going down. I'm scared, Dad. For you. For me. I can't stand the idea of losing you again."

His daughter had gone through a physical puberty and a mental evolution in the time he was away. The second part of it accelerated by a public trial, headlines, trash TV, and separation. She had always been precocious, but now talking to Maggie was like talking to an adult. Still, he had to be careful: she had an adult mind controlled by a teenager's emotional circuit board.

"Look," Bobby said, "some of the stuff you found out for me has already helped me put big pieces of this puzzle together. I'm your old man, but you are still a kid. So I'm gonna tell you what I think you can handle."

"Okay," she said.

So as they walked through the park, he told her about Barnicle, Tuzio, and Farrell, possibly all working together in a pension scam to raise money for the Stone for Governor Campaign. "These two cops, Kuzak and Zeke, collect the money and the three-quarters pension applications. The money goes to the Stone campaign. The applications wind up at the police medical board in Rego Park, Queens. Maybe you can find out who's on that board so I can check them out."

Maggie said she would. Then Bobby made her swear she wouldn't repeat any of this to anyone, including her mom or Trevor. He told her that when he started asking questions about this racket a year and a half ago, they framed him for Dorothea's murder. He didn't tell her about the meeting he'd had with her mother and left out the part about the cops trying to kill him out in Rockaway and the attack on the boat. He did tell her about Tom Larkin and Carlos at the Brooklyn crematorium and the medical examiner whom he would see on Friday. He told her a little about Gleason and how well Herbie could cook. He didn't tell her about Sandy and the baby with the mystery father. But at some point, he thought, Maggie should meet Sandy. The girl's intuitive take on Sandy might be better than his.

"Okay," Maggie said. "My bullshit detector tells me you're telling me the truth. At least I know you're making some progress."

She stopped in front of a bench just down the hillock from the parking lot of Tavern on the Green. "Trevor bought me this amazing new IBM notebook with built-in cellular modem and miniature printer," she said, removing the small, three-pound compact piece of wizardry from the JanSport bag. "Thanks to satellites, I can access and download from just about anywhere in the universe except the subway, which Mom wouldn't let me take anyway. That's another story. But I have a few things I want to check . . ."

She took out a bagful of software discs labeled "Department of Motor Vehicles," "FBI," "NYPD," and started shuffling through them.

"How much did Trevor spend on that thing?" Bobby asked, feeling a tinge of inadequacy, a dent in his macho armor.

"Chill, old man," Maggie said. "It's just a *thing*, Dad." She hefted the little computer. "A tool. Meanwhile, he's up there waiting to speak to you."

"Who?"

She pointed up the knoll to Trevor Sawyer, leaning on his Rolls-Royce Silver Cloud limousine, checking his gold Rolex.

"He signed me out of summer school for lunch on the proviso that I bring you to see him," Maggie said, with the IBM notebook opened on her lap, punching keys on the elaborate keyboard. "You're wasting time. Go see him, and then he'll take me back to school. I'll be okay right here."

Bobby climbed the hillock and shook hands with Trevor Sawyer. His uniformed chauffeur sat inside the Rolls-Royce and rolled up the windows as Bobby approached. Father and stepfather stood with their backs to the car, keeping Maggie in plain sight.

"I'd like to pay you for that gizmo you bought her," Bobby said, pulling from his pocket what was left of the five-thousand-dollar wad of cash Gleason had given him.

"Please, don't insult me," Trevor said. "Your kid's love isn't for sale. In fact, the quickest way to Maggie Emmet's heart is through yours."

Bobby felt abashed, crumpled the wad of money in his hand, and looked from Trevor to Maggie. He said, "Sorry. I'm not trying to insult you. It's just . . . She's my kid and I want to pay . . ."

"Please, Bobby," Trevor said. "I was born into the filthy shit. I'm not here about *money*. Not yours anyway."

Bobby shoved the money back into his pocket, satisfied that he'd made the feeble, awkward gesture. He didn't want to like Trevor. Everything in his being said he should loathe this man who slept with the woman he used to love, who lived under the same roof with his only child. But Trevor just seemed like a nice fella, in spite of his shitty money. Still, how could you ever trust someone who never dreamed of winning the lottery?

"The best part of marrying Constance—"

"Is that really what Connie wants to be called now?"

"It's how she introduced herself," Trevor said. "It's hard to call her anything else. I wish it was 'Connie.' Or 'Dot' or 'Mousie' or 'LuLu,' something sweeter. But anyway, the best part of marrying her was Maggie's arrival in my life. She let me know from jump street, as she would say, that if I wanted to be her *friend*, I'd have to help her father who was jammed up. . . ."

It finally clicked. He glanced at Maggie, fiddling with her laptop.

"You put up my bail, didn't you?" Bobby said. "You contacted Gleason. . . ."

"It was the least I could do," Trevor said, loosening his tie as the sun dialed its way toward the hottest hour of the day. "And don't start reaching for the damned money again. My bail is safe. I know as long as Maggie is around, you aren't going anywhere."

Bobby was really glad now that he had turned down Connie's amorous offer. This guy didn't deserve to be cuckolded. *On the other hand, he could have bailed me out to have me whacked out here,* he thought.

"This what you wanted to see me about?" Bobby asked.

Trevor smiled. "No. I wanted to tell you about a party I went to in Luke Worthington's apartment the other day. . . ."

"The big Republican fund-raiser?"

"The one and only," Trevor said. "Of course, I give to both sides. Constance refuses to go to political events. So I brought my checkbook. However, this gathering was odd. More than a hundred people, food, a string quartet, champagne. But no one asked for a cent. The primary is six days away, the race is neck and neck. Stone is saturating the airwaves with ads, but I don't know where his campaign is getting its money. None of the usual suspects—and I'm one of them—are being hit on. It's as if they wanted to send a signal: a Stone administration will be indebted to no one."

Bobby knew where Stone for Governor was getting some of its money but said nothing. Was Trevor sniffing to see what he knew, Bobby wondered.

"That doesn't sound like the worst idea in politics," Bobby said. "But what's all this have to do with me?"

"Well, Sol Diamond was there, of course," he said. "And Daniel Barth . . ."

"The little bulldog-looking media guru?"

"Yes, that's him," Trevor said. "Anyway, as I nosy-moseyed toward Worthington's study to see what new paintings he'd bought lately, I heard Diamond and Barth involved in a rather hushed but agitated discussion of your case. I stopped in the foyer and listened. I'm a nosy swine like that. Barth is a genius, but he's a hothead and he's too fond of Jack Daniel's—the drink, not the person—and he was lashing into Diamond about how your case was handled. About how you got out on bail. Diamond tried to explain that it was a Democratic-stacked appellate court that overturned the conviction. He actually said, 'Unlike Brooklyn judges, I can't control appellate judges.' Barth chided him for taking too long to schedule a new trial, how they could all feel the political reverberations for a long time to come if it wasn't tidied up pronto."

"What did Diamond say?" Bobby asked.

"Well, he was trying to tell Barth that it wasn't the time or place to discuss this," Trevor said. "Diamond said they were trying to get your case on the calendar ASAP. Then Diamond tried to walk away, nip the conversation in the bud. But Barth grabbed him and asked when the brand-*new* charge would be lodged, one that would revoke your bail."

"What *new* charge?" There was a blade of fear in Bobby's voice.

"I don't know," Trevor said. "I wanted to ask you. Because, at that point Diamond was so angry he just stormed out of the study and left the party. I ducked into the dining room before he could see me. A few minutes later, some aides whisked Barth out as well. He was a little too drunk for everyone's good. It was a delightfully nasty little piece of business. And, I thought, one significant enough that I should pass it on to you in person. The purpose being, watch your ass. I think they might be looking to frame you for something *new*, in addition to your lady friend's . . . death."

"Thanks," Bobby said, wondering if this was a warning coming from *him.*

"I don't want to see that little girl hurt any more," Trevor said, nodding down toward Maggie, who was still working the notebook computer.

They shook hands, and Bobby thanked him for being so kind to his daughter and for the information. Before Bobby turned to walk back to Maggie, Trevor said, "One more thing."

"Yeah?"

"The other day on the boat," Trevor said. "Thanks for not fucking my wife."

Bobby stared at him in disbelief.

"You spied on us?" Bobby was incredulous, didn't know whether to be angry at Trevor or himself for not realizing that the Japanese tourist with the video camera was a tail.

Trevor smiled and said, "I always have someone keeping an eye on my assets. For whatever reason, you didn't reclaim my wife. For that I owe you a lasting gratitude. I love Constance and want our marriage to work."

"She loves you, too," Bobby lied. "So you've been in touch with Izzy Gleason all along?"

"He's quite the character, isn't he?" Trevor said. "I had warned him that if I thought you would interfere with my marriage when you were out, I would do everything in my power to have you sent back to jail. He assured me you were an honorable man. I called him the other day, when you lived up to that honor, to say if there was anything else I could do, that I would. He said there was something I could do. . . ."

"What was that?"

"He asked if I could set him up with Naomi Campbell," Trevor said. "Do you think he was serious?"

"Oh, he was serious all right," Bobby said with a smile.

"I must give him some work down the line if I can ever find anything suitable to his particular type of law," Trevor said.

"I don't wish that on you," Bobby said.

"Send Maggie up for the ride back to school," Trevor said. "If Constance knew I'd taken her out to see you, she'd be livid because of all the tabloid reporters. So keep this little rendezvous under your hat. Anything you need, call."

Trevor climbed into the back of the limousine and closed the door. Bobby liked him even more now than he had before. Which made him trust him even less.

Bobby called to Maggie, and she folded her computer notebook, put it back into the JanSport bag, and held a long scroll of printed paper in her right hand. When she reached Bobby, he put his hand around her shoulder.

"I forgot to tell you that one of Dorothea's girlfriends visited me," Bobby said. "I don't know what she knows or if I can trust her. Her name is Sandy."

"Let me meet her, Dad," she said. "I'll check her out for ya."

"I was thinking the same thing," Bobby said.

"Make it Coney Island on Saturday," Maggie said. "The Cyclone, Nathan's hot dogs, Wonder Wheel. Like old times."

Only a rotten divorce and a little dash of murder could make a fourteen-year-old talk about the good old days.

"A deal," Bobby said.

Maggie handed Bobby the printed sheets from her IBM computer.

"What's this?"

"The names and brief bios of the three doctors on the police medical board you told me about," Maggie said. "Public record. Wasn't anything in the *New York Times,* so I checked the back issues of *The Civil Service Gazette,* which is on-line. I found a story about the medical board. Story says two of those three doctors have to approve each medical pension."

Bobby looked from Maggie to the printout news story, then back to his kid.

"You're some piece of work," Bobby said.

"Adore ya," she said, kissing his cheek as she climbed into the back of the limo. "Gonna be late. Bye."

"Love ya, kiddo," Bobby said as the limo pulled away. Then he studied the printout, focused on the name and smudgy photo of a young doctor named Hector Perez.

35

Bobby stared up at Tom Larkin, who was swinging from the ceiling. A pair of handcuffs were yoked around his purpled neck. His belt was looped through the two metal handcuff hoops and tied to an overhead water pipe. His mouth was puffy with cotton and gauze, his eyes demented in death. A trash barrel lay on its side on the floor of the men's room as if he had stood on it before it was kicked out from under him.

Bobby had seen the crowd and the flashing lights before he reached the Kopper Kettle. The diner was on Fourth Avenue, three blocks from the 72nd Precinct, where Tom Larkin worked. Bobby was supposed to meet him here at four PM. It was 4:08. Larkin must have arrived early.

While Bobby was parking his Jeep, he'd noticed Max Roth in the crowd, scribbling into a notebook. The new crime scene had not yet been taped off, and Roth had led Bobby through the parking lot, behind the diner, to a spot where they could look through the open men's room window.

Now, the crowd was beginning to swell, and uniformed cops and plainclothes detectives were starting to push people back. A morgue wagon pulled up. The NYPD criminalists and a forensic crew would soon scour the men's room for clues, taking pictures, dusting for fingerprints, taking measurements.

"I was doing some of that research you asked me to do down in the Brooklyn courthouse when I got a beep saying a cop named Larkin had committed suicide here," Roth said. "I drove right out. By the way, I found out that both Farrell and Tuzio once clerked for Judge Mark White."

"My judge?"

"Yep," Roth said. "These two graduated college together, like you said, and then they were sucked right into Brooklyn politics. It was a good hunch on your part to see if they worked together."

"I never expected it to be for the same judge," Bobby said. "The one who sentenced *me*. I gotta tell Gleason. . . ."

"Remember, I get first dibs on this story, Bobby," Roth said.

"Of course," Bobby said. "But wait till Gleason says it's okay."

"Fine. Meanwhile I gotta write this fast for deadline."

Bobby widened his eyes and stared up at Larkin. "No way he committed suicide," Bobby said softly.

"Why's that?"

"See the gauze in his mouth," Bobby said, pointing to Larkin's mouth.

"To muffle his screams?"

"He had a root canal this morning and still went to work," Bobby said.

"You sure about the root canal?"

"I was supposed to meet him here at four this afternoon, Max," Bobby said. "He was excited about some news he had for me."

"He met his maker first," Max said.

The Internal Affairs guys were busy interviewing a few cops who had been dining and who were still on the scene. Bobby stood in the parking lot of the diner, quietly telling Roth about his final message from Tom Larkin. "He said something about an old kidnapping case involving someone named Kate Clementine," Bobby said. "Somehow connected to a missing architect. The Ukraine. . . ."

"Was Larkin on painkillers for his bad tooth?" Roth asked. "This sound like pretty stream-of-consciousness stuff."

"But please don't mention that in the column either until we check it out," Bobby said.

"The Kate Clementine thing sounds familiar to me," Roth said, tapping his right temple with his Bic pen. "But I think it goes way back."

"Seventeen years," Bobby said. "Check it out, Max, will ya? Also see if you guys ran any stories on some missing architect. More recent. Maybe a Ukrainian architect. I don't know. . . ."

"The Clementine thing would be before the paper had computers," Roth said. "I'll check the clips, but it'll take some time. Right now I gotta get as much here as quickly as I can and dump it into the paper."

An investigator from the medical examiner's office closed the men's room window, blocking the ghastly view of Tom Larkin. It reminded Bobby that he still had to see the assistant ME named Franz. Bobby was feeling empty, hollow, slightly nauseous. He had contaminated someone else now. It had gotten his father's friend killed.

The black IAB detective that Bobby recognized as Forrest Morgan walked up to them.

"The Bobbsey twins," he said. "One leaks; the other pisses. Into print."

"Nice to see you, too, Morgan," Bobby said.

"Is that quote on or off the record, Morgan?" Roth asked.

"What the hell are you doing here, Bobby?" Morgan asked. "I'll need a statement from your sorry ass."

"I need one from you," Roth said to him.

"No comment," Morgan said.

"Same here," Bobby said. "I'm not on the job anymore. So why would I want to talk to NYPD Internal Affairs? As a private citizen, I'll talk to *Homicide* if you want."

"Right now it's being treated as a suicide," Morgan said. "The handcuffs around his throat were his, had his initials scratched into them. The belt was his . . ."

Roth wrote these details into his reporter's notebook with the Bic pen. No serious reporter ever carried an expensive pen on assignment. They always disappeared before the story made print.

"So was the root canal he had this morning," Bobby said. "Who bothers to get a root canal if you're gonna commit suicide? He had a girlfriend he was crazy about. Said he was gonna propose. He had two years to retirement. Larkin didn't hang up, Morgan."

"I'm using that root canal bit," Roth said, still scribbling in his notebook.

"No, you're not," Morgan said.

"Excuse me, did someone also lynch the First Amendment in this diner? Because if they did, I'd sure like to report that, too."

"I told you nice not to write that," Morgan said, stepping past Bobby and staring into Max Roth's eyes like a warden to a con.

"I'm telling you that I have an obligation," Roth said.

Bobby stepped in front of Morgan, who was trying to intimidate Roth. "Why don't me and you walk around the block," Bobby said.

Morgan looked from Roth to Bobby and sidestepped past the newspaperman, and Bobby followed, catching stride with him.

"I don't like that nasty little man," Morgan said.

"He's a columnist," Bobby said. "If everyone liked him, he wouldn't be doing his job. Sort of like working Internal Affairs."

Morgan gave him a sideways glance, smiled, nodded.

"All right, I hear that," Morgan said as they strolled down toward Third Avenue, over which ran the rusting Gowanus Expressway, thundering with trucks and cars. "But I'm trying to do an investigation, and your buddy is fucking it up."

"If he doesn't get it down as a possible murder, which I know it is, then nothing will happen," Bobby said. "I liked Tom Larkin, liked him a lot. He was one of the few guys on the job who believed in me."

"Not the only one," Morgan said. "I don't think you killed that girl."

"Thanks," Bobby said. "But you never stepped forward."

"For what? How was I gonna help you? I'm disliked in my own community for being a cop. I'm disliked by cops for being IAB. I'm disliked in IAB for being black and 'off agenda.' You can't get any more nigger than a black IAB cop, baby. But it's what I do. And I do it well. And it still doesn't get me any promotions. So, I don't see how I could have helped your case. First, it was handled by Homicide and then the Brooklyn DA's office. It wasn't an internal police matter. But what I saw in your file, and I looked the same way I look at the old fight films, they didn't make a good case against you. Just like you never really beat me. But you went the distance four times. And anyone as good with his hands as you are would never use a knife. Especially on a woman. Some things just don't jibe."

They walked along Third Avenue, under the highway that cut this neighborhood in half. A group of Hispanic men sat on plastic milk crates playing dominoes on the traffic island amid the rusted hulks of abandoned and crashed cars. As they strolled, Bobby told Morgan as much as he thought the big cop could digest in one feeding. Without naming names. He told him about the three-quarters pension scam, about certain cop bars where the pension papers and the cash were picked up, about a corrupt assistant district attorney, and defense attorney, a private security firm that ran a mini-militia of corrupt three-quarters cops.

"I think you need me now as much as I need you," Morgan said. "What other cop you gonna call?"

Morgan was itchy for names and hard facts. But Bobby was cagey, just tantalizing him with a sketch, doing a rope-a-dope, inviting his old opponent onto the ropes with him. Bobby wanted him salivating for a later time, when he would need an ally.

"I've been trying to crack open the three-quarters scam for years," Morgan said. "We've nailed plenty of individual phonies, of course. Guys weight-lifting with bad backs. Arrogant assholes with three-quarters fighting in the Golden Gloves! But I've suspected for some time that there was some kind of an organized crew. Now, if you're saying these same people are associated with Tom Larkin's death, then maybe me and you have some more serious talking to do."

"We do, but I'm fighting this one by my rules, Morgan," Bobby said. "My ass is on the line here. My life. I have a kid I might never see on this side of prison bars again. And the woman I love is missing. I have to know I can trust somebody before I can confide in him."

"You can trust me," Morgan said as they circled back to the parking lot of the diner. The parking lot was now filled with uniformed cops from the 72nd Precinct. Bobby noticed Caputo and Dixon in the crowd. Bobby's Jeep was now covered with dozens of thin slices of American cheese, melting in the late summer sun.

"That's the sign of a rat," Morgan said. "A cheese eater."

"I know what it means," Bobby said. "Talking to you only confirms it for them."

"You want protection?" Morgan asked.

"Yeah, from you?" Bobby laughed. "You butted me in the last round of our last fight."

"That was a goddamn accident," Morgan said, angry and insulted. "I never fought dirty in my life. Never had to."

"With these people you might have to," Bobby said.

"This is different," Morgan said. "Dirty cops are my business. They're worse than ordinary mutts. They're skells who hide behind a badge. That ain't fair and makes them mutts times two. And if they don't fight fair, why should I?"

"Aw shit, I knew the butt was an accident," Bobby said. "I just wanted to hear you say it, Forrest. You never apologized for it."

"Why should I apologize?" Morgan said, incredulous. "The judges gave you the decision even though I won."

"You won? Are you crazy? I won every fucking round."

"You ran like a rabbit," Morgan said.

"I boxed your ears off," Bobby said.

"We could do it again," Morgan said, stopping in his tracks, nodding his head, fists balling, serious.

"If I climb back in the ring with you," Bobby said, "we'll be fighting side by side."

"I hear that," Morgan said. "But get it straight. I'm not your friend. I ain't your enemy, either. That's the way it got to be in my job."

"Sounds fair," Bobby said.

"Now, can you keep this Max Roth from printing the shit about Larkin's root canal?"

"No," Bobby said. "He's already on the way back to the office, dictating it in from the car phone."

"This could fuck things up," Morgan said.

"I think we need to make people sweat," Bobby said. "I also want you to note for the record that I've been told I might be set up and framed for another crime. What and who or where— I obviously don't know."

"You gonna give me some names?"

"When the time is right," Bobby said. "Meanwhile, I think you have a whole precinct to interview. I was you, I'd start with a couple of shitheads named Caputo and Dixon. They didn't exactly get along with Tom Larkin. I wouldn't bet they were regular contributors to the United Negro College Fund, either. If you catch my drift."

Forrest Morgan wrote down the two names, and Bobby held out his hand for him to shake. Morgan looked down at it and said, "I'll do that when you're ready to come out fighting."

36

Bobby recognized William Franz as soon as he saw him walk in from his six PM snack break. Bobby had been waiting for almost a half hour in the lobby of the Brooklyn medical examiner's office of Kings County Hospital. Over the years, especially in the crack-infested eighties, Kings County had become like a MASH unit in a war zone. It was also the hospital where Bobby's father, Sean Emmet, was officially pronounced dead, all those years ago.

Working on cases, Bobby had been here too many times. Somewhere downstairs Tom Larkin's body was probably in a zipper bag in a walk-in freezer, waiting to be cut open for autopsy.

The ME's office was at ground level, but the autopsy rooms

were in the cool, discreet basement. Most of the crime victims
who died in ER were shipped downstairs to the morgue. Bobby
had seen them: people who had been killed in shootings, blud-
geonings, overdoses, poisonings, knifings. They all wound up on
the stainless-steel tabletops there, cut from hip to hip, nipple to
nipple, and then straight down the center of the torso, opened
up like human envelopes, the elaborate contents examined for
causes of death.

But in the case of the cremated woman whom the authorities
convinced a jury was Dorothea, there was no body to cut, no
brain to explore. Just a pile of beige dust. But Carlos from the
crematorium had also given the Brooklyn deputy chief ME, William Franz, the charred but intact teeth that had survived the
final flames. Bobby wanted to know what had happened to them.

Bobby remembered Franz from the days when Bobby was still a
cop with Brooklyn South Narcotics and often brought the chubby,
bespectacled little man NYPD forms to sign in connection with various cheap homicides. Not much talk, just bureaucratic cop-to-ME
formalities. Bobby remembered him for his high-pitched laugh
and for always smelling of onions—of the hot-dog-with-everything-
on-it variety. He'd hate to witness Franz's own autopsy. Now
Bobby rose to greet Franz, who still smelled of onions. He wore
black-framed glasses with lenses as deep as glass bricks.

"Ah," Franz said, rocking a toothpick in his mouth as he
walked with short, quick paces past a female receptionist, "I was
wondering when you'd get around to me, Mr. Emmet."

He waved to the receptionist and a hospital security guard and
said, "He's okay."

Bobby followed him through a heavy metal door. Franz
grabbed two white lab coats from a wall hook, tossing one to
Bobby and pulling on his own as he clicked down a hospital-
green corridor to another door. Bobby then trailed Franz down
a flight of steps and was immediately overwhelmed by the smell
of formaldehyde and death.

"You remember me from the old days, Brooklyn South?"
Bobby asked. "Or the goddamned newspapers?"

"Cops faces I don't remember," Franz said, inspecting the tip
of the toothpick for salvage. "Killers I do. So tell me, did you
kill her?"

He stopped on the stairs and turned and smiled at Bobby

through thick lenses. Buried deep in the distorted wavy abyss behind the glasses were two little dark, dilated eyes.

"No," Bobby said, "I didn't."

"I didn't think so," Franz said with a silly high-pitched laugh that made him sound like a grade-schooler, and then he click-clacked down the remaining steps.

Bobby recoiled as they passed through another door into a scrub room outside the morgue. He handed Bobby a pair of surgical gloves and a surgical mask. They both donned the pro-tective gear to ward off airborne bacteria from the exposed corpses inside. Bobby then followed Franz into the sprawling, brightly lit lab of antiseptic stainless-steel sinks, linen hampers, and scattered gurneys. Bobby scanned a row of autopsy tables equipped with overhead Luma-Lite lamps, dangling micro-phones, and Stryker saws and instrument tables where handsaws, files, forceps, scalpels, and other stainless-steel tools of the death trade were neatly arranged. The lab was lined with several glass-enclosed offices, covered with vertical blinds. The two men crossed the autopsy area, where space-suited medical students were working on cadavers. One medical student looked up from a corpse, through the window of his headgear, and seemed to recognize Bobby. He nudged another student. The two of them stared like celebrity hounds. Bobby hoped the body wasn't the remains of Tom Larkin.

Franz then entered his small, cramped office and took a seat behind his desk. He wheeled himself in his office chair to a Mr. Coffee that rested on top of a low file cabinet and poured himself a cup.

"Coffee?"

"No thanks," Bobby said.

Franz sprinkled in a half packet of Sweet'n Low and wheeled himself back behind his desk. "Did you know that every little pink packet of Sweet'n Low in the world is made right here in Brooklyn?"

"You don't say?" Bobby said. "So, why don't you think I killed her?"

"A voice from the grave," Franz said with his high-pitched laugh. "You're here about the teeth, no?" Franz sipped the cof-fee, pushed the steam-fogged glasses a little higher on his little sweaty snout.

"Yes, I am," Bobby said.

"About a year and a half late," Franz said, the smell of the onions still drifting from him.

"Oh?"

"I turned the teeth over to the district attorney's office," Franz said. "Funny how they were never used in evidence."

" 'Funny' is the wrong word," Bobby said. "I spent a year and a half behind bars."

"Oh, I know, I know, I know," he said. "I don't usually follow most of the homicides that come through here, anymore than a baggage handler follows what happens to a piece of luggage. I don't mean to sound insensitive, but you get numb to the endless conveyor belt of domestic violence, drug killings. Children I always remember because every one is an innocent. Yours I remember, too, and not just because it made headlines."

"Why, then?"

"Because, how often do we get ashes here?" he asked, blurting the silly high-pitched laugh again.

"Not really ashes," Bobby said. "It's bone dust."

"Ah, you've done your homework," Franz said, impressed, sipping his coffee. He added a little more Sweet'n Low.

"Who did you give the teeth to?" Bobby asked.

"Cis Tuzio herself. An unpleasant woman."

"Do you have a voucher for it?"

"Yeah," Franz said. "The teeth were never returned. I was told they were lost."

"Convenient," Bobby said.

"They said it made no difference because Dorothea Dubrow had no available dental records to compare them to," Franz said.

"My attorney might be subpoenaing you," Bobby said, standing to leave. "That okay with you?"

"Anytime," Franz said. "I'd like nothing better. Because those teeth spoke to me like they still had a tongue attached to them. Spoke to me with a New York accent."

Bobby leaned on his desk and tried to find the eyes behind the thick kaleidoscopic glasses. "Explain all that to me, Mr. Franz," Bobby said very softly. "Please . . ."

"Was your girlfriend a smoker?"

"She hated cigarettes," Bobby said. "She was a health nut."

"And she was supposed to be from the Ukraine, no?"

"That's right."

Franz wheeled himself to the file cabinet under the Mr. Coffee and pulled out a drawer, removed a file, and opened it as he rolled himself back behind the desk.

"The DA's office might have lost the teeth," Franz said, perusing the official documents in the folder. "But I didn't lose the lab tests. Judging by the high tar and nicotine content in the teeth, the person who belonged to those teeth was a heavy smoker. American cigarettes, because of the ammonia additives that American tobacco companies use to boost addiction levels. She would probably have lived in New York most of her forty years, judging by the amount of fluoride in her teeth. It's the same type of fluoride we use here. I haven't been able to find anywhere else in the world besides New York that uses the same chemical formula of fluoride as was found in those teeth." He paused and giggled and put on a mock accent, "Yo, dem teet' tawk wit' a New Yawk accent."

Franz started to giggle with the high-pitched voice again. "New Yawk, New Yawk, helluva town," he blurted, and began giggling some more and then stopped abruptly when he saw that Bobby Emmet was deadly serious.

"Dorothea didn't smoke," Bobby said. "She was twenty-five, and she had lived in New York for less than a year."

"Then they better arrest you for killing someone else," said Franz, and then he started to nervously laugh some more, putting his hand to his mouth to stop himself.

"Can I get a Xerox of these tests?"

"My pleasure," Franz said.

37

Friday

Gleason was supposed to meet Bobby aboard *The Fifth Amendment* the next morning at nine. He arrived at 10:12 AM.

"Sorry I'm late," Gleason said. "I got caught in an argument with the broad. . . ."

"Alana?"

"My candy jones was driving her crazy, so I cut down to two Hersheys a day," he said. "Detoxing. Now she says if I don't see a shrink about gnawing the inside of my face, she's gonna split. I ain't seein' no doctor. So I started smoking three packs a day again. You mind?"

He lit a Kent 100 before Bobby answered and threw the match overboard into the morning wind.

"As long as it's out here on deck," Bobby said, watching the flight of the match. "Speaking of doctors, I have to tell you about Franz, the first deputy chief ME in Brooklyn."

Gleason blew out a lungful of smoke, took a *Daily News* from his back pocket. It was folded to the Max Roth column about Tom Larkin's death. He said, "Tell me about this, too."

Bobby told him about Franz first, handing Gleason the photocopy of the lab report on the teeth, about how the little man had said the teeth were from a woman in her forties, a New Yorker and a smoker. Gave him all the little details about American cigarette ammonia additives and New York City's unique fluoride formula.

Gleason leafed through the file, walked to the edge of the Silverton, grabbed the railing, and took a drag of the cigarette.

"I checked on the pacemaker thing," Gleason said. "Tuzio was savvy enough to log it as evidence. No suppression there. It was up to her to use it; she chose not to. But it doesn't explain why Moira Farrell never used it. It did fall into the category of exculpatory evidence.''

Bobby went through the whole Tuzio-Farrell connection that went all the way back to their high school days in Scranton.

"Collusion," Gleason said. "Conspiracy. Jesus, I can make a dog and pony show out of that alone.''

"It could mean the judge, too,'' Bobby said. "Max Roth was in the Brooklyn courthouse yesterday doing some research, which showed that *both* Farrell and Tuzio once clerked for Judge Mark White, who presided over my trial and sentenced me.''

"My next press conference is gonna be a fuckin' doozy,'' Gleason said, slapping the rolled file folder against his palm. "I might hold this one on the fuckin' Brooklyn Bridge. They've tried to sell the public everything else. Tell this Franz guy I want to depose him on Sunday if he's available. Same with Carlos Orosco from the crematorium. I need a few hours each of their time.''

"I can arrange that,'' Bobby said.

Then Bobby told him about Larkin. About the message on the answering machine asking him to meet him in the Kopper Kettle.

"Well, you already know what he said. . . .''

"I do?'' Gleason looked confused.

"You know, about the Kate Clementine kidnapping case,'' Bobby said as if familiarizing Gleason about what he already knew. "Some missing architect? The Ukraine? I don't have to tell you what he said, you heard it yourself, Izzy. . . .''

"When the fuck did I hear it?'' Gleason said. "The only thing I heard the last few days was Alana sayin', 'No checks, no sex!' And 'stop cussing and stop eatin' candy and stop smokin'.' What the hell you mean I 'heard it'?''

"Didn't you check the messages on the machine in the office the other night?'' Bobby asked.

"I told you, I have no fuckin' idea how that machine works,'' Gleason said.

"Well, someone was using the remote code to check the messages the other night when I went there to get the gun,'' Bobby said, walking to the edge of the boat and looking downtown on the calm river.

"It wasn't me,'' Gleason said. "If you check the outgoing message on the machine, it says that if you need to get in touch with me for professional reasons, to call my Chelsea Hotel number.

Clients don't call me at the office. I have them call the Chelsea because there's a switchboard. Human beings who answer the phones when I'm out. I told you I have no fuckin' idea how to work them machines. Especially from the outside.''

"Then who the hell was checking the messages?" Bobby wondered out loud.

"Who else did you give the remote code to?"

"I didn't give the code to anyone," Bobby said. But he suddenly thought of one person who might know it.

"Whoever had the remote answering-machine code knew Larkin was gonna connect the dots for you," Gleason said. "This person also knew where and when you were gonna meet him. And got there first. Me, alls I remember about the Kate Clementine case was that some crazy relative abducted her or something. It's going back a while. One thing for sure: 'Clementine' ain't no fuckin' Ukrainian name.''

"I have some people to see," Bobby said.

"I'll check and see if Tuzio ever logged the teeth," Gleason said as he squinted downriver, the wind flattening his hair. "If she didn't, then we got us a suppression of evidence case to go with the conspiracy. The pacemaker is interesting, but without a body or medical history there is no way to know if Dorothea ever had one. Only your testimony to the contrary. Which without corroboration is meaningless. The teeth are different. That evidence is clearly exculpatory and corroborative, because even though there is no body, we have an expert witness ready to say these teeth came from a forty-year-old woman. A lifelong New Yorker. Which contradicts the prosecution's description of Dorothea Dubrow as a twenty-five-year-old native Ukrainian who was only in this country less than a year."

Sometimes, in moments of lucidity like this one, Bobby felt safe in Izzy Gleason's hands.

"I'll keep in touch," Gleason said, and hurried off *The Fifth Amendment.*

At noon, Dr. Benjamin Abrams sat on a bench, feeling the sun beat on his face. He had arrived five minutes earlier and taken a seat at the bus stop on the corner of Flatbush Avenue and Avenue U, across from the Kings Plaza Shopping Center, just as he did every Monday and Friday. Immediately after sitting down, he put on the special glasses, plunging himself into inky darkness.

They were wraparound glasses with light-tight frames that softly bit into the skin and bone surrounding his eyes, the lenses made with pure black glass that blocked out all view. Although they looked to others like sunglasses for the blind, they were designed so that the wearer could see absolutely nothing.

Dr. Abrams never dared trying to peek or to alter the glasses. He had no desire to know his blackmailer's identity. As long as he went along with the blackmailer's simple requests, his life would proceed smoothly. No hassles, no interruptions, no angst. He would never be dragged into court for murder. Never subject his wife or daughter, Rebecca, to the humiliation. Never have to do a day of jail time. All he had to do was sign those silly "91" pension forms when they came in and report here to this bus stop twice a week with his little black doctor's bag. He was always approached by the same soft-voiced gentleman, who escorted him into a car that always smelled new, where he was buckled into a deep leather seat.

Today was exactly the same as all the other Fridays and Mondays. The man pulled up to the bus stop, walked to Dr. Abrams, led him into the car, buckled him in. They drove in silence for another fifteen minutes. Abrams was unsure which direction, as the driver always made a series of turns.

Then he was escorted by the driver into a building, led along a very narrow corridor, through a low door and down an even more cramped, very steep stairwell into this comfortable, sound-proof subterranean bunker–living quarters.

The twenty-by-twenty-foot underground room was equipped with a bathroom, shower, kitchenette, a living room area, a stereo, a TV with a special chip to block out normal programming but hooked up to a VCR, a bookcase filled with books. There was a stationary bicycle and a StairMaster. The room was stuffy, but a steady whir of fresh air blew through a tiny duct in the kitchen area.

Off the living room area was a small alcove with a full-sized bed, neatly made. In another corner was an overstuffed armchair.

When the blackmailer was safely in his armchair, with a spotlight behind him to shroud him from view, he would tell the doctor that he could remove his blindfold glasses. When he did,

Abrams would always find Dorothea Dubrow sitting on the sofa, staring at him with the same sad dark eyes.

"Hello, Doctor," she said. "Today I am feeling cold. Is the sun out?"

Dr. Abrams placed a thermometer in her mouth. He'd recognized her from the photographs that came out at the time of the trial. Dr. Abrams knew that Bobby Emmet was accused of killing this poor woman, who had been held captive here for the past eighteen months. But precisely because of what these same people had done to Emmet, Dr. Abrams would never mention a word of her existence to anyone. He had no desire to know who was behind all of this. Life and freedom were too precious. Suppose they did the same to his own daughter?

Besides, every time he examined Dorothea Dubrow she was in generally good health. The three-milligram Haldol tablets that he prescribed for her kept her as docile as a parlor cat. There were never any signs of abuse. She obviously ate well and did exercise. He always gave her a multivitamin shot, to be certain she did not become malnourished. Her beautiful teeth were regularly brushed and flossed. There was no sign of rape or mistreatment at all. The blackmailer even provided her with sunlamps to keep her from growing too pale. But today she was trembling, her teeth chattering.

He checked the thermometer: 102.6. Not deadly, but not good.

Dr. Abrams checked her pulse, her heartbeat, her reflexes. She obeyed all his polite commands with a mannequin's pasty smile. The drugs and so much time down here had made her listless and accustomed to a simulated one-note life that was like a human dial tone.

But none of that bothered him. She was still a basically healthy woman. She was the least of his troubles. She was alive, unlike the butchered woman in the videotape that the blackmailer held over his head.

"She has a fever," Dr. Abrams told his blackmailer, who sat in his shadowy chair behind the shield of light.

"Will she be okay?"

"She has to be kept warm," Dr. Abrams said. "Give her Tylenol and lots of juices. I want to keep tabs on her. Contact me immediately if she gets any worse."

"There's a possibility we might have to travel soon," the man in the shadows said. "Is she up to that?"

"Check with me first," Dr. Abrams said. "Any change in environment could exacerbate the fever."

"All right," the blackmailer said.

"I'm finished here," Dr. Abrams said as he closed his small doctor's bag, patted Dorothea Dubrow on the shoulder, and put the wraparound glasses back on. "Remember to keep her warm."

"Is the sun shining today, Doctor?" Dorothea Dubrow asked, her teeth chattering.

He was startled to hear the question again. Then he said, "Yes, yes, it is."

"Feel it for me," she said.

Then the blackmailer led Dr. Abrams blindly up the stairs.

38

The room was ripe with too many flowers.

The wake was only one night, in Walter B. Cooke's in Bay Ridge, the most popular funeral parlor for those few cops who still lived in Brooklyn. The PBA had made all the arrangements for the wake and burial.

The undertakers had done a good job on Tom Larkin, repairing the ruined neck and adding color to his gaunt, dead cheeks. Old-time retired cops filed past the coffin, kneeling, blessing themselves, saying silent prayers. Larkin had been the only one of his contemporaries to keep working. Most got out after twenty years or less, depending on whether they got three-quarters, and called it a career. Larkin, who was still on the job when he died, called it a life.

Bobby greeted Rose Morse, the woman who had been dating Tom Larkin, as she sat in stunned bereavement. Larkin was the second man in her life to die in the past five years. "Good men

are harder and harder to find as a woman gets older," she said
to Bobby as she clutched his hand. "I'll never find another one
like him. . . ."

Bobby was fumbling for words. "He was crazy about you,"
Bobby said. "You gave him a last dance he didn't even know he
had in him."

That sent her cascading into tears, and Bobby felt terrible.
Some other women in the funeral parlor came to her side to
comfort her with Kleenex, hugs, and soothing words.

Bobby retreated to the back of the reposing room, where he
found John Shine standing, the way men do at bars, talking softly
to a few saddened old-timers. Then he glimpsed Forrest Morgan
in the corridor near the entrance to the viewing room, signing
his own name and then tracing his finger down the list of other
signed names. Bobby exchanged glances with Morgan, and he
and Shine drifted to the rear wall of the parlor, where they could
converse in whispers. Shine leaned against the wall and sighed
with grim relief.

"I can't stand for long periods," he said.

"I can't stand what's going on," Bobby said.

"You think they killed him, don't you?"

"Positive," Bobby said.

"But who the fuck would hurt old Tom? He was ready for
pasture."

"He was onto something," Bobby said.

"What? What could he possibly have known?"

"He was looking into what happened to Dorothea."

"You actually had him working that?"

"You're the one who told me I should see him."

"Yeah," John Shine whispered, arching his back, trying to get
comfortable. "I thought he might have a useful hunch or two,
that he was spinning some wacky theories. But I didn't know he
was actually *working* the case."

"He was just nosing around."

"So why would someone kill him?"

"Maybe because he was raising the dead, John," Bobby said.

"Riddles I don't need, Bobby," Shine said. "You were in touch
with him. What the hell was he telling you?"

"About some old case."

"What case . . . ?"

Bobby was interrupted when Lou Barnicle appeared with a flourish, followed by a badly limping Kuzak, who favored his crotch area with a protective stoop. Then came Zeke, O'Brien, Flynn, Levin, Lebeche, Daniels, and two new additions—Caputo and Dixon.

"Where do they get the balls?" Bobby asked.

"It is a disgrace," Shine said. "You start at one end. I'll start at the other. We'll toss the whole shit pile of them onto the sidewalk."

"I'd like nothing better," Bobby said. "But not here."

"Tom would love it," John Shine said, twisting his torso for relief. "A real fuckin' Irish wake. We'll kick ass and take names and leave the dead for the sweepers."

Bobby laughed and a few heads turned.

Forrest Morgan, the only black man in the room, watched each of the three-quarters crew sign in. His and Bobby's eyes met again, and then Bobby glanced toward Caputo and Dixon. Morgan acknowledged Bobby's barely perceptible signal and tapped those two on their shoulders and pointed out toward the lobby. Caputo and Dixon appeared startled and looked to Lou Barnicle as if for guidance. He shrugged and nodded for them to accompany Forrest Morgan.

Barnicle then looked at Bobby and Shine. Bobby stared right back, watching him dip his hand in a holy water font and bless himself, kneel at the casket, clasp his hands, and bow his head over the body of Tom Larkin.

"Hypocritical bastard," Shine said. "He had no use for Tom. Never did."

"The feeling was mutual," Bobby said. "Let's get some fresh air."

They walked out of the reposing room into the lobby. John Shine seemed happy to be in motion, his movements growing more fluid with each step.

"Barnicle is in nose deep, John," Bobby said, as they crossed the lobby and pushed through the glass front doors onto humid Fourth Avenue, alive with honking horns and the lights of the Brooklyn night. "But I think he's working for even worse people."

"I think you better keep me in the loop," Shine said. "You're gonna need all the help you can get."

"I appreciate that," Bobby said, as he saw Forrest Morgan grilling Caputo and Dixon beside a fire-alarm box on the corner.

"Start by telling me what Tom was looking into that could have gotten him killed," Shine said.

"Funny," Bobby said. "This wake got me thinking. Both of us lost women, the loves of our lives, and neither of us had a body for a wake."

John Shine looked at Bobby oddly. "What a morbid thought," he said. "Talk to me instead about what could have gotten Tom killed. What was he looking into?"

Before Bobby could answer, Forrest Morgan strode quickly across the sidewalk and pointed to Caputo and Dixon.

"Did you witness these two men having any kind of altercation with Tom Larkin in the last week or so?" Morgan asked aloud, as Caputo and Dixon stood looking at Bobby and Shine.

Bobby stared at Caputo and Dixon with disgust and then looked back at Forrest Morgan, who stood, big and powerful and sweaty, in front of him.

"I don't talk to Internal Affairs," Bobby said, and winked at a smiling John Shine.

39

Saturday

Trevor Sawyer sat next to Bobby Emmet as they made their third trip down the thunderous Cyclone ride in Coney Island, making sixty-mile-an-hour hairpin turns on the oldest wooden roller coaster in America. Sawyer, a native New Yorker, had never been on the Cyclone before. Bobby thought this man who had everything must have had a very sad childhood. "Never been to Coney Island before," Sawyer said. "Of course, I sailed past with father a few times. But when Maggie asked me to take her here from Southampton—without her mother's knowledge, of course—I jumped at the chance. I'm delighted I did."

"Consider yourself baptized," Bobby said. "A born-again New Yorker."

F. Scott Fitzgerald was right, Bobby thought. The rich really are different. And not just because they had more money than everyone else, as Ernest Hemingway had snidely replied to Fitzgerald's comment. It was because the money *owned* them. And often distanced them from some of the best things in life. Like simple fun. And what good was Hamptons money without Coney Island fun? The rich were raised with the belief that if it didn't cost a lot, it couldn't be good. And they remained impoverished in the soul.

"Thanks for showing me around," Trevor said, his eyes pin-wheeled like a kid's, as they moved past the barkers of the arcades and the other frantic rides of the amusement park.

"You don't have to be poor to love 'The Poor Man's Para-dise,'" Bobby said. "Coney is yours, too. It belongs to the citizens."

"I'm glad something does," said Trevor.

Earlier, Bobby had tried to explain that this was more a state of mind than a place. A symbol of freedom that attracted the immigrant masses. What beat poet Lawrence Ferlinghetti called "a Coney Island of the mind." Bobby told Trevor that Coney Island, even now in its shabby elegance, was still a perfect Oz that managed to survive the foulest of political neglect over the years.

"What's troubling you?" Bobby asked as they walked, looking for Maggie, who had wandered off with Sandy Fraser and her little boy, Donald, into the Kiddieland park. Maggie had volunteered to help with Donald, but Bobby knew she was really trying to get a read on Sandy for him.

"I was at another political gathering," said Trevor. "Again for Stone. Again no monetary solicitation. It makes me nervous."

"Because the rich might not control the next governor?" Bobby asked, a drop of acid in the remark.

"Because no one will. A politician who doesn't solicit money doesn't just want to be elected. He wants to be crowned. And once again your name came up."

"From Sol Diamond?"

"Yes."

They walked up to the three-mile stretch of boardwalk that was still the best stroll in the city, with the salt breeze blowing in off the Atlantic, the smell of hot dogs, french fries, corn on the cob, wafting in the air. Bobby bought Trevor a hot dog and a cup of beer from a stand called Gregory and Paul's. He remembered years back, when he was new on the NYPD, a police captain in the Coney Island precinct had been fired from the job for getting caught by Internal Affairs taking free coffee and ice cream from this food stand. Today you could rip off a lifelong, tax-free pension and get away with it. But, as John Shine always said, "A corrupt cop always starts with that first free cup of coffee."

"How'd my name come up again?" Bobby asked.

"In relation to the old cop who committed suicide," Trevor said, holding the beer cup in one hand and eating the hot dog with the other.

"Tom Larkin," Bobby said.

"The one Max Roth in the *Daily News* is saying was a murder. It has people very nervous."

"Good."

"No, it's not," Trevor said, wiping mustard off his mouth with the back of his hand and swallowing. "Because it also makes me nervous. It comes right back to you. If they are going to deal with you, it will have to be soon. Before the primary. Which is four days away. And if anything happens to you, it will crush little Maggie's heart. Which would destroy Constance. And probably my marriage. I don't want anything bad to happen to you."

"I appreciate your concern, Trevor," Bobby said, staring the millionaire in the eyes, this time believing him completely.

They walked down toward the amusement area again. Maggie and Sandy were in the kiddie park, chatting and laughing. Maggie caught Bobby's eye and waved. Sandy's little boy, Donald, pulled furiously at the chain of a bell on a miniature fire engine ride. Bobby and Trevor stood by the spook house, listening to a mechanical devil cackle at a group of passing homeboys who strutted with teenaged girlfriends carrying Kewpie dolls that the guys had won for them in the arcades.

Trevor finished the last bite of the hot dog, washed it down with a big gulp of beer, and tossed the cup in a trash barrel. "Now I think I'll give that Cyclone another whirl. Care to join me?"

"I think I'll sit this one out," Bobby said as Maggie drifted over from the kiddie park.

"Come on, Mag," Trevor said.

Maggie smiled and winked at Bobby and hurried after Trevor to the roller coaster. Bobby was now convinced Gleason was wrong about not trusting Trevor. He was just too sad and insecure to be diabolical.

Bobby sauntered across the amusement park to Sandy, who was strapping little Donald into a seat on a small kiddie carousel. Bobby hopped on board, holding on to a brass pole as the ride spun to life.

Sandy was dressed in tight faded denim shorts and a scoop-neck white summer T-shirt, her thick hair pulled back with an elastic band, small elegant sunglasses perched on her perfect nose. Her white Reebok sneakers were well broken in but bleached bright white. She was even more beautiful in the bright sun than in moonlight.

"That Maggie's some kid," Sandy said. "You must be very proud."

"I am," Bobby said. "This little guy is adorable, too."

"He's the core of my life," Sandy said, looking away as she spoke, a small fracture in her voice as a trouble-free Strauss waltz gurgled from the pipes of the carousel.

"Weeeeeeeeee," said Donald as the ride picked up moderate speed and wooden horses with terrifying faces pumped up and down on greased pistons.

"His father must be very proud," Bobby said.

"Unfortunately, he's not."

"Hard to believe."

"It's like he doesn't know he exists. Resents him."

Bobby could see her eyes water. He handed her a napkin from the hot dog stand, and she lifted the glasses and dabbed her eyes.

"How did you get away from Barnicle and the nanny today?"

"I put laxatives in the nanny's vitamin C bottle," she said, and laughed through the tears. "She takes four capsules every morning. I don't think she's been out of the bathroom all morning."

Bobby smiled.

"You can run now. Come with me."

"No," Sandy said. "You don't understand. It's too late for that. They still have the evidence from the medical board against me that could put me in jail. I couldn't live as a fugitive. I couldn't weather a custody fight with Barnicle. I have no money. Plus they'd look for me. He has connections everywhere. Besides, it's not forever. Eventually they won't need me anymore, and they say they'll pay me off and leave me alone."

"I think maybe you should tell me a few more things, Sandy," Bobby said.

"Bobby, you know I can't. The baby . . ."

"Barnicle sent you to me the other night, didn't he?"

She looked at him with the raw eyes, as if asking for forgiveness.

"I know you were lying, because you said you traced the boat to my lawyer's name," Bobby said. "It's not in his name. So my guess is Barnicle told you where to find me, sent you to come and play the weakest card in an ex-con's hand. Told you to try to *fuck* information out of me."

This wasn't indiscriminate vulgarity; this was the operative verb in question.

"Okay, that's true," she said with a trembling lower lip, as the carousel spun. "But, I couldn't do that to Dorothea. She loves you. I know you love her. But I needed some human affection. Needed someone to *talk* to. I wanted someone to see that Donald was taken care of in case something happens to me. I love my kid the way you and Dorothea love each other. I never wanted to hurt anyone. But these people are capable of anything. You have no idea. . . ."

"You keep talking about Dorothea in the present tense," Bobby said as the carousel twirled, the music soaring, the pistons pumping, Donald squealing, the world zipping past them— streaks of blue ocean, black faces, other amusement rides.

She nodded. "I think she's still alive."

"Why?"

"Because of the blind man," she said, still dabbing her eyes.

"What blind man?"

Now little Donald saw that his mother was crying, and he immediately joined in the sobbing, stretching his arms out to her as the ride began to slow. Bobby bent and unstrapped him and lifted him up in his arms, considered his vaguely familiar looking face, studying him for a long moment as the kid whined for his mother. Bobby tried to place the face. It was like an artist's composite sketch that needed a few more specific details to bring the image into focus. The kid's face began to haunt him.

When the carousel stopped, he handed the boy to Sandy, and she held him in her arms until he calmed down, and then she strapped him into his stroller. Bobby bought some cotton candy from a wagon and handed the immense spun-sugar cocoon to the kid, who pushed it into his face like a pillow, mouth open. The kid was soon giggling as the candy melted in his mouth, his face as sticky as flypaper.

They climbed up to the boardwalk, and when they strolled past West Eleventh Street, they paused near the railing on the street side, near a rank of public telephones. Bobby looked both ways on the boardwalk, making certain they weren't being watched.

"Now, tell me, what blind man?" he said.

"The one that arrives at John Shine's house every Monday and Friday," she said.

"John Shine's house?"

"I spend a lot of time down in Windy Tip, mostly doing nothing, because most days Barnicle doesn't give me anything to do. I do clerical work in Gibraltar Security three mornings a week, making up payrolls, billings, mail. Mostly I sit on the balcony down Windy a lot, watching the world go by. What little of it there is in my life. That's where I saw you swim in from the boat to John Shine's house."

"I know."

"Well, over the last year or so, I started noticing that every Monday and Friday afternoon, at about a quarter after twelve, Shine would show up and help a blind man out of his car. The blind man always wears big dark glasses and carries a small black bag, like a doctor's bag. They go in the house together. About a half hour later they come out. They get back in the car, and Shine drives away and returns alone. Twice a week."

Bobby watched little Donald gnaw deeper into the sugary nest of cotton candy. He looked out toward the horizon, trying to match a straight line against this new information he was hearing. It was like putting a level on a canoe. Bobby turned back to Sandy. She was wearing her sunglasses again.

"What does that have to do with Dorothea?"

"I'm not sure," Sandy said. "It's just weird. Besides the blind man, I never saw another person go in that house until you did. Women love Shine. He dates them, all right; dinner, a show, a movie. But he never sleeps with them. I know because a few girls who wanted to sleep with him told me they never got to first base. And these were pretty girls. He never brings a woman in there. And I don't think he's gay either."

"Well, he says he's still in mourning for the one great love of his life," Bobby said. "Some men do have *feelings.*"

"Okay, maybe that's true. But, no offense, who has a blind doctor? And why go pick him up? Why not just drive to his office? Who picks up a blind doctor to do a house call? And then drives him back to wherever he came from? I'm telling ya, it's freakin' *weird.*"

"Maybe he's just a friend," Bobby said, trying to make sense of this oddity. Maybe she was lying again. For Barnicle. Literally leading Bobby down a blind alley.

"Yeah," she said. "So how come he carries that little old-fashioned black doctor's bag all the time?"

"So John Shine has a doctor come visit him," Bobby said. "He does have a very bad back. Maybe this blind doctor has magic fingers, a chiropractor But what's this got to do with Dorothea?"

As he talked, he knew there might be something very ugly and scary going on here. He controlled his emotions, reminding himself that Sandy could also still be trying to throw Bobby off Barnicle's scent. Trying to make him suspect one of his closest friends. Using sweetness and guilt and apologies and even her own child to mask yet more deceit.

"What if Shine has Dorothea hidden in his house and uses the doctor to check on her?" Sandy asked. "That's what I think might be going on."

Bobby imagined Dorothea as a captive inside that house. But where? He thought of the attic; the mad scratching of squirrels. What if it hadn't been squirrels? But Dorothea clawing to get free.

"I'll look into it,' Bobby said. "Is there anything else you want to tell me, Sandy? Like who the real father of your baby is?"

"If I revealed that, and they found out, they might kill Donald," Sandy said.

He studied her, hoping she wasn't lying about everything.

"What else can you tell me?" Bobby asked.

"Whenever Barnicle gets a call on the special security phone—I call it the Batphone because he has it swept twice a week for taps—from one particular person, he makes me leave the room,"

Sandy said. "But I eavesdrop as best I can. Your name comes up a lot. As someone who is in the way. I heard him say he understands that they can't wait six months or a year for a new trial and risk an acquittal. I think they have other plans. I'm not sure what or with who, or when. But I think they intend to frame you again. Soon. Today. Tomorrow. Before the election."

"I heard that, too," Bobby said.

"They also use the phrase 'accelerated operation' a lot these days, since you got out on bail. I think they're trying to collect a really huge haul of cash as quick as they can. I know you know about the three-quarters scam. They know you know. So I see lots of cash. They're accelerating that operation. And they want to frame you for something *new.*"

Bobby trembled in the hot sun. The music and fun suddenly went out of the mindless day. He looked both ways on the boardwalk, searching for unfriendly faces. *Maggie,* he thought. *I better get back to her.*

Sandy checked her watch.

"God, it's almost two," Sandy said in a quiet, resigned voice. "I gotta go before *himself* gets home."

The sun shone on her face and sparkled in her dark glasses, in which Bobby could see his own reflection. The fear he saw on his own face startled him. Sandy elevated herself to her tiptoes and leaned in to kiss him good-bye. He unconsciously turned his head, and she planted it on his cheek. She looked mildly wounded.

"In spite of all she's been through, Dorothea is one lucky girl," she said as little Donald smacked his lips and jabbered nonsense syllables. "I hope you find her. I hope she's finally honest with you about who she really is. I could never really nail her down. I guess I've said enough. Too much, for my own good. Be careful, Bobby. I better go."

"I better get back to Maggie," he said.

"I'd say that's a very good idea, Bobby," Sandy said, almost like a warning. "I'd get her out of town, I was you."

With that she spun, and Bobby watched her wheel her stroller down the ramp from the boardwalk. She looked absolutely beautiful, scared, and alone. He walked back toward the amusement park to find his daughter.

* * *

Bobby did not see Sandy pass the white van with the dark-tinted windows, in which sat Lou Barnicle, Kuzak, and Zeke, but they had just witnessed Sandy Fraser kissing Bobby Emmet on the Coney Island boardwalk and watched her and the boy get into her car.

"What now?" Kuzak asked as Sandy climbed behind the steering wheel.

"We make sure nothing happens to that kid," Barnicle said.

After his third visit to Nathon's Famous and his sixth Cyclone ride, Trevor Sawyer looked as if he needed a rest from his new-found childhood. He climbed into the back of his Rolls, his face draining of color. Bobby could almost see his guts boiling like the Coney Island surf, with hot dogs, raw clams, french fries, sausage and peppers, and pistachio-flavored custard. He had been the proverbial kid in a candy store, thirty years too late.

"Give me a few minutes," Bobby said to Trevor as he took Maggie by the hand. The rich man just waved and covered his eyes with his right arm.

"What's your read on Sandy, my amazing child?"

"I think she's a straight shooter. The reason I think she's sincere is that she didn't try to make me think she was. She was just normal, worrying mostly about her baby. He's adorable."

"Yes, he is," Bobby said. "Does he remind you of someone? Someone you know?"

"He has one of those faces, all right," Maggie said. "I can almost place it. But, anyway, back at the ranch, I don't think that Sandy would do anything that would come back to haunt her and her kid. But that's just my bullshit detector at work."

Bobby took a deep breath and watched the roller coaster dip down the steel rails.

"She's in some kind of trouble, isn't she, Dad?" Maggie said.

"Yeah," Bobby said.

"I could tell that, too. Is there anything you can do to help her?"

"I hope so," Bobby said, also not wanting to believe what Sandy had told him about his friend John Shine.

"I don't care if I sound like some awkward, pubescent, spoiled rich brat," Maggie said, staring at her father with watery eyes.

"I'm still worried about you, and I want an old-fashioned hug before I leave."

She threw herself into Bobby's arms, and he lifted her off her feet and squeezed her tightly to him and turned her around in the Coney Island sun and whispered in her ear, "Everything will turn out okay. Promise, kiddo."

He placed her down, and she ran for the limousine without turning her teary face back toward him.

40

Bobby needed to digest what Sandy had told him about John Shine. The rugged, brilliant cop had been more than his *friend*. He was a mentor, like a big brother or an uncle. And now Bobby was confronted by dark, uneasy thoughts about the man who lived alone spouting Emerson in a house by the sea. As Bobby drove along the Belt Parkway, he imagined this blind doctor checking on Dorothea, stashed in his friend's house. Could Shine be that monstrous? That diabolical?

But this was the same John Shine who saved his life just two days ago, Bobby thought, and then told himself to think harder.

Then Bobby completed the memory.

Right after he had been beaten by the Barnicle crew on the beach in the rain, Bobby had got into his Jeep. John Shine had climbed in next to him. Bobby had dialed the message machine at Gleason's office. He punched in the remote code—378, the same as the office room number. Shine could easily have watched the numbers he pushed. Bobby had then listened to Tom Larkin's message. With his guard down, after Shine had saved his life, Bobby had even told Shine the gist of Larkin's taped message. About some seventeen-year-old kidnapping case, a more recently missing architect, the Ukraine. Later, when he arrived at the office at the Empire State Building, someone was checking the machine with that remote code.

Had it been Shine?

He was inching along the Gowanus Expressway now, toward the Brooklyn Battery Tunnel, oblivious to the traffic.

Had Shine checked Bobby's messages? Discovered where and when Tom Larkin would be meeting Bobby? And then sent someone there to kill Larkin? Before Larkin could tell Bobby what he knew?

Then Bobby remembered the well-thumbed *Complete Emerson* that Shine had sent him in jail. Bobby had always been troubled by the single passage in the Emerson essay called "Friendship" that Shine had chosen to highlight with a yellow marker: *"We walk alone in the world. Friends such as we desire are dreams and fables."*

Why, out of an essay that glorified friendship as one of the great treasures of human existence, would Shine highlight such a negative passage?

Why? he asked himself over and over as he paid the toll for the tunnel and sped toward Manhattan. He kept asking himself the same question until he arrived back at the Seventy-ninth Street Boat Basin.

When he checked his new messages, he found one from Max Roth. He said he had some information Bobby'd asked him to get from the old clips. Bobby called Roth and they met at an old-fashioned Greek diner on Broadway.

"The old clips are warehoused, but I managed to dig out a very yellowed second-day story from the photo files on this Kate Clementine," Roth said. He poked at the fruit salad and gave it a one-word culinary review: "Canned."

He dropped his spoon, refusing to eat.

"A kidnapping, no?"

"Yep," Roth said, checking his drinking glass against the ceiling light for stains. He made a face and then unwrapped a sanitary drinking straw, poked it into the can of club soda, and sipped.

"It was a little like the recent Katie Beers case," Roth said. "The little girl in the underground chamber out in Long Island. But this was different. Kate Clementine was buried in an underground bunker by an obsessed uncle for two years and came out alive. The girl's boyfriend was the main suspect all along. But it turned out to be the uncle, who said he was only trying to preserve her virginity and her wholesomeness. She's been in and out of mental hospitals ever since."

"Poor kid," Bobby said. "But what—"

"And buried deep in the next to last graph of the jump I come across a name that gives me brainfreeze."

"Who?"

"He was still a patrolman then," Roth said. "He wasn't in charge of the case. But he was one of the cops who discovered the underground bunker and set this Kate Clementine free and arrested her wacky uncle."

"His name, Max," Bobby said, hoping he was going to say Lou Barnicle but fearing he was not.

"John Shine," Roth said, staring Bobby in the eye.

Bobby closed his eyes as the steam from his coffee rose around him. The name resounded in the air. He took a deep breath and told Roth again about how Shine had saved his life from the three-quarters crew out in Rockaway. "But, thinking back, afterwards Shine pumped me for information about what I knew. That wasn't unusual. He was always an information freak. . . ."

"Maybe he saved your ass in case you'd told someone else, like me," Roth said, sipping his club soda. "So he could prepare himself. Go to Plan B."

Then Bobby told Roth what Sandy had said about the blind man who carried a doctor's bag into Shine's house every Monday and Friday.

"Maybe the sheen is coming off your buddy Shine a little, no?" Roth asked.

"Max," Bobby said, "I want you to find out everything you can about Shine's police department record."

"I know a guy who can expedite a Freedom of Information press request," Roth said.

"Also run a Lexis legal history on him from the paper's computer," Bobby said. "Jesus, Max, what can his motive be?"

"It can't be greed," Roth said. "He already won the lottery."

"If it is him," Bobby said, "it must be some kind of weird revenge. Or obsession. Some dark part of his personality I never knew."

"I'm glad you're thinking sanely, here," Roth said. "In fact, as much as I dislike the weasel, I think you better track down

Sleazy Izzy and tell him everything. About Shine, the blind doctor, Sandy and her baby with the mystery father."

"I will," Bobby said.

"I better get cracking," Roth said, getting up from the booth.

"I'm more spooked now than I was before," Bobby said.

"Why?" Roth said.

"Dead, I knew there was nothing more they could do to Dorothea," he said softly. "Alive, they can kill her all over again."

Bobby had to take another look inside that house.

He spent the afternoon shopping for the supplies he'd need. That evening he took the boat out to Windy Tip and moored it at a buoy far enough out so that he wouldn't be noticed in the dwindling light. He used the binoculars to watch Shine leave, setting his elaborate alarm system, dressed for the dinner shift at The Winning Ticket. Shine drove off in the Mercedes.

Bobby waited until darkness fell and then pulled on a pair of surgical gloves, fastened a small but sturdy pinch bar to his belt, shoved a small watertight flashlight into his right pants pocket and a tube of Vaseline into his left pocket, and looped a nylon scaling rope with a three-pronged grappling hook around his waist. He dove off *The Fifth Amendment* and swam to shore in the tame tide. He came up on the far side of Shine's house.

He stealthily made his way to the westernmost wall that faced the open bay and the distant lights of the Coney Island amusement rides. Bobby hurled the grappling hook up to the high roof of the house and, after the third try, managed to secure a firm bite around the base of the red-brick chimney. He scaled the face of the house, his great strength easily hoisting him to the slanted roof. He pulled the rope up behind him and scurried across the roof tiles. He found the open attic window through which the squirrel came and went without triggering the alarm.

The attic wasn't wired. Shine had told him he left the window open a crack to allow an even flow of air into the hot, confined space. To prevent spontaneous combustion.

The window was even smaller than Bobby had imagined. He rubbed the Vaseline on his bulky shoulders and the frame of the attic window. Getting through the window was like deflowering a virgin, he thought. A series of patient false starts, gentle maneuvering, delicate shiftings of position, incremental penetration, being careful not to be too rough.

Finally Bobby was safely inside. His shoulders were raw with friction burns.

In the darkness, he heard the scurrying of the rodents. Bobby played the beam of the penlight across the plywood flooring. The attic was an innocuous disarray of old cardboard boxes, unused furniture, discarded lamps. He even saw John Shine's old NYPD dress uniform hanging in a plastic suit bag, adorned with award ribbons for bravery above and beyond.

Dorothea wasn't being kept in the attic.

Bobby found the attic trapdoor, an elaborate one with folding stairs. He grabbed the handle and twisted, but it would not move. Locked from the other side. He used the pinch bar to pop the catch. It gave, and the trapdoor ladder unfolded down to the landing of the top floor.

Bobby descended into the eerily quiet house and began his furtive search. He made a cursory examination of all bedrooms. Empty. As was the office. Using the penlight, Bobby looked through the paperwork on Shine's desktop. Most of it appeared to be legitimate accounting work for The Winning Ticket. He had no time to pore over documentary evidence. He was looking for Dorothea.

Bobby made his way to the first floor and got down on his hands and knees, placing his ear to the floorboards to listen for sounds of human life. "Dorothea," he whispered. "Dorothea, can you hear me?"

There was only silence and the crashing of waves on the shore. Far off he could hear the raucous echoes of country music, laughter, and shouting coming from The Central Booking Saloon. He was certain no one could hear him in here, so he moved across the floor on all fours, peeling back throw rugs, searching the floorboards for trapdoors, knocking on the planks with the pinch bar, tapping on the walls, listening for hollow echoes. *Nothing.* The house was as solid as its owner. He stamped his feet across the floors of the living room, dining room, kitchen, hoping Dorothea might hear him and knock back.

He carefully examined the corridor between the stairs to the second floor and the living room wall. He banged on all the tongue-and-groove work along the narrow corridor. Nothing. The empty space under the stairs was a walk-in closet. He tapped on all the plaster walls. No break in the seams, no hollow echo.

He scanned the floor-to-ceiling, wall-to-wall bookcase in the living room. Wiggling the oak moldings, touching books, feeling behind them for secret levers like the ones he'd seen in old Vincent Price movies. Nothing.

Then something odd caught his eye. On one shelf, under the alphabetized section of *E*, he found two shelves of Ralph Waldo Emerson. Some were leather-bound original editions. Some were hardcovers. Some paperbacks. Some in Italian, Spanish, French. He hadn't known John Shine could speak any other languages. John Shine loved Emerson and collected his works the way others collected stamps or coins or baseball cards.

Then Bobby noticed one particular edition of what he was certain was "Self-Reliance." A thin cheap paperback, but Bobby removed it from the shelf because of the odd Cyrillic script on its faded spine. He took the book from the shelf with trembling fingers and opened it to the copyright page. There, in tiny print, he saw where the book had been printed. An icy shiver moved through him when he recognized the word for *Ukraine*. There were handwritten initials on the inside of the cover: DD. It looked like Dorothea's handwriting.

He thought of murdered Tom Larkin's muttering about something concerning the Ukraine. He held the book for a long, anguished moment, imagining a trapped and bewildered Dorothea somewhere in this house. He replaced the book carefully on the shelf.

"Dorothea!" Bobby shouted, standing in the center of the empty, ominous house. "DOR-O-THEA!"

There was no reply. Just squirrels scratching in the attic.

He checked his watch: 9:10 PM. John Shine had said he never stayed in The Winning Ticket past nine, which meant he would already be on his way home. Bobby left the house as he'd entered, careful to erase all traces of his visit.

41
Sunday

Gleason sat in the passenger seat, chewing on the inside of his face. Since Bobby had picked him up at the Chelsea Hotel a half hour earlier, Gleason had been mute, looking hungover and tired. They were heading north on the Sprain Brook Parkway in Westchester County. Gleason gave directions.

"Where're we going?" Bobby asked.

"I'll tell ya when we get there."

"Where's Alana?"

Gleason mopped his face with his open hand, muffling the answer into an unintelligible garble.

"I said, what happened to Alana?" Bobby said, louder.

"The ingrate bitch left me for the fucking dentist!" Gleason shouted.

"Why?" Bobby tried to hide his smile.

"Soon's he took off the temporary veneers and he put on the permanents, she smiled at me like a movie star, batted her eyes, and said, 'Fuck you, Gleason, you revolting piece of shit.' This is the bitch who tells me to watch my fuckin' language! Who drank my champagne, ate my meals in the best restaurants in town, shopped with my money in Blooming-fuckin'-dales! And she calls me a revolting piece of shit!"

"But I thought you were doing a barter with the dentist on the divorce," Bobby said.

"I was," Gleason said. "I used Herbie to track his wife. He did. He stomped down a motel door and took pictures of the wife with the dentist's sister's husband. The two in-laws banging each other like minks in a motel in Sheepshead Bay. Once the dentist got these pictures from me, he figures he doesn't need me anymore, so he starts banging *my* dame."

"Somehow this all seems to fit you like a glove," Bobby said.

"At least I got another client out of it," Gleason said.

"Who?"

"The dentist's sister. I'm using the same photos in her divorce from her husband, who was humpin' the dentist's wife. But somehow in the middle of all this, I got fucked in the heinie, too."

"So where the hell are we going now?" Bobby asked, trying to find a destination amid the murk.

"North," Gleason said. "Drive north. And tell me alls about John up-fuckin'-standin' Shine and this here other bimbsky, what's-her-face, Sandy. And Kate Clementine, who I remember because the case came up as a precedent in an insanity defense I used once."

Bobby gave him the fill on Sandy, John Shine and the blind man, Barnicle and the mystery kid. And reluctantly told him about breaking into John Shine's house.

"You're an asshole, know that?" Gleason said. "First of all, you got caught doing a B and E, your bail is revoked. But second, if Dorothea *is* in there, this crazy fuck could have the place booby-trapped. If you found her, it could have killed you both!"

"It was a chance I had to take," he said.

"Well, I checked your case file," Gleason said. "Cis Tuzio never logged the teeth from the crematorium. So, I'll tell ya what I'm gonna do. As much as I hate that bastard Roth, I want you to let him go to print in two days, saying that I'm gonna make a preemptive motion to quash in advance all further proceedings in the matter of the State of New York versus Robert Emmet on the grounds of suppression of evidence, namely those teeth, lab reports, and witnesses William Franz and Carlos Orosco, on the part of the prosecution in the previous trial. Evidence which would have exonerated you. I am going to charge that Moira Farrell, Tuzio's childhood friend, college roommate, former co-clerk for the presiding judge, Mark White, acted in concert in a conspiracy against you for the murder of Dorothea Dubrow, who we don't even think is dead! We are gong to take depositions from this Carlos Orosco and this here Franz guy about physical evidence they gave to Hanratty and Tuzio at the Brooklyn district attorney's office that was never introduced at trial. We'll leak it all to Roth first. Then I am going to hold a lalapalooza of a press conference in front of the Brooklyn DA's office on Primary Day, demanding that the state attorney general investigate all these allegations. You are going to walk, and I am going to run, all the way to the fucking bank!''

Bobby didn't care what Gleason's motives were. He liked what he was hearing.

"You want Roth to go with *all* of it?" Bobby asked.

"The whole shootin' match," Gleason said, pointing to the exit that was coming up. "Page A-freakin'-one! The *wood!* We're gonna demand that criminal charges be brought against all of them. Lock 'em up and put 'em in *your* old cell! The Pulitzer!" He glared at a road sign. "Get off here, make a left at the first light after the traffic circle, and go about a mile and a half."

Bobby followed the instructions as Gleason nervously drummed his fingers on the dashboard.

"That story will cause a political earthquake from Albany to Staten Island," Gleason said, this time pointing to a pair of white stone columns supporting a pair of wide white gates. A raised wood sign on one column read HUDSON HEALTH MANOR. "In there."

Bobby followed a winding gravel path up to a magnificent Gothic house that sat splendidly on a large knoll, shaded by a weeping willow. "Nutritionist who owns the joint is in deep ca-ca with the IRS," Gleason said. "It's a strictly cash operation. The Feds planted some two-ton agents in here who paid cash that was never declared on the owner's taxes. Me and you, we're gonna keep him out of Leavenworth."

"Another one of your amazing barter deals?" Bobby growled.

"He's already come through with his part of the bargain," Gleason said. "Good thing, too, because I gotta start getting the brief for your motion typed tonight."

"We're coming all the way up here to get a typist?"

Bobby pulled to a stop in front of the house. Standing on the steps was a beautiful Latina vacuum-packed into a size seven red minidress. She wore red high heels and stylish Guess sunglasses, and she beamed when she saw the Jeep pull up. Behind her was a collection of very large, overweight women.

"Izzy, that's not the adorable Venus, is it?" Bobby asked.

"Yeah, but look at that herd of bison behind her," Gleason said. "My Venus looks like their lunch."

Gleason ejected himself from the front seat in one frantic motion, and Venus ran into his arms. The compact lawyer swept the now svelte Venus off her feet and spun her around as she kissed his face, leaving lipstick imprints all over his cheeks. Gleason and Venus kissed passionately in front of the crowd of heavyset women, who broke into applause.

"Bobby, you remember Venus, don't ya?" Gleason said as Bobby looked at a portion of the woman he had met a little over a week before.

"Hello, Venus," Bobby said.

"Pleased to seeing you again, Mr. Bobby," she said. "I am losing the weight and listening to the tapes of the English. I never feel the better in your life."

"Take us home, Jeeves," Gleason said, climbing into the back with Venus, mauling her like a teenager at a drive-in.

42

Gleason again warned Bobby not to jump the gun with John Shine. Everything Sandy had told Bobby about the blind doctor and John Shine could be lies, concocted by Lou Barnicle to throw him off his scent. Gleason told him to proceed with caution or wind up with his bail revoked.

That afternoon, Gleason took depositions from Carlos Orosco and William Franz. Venus typed the motion Gleason would make to the court. Max Roth awaited the reply from his source inside One Police Plaza to his Freedom of Information request to the NYPD on John Shine. As he awaited the file, Roth prepared his exclusive story about the Gleason motion, which would run on Tuesday, Primary Day.

At the same time, Bobby and Patrick used two rented cars to tail two separate teams of Gibraltar Security workers to the cop bars in all five boroughs. Although Tuesday was their usual pickup day, the Gibraltar teams—Zeke and Kuzak in one car, Flynn and Levin in the other—picked up Sunday envelopes from off-duty cops, who were actually lining up as if this were a going-out-of-business fire sale. Patrick and Bobby used camcorders to film the collections.

The Emmet brothers kept in contact with cell phones, using personal coded shorthand, referring to each other as "Charlie" and "Sonny." By late afternoon, all the envelopes wound up back in Gibraltar Security.

On a few occasions during the long day of surveillance, Bobby felt certain he was also being tailed. He made the routine elusive maneuvers, four rights to spot a tail, driving a full 360 around a traffic circle, making U-turns in cul-de-sacs, checking for more tracking bugs on his Jeep. He always came up blank. But he still had the feeling they were being watched. If someone was following him, the tail was very, very good. Certainly no one he'd met in the three-quarters crew was capable of pulling it off. He chalked up the feeling to paranoia.

A few minutes before four o'clock the two brothers sat parked across the street from Gibraltar Security in Bobby's rented Caprice. They watched the Gibraltar teams bringing in the envelopes.

"Sandy is right," Bobby told Patrick. "They are certainly accelerating the operation. Millions in a single day."

"Why the big push?" Patrick asked.

"The primary is Tuesday," Bobby said. "A media blitz. And for a war chest for the general election. I dunno. . . ."

"You think it's also because they know you're onto their game? That you'll expose it all to Max Roth in the *Daily News* or from the witness stand? To get as much as they can while the getting is good?"

"Maybe," Bobby said. "But there's something even more desperate going on."

"And that has to do with the blind doctor, doesn't it?" Patrick asked.

"Yeah," Bobby said. "If Sandy is right, the doctor arrives tomorrow at noon."

43

Minutes before seven PM Bobby met Max Roth in the small park across the street from the United Nations.

Roth had a ream of papers in his hand, and he insisted on walking as he told Bobby what he had learned from the Freedom of Information request to the NYPD on John Shine and from a Lexis legal-history computer search on him.

"First of all," Roth said as they passed an old lady feeding pigeons and a small group of protesters across the street chanted about China's human rights abuses in Tibet, "Shine was never married."

"What about the wife and kid he always talks about?" Bobby asked. "The ones he said drowned in a boating accident."

"I thought you said they disappeared," Roth said.

"Drowned, disappeared, whatever."

"You of all people should know the difference," Roth said. "But more about that in a minute. Let's talk about the year 1991: the year John Shine first applied for a three-quarters pension. . . ."

Bobby stopped in mid-stride, in front of two homeless men who were fighting over the last sip of a forty-ounce bottle of Olde English malt liquor.

"Shine told me he never applied for a three-quarters pension," Bobby said.

"Bullshit," Max Roth said, and continued walking, slapping the papers against his open palm. "He applied three times in the same year. Each time he was turned down. Shine claimed he injured his back wrestling with a crazed crack dealer."

"He told me about that," Bobby said. "That's how he ruined the disks in his back. Said he never put in a claim because that was for crippled heroes who couldn't work."

"Well, he put in his three-quarters papers, and an internal

247

investigation revealed that he messed up his back on a ski trip up to Hunter Mountain," Roth said. "In his Internal Affairs interview, Shine claimed he was sandbagged by a certain captain he didn't get along with."

"His name wasn't Barnicle, was it?"

"The one and only," Roth said.

"Who were the doctors who disapproved him?"

"One was named Dr. Frederick Jones," Roth said.

"No data," Bobby said, shrugging, tapping his right temple.

"He died in a car wreck a couple of months ago," Roth said. "I vaguely remember it making a blip on the wires. But the second doctor who turned John Shine down was one Dr. Benjamin Abrams."

"Okay," Bobby said, recognizing the name from the printout Maggie had made for him on her laptop in Central Park. He looked over at the East River, busy with afternoon boats.

"Dr. Jones was replaced by a guy named Dr. Hector Perez," Roth said.

Bobby also recognized this name from the printout.

"It should be no surprise that John Shine is never with the same woman more than once," Roth said.

"He claims it's because he can never replace the love of his life," Bobby said.

"That might be true," Roth said as they walked toward the glittering glass UN building. "But whether he hurt himself in a ski lodge or in a fight with a crack head, according to his file, John Shine ruined four disks in his back, which also left him sexually impotent. Shine produced three affidavits from different doctors to verify this. Even the city's doctors agreed that part was true. They just said the injury happened off duty, so they turned him down for three-quarters three times."

"The irony here is that he probably did get hurt on the job," Bobby said. "And Barnicle sandbagged him. So what we have here is a good cop who gets denied a legit claim and to get even he decides to concoct one of the biggest pension scams in city history."

"Think of the dramatic dynamics here," Roth said with a whoop of a laugh. "A good cop is hurt on the job busting a mutt, left impotent, then turned down for a legitimate medical pension, and to get even he's *fucking* the whole department for fucking him."

Bobby stopped, looked at Roth, and said, "John could think like that. He is grandiose."

"Plus, he's using Barnicle, who *sandbagged* him, as his bag-man," Roth said with a measure of dark admiration. "This guy big on poetry? Because there is some badassed poetic justice in his madness."

"He loves Emerson," he said.

"Well, that explains it," Roth said, rattling the printed pages. "If all this is even half right, he is definitely one sick *individual.*"

"You said there was a woman in his past," Bobby said.

Roth pointed to an NYPD kiosk box outside the UN, where a uniformed cop stood on duty, a young sentry assigned to look out for crazies who might take potshots at world leaders and diplomats. Then Roth leafed through the paperwork in his hands.

"According to his file," Roth said, "Shine had that duty for a couple of years early in his career."

"Yeah," Bobby said. "He's mentioned it in passing a few times. No secret there."

"What he probably didn't mention was that while assigned here, he had a steamy affair with a diplomat's wife," Roth said.

"It's been known to happen," Bobby said. "I met Connie while assigned to protect her. Patty Hearst married the cop who was assigned to bodyguard her. They say Princess Di even had a fling with her bodyguard. So . . ."

"So, in Shine's case, it caused a mini diplomatic shebang, and FBI and CIA got involved," Roth said. "The diplomat, whose name was Slomowicz, was from the Ukraine. . . ."

Bobby stopped and looked at his friend and swallowed hard.

"Where Dorothea was from," Bobby whispered. "Tom Larkin kept asking me if I was certain she was from the Ukraine. . . ."

"Silly accusations of espionage were exchanged," Roth said. "This was in the seventies when the Iron Curtain was still rust free. But according to this report, which has lots of blacked-out National Security sections, it looks like it was just sex. The diplomat's wife, who was a brilliant linguist with great breeding, claimed she was tired of her husband being a New York nightlife whoremaster. The diplomat was apparently out banging every-thing that moved, and Shine, a poor bored, single young cop, wound up laying a little log on the jilted bride. Probably just a vengeance fuck on the wife's part. Most of the record is sealed because of National Security classification. But it couldn't have been too politically serious, because all Shine lost was a month's pay and he was transferred—with a solemn promise never to attempt any further contact with the woman or he would be fired from NYPD and arrested on federal espionage charges. The diplomat and his wife were recalled back home. In her case, probably to a fucking salt mine. More likely house arrest."

"Shine never mentioned a word about any of that," Bobby said. "And I worked with him for four years."

"I'm not surprised," Roth said. "But that's as close as his file comes to John Shine ever having a woman or any other kind of significant other in his life. He never claimed a wife or kid on his medical insurance, income taxes, or anything else. And in his Lexis file, which is his legal history done by Social Security number and date of birth, there's no record of a marriage. Although it does say that he employed an attorney to get him a visa to visit the Ukraine after the Iron Curtain fell in eighty-nine. He used the same lawyer when he won the lottery, to help him get his liquor license, set up his corporation, close on the Bay Ridge saloon and the Windy Tip beach house. The lawyer was, I'm sure you'd also like to know, none other than Moira Farrell."

"Jesus, the world shrinks by the sick second," Bobby said.

"Now, I remember clear as a bell, because I wrote about this, that Moira Farrell also defended a crew of Bensonhurst wise guys who laundered money by buying lottery tickets from actual winners," Roth said. "A legit guy wins, doesn't want to pay all the taxes, or let his ex-wife find out. So he sells the ticket to a mob guy for seventy-five percent of face value, in *cash*. This way he doesn't have to pay forty percent in income taxes. He's up fifteen percent and remains anonymous. Bill collectors, the IRS, or his ex-wife never learn about him winning. No record of it. The wise guy, on the other hand, cashes it at the official lottery office and makes some of his dirty drug or gambling money clean and legal. Capisce?"

"You think Shine did that to launder some of the dirty three-quarters pension money?" Bobby asked.

"Yes," Roth said. "With Moira Farrell's client's help. Shine buys a legit winning lottery ticket with the dirty three-quarters cash, sets himself up legitimately with a saloon, beach house, Mercedes. These people are better connected than Ma Bell."

They walked across First Avenue and up Forty-first Street,

where Roth had his car parked in the press parking zone alongside the old *Daily News* building.

"What else did you learn about this Kate Clementine case?" Bobby asked.

"I have a call in to the architect who designed that house of horror," he said. "I want to see if she's designed anything else like it."

"I have to update Gleason," Bobby said, "and at least one cop I know who I can trust."

"Don't tell me it's that Forrest Morgan asshole."

"He's not a big fan of yours either," Bobby said.

"I don't like any of your friends," Roth said. "They all have a habit of coming up dirty."

"Dirt is your life," Bobby said.

"This is true," Roth said. "Anything else?"

"Do you have a connection at the State Department?" Bobby asked.

"Yeah," Roth said. "Through our Washington bureau. Why?"

"At my trial they said they had no record of a Dorothea Dubrow entering the country," Bobby said. "Let's see if she entered under another name."

44

Monday

In the morning, Bobby borrowed a twenty-five-foot cabin cruiser from Doug the dockmaster. He knew that Shine or Barnicle could now recognize *The Fifth Amendment*. He steered the cabin cruiser out to the calm waters off Windy Tip. At 10:28 AM he dropped anchor. He used the zoom lens on the camcorder to get a good look at John Shine's house. He saw that Shine's Mercedes and his red Land Rover were both in the driveway alongside the house.

Bobby called Patrick on the cell phone. Patrick was parked in a rented Plymouth at a rest area on the side of the road outside the security gates of Windy Tip.

"Stand by, Sonny," Bobby said, using the Charlie Chan code they'd worked out. "He's home."

"I'm waiting, Charlie," Patrick said.

Bobby kept watching Shine's house until he stepped out at 11:41 AM. Bobby began taping him as Shine eased into his Mercedes. Then he phoned Patrick and told him Shine was on his way out of Windy Tip.

As Bobby waited for an update from Patrick, he used his viewfinder to pan the beach. He saw that The Central Booking Saloon was opening for business, several daytime drinking desperados piling in for eye-openers.

Patrick phoned again, saying he'd picked up John Shine's tail and was following him into Brooklyn.

Then Bobby focused his camcorder on Barnicle's spectacular beach house and spotted Sandy Fraser stepping out onto her balcony with her son, Donald. She wore a skimpy yellow bikini, which made her deeply tanned and oiled body gleam in contrast in the sun. He studied the little boy's face again, trying to match a father's older face to it with some genetic imagination. It still eluded him.

The cell phone rang again. "Shine just picked up a blind guy from a bus stop on Avenue U and Flatbush," Patrick said. "Across the street from the Kings Plaza shopping mall."

Bobby swung the camcorder back toward John Shine's house. Twelve minutes later, at 12:01 PM, Bobby hit the record button when he saw Shine's Mercedes swing into the blacktop carport alongside the red Land Rover. Bobby watched Shine walk around to the passenger side of the car, open the door, and help out a man wearing a hat and big dark glasses. He led him awkwardly into the house. The blind man carried a small black doctor's bag, just as Sandy Fraser had said.

He felt suddenly guilty about doubting Sandy and swung the camcorder back toward her on the sundeck. She was now engaged in an animated argument with Lou Barnicle. Sandy was trying desperately to talk into a cordless phone. Barnicle wrestled the phone from her hand, poking her, then pointing to the wailing baby, waving a finger, shouting. Bobby saw young Donald crying and Sandy picking him up and shouting right back in

Barnicle's face. Now the housekeeper came out on the porch, and she and Sandy had a small tug-of-war over the child. With Barnicle's help, the housekeeper won. Young Donald seemed hysterical as he was detached from his frantic mother.

Barnicle forced all of them into the big house. Once inside he slid the heavy glass door shut and pulled a curtain across it. Bobby felt hollow and a little nauseous. The woman who had warned him of his own danger was now in some kind of trouble. These people he'd been spying on the last few days all seemed suddenly desperate.

A police launch chugged past. A cop stood near the edge of the boat eyeing the surf through binoculars. The cop politely nodded to Bobby. He nodded back. Another cop stood on deck, his back to him. The police boat kept going.

Bobby thought of pouncing on Shine's house right then. Swimming ashore, kicking open the door, and seeing what the hell the doctor was doing. But Gleason's warning haunted him. Forget that he would be illegally entering the house, which could get him arrested and his bail revoked. It was the other fear that Gleason had put in him. The fear that if Dorothea was in there, being held prisoner, Shine might kill her. Kill them all with a booby trap.

If Sandy was right and Shine was bringing Dorothea a doctor for regular checkups, it meant she was being cared for in some sick, demented way. There was no immediate need to act.

Bobby knew he had to do it right. Legally if he could. With backup. He needed to get the doctor alone. Pick his brain, crack him like a coconut.

Sixteen minutes later Bobby filmed John Shine as he led the same blind man out of his house and into the Mercedes. Bobby phoned Patrick, and a few minutes later his brother called back to say that he had picked up Shine's tail again and was following. Bobby fired the motor of the cabin cruiser. "I'm gonna cruise over to the marina behind Kings Plaza, near where the blind man was picked up," Bobby said. "I'll meet you over there. I want to find out who this doctor is."

Patrick said, "They're heading down Flatbush Avenue in that direction now."

The sick feeling in Bobby's gut returned. He was beginning to think Sandy was absolutely right about Shine having Dorothea stashed in that beach house. But why? Was she in on this monstrous scheme? Faking her own death to get rid of him and make off with a bundle? Or did Shine have some sick obsession with her, the way Kate Clementine's uncle had, all those terrible years ago?

He would need to get into that house, one way or the other.

As he neared the back of the giant shopping mall located on a busy marina in southern Brooklyn, he also worried about Sandy and her child, alone with Barnicle. *I should call the cops,* he thought. Except they *were* the cops. In this part of Brooklyn, Barnicle was beyond the law.

"He's dropping him at the same bus stop," Patrick said on the cell phone as Bobby pulled into an empty slip at the marina behind Kings Plaza and tied up, which would cause a ruckus if the slip's owner came back any time soon.

"Shine left him sitting there on the bench," Patrick said as Bobby carried the cell phone with him up onto the dock, making his way toward the stairs to the street, passing the boat people, who were a species unto themselves, talking about winds and currents and marina taxes that would never affect the ordinary citizen too poor to own a boat.

"Bobby, he's taking off those goddamn glasses now," Patrick said with alarm, as Bobby climbed the last steps onto Flatbush Avenue. He spotted Patrick's tan Plymouth parked across the wide six-lane avenue, about seventy-five yards from the man with the small black doctor's bag. The man stood and began to jaywalk across the street toward the parking lot of Kings Plaza Shopping Center. No longer blind. Dodging traffic.

Patrick got out of the Plymouth as the man quickly passed Bobby, who turned his head, as if looking for a bus that would never come. But Bobby had glimpsed the man's face. It looked an awful lot like one of the faces in the pictures accompanying the on-line *Civil Service Gazette* clipping that Maggie had downloaded from her portable laptop in Central Park. *Abrams,* Bobby thought. *Dr. Benjamin Abrams.* One of the two doctors who had turned Shine down for his three-quarters pension in 1991.

Patrick joined his brother as they entered the parking lot. An armed security guard on a scooter passed them, winding through the aisles of parked cars, searching for thieves, muggers, and car-jackers.

The man with the doctor's bag walked up a wide traffic ramp, and Bobby and Patrick followed at a distance of about fifty feet.

"Let's grab this guy and squeeze some information out of his neck," Patrick said.

"Love to," Bobby said. "But if I'm right, his name is Abrams. Dr. Benjamin Abrams, of the police medical board."

"Fuck 'im," Patrick said. "Let's put the bull on him. . . ."

"He's a deputy inspector in NYPD," Bobby said. "You can get fired. I got nothing to lose. Go wait in the car."

"Let me do this with you. . . ."

"Wait in the car," Bobby said with big-brother finality.

Bobby followed the man with the doctor's bag into the dark, cavernous indoor parking lot and up a ramp to the second level. His footfalls echoed, and the man turned once. Bobby turned his back, jangled his keys, and pretended to be searching for his own car. He saw the man unlock the driver's door of a BMW and toss the bag into the front seat before climbing in. Bobby approached silently.

"Dr. Abrams?" Bobby said.

The man turned, saw Bobby standing there in the half-gloom, and said, "Yes, who's that?"

"Where is she, Abrams?" Bobby asked. "Where's the woman? Where is Dorothea Dubrow?"

The startled doctor quickly bent into the car, popped the glove compartment latch, and tried to grab his .38 caliber service revolver. Before he could reach the gun, Bobby yanked Abrams out of the car and slammed him against the back door. The wind blew out of the middle-aged doctor.

"I have no idea what you're talking about," said Dr. Benjamin Abrams. "I know who you are. You're Bobby Emmet. Boy, oh, boy, are you in trouble now, fella. . . ."

"It's all here on tape," Bobby said, waving the tape he had removed from the camcorder.

Abrams looked at the tape with horror, his lips trembling, and said. "What do *you* want?"

"Dorothea Dubrow," Bobby said.

"I can't take any more of this. . . ." He closed his eyes as his face reddened and sweat formed on his brow.

"It's all here," Bobby said, waving the tape.

"Please, not another tape . . ."

"I have John Shine picking you up on tape . . ."

"Who the hell is John Shine?" Dr. Abrams seemed to be genuinely baffled by the name.

"The guy who takes you blindfolded into the beach house," Bobby said.

"I . . . have . . . no . . . idea . . ."

"Forget the name. Where does he have her stashed, Doc? She in on it?"

"You have nothing on that tape that shows I've done anything wrong . . ."

"Come on, Doc, how many phony three-quarters pensions do you approve in a month?" Bobby asked.

Abrams stared at him in silence.

"What's your take?" Bobby said, taking the doctor's shirtfront in his hand. "Or do they have something on you? On some other tape, maybe?"

"You are making an extremely serious accusation," Dr. Abrams said now, trying to free himself from Bobby's grip.

The security guard on the scooter puttered up the ramp. Abrams looked at him. Bobby loosened his grip on the doctor.

"Everything all right there, folks?" the security guard asked as he stopped on the ramp.

"I can have you arrested right now," Abrams said, suddenly filled with bravado. "I'll have you know, I am a deputy inspector of the New York City Police Department!"

Dr. Abrams quickly climbed in his car, locked the doors.

"When you get to the joint, Doc, I wouldn't advise you to spread that news around," Bobby said.

45

From the fly deck of the cabin cruiser, Bobby watched the yellow crime-scene tape rising and falling in the river wind. It cordoned off his boat slip, making *The Fifth Amendment* look like a diseased ship in quarantine. It was three PM, and the sun blazed on the rollicking Hudson flowing past the Seventy-ninth Street Boat Basin. Bobby walked along the narrow, wet walkway, and ahead of him he saw uniformed cops and detectives in suits and ties and a forensic crew with cameras and evidence kits. His heart beat with fear. Only a corpse would bring out this group.

Thank God I don't have the gun on me, he thought. *They'd nail me with a gun charge for shit sure.* When he'd seen all the activity from the fly deck of Doug's boat, he hid the .38 on board.

Now he hurried down to *The Fifth Amendment.* Hanratty approached him first, walking with a cocky swagger.

"This time, shitmouth, we got us a body," Hanratty said. "And you're going back where you belong. Into a cage."

Hanratty grabbed him by the arm, and Bobby yanked himself free and hurried past him toward the boat. Cis Tuzio stood with her hands in her baggy pants pockets, her thin lips gathered together like a Boy Scout knot, her cheeks hollow with authority. She untied her lips to say, "No flamboyant lawyer or loud-mouthed newspaper columnist is going to get you out of this one, Mr. Emmet."

"If you're charging me with something, maybe you better tell me what it is," Bobby said.

She motioned to a uniformed cop who nudged Bobby up the gangplank. A bevy of cops walked in front of and behind him. He was led across the deck and down into the cabin, into the master stateroom. The room was speckled with blood. Bobby felt his guts tighten and his mouth go dry as a forensic photographer popped a picture and stepped aside.

"Ah, Jesus . . . no. . . ."

Sandy Fraser lay across Bobby's bed. Nude except for white sandals. Her throat was slashed in a vicious semicircle, so deep Bobby could see the dull white of the spinal cord. Her eyes half open in death, as was her right hand. In that hand were three shiny quarters. Bobby stared at the quarters. They were all dated 1991.

"Ah, Jesus, no. . . ." Bobby whispered again.

"Jesus, no," Tuzio said. "Bobby Emmet, *si.* You're under arrest, fella."

Hanratty twisted Bobby's left hand behind his back and snapped a handcuff over his thick muscular wrist. Bobby heard the awful ratcheting sound of the cuffs tightening, felt the pincers biting his flesh. He could almost hear the banging of the steel.

"This is so obvious a frame that it could hang in the Louvre," Bobby said, the words fuzzy from his dry mouth.

"Robert Emmet, you are under arrest for the murder of one Sandra Fraser," Hanratty said as he reached for Bobby's other wrist to manacle. "You have the right—"

"He has the right to be let go right now," came a voice from the entrance of the cabin. Tuzio, Hanratty, and the others turned to see Forrest Morgan standing in the doorframe, blocking most of the afternoon light. His tired black face was furrowed with contempt. He pinned his badge to his rumpled suit jacket and stepped past Bobby and Hanratty to take a look at the corpse. It was being delicately examined by a deputy medical examiner. Bobby stared down at Sandy and felt himself swoon from the smell of feces, stale whiskey, and close air in the tight room. *This poor woman reached out to me for help,* he thought. *She tried to help me. Help find Dorothea. Tried to protect that little kid Donald. And they slaughtered her. To shut me up. She died because of me. . . .*

Morgan tapped the coroner on the shoulder and said, "How long she been dead?"

"Judging by the temperature of the liver I took with the incision thermometer, I'd say one to three hours," the deputy medical examiner said.

Morgan turned to Tuzio and said, "Mr. Emmet has been under constant Internal Affairs Bureau surveillance for the past thirty-six hours," he said. "On land and sea. And he certainly hasn't been here with a woman in all that time. He's been out tailing other people. Law enforcement people. Some of them are in this room. . . ."

He glared at Hanratty, who attempted a cocky sneer.

"You know who you are, and it'll all be in my report," Morgan said, looking back at Tuzio with a slow shake of his head. "In the meantime, ladies and germs, I am Robert Emmet's alibi, like it or not."

Hanratty's sneer had turned to a look of dread. He unlocked the handcuff from Bobby's left wrist. Bobby turned to Hanratty.

"I think you better get a lawyer," he said to the red-haired cop.

Then Bobby looked at Tuzio. "You have a lot of explaining to do, too, Cis," Bobby said. "Maybe you should check this dead woman's *teeth.*"

Tuzio looked Bobby in the eye, her lips clamping into a wrinkled bud that never managed to blossom. "I'm not finished with you yet," she said, and turned and stormed out of the cabin, followed by a nervous Hanratty. Bobby glanced at Morgan. The black cop shook his head.

"Bag her up," said the assistant coroner, and the morgue crew in jumpsuits walked to Sandy Fraser. Bobby watched them roll the nude and savaged woman onto a plastic sheet and roll her again like a human sausage. The same woman who'd come to him for help and human affection only a few nights before. Who'd slept on that bed. The woman who'd told him about John Shine and the blind doctor and Barnicle and the accelerated three-quarters operation. The woman too terrified to name the father of her now motherless child.

He felt a generalized lousiness spread through him, his skin suddenly clammy and itchy, his mouth pasty and his throat parched, a wave of nausea building in him, a malaise not unlike the one he'd felt on the morning he was arrested for the murder of Dorothea.

"This is going to be a closed crime scene at least until morning," said one of the criminalists, an Asian man with a name tag that said Woo. "You'll have to find another place to stay tonight, guy."

Bobby did not object. He wouldn't be able to sleep there again anytime soon. He turned to Forrest Morgan as he heard the zipper being crackled closed on the body bag behind him.

"I could have prevented this," Bobby said.

"I don't think so," Morgan said. "But you might be able to prevent another one if you tell me what the fuck is going on, man."

They went up on deck, and Bobby inhaled the fresh air, watched the river flow past. It was too beautiful a day to die, Bobby thought. Especially like that.

"She had a beautiful kid," Bobby said to Morgan.

"I know," Forrest Morgan said. "I saw her and the kid with you in Coney Island. . . ."

"Sandy has an aunt in Jersey," Bobby said. "See if you can track her down. Please. That kid was at Lou Barnicle's house, where Sandy lived. He's an important little boy to some very dangerous people, and somehow he's tied to all this. I wish I knew more than that right now, but I don't. But Sandy said the kid isn't really Banicle's. He shouldn't wind up conveniently lost in the foster system or a body bag. Can you find the kid and then this aunt?"

"No problem," Forrest Morgan said. "But I have to go through Child Welfare for that. That agency is a crossword puzzle of jurisdictions. But you know I'm on Barnicle's tail anyway. I got a good idea what's going on from following you around. I'm just waiting for the last shoe to drop."

They walked down the gangplank, passing Tuzio and Hanratty, who whispered together on the dock.

"Now, why don't you tell me *everything*," Morgan said.

"*Everything* will be in Max Roth's column in the morning," Bobby said, loud enough for Tuzio and Hanratty to hear him.

46

The whole operation was coming unraveled. In the last two hours Lou Barnicle had received one phone call after another.

The murder of Sandy Fraser was bungled, he thought. *What a pity. Great piece of ass wasted. Bobby Emmet has an alibi. The* Daily News *guy, Max Roth, has a big story ready for the morning paper.*

A real fucking mess. Those assholes of mine fucked it up again.

Now I have to figure out what to tell The Fixer when he calls. He'll be pissed off that it was bungled. Again. He'll call me an incompetent, a cretin. Wait'll I get my hands on this cocksucker when this is all over. . . .

Meanwhile, I'll assure this pompous prick that I did a masterful job of damage control with the homicide cops; told them that I was at work all morning, had lunch with my parish priest, who wouldn't forget the five grand I palmed him, at the estimated time of Sandy's murder. That because I have a funeral to arrange, the kid, Donald, is with the nanny. That the cops were apologetic, even called me Captain. Said they'd be in touch with any new developments.

But my dream's in jeopardy, he thought. *If I can hold this operation together, I'll be running the State Division of Police, in charge of all the state troopers. With a finger in the pie of every local police force in the State of New York. A fucking army of cops and untold millions in pension funds.*

At 4:09 PM the phone rang.

"The business with the woman was badly handled," The Fixer said. "Get the child somewhere safe. This thing is coming to a head."

"The Max Roth story scheduled for the morning paper worries me," Barnicle said.

"Everything will turn out all right so long as we have the kid," The Fixer said.

"I still get my appointment?" Barnicle asked. "And my share of the money?"

"Of course," said the man, whose steady, calm voice was reassuring on the other end of the line. "Just be sure he's somewhere safe, and you will get everything that is coming to you."

"The kid is already safe," Barnicle said.

"Where is he?"

"At the nanny's house in Rockaway," Barnicle said, and gave The Fixer the address.

"Good."

"When do I get to finally meet you?"

"In two hours," said the man. "Bring the last of the money to the transfer point. The other main players have been contacted and will be there."

"I'll be there. With the money."

Barnicle smiled. He was certain that despite these minor setbacks caused by Bobby Emmet, everything would work out as planned. The campaign would get what money it needed, and the leftover cash would be split evenly among the fund-raisers. Then the political appointments would come after the November election. *Then I'll fix this fucking Fixer,* Barnicle thought. *With pennies on his eyes . . .*

"One more thing," The Fixer said. "Use your best men. Emmet must cease to be a problem ASAP."

47

At 4:35 PM Bobby accompanied Forrest Morgan into the police medical board to see Dr. Benjamin Abrams.

On the way there, Bobby had filled Morgan in on all he knew about the doctor's involvement in the pension scheme.

Morgan said that while he had had Bobby and Patrick under

surveillance, he had witnessed the blind-doctor routine and traced Abrams's and John Shine's license plate numbers.

"Like I told Tuzio," Morgan said, "I had you under surveillance the whole time. I was on the police boat that cruised past you this morning when you were spying on Shine's house. So, what's up?"

"I'm not really sure," Bobby said, unwilling to give him more than he already knew, yet. He didn't want Morgan charging into that house cowboy style for a cheap promotion and risking Dorothea's life.

"You ain't being straight with me, Bobby," Morgan said.

"I really don't know for sure," Bobby said. "Maybe Abrams can tell us what we need to know. He's the answer."

They stepped off the elevator and approached the reception desk. Morgan flashed his gold IAB badge.

"Would you tell Dr. Abrams I'd like to see him?" Morgan said. "I'd also like to see all the files for all three-quarter medical pensions in the last couple of years. Just the approvals, ma'am."

The receptionist swallowed a dry knot, got up from her desk, and walked down the corridor, then knocked and entered the office door bearing Abrams's stenciled name.

Bobby looked at Morgan, who stood rocking on his heels.

"How many years you got left before you put in your papers, Forrest?" Bobby asked.

"The duration, baby," Morgan said. "Where the fuck am I gonna go?"

Bobby looked uneasy when he heard Abrams's office door being frantically locked as the woman told them, "The doctor said he would be out in a min . . ."

Bobby barreled past her, Morgan right after him. Dr. Benjamin Abrams ended his life before the receptionist could end her sentence. The gunshot was low and muffed but loud enough to send Morgan and Bobby crashing through the locked door, the doctor's stenciled name shattering with the glass.

Dr. Abrams was bent forward in his swivel chair, his forehead on the desktop, the barrel of his service revolver buried in his mouth, both thumbs looped through the trigger guard, smoke leaking out of his open mouth and trailing through the exit wound at the base of his skull. The ceiling was splotched with blood and brain matter.

Bobby moved closer and saw the hastily written note on the desktop, scrawled on NYPD stationery that was sprinkled with blood: "Dearest Rebecca, I love you. I'm sorry. Love, Dad."

The Montblanc pen lay beside the note. There had been no time to write more. There was nothing else to say. On the TV Bobby saw a lurid videotape playing. It showed Dr. Benjamin Abrams in a blood-soaked bed with a naked woman. Her throat had been cut—just like Sandy's, Bobby thought.

Bobby looked from the TV and stared at Abrams and felt another wave of guilt crash through him.

"Je-sus Christ, we should have gotten his gun first," Bobby said.

"Corrupt cops always have a second one," Morgan said, watching the videotape as a horrified Abrams got out of bed and began dressing. "For their last meal."

"For Chrissakes, Morgan, he was a *doctor,*" Bobby said angrily. Bobby watched the video and noticed a convention lapel name tag pinned to the doctor's suit jacket: DR. BENJAMIN ABRAMS, American Association of Police Physicians, Boston Sheraton.

"He was *dirty,*" Morgan said. "He died like he lived."

Bobby took a step closer to the TV screen as something odd caught his eye. He now noticed that in the dead woman's hand there were some coins. Quarters. Three of them.

"The doc here was obviously being blackmailed," said Morgan. ". . . Something you see there that I don't?"

Bobby shook his head, said nothing. He turned away from the TV and the dead doctor. Standing silently in the doorway of the office was an astonished Dr. Hector Perez. Morgan saw Perez and walked to him.

"Doctor . . . Inspector, . . . at some point I'm going to need to speak to you and the other doctor on the medical board, too," Morgan said, pulling a business card from his vest pocket and handing it to Perez. "All the records here are going to be examined. Please check your schedule for tomorrow and see what time is convenient for you, sir."

Perez looked at the card and then at Morgan, blinked, nodded, said nothing.

Uniformed cops now arrived from the lobby of the building. Ms. Burns was hyperventilating in the outer office. Forrest Morgan told one of the uniformed cops to call the morgue and a forensic unit. Morgan picked up a phone to call his own office and turned his back to Bobby.

Bobby knew Morgan would be tied up there for hours with the Abrams suicide. Without saying good-bye, Bobby walked for the exit in the confusion. Before he left, he made eye contact with Dr. Hector Perez. The doctor looked like a condemned man staring at the gallows.

On the Queensboro Bridge back to Manhattan, Bobby called Gleason and told him about Sandy and Abrams and what he had seen at John Shine's house. Gleason told him to meet him at the basement office in the Empire State Building at 8:30 PM. He made Bobby promise not to make any more moves until they met. Then Bobby received a call from Max Roth, who told him to pick him up outside the main library at Forty-second Street and Fifth Avenue. He said he had tracked down some of the information Bobby had asked him to find out. He could show him what he learned on the way to the *Daily News*.

Then Bobby called Patrick.

"Remember last week, the day I got out of jail, they found a dead hooker in a hotel in Manhattan?" Bobby said.

"Yeah, the Hotel St. Claire," Patrick said.

"She had three quarters in her hand . . ."

"Christ, I never put that together with this. . . ."

"There was a convention of police physicians going on in that hotel that night," Bobby said. "I want you to check the guest list."

"Who we looking for?" Patrick asked.

"A doctor named Hector Perez," Bobby said. "Deputy inspector, NYPD."

Dr. Hector Perez had received a phone call at the office just a half hour after Dr. Abrams took his own life. Bad news traveled that fast. The report was obviously picked up on the police radio band. Perez was still damp with fear when he'd answered the phone. The blackmailer on the other end told him that he needed him that night to do a final piece of business for him. It would be the last thing he would ever ask of him.

Perez had refused. He had told the blackmailer that he could no longer do what he asked, that IAB was still there, that they were wise to the three-quarters scheme, and hung up on him.

When he left the building to drive home to Brooklyn, a shaken Dr. Perez climbed into his Lexus. On the passenger's seat was the pillowcase from the Hotel St. Claire, filled with bloody sheets. Perez screamed when he looked into the pillowcase. Also on the seat was a pair of blindfold glasses, identical to the ones Dr. Abrams had worn. The car phone rang. Dr. Perez was afraid to answer. After three rings he snapped it up.

"I still have the razor," the blackmailer said. "And the video-tape. Don't force me to give them to the police. Don't do that to your wife and your beautiful unborn baby."

"What the hell more do you want from me?" Perez screamed into the phone as he sat on the street in his car.

"I need you to wait on a bus stop on Flatbush Avenue and Avenue U tonight at midnight," the calm voice said. "Wear the glasses and bring your doctor's bag to give someone a checkup. She's running a fever, and I want to be sure she's ready for travel."

"That's it?"

"That's it."

"Then we're finished?"

"I'll give you the razor and the original videotape," the black-mailer said. "We'll be finished."

"I'll be there," Perez said.

48

At 7:05 PM Moira Farrell popped the cork from a chilled bottle of Roederer Cristal and filled five gleaming fluted glasses. She had gathered together the main players involved in the three-quarters cash operation of the Stone for Governor Campaign in her plush Court Street office.

She handed a glass each to Cis Tuzio and Hanratty, who sat on one green suede couch opposite Barnicle on an identical couch. Moira Farrell handed a third glass to Barnicle and picked one up for herself.

She placed the fifth glass on the end of the large coffee table. Also on the table sat two very large unzipped duffel bags with dangling shoulder straps. Each bag was stuffed with five million dollars in neat bundles of one-hundred-dollar bills. The result of two hundred fraudulent three-quarters medical pensions, at fifty thousand dollars per. The money was to be used as a slush fund in the general election for the Stone for Governor Campaign.

"So who is he?" Barnicle asked Moira Farrell as he pointed at the fifth glass of champagne.

"He's on his way up on the service elevator," Moira Farrell said.

"I want him to look me in the eye and tell me that I will be the new state chairman of police," Barnicle said.

"I'm looking forward to meeting him, too," said Tuzio. "I want an assurance that this meatball charge of suppression of evidence in the Emmet trial won't stand in the way of my state supreme court judgeship. And Hanratty here goes where I go, of course. And Sol Diamond can get his seat on the court of appeals."

"Of course," said Moira Farrell as she heard sounds coming from an inner office behind her. "Well, then, I think it's time you all finally met the man who made all this happen."

Moira walked across the opulent office and opened a large teak door, and John Shine stepped into the room, wearing faded dungarees, a pair of Top-Siders, a Yankees hat, and a plain zippered jacket.

"This some kind of fucking bad joke?" Lou Barnicle snapped, staring at Moira Farrell. "I used to boss this asshole around for cheap laughs. If he's Mr. Big, I'm the goddamn pope."

"Who *is* he?" asked Cis Tuzio, totally baffled, looking from Barnicle to Moira Farrell to Hanratty.

"He came to me as a client and presented this ingenious scenario," Moira Farrell said.

"His name is John Shine," said Barnicle. "A weirdo lone wolf who quotes dead poets and runs a saloon in Bay Ridge. He's a busted-down cop, retired."

"Sandbagged is the word, Lou," John Shine said. "Not retired."

Barnicle squirmed in his seat. "Something's wrong here, Moira."

"Sit down, Moira," John said. "Let's get the finishing touches over with as quickly as possible."

Moira took a seat on the suede couch next to a perplexed Barnicle.

"Is everything on track?" Cis Tuzio asked. "With the campaign? The appointments? This Bobby Emmet is trouble."

"There's supposed to be a big story in tomorrow's *Daily News,*" Barnicle said.

"Well," Shine said, "there is a problem with this Bobby Emmet. . . ."

"He was your fuckin' buddy boy on the job," Barnicle said. "I've seen you with him, still pallin' around with him. Just the other day down Windy—"

"Yes," Shine said. "That's why I put you in charge of disposing of him. On a personal level, I simply like him too much to do it myself. But you blew it, Lou, repeatedly. And you, Miss Tuzio, you left a trail that only Bobby Emmet could trace. But he did. Right to me! Which makes sense, since I really can't rely on anyone but myself. It always comes down to self-reliance, doesn't it? Even you, Moira, as sweet and brilliant and beautiful as you are, you were exceedingly sloppy with one very tenacious cop."

"I was told to make sure he was convicted," Moira said. "He was. It's not my fault this Gleason freak came along . . ."

"Now, wait a minute," Tuzio said. "What does all this rambling mean? Tomorrow is the primary. Is everything going to work out? Are we on track, on schedule? What's it all mean?"

"It means I presented a foolproof schematic for success, and you fools have consistently blown it," Shine said. "As Mr. Emerson once said, 'A foolish consistency is the hobgoblin of little minds, adored by little statesmen and philosophers and divines. With consistency a great soul has simply nothing to do.' I'm a great soul. You're all lost souls. I have something I must do."

Shine smiled, grimaced, raised his flute of champagne.

"Fuck is he talking about?" Barnicle demanded of Moira Farrell. She just shook her head, baffled, concerned.

"But it will all turn out fine in the end," Shine said with a smile. "To the new governor."

He raised his glass in a toast.

The others, too confused to do otherwise, awkwardly raised their glasses to sip. As they did, Shine placed his glass on the coffee table and quickly removed two silver pistols, one from each jacket pocket, each equipped with a silencer. He shot Barnicle first, through the right eye, with the gun in his left hand. The second bullet pierced Moira Farrell in the center of her chest. He turned his head quickly, wincing with back pain, aimed the right-handed pistol and shot Cis Tuzio in her open mouth as she attempted to scream. Shine caught an astonished Hanratty in the heart.

With gunsmoke wafting in the air, the four corpses sagged in bewildered final poses on the expensive couches, champagne glasses softly trickling bubbly over their lifeless bodies. Shine took out a hankie and wiped his prints from both guns and pulled on a pair of soft leather driving gloves. He walked to Barnicle and placed the left-hand pistol in his right hand. He placed the second pistol in Hanratty's hand.

He took five stacks of cash from the many bundles in the bags and cracked one of them open, scattering scores of hundred-dollar bills between the dead bodies to make it look as though these four had quarreled over money. He dropped the other four bundles on the coffee table. The only object he had touched in the room was the champagne glass. He lifted the glass and washed down a painkiller with the last of the champagne. He put the glass in his jacket pocket, zippered both big bags, and placed a shoulder strap over each shoulder. Shine knew from experience that a million dollars in one-hundred-dollar bills weighed exactly twenty-two pounds. That would mean that each five-million-dollar bag would weigh one hundred and ten pounds. The unwieldy weight of the two hundred and twenty pounds of money was murder on his bad back.

He took one last look and then was quickly gone.

49

After Bobby picked him up outside the library, Max Roth said, "The architect, the one who built the house where the wacko stashed Kate Clementine, was a woman name of Barbara Lacy. It was in the old clips."

"Is she the missing architect poor Larkin was talking about?" Bobby asked, quickly changing to the center fire lane to avoid the buses in the right lane. The dashboard clock said it was 7:25 PM.

"Yes, I think she's the same one," Roth said, pulling some newspaper clips and copies of microfilmed documents from a big *Daily News* manila envelope. "Her family finally called me back. This woman went missing about nineteen months ago. . . ."

"About the same time as the corpse showed up in the crematorium," Bobby said, swerving to avoid a cabbie. Roth braced himself, looked at Bobby's animated face, and flicked through his notebook and old newspaper clippings.

"It was a two-day story buried in the middle of the paper," Roth said. "Buried because you and that pile of ashes in the cemetery were scattered all over the first five pages."

"I don't need to be reminded," Bobby said.

"I called the city desk a few minutes ago, and they said the story about the dead woman on Gleason's boat is moving on the police wires," Roth said. "But it says you have an alibi this time."

"I don't have an excuse for letting it happen," Bobby said, making a squealing right-hand turn though a light that switched from yellow to red at Thirty-fourth Street. He drilled the Jeep west toward the *Daily News* building. "I can't let it happen to Dorothea."

Max Roth cleared his throat, rustled the newspaper clippings, and read from his notebook as they approached the crisscrossing intersection of Herald Square, where traffic was always snarled and the shoppers from Macy's clogged the streets.

"Anyway, seventeen years ago, back at the time of the Kate Clementine case, this Barbara Lacy told reporters that she built the 'house of horror' to specifications for the mad uncle, who said he was afraid of a nuclear attack," Roth said. "He claimed he wanted an underground bunker that would keep out radiation and shield him from the atomic explosion. She thought he was a crackpot, but she was a young kid out of Pratt Institute, and she needed the work. So she built it."

"And she disappeared nineteen months ago," Bobby said, screeching to a stop at Broadway. "What did you learn about her?"

"She was a heavy smoker," Roth said. "She had a brownstone in Brooklyn Heights. And yes, she was born and raised and still lived in New York. And probably drank the fluoridated water regularly."

"Like the woman whose teeth were found in the crematorium," Bobby said, staring at Roth. "Jesus, the poor woman . . ."

Horns honked from behind him the nanosecond that the light turned green. Bobby floored the pedal and zoomed through the intersection, dividing a crowd of angry shoppers.

"Family said it was the cigarettes that gave Lacy her first heart attack at the age of thirty-nine," Roth said, bracing his foot against the dashboard for leverage as Bobby swerved around a traffic cop. "They installed the pacemaker in NYU Medical Center. All these months the family figured she had a heart attack somewhere and was considered a homeless Jane Doe and was buried in some potter's field grave . . . which is where we'll wind up if you don't slow the fuck down!"

"Ah, Je-sus, Max, it is her," Bobby said, forcing an oncoming cabdriver to skid to a halt in the middle of the intersection as Bobby made an illegal left onto Seventh Avenue. "They killed this poor woman, cremated her, and made it look like Dorothea . . ."

"I naturally asked the family what the last architectural work she did was," Roth said, clutching the overhead handgrip as Bobby made a shrieking right onto Thirty-third Street. "This took them a while to find, but they were more than eager to help because they do want a fresh story in the paper. I didn't have

271

the heart to tell them she's in an urn with Dorothea Dubrow's name on it in the Kings County evidence room.''

"So what did she design?'' Bobby asked, eagerly, passing the delivery trucks outside the General Post Office on Thirty-third Street just west of Eighth Avenue.

"Well, she redesigned a SoHo loft,'' Roth said. "She rehabbed a Brooklyn Heights condo . . .''

Bobby rattled off an address Maggie had given to him and asked if it was the same one where Lacy did the work.

"How'd you know?'' Roth asked.

"It's the address where Tuzio and Farrell live,'' Bobby said, coming to a stop at a light on Ninth Avenue.

"Jesus Christ,'' Roth said. "And it gets better. Then Lacy over-hauled a restaurant in Bay Ridge . . .''

"The Winning Ticket,'' Bobby blurted.

"Yep,'' Roth said. "Then she drew up a whole set of plans for Shine for a beach house in Windy Tip.''

"Does Shine's house have a basement, a bomb shelter?'' Bobby asked, excited. "Something like that?''

"Ordinarily they can't dig anything like that in the sand down there,'' Roth explained. "But according to the plans, the house sits on top of part of an abandoned post–World War Two Nike Hercules missile silo, one of many that were dug by the Army Corps of Engineers to defend New York Harbor. I found most of this on record in the library.''

"The silo provides enough space for an underground quarters?''

"Oh, yeah,'' Roth said. "Some of them used to be manned, waiting for the Red Menace and the Yellow Peril.''

"This is part of what Tom Larkin wanted to tell me,'' Bobby said. "Larkin probably tapped into Shine's folder. Found out about his bogus past. About how his three-quarters was repeatedly denied. And when he started checking into Kate Clementine, he also found out that Shine worked on that case and had used Moira Farrell as his lawyer and Barbara Lacy as his architect, before she disappeared.''

"Disappeared at the same time Dorothea did,'' Roth added. "Then Shine somehow found out that Larkin was onto him. . . .''

"Found out from me, that bastard,'' Bobby said. "Shine sent me to Larkin, just to find out what he *knew!*'' The light turned green, and he lurched through the intersection. "When I inadvertently let him know that Larkin was getting too close to exposing him, Shine had him killed."

Roth took his foot down from the dashboard as Bobby approached the *Daily News* building near Tenth Avenue and pulled into the yellow-lined truck-loading zone. Then he looked Bobby in the eyes.

"Look, I have to finish filing my piece for tomorrow," Roth said.

"Hey, Max," Bobby said. "Thanks."

Roth took a deep breath.

"But I have something else that's even more disturbing I gotta tell you," Roth said. "I don't want you to do anything stupid with that gun I know you're carrying around."

"What, Max?" Bobby said, looking at the clock on the dashboard that said it was 7:43 PM. "Come on, man. This is coming to a head. I gotta go!"

"You asked me to check with the State Department . . ."

"Yeah?"

"Well, they have a record of a woman named Dorothea *Slomowicz* entering the country from the Ukraine twenty-two months ago."

"And?"

"And 'Slomowicz' was the name of the Ukrainian diplomat whose wife had an affair with John Shine," Roth said. " 'Dubrow' was her maiden name."

Bobby sat frozen for a long moment, staring at the river two blocks west. He cleared his throat, tried to swallow what Roth was saying.

"Max, are you saying it's possible John Shine is Dorothea Dubrow's father?" Bobby asked.

"I think it's more than a possibility, Bobby," Roth said. "What are you gonna do?"

"I have to meet Gleason, and then I have to get back into that fucking house," Bobby said. "Tonight."

50

Bobby arrived to meet Gleason at the Empire State Building at 8:14 PM. He didn't want to risk the chance that someone was lying in wait for him in the underground garage, so he parked the Jeep on the street. It would make for a quicker departure anyway. He put the NYPD pass in the window.

Gleason would be meeting him in the basement office to work out a plan on how to enter Shine's house. To find Dorothea.

As soon as Bobby entered the lobby, he thought there was something wrong. The security guard who usually sat at a large metal reception desk wasn't on duty. And there was something cockeyed about the two janitors. First of all they were white, and he hadn't seen any white janitors here before. They had their backs to him, and the one with the mop moved with a half-stooped shuffle, as if he was favoring a rather tender injury. He also sported highly polished leather-soled loafers, too fancy to be wearing while slathering ammonia and disinfectant in an office building lobby.

Bobby took several steps to his left, using the black-backed glass of the wall directory as a mirror to get a better gander at this big janitor. The two janitors drifted to either side of Bobby. In the reflection he recognized Kuzak immediately, but before he could remove his .38 from his pants pocket, the second janitor raced from his left and whacked him with an industrial broom across the side of the head. Bobby fell to his hands and knees, from where he now saw the security guard handcuffed behind the metal desk, his mouth taped, terrified.

Bobby looked up, saw Kuzak and Zeke produce pistols from their overalls and take aim. Bobby toppled the security desk in front of him, the metal desktop deflecting the first two bullets. He rolled across the floor and pulled the .38 from his pocket, fired blindly, scampered across the lobby away from the vulnerable security guard, and took refuge behind the display advertisement for *Guinness Book of Records*.

He fired at Kuzak. The bullet shattered a display case holding King Kong memorabilia. He fired twice in Zeke's general direction. It had been so long since he'd fired a gun that it felt tiny and toyish in his hand. Zeke pulled the security guard to his feet and used him as a human shield as he advanced toward Bobby, firing. Kuzak did the same with a petrified real janitor who was stripped to his underwear. The *Guinness Book of Records* display case shattered. Bobby dashed past the elevators for the fire stairs. He wasn't going to help kill a security guard or a janitor. And he knew Kuzak and Zeke weren't going to drag these poor working stiffs *up* several flights of stairs in pursuit. So he hoisted open the fire door and thought for a moment of running downstairs toward the office, where he could call 911.

He heard someone shout from below, "Who the fuck's that?" The voice sounded vaguely familiar, but the timbre was too deep to be Gleason's, so he ran upward. Up into the winding spine of the most famous skyscraper in the world, up toward the red blinking light.

After a flight and a half, he paused, heard Kuzak and Zeke firing blindly up the stairs. The gunshots echoed in the great hollow enclosure, the bullets pinging around the metal banisters, overhead pipes, and old stone steps.

"You're dead, Emmet," Kuzak screamed. "I'm gonna cut your fucking cock off and force-feed it to you."

"I'm here," Bobby taunted, hoping to draw them higher. He knew his wind was better than theirs. He could take them when they were half spent. "Two against one is shitty odds," Bobby shouted, "for you two pussies."

Kuzak fired a shot up the narrow space between the banisters, the bullet ricocheting like a pinball.

Bobby kept taking stairs two at a time, saving his last two bullets for when he would really need them. At the eighth floor, he could hear the ex-cops groaning and puffing. This was as good a place as any to make a stand, Bobby thought.

He flattened himself against the cement wall on the eighth-floor landing, listening to the huffing grow nearer. He had his gun cocked, ready to fire. But he realized he was now listening to only one set of footfalls, one panting mouth. And it wasn't Kuzak's pained wheeze. The footfalls were lighter.

Bobby waited until he heard a foot scraping the landing below him, and then he twisted in one motion to fire. As he did, someone burst through the fire door leading from the eighth floor onto the landing. The swinging door startled him and made his shot go awry. Zeke fired a wild round from below. Bobby squeezed off a second shot just as Kuzak lunged through the open door and grabbed Bobby in a powerful bear hug. Zeke crouched, pulled the trigger. Out of ammo. He quickly produced and flashed a seven-inch switchblade. The sound of the steel blade locking into place sent a jailhouse shiver up Bobby's back. Zeke charged at Bobby to gut him while Kuzak held him from behind. But as Bobby had done on more than one occasion in prison when attacked from behind, he managed to wiggle his hand backward far enough to grab Kuzak's already damaged crotch. He squeezed hard, and Kuzak howled in agony and loosened his grip. Bobby spun Kuzak around in front of him as Zeke's blade plunged downward. The silver blade disappeared deep into Kuzak's chest. Bobby felt the big man vibrate and surge, and then Bobby knew Kuzak wasn't alive anymore.

But Zeke was fast with a blade, the way small mean men often are, and he came at Bobby from the side, this time the blade ready to descend into his neck. As he made his flashing move, Bobby saw a flying bulk sail past him from the stairs leading down from the ninth floor. Herbie Rabinowitz smashed into Zeke with a blind-side tackle that crushed the astonished smaller man.

"Fuckin' wop bastard!" yelled Herbie Rabinowitz, who twisted Zeke's grossly overmatched arm until the big knife dropped to the floor in a rattle next to Kuzak's lifeless body. Kuzak lay across the threshold, jamming open the fire door to the eighth floor.

"Herbie," Bobby shouted. "We need to hold on to him . . ."

But Herbie was lost in the white-hot zone again. Bobby watched Herbie lift the moaning Zeke over his head by the crotch and the throat and run with him into the corridor of the eighth floor.

"Find me a fuckin' window!" Herbie shouted, kicking at locked office doors. Zeke made choking noises and kicked madly to get loose, but the big man was too strong. Bobby ran after Herbie.

"Herbie, *nooooo!*" Bobby shouted as Herbie stomped open an office door and charged inside as if running with the World Cup.

Herbie ran across the dark, cluttered office, heading for a wall of windows that looked out over the neon-charged night of Thirty-fourth Street. He did a crazy twist in preparation to hurl the terrified Zeke through the window, a loud primordial bellow escaping from deep in Herbie's guts.

"Herbie," Bobby screamed. "Listen to me! There's a better way! One your mother would have been proud you thought of."

Herbie stopped and looked at Bobby with a wave of sudden sadness in his eyes. Zeke writhed and gagged above his head.

"Talk fast," Herbie said, veins jumping in his neck.

"Let me ask him some questions," Bobby said. "He can help us. Please."

Herbie reluctantly slammed a terrorized Zeke down onto his back on a desktop with a loud thump. Then he gazed around the darkened office. Mock-ups of detergent ads were pinned to the wall above the desk.

"How'd you know to look for me here?" Bobby asked, wrenching Zeke to a sitting position.

Zeke didn't answer, clutched his throat, trying to catch his breath. Herbie twisted his ear like a beer cap.

"Barnicle hit redial . . . on the phone . . . that the Sandy broad dialed . . . and this number come up," Zeke said, panting desperately for the air necessary to form the words. "She tried to call you. . . . We used the reverse directory . . . figured out it was Gleason's office. . . . We laid for you . . ."

"Why'd she call?" Bobby asked.

"Something about that brat kid of hers," Zeke said, breathing easier now. "How the fuck am I supposed to know?"

"There's been a big push the last few days to collect three-quarters money?" Bobby asked. "Why?"

"They don't tell me shit like that," Zeke said. "But you'd have to be one dumb prick not to know why. The fucking Stone campaign. I know that. Everybody was promised jobs. Us, too. No-show jobs. Dick-work titles. Seat-belt inspectors. Water-bill adjusters. Government cars, cherry dome lights to get through the fuckin' rush-hour traffic, parking passes. Plus the three-quarters city pension, the SSI. And what Barnicle pays us off the books.

277

House down Windy, a boat, no yoms. Kiddin' me? Set for fuckin' life.''

"All you had to do was kill Sandy," Bobby said. "Then kill me. Great citizen."

"All that was never spozed to happen," Zeke said.

"Where's Dorothea Dubrow?"

"Fuck kinda question's that?"

Bobby walked to the big window overlooking the street and then looked back at Zeke, who saw him nod to Herbie and then hook a thumb over his shoulder and start to walk for the office door. Herbie grabbed Zeke by the ear.

"No!" Zeke screamed.

"Where's Dorothea Dubrow?" Bobby said, turning.

"You killed the broad, last I heard," Zeke said, tenderly touching his ear, examining his fingers for blood.

"Who killed Sandy Fraser?" Bobby demanded.

He hesitated, looking trapped and defeated, and then Herbie corkscrewed the ear again.

"I got a flat tire I could patch with this here ear," Herbie said.

"Caputo and Dixon did that piece of work," Zeke said, leaning away from Herbie. "To make their bones with the crew."

"You guys even use the same jargon as the mob guys," Bobby said. "What's John Shine got to do with all this?"

"Shine? Nobody likes that fuckin' guy," Zeke said. " 'Specially Barnicle, far's I know. He's a fuckin' flake."

"Why is Sandy's kid so important?"

"No idea," Zeke said. "Square business. Alls I know is they treat him like the fuckin' Christ child."

"What else should I know that you know about Barnicle and his operation?" Bobby asked.

"What's to know? You do what you're told, you could get rich," Zeke said. "Hey, it beats chasin' jigs in the dark for chump cop change."

Bobby pulled him off the desk and onto his feet and nudged him forward, walking him back down the corridor. Herbie walked behind them.

"Let me ask you a question, Zeke," Bobby said. "And I want an answer, a real answer. *Why?* Why did you cross the line? From cop to skell? Why? Why did so many of you turn your backs on your badges? Flip from good cops to bad guys? *Why?*"

Zeke looked Bobby in the eye and cupped his sore ear as he walked.

"Why?" Zeke asked incredulously, stumbling up the corridor. "The question should be, why not? Why shouldn't *we* have a taste? They send us out there; they let us see it all—money, pussy, power, million-dollar homes, fancy boats, foreign cars. Rich, dumb high-school-dropout spades selling dope, flashing wads that could raise my family for a year. Ex-mayors with talk shows, writin' books, gettin' fuckin' rich. Ex-police commissioners getting twenny grand a pop for asshole lectures. Skells with beautiful babes half their age on each arm, some of them even *white*. All tits, high heels, and lipstick. Fancy restaurants from the *New York Times,* fancy nightclubs with big-name celebrities." Zeke stopped and spread his arms for emphasis, and Herbie pushed him up the corridor. "They put us up in front of all that," Zeke said, on a roll now, as if looking for sympathy. "But none of them cocksuckers ever lay awake nights, wondering where the money for the orthodontist is gonna come from for my kid in parochial school. And when summer rolls around, hunrid and ten degrees, how come I can't take my kid to a nice beach house with an Olympic-sized pool? In a spanky new Explorer instead of an eight-year-old Pontiac with a hunrid sixty-two K on the odom that I gotta drive a hunrid eighty-nine miles round trip every day from Cornwall to chase spades through crack alleys in Brownsville."

Zeke stopped again, touching his ear, touching his fingers together and shaking them as he hunched his shoulders. Bobby looked at him with cold eyes. "You ask fucking *why?*" Zeke said, incredulous. "Why shouldn't we have a taste of all that? We protect this shit-hole city, us, so that these pricks can live it up? Fuck that. Okay, I mean, I'm not gonna sell dope to schoolkids or put hos out on the corner to get *mine,* what's coming to *me.* But what the fuck is so wrong, Bobby, about taking a decent pension from the city I give my best years to, huh? *Why* does everyone else get theirs but not *us?* What, are *we* the wrong fuckin' flavor? We want at least three-quarters of what everyone else gets. That's the fuckin' *why.* "

They reached the fire exit where they had entered the eighth floor, where Kuzak lay in a pool of blood.

"And you're willing to kill for this sick, twisted line of reasoning?" Bobby said.

"It wasn't planned that way," Zeke said. "If it wasn't for you, it would never have come down to bodies. But when you think about it, on *the job* it's okay to kill for a whole lot less. I mean, what the fuck?"

"What the *fuck* about the fucking law!?" Bobby screamed.

"Like Lou says," Zeke said, shrugging, "sometimes the law is out of order. But one thing I know. Unlike you—me, I ain't going to no fuckin' joint. I got kids, so I'm turning state's in a New York minute."

"I can still heave him into the street for the Sanitation," Herbie said.

"He ain't worth the OT," Bobby said. "But I don't need him awake anymore."

Bobby stepped aside, and Herbie nonchalantly coldcocked Zeke with a single backhand blow. Zeke collapsed to the stairwell landing. Inert. Bobby took a pair of handcuffs from Zeke's belt and handcuffed the unconscious killer to a standing hot-water riser a few feet from Kuzak's blood-saturated body. He put the handcuffs' key in his own pocket.

The knife Zeke killed Kuzak with lay at least eight feet away, far from Zeke's reach.

"This clown's prints are on the knife," Bobby told Herbie. "He gets charged for killing his own pal and dimes on everyone else."

"You're right," Herbie said. "Ma would have liked this way better."

"What the hell are you doing here anyway?" Bobby asked.

"I'm still hiding from the racket guys," he said. "When I heard you go up, I shouted, but you didn't answer. Then I hear one of them shout your name. So I took an elevator up to head you off and came down the stairs. One of these bums obviously had the same idea and took a different elevator. I thought they were the . . . Italians."

"No," Bobby said. "Just a pair of dirty cops."

"Even better," Herbie said.

Bobby handed Herbie a few hundred dollars. "Herbie, there's a Day's Inn on West Fifty-seventh Street. Go check in. Stay put."

51

Bobby hurried down the stairs, and at 8:33 PM he found Izzy Gleason waiting in the basement office.

"You're late," Gleason said, sitting in the swivel chair behind the desk, blowing smoke at the buzzing light on the ceiling.

"How'd you get into the building?" Bobby asked.

"Through the underground garage," Gleason said. "Why?"

Bobby gave Izzy a quick fill on everything that had happened. He told him about the blind doctor at John Shine's house, confronting Abrams, Sandy's murder, then Abrams's suicide. He told Gleason everything Roth had told him about John Shine's past. Kuzak and Zeke upstairs.

"If Dorothea is in that house," Gleason said, "there's no more time to fuck around. Shine has to be ready to fly the coop. Either with her or without her."

Bobby said, "If I have to, I'll go into that house with a fucking jackhammer to find her. . . ."

"You can't go in there alone," Gleason warned. "Somehow you need to get Shine to invite you back in there . . ."

Bobby's cell phone rang. It was Patrick. "I checked last week's police physicians convention at the Hotel St. Claire. Same night the hooker named Karen Anders got wasted. Just like you thought, Bobby. The only one from the NYPD Medical Board on the list was Dr. Hector Perez."

"He has to be the second doctor in the bag," Bobby said.

Patrick gave Bobby Dr. Perez's home address and phone number that he'd gotten from NYPD personnel files. Bobby thanked Patrick and told him to make himself available because he might need him later. He hung up and told Gleason what he'd learned.

"I have a hunch this Dr. Perez can get us in," Bobby said.

In the Jeep on the way to Brooklyn, Gleason lit a cigarette, and Bobby's cell phone rang again. It was Maggie. "Dad, I heard on the news about Sandy. . . . I can't stop thinking about her baby. . . ."

"Someone will pay for it, Maggie," Bobby said as he sped over the Brooklyn Bridge, the lights of the harbor twinkling, ferries moving across the dark waters, Lady Liberty's torch burning a hole in the New York night. "The police know I had nothing to do with it. Don't you worry."

"I just worry about that little boy," Maggie said. "I kept thinking about what we talked about. That he looked so familiar, just like someone we know . . ."

"Yeah," Bobby said. "Like a face you know you've seen on *America's Most Wanted* . . ."

"Well, I think I know who Sandy's baby looks like," Maggie said.

"Who?" Bobby said.

"That guy that's running for governor," Maggie said. "Little Donald looks just like that guy Gerald Stone. . . ."

52

At 9:52 PM, after she had bathed and he'd blow-dried her hair, Shine was ready to give Dorothea another Haldol pill, just as he'd been doing three times a day for the past eighteen months. Tonight he would give her a fourth, Shine thought, to make her sleep on the trip to Miami. He would refuel and then fly two hundred miles southeast to the tiny Bahamian Island called Norman's Cay, forty miles southeast of bustling Nassau. In the 1980s Norman's Cay was one of the main money-laundering and smuggling ports of the cocaine cartels. Most of those people were either dead or doing life, but there were still enough marginal players left there who knew their way around a crooked dollar to attract John Shine.

The bags were already packed. Nothing much for him. Just some of the rare Emerson editions, some shirts, underwear, and trousers. Equally light for Dorothea. He'd buy new wardrobes in the islands to go with their new identities on the new passports. A whole new identity—Social Security Card, passport, INS green card, driver's license—could be purchased on the streets of neighborhoods like Sunset Park for five thousand dollars apiece. The craftsmanship was excellent, he thought.

Even the one for Sandy's baby, Donald, was perfect. He'd bought that one, too, in case he was ever forced into this contingency plan. Barnicle's nanny was packing a bag for the child at her Rockaway home, preparing little Donald for the trip to the Bahamas.

Shine had been redirecting the three-quarters money to his tiny bank in Norman's Cay for the past two years via convoluted international wire transfers originating in Mexico. His flagship bank account was in Mexico City, which he had opened two years ago with the fifty thousand dollars from his very first "91" three-quarters operation. Since then he'd made the rest of his deposits at a branch of the Mexican bank in Manhattan. Through this branch he routinely redirected the money to Singapore. In Singapore it was transferred to a numbered account in Switzerland. Then finally it was sent to the account of "Ralph Emerson," collector of rare books, in Norman's Cay. The name on the account matched the name on his new passport.

There was already five million dollars in Ralph Emerson's Norman's Cay account, and Shine had called his banker there earlier in the day to say he would be arriving in a private plane in the early morning. He told him he would be carrying a substantial cargo of American currency that he wanted to deposit in his bank. It would bring his total to fifteen million dollars.

"I'll be arriving with a small child and my adult daughter, who is not in the best of health," Shine had told his banker, who also held the unofficial title of *island manager*.

"I'll personally be waiting at the airport for you," the banker had said. "I'll just debit your account for any special VIP customs tariffs."

Here in Brooklyn, Shine's private twin-engine Cessna would be waiting at Floyd Bennett Field, the old airfield that was now part of Gateway National Recreation Area at the southern end of

Brooklyn, just five miles from Windy Tip. Floyd Bennett Field had once been the most heavily used airport in New York, the place where Wrong Way Corrigan took off on his way to California and wound up in Ireland. It was also once a favorite airstrip of Amelia Earhart's. Today it was used for air shows and to train the NYPD Aviation Unit, where Shine first learned to fly.

Shine knew the deputy director of Gateway, and a yearly contribution to the Park Alliance gave him unlimited, unrecorded access to the airport for his private plane. Shine had used the plane only three times in two years; twice to travel to Norman's Cay to meet his banker–island manager and to buy a condo on the sea. And once, two years ago, to do a piece of business in Boston.

Sandy Fraser's child would be placed with a good expatriate American family, Shine had decided. Where Shine would personally see that the boy was well taken care of. And kept available in case Shine ever needed him. No one would ever find the child or John Shine or his daughter, Dorothea. In the Bahamas or later—when they traveled together through the four-star hotels, the best restaurants and VIP galas throughout the world—he'd find his daughter an appropriate husband, he thought. The man certainly would not be some dead-end cop like he was. Or Bobby Emmet.

As good a guy as Bobby was in John Shine's eyes, he was still just a *cop. Not for* my *daughter,* he thought.

No, Shine's daughter would have the privileged life her beautiful mother was denied because she got involved with a New York City cop. In the Ukraine they'd banished her to a life of disgrace, ridicule, and destitution. Not their daughter. She'd live like a queen.

Shine reflected on his plans to create a governor, to own and manipulate a man who could run New York and maybe, someday in the next century, even sit in the White House. He was taking Stone's bastard child with him in case Stone somehow managed to weather the storm Bobby Emmet had created. *If Stone does get elected,* he thought, *then I can always use the kid by remote control in the future.*

If Stone was defeated, the kid would still have a good life. It was the least Shine could do now that his mother was gone. He would pick the child up at the nanny's house on the way to the airport. *Unfortunately for her,* he thought, *she's another loose end. . . .*

"Open, my treasure."

Dorothea opened her mouth and stuck out her tongue like a congregant ready to receive Holy Communion. Shine placed the sedative on her tongue and handed her a cup of hot, sweet tea. Although dressed in jeans and a heavy wool sweater, Dorothea trembled with fever, holding the teacup with two hands for warmth. She swallowed the pill with a grimace.

In addition to the three-milligram Haldol, John Shine gave Dorothea an antibiotic and two aspirin for the fever. And a multivitamin and an assortment of other vitamins and mineral supplements that Dr. Abrams had prescribed. She swallowed the pills, washing each one down with a sip of tea.

"Daddy, I'm scared," she said in a thin singsongy voice.

"Scared of what, darling?"

"I'm cold and afraid," she said, a spasm quaking through her, making her spill some of the tea. "I'm afraid I'll never be warm again. Mommy was always cold . . . always cold . . . never warm . . ."

"Drink your tea, Darla," Shine said. "That's your new name. Your American name. Darla. Short for 'my darling.' Okay? Daddy promises you'll be warm again. Very, very soon."

"I miss the sun," she said. She took another sip of tea.

"Cheer up, baby," John Shine said. "We'll be leaving very soon. Going away."

"Away?" Dorothea asked, clinging to the warmth of the teacup. "Where is that? Where are we now? Will there be sunshine?"

"You're here with me, darling," John Shine said. "Where no one can hurt you. I'll take you away where we'll be even safer."

"Will there be sunshine?"

"Yes, there will be sunshine," John Shine said. "Every day."

"Will Mother be there?"

"Mother is dead," John Shine said. "That's why you searched and found me. Now no one will ever break us apart again, angel."

"Mother is dead," she said, and a tear came from her glazed eye. "That's why I came to America to find you . . ."

He dried her eyes and looked at Dorothea. God, he thought. She's beautiful. As beautiful as her mother. And now he had the money to give her the life her mother was denied, the life she deserves.

The police department didn't know what a favor they did me when they denied me my rightfully due pension, John Shine thought. He'd promised himself he would get even. And it was so simple. He'd got even with Lou Barnicle, his former captain, who sandbagged him. Got even with the medical board, with their petty power. Got even with all the phonies in the brass. Now he'd taken more money from them than they would ever know. And he'd got even with them for making him stop seeing the woman he adored. Although the one true love of his life was now dead, driven to her grave in disgrace with a broken heart, John Shine had gotten back the next best thing, Dorothea.

No one will ever take her away from me again, he thought. He was sure she would forget about Bobby Emmet, who would soon be dead or in jail forever. Even if Emmet eluded both fates, he'd never find them, living under brand-new names, in a brand-new country.

After she finished her tea, John Shine lay Dorothea on the couch and kissed her forehead. He placed a throw blanket over her. "Try to sleep, darling. I have to go make last-minute arrangements for our trip. A new doctor will also have to check you one last time."

"Promise there will be sunshine, Daddy?"

Bobby pulled the Jeep to the curb on Eleventh Street in Park Slope, Brooklyn, across the street from Dr. Hector Perez's brownstone. He saw a Lexus with an MD license plate in the driveway. He called Perez on the cell phone.

"Dr. Perez, I know all about the blackmail scheme, the three-quarters pension racket," Bobby said. "I need to talk to you about it before you wind up doing what Dr. Abrams did."

"Who is this?" Perez asked.

"Come outside," Bobby said. "I'll meet you on the street. I don't want to embarrass you in front of your wife."

Less than a minute later Dr. Perez emerged from the ground-floor vestibule. Bobby got out of the Jeep and approached him on the street. Now Gleason sauntered across the street, and the three men stood by the carport.

"We better talk right now," Bobby said softly.

"I know who you are," Perez said defensively, looking from Bobby to Gleason. "I don't have to talk to you guys."

"I didn't say you had to," Bobby said. "I said I think you better."

"Of course, you'll have to talk on the stand when I subpoena your corrupt ass," Gleason said.

"What the hell do you want?" Perez asked, nervous, looking at his front door, hoping Nydia wouldn't see them.

"Okay, asshole, let's talk about the blackmail tape in Abrams's office," Gleason said.

"The dead hooker had three coins in her hand," Bobby said. "Quarters. As in 'three-quarters.' "

"From the police medical pensions you've been signing like Mickey Mantle autographs," Gleason said.

"You saw the videotape in Abrams's office," Bobby said. "Familiar? You have one, too, don't you? The dead hooker in the St. Claire last week had three quarters in her hand. Just like the dead hooker in the Boston Sheraton where Dr. Abrams stayed two years ago. I know you were at the St. Claire that night last week. Homicide and IAB haven't put it together yet. But they will."

"If you wait for them to build a case, forget the corruption charges," Gleason said. "Conspiracy to murder. Time they stop countin', there'll be more bodies in your indictment than you saw in medical school."

Perez looked at Gleason and then at Bobby in a trembling, sweaty panic. His throat clicked when he tried to swallow, and his Adam's apple rode up and down in his neck as if it were attached to a pulley.

"I didn't kill that woman," he said.

"They got you on tape, though, don't they?" Bobby said. "In bed with her. The way they got Abrams on tape."

"I woke up and she was there and . . ." Perez broke down.

"Actually, I might be just the guy to help you with all of this," Gleason said, doing a sudden sales pitch.

"You think you can?" Perez asked with hope.

"I mean what did you really do?" Gleason said. "You okayed a few pension forms under terrible duress. You failed to report a homicide. But you were set up, a victim. I mean you might lose the city job. The AMA might suspend you for a year. But I can't see any jail time. I can even see immunity. If you turn state's evidence on these bastards."

"I know what it's like being a cop in jail," Bobby said. "No offense, but you're just not built for the showers, Doc."

Perez considered this a moment, and it registered like a life-long recurring nightmare. He turned to Gleason and said, "And you'll represent me?"

"You own this house?"

"Yeah," Perez said.

"Of course I'll represent you," Gleason said.

"I'm supposed to wear special blindfold glasses and wait on a bench . . ."

". . . on the corner of Avenue U and Flatbush," Bobby said.

"How'd you know that?" Perez asked.

"Never mind," Gleason said.

"I'm supposed to check on some woman," Perez said.

Bobby's pulse started quickening. He and Gleason exchanged a knowing nod. "He said it was a woman?" Bobby said.

"Yes," Perez said, checking his watch. "I'm supposed to meet him in an hour."

54

John Shine's Mercedes passed them on the road out of Windy Tip as Bobby, Gleason, and Forrest Morgan sat in the Internal Affairs cop's unmarked Lumina on the shoulder of the road two hundred feet from the security gates.

Bobby dialed Patrick on the cell phone and said, "Shine is heading your way, Sonny."

"I'm waiting, Charlie," Patrick said to Bobby on the other end, parked two miles away in a PAL minibus outside of Kings Plaza Shopping Center. Patrick was watching the man with the dark glasses who sat alone on the bench at the bus stop across the street. In the PAL bus with Patrick was a father and son from the Coney Island projects, eager to play a little midnight basketball in Windy Tip. The kid's name was Walters. The father was a subway track worker who was even taller than his six-foot-three son.

"You really think the cops who stole my father's birthday money might be there tonight?" Walters asked Patrick.

"If the police photos you identified for me are correct," Patrick said, "chances are very good."

"I wanna meet these two," the father said.

"I wanna play them," his son said. "A little one-on-one . . ."

"You just ID them, for me," Patrick said.

"I can't go in there without backup, Bobby," Morgan said as he shifted in his seat. He waited with Bobby and Gleason in his car near the gates of Windy Tip.

"I know John Shine," Bobby said. "He's a man who refuses to lose. He'll kill Dorothea if he's trapped. I know if we wait for him to come out of the house with her, he'll lead her out first, using her as a human shield in case anyone is waiting. He'd use her as a hostage. He'd also blow her away if he had to. So we need to surprise him where he least expects us to show up."

"But without a fuckin' warrant?" Forrest Morgan said, looking at his watch for the third time in five minutes. It was a few minutes before 11 AM. "There's this little thing called the Fourth Amendment, man."

He yanked up the door handle and stepped out onto the road for air. Bobby climbed out of the front seat. Gleason got out of the rear door.

"Come on, Morgan," a nervous Gleason said as he unzipped his pants and proceeded to urinate on the side of the road next to the Lumina. "You know the law. You can enter any premises and use the Fourth Amendment for a doormat if you're following a suspect that you know is involved in the commission of a felony. There's not a judge in Sol Diamond's Brooklyn who'd give you a search warrant. But this Shine is ready to fly the fuckin' coop. He knows the jig is up, excuse my French. But you know that when Perez enters that house, he is participating in the commission of a felony called blackmail, participating in a conspiracy called kidnapping, pension rigging, and even murder. That gives you probable cause. How many more dead bodies do you need before you justifiably move your sorry ass past the Fourth Amendment?"

An agitated Morgan looked Bobby in the eye. "I don't like this arrogant, nasty-mannered little man," Morgan said, pointing at Gleason with disdain. "He's not only pissing me off; he's pissing on my fucking car!"

"City car," Gleason said. "I got the jitters. I usually don't help bust people. I'm used to unbustin' 'em. But duty calls."

"Izzy, put away your prick, will ya?" Bobby said.

Morgan paced across the deserted road, carrying his police radio in his hand, trying to make a decision.

Patrick saw Shine's Mercedes slow on Flatbush Avenue, watched it make a U-turn and park in front of the bus stop. Shine got out of his car, walked to the bench, and guided Perez into the front passenger seat. He slammed the door shut and then glided back into his car. Patrick dialed Bobby on the cell phone.

"Pickup made, Charlie," Patrick said. "I'll wait three minutes and follow. I'll proceed to prearranged place."

"Shine's on the way with Perez," Bobby shouted across the road to Morgan. "This is it, babe. You have the chance to blow open the biggest three-quarters scam in NYPD history. Hundreds of dirty cops that make all the tens of thousands of good, honest, noble ones look like pieces of shit. Page one, *Daily News,* big picture."

Morgan glared at Bobby and flapped his arms. "Don't you think I know all that shit?" he said.

"Then shit or go blind," Gleason said.

"We have three minutes," Bobby said. Morgan walked on the other side of the road, waving his hands, talking to himself, throwing left hooks at imaginary opponents. An urgent report crackled over his police radio, and Morgan put it to his ear and listened in glum, motionless silence and then walked quickly back toward Bobby and Gleason, his face stunned with awful surprise.

"What?" Bobby asked.

"Dunkin' Donuts go out of business, Morgan?" Gleason asked.

Morgan looked at Bobby, waving his index finger, and said, "Good thing I still had you under surveillance last night, Bobby."

"Yeah? Why?"

"They just found Barnicle, Tuzio, Hanratty, and your first law-yer, Moira Farrell," Morgan said. "All shot dead in her office on Court Street."

"There goes the neighborhood," Gleason said.

"I told you I didn't like this despicable little man," Morgan snapped, pointing the radio at Gleason.

"Dorothea will be next," Bobby said. "Now do we go in?"

All the old battle scars around Morgan's tired eyes appeared to converge into one final blink.

"We go in," Morgan said.

55

Two minutes later Shine's Mercedes rolled past them on the road, heading toward the security gate of Windy Tip.

"You follow my lead, Bobby, is that a ten four?" Morgan said.

"Ten four," Bobby said, from the passenger seat.

"What's this, fuckin' *Dragnet?*" scoffed Izzy Gleason from the backseat.

"When we get out there, Izzy," Bobby said, "I want you to stay in the car. The last thing I need is to be worrying about you. But I want you there to make sure my ass is covered by the letter of the law."

"We should have brought Herbie," Gleason said.

The security guard recognized John Shine and mechanically lifted the security arm to let the Mercedes pass through the gates. Less than a minute later Forrest Morgan pulled up in his Lumina. The elderly security guard looked at Morgan and said, "Lost?"

"Actually I'm here for some watermelon and ribs," Morgan said, and flashed his badge. The security guard held his hands up in mock surrender.

"Enjoy your meal, bro," he said, and lifted the security arm.

John Shine parked at the carport beside his beach home and helped Dr. Hector Perez from the passenger's seat and up the stairs to his deck and through the back door. He walked him through the living room and then down a narrow corridor between the stairs leading to the upper floor and the wall of the living room. On the right-hand side of the base wall of the staircase, John Shine pressed firmly on a three-foot-by-six-foot panel of oak, right where the wooden tongue met the groove of the next gleaming panel. A firm double counterpress released the magnetic catch-lock, which allowed Shine to swing the section inward. In front of him was a flight of steep stone steps leading into the earth beneath the beach. Nothing, not all the reinforced concrete and soundproofing in the world, could lock out the smell of the sea that seeped through the three-foot-thick missile-silo walls. John Shine flicked on a light switch and led Dr. Perez through the entrance.

"Watch your step, Doctor," John Shine said. "These stairs are rather steep. Let me lead."

At the bottom of the steps, John Shine unlocked a ten-inch-thick door, consisting of solid soundproofing foam sandwiched between two sheets of two-inch plywood. He pushed open the door, which gave way with a sigh.

"Daddy, I'm cold," Dorothea said.

"The doctor is here, darling," Shine said. "Everything will be fine."

Forrest Morgan parked on the beach road with a clear view of the stately house. Stars twinkled in the sky above Jamaica Bay, and the far-off strains of the Coney Island amusement parks carried on the soft night wind.

"Okay, Counselor, we watched him walk Perez inside," Morgan said.

"Then you witnessed conspiracy, extortion, blackmail, and a victim under duress," Gleason said. "You can legally follow them inside. That's my whole fuckin' contribution. See ya in court. I'm going down to that gin mill for a fuckin' Yoo-driver."

Gleason made a move to get out of the car. Bobby stopped him.

"You gotta wait right here, Iz," Bobby said. "That's enemy territory."

"You ready?" Morgan asked.

"Let's do it," Bobby said and walked toward the back of the house.

Patrick stopped at the Windy Tip security gate in the PAL bus. The security guard looked at him and then at the two black faces with him. "Sorry, ace," the security guard said. "You musta missed the turn for Riker's Island."

Patrick flashed his badge. The security guard looked at it.

"You can go in," he said. "But the help stays where they are."

Patrick smiled, floored the accelerator, and smashed through the security arm and into Windy Tip.

Dr. Perez checked Dorothea Dubrow's heartbeat and her pulse as John Shine sat in an overstuffed armchair in the shadowy corner of the subterranean living quarters. A spotlight behind him shone directly into the room, casting him in shadow and shielding him from Perez's view.

Perez put an ice pack on Dorothea's forehead and placed her hand on it to secure it.

"I need you to do this as quickly as possible," John Shine said from the shadows. "I have a child to collect and a plane to catch. I need to know if she is ready to endure a long trip."

"What drugs is she on?" Perez asked.

"Haldol," Shine said. "Three milligrams three times a day."

"Enough to keep her in a prolonged semiconscious zombie state," Perez said. "She must be a hell of a strong woman to still have a pulse and heartbeat like she has. Her fever is bad. But not dangerous. Still, I don't recommend travel."

"Can she endure a four-hour trip?" Shine asked.

"Yes," Perez said. "But I'm going to give her a vitamin B shot. Her fever might worsen if she sleeps." Perez was lying, sweating, checking his watch, looking over at the stairs' door beyond John Shine. Instead of vitamin B, he gave Dorothea a low-dose injection of a mild amphetamine, to bring her out of her Haldol stupor. He knew that anything could happen in the next few minutes. Where were they? He stalled for time. He crossed Dorothea's legs, checking her reflexes, which were weak but satisfactory. The amphetamine was already beginning to counteract the Haldol.

"She comes from excellent stock," John Shine said, beaming with pride.

Bobby slid open the back door of the beach house. After leading Perez inside, John Shine had not locked it or set the elaborate alarm. He was obviously planning a quick departure.

Bobby and Forrest Morgan stepped quietly into the house, guns drawn. Morgan cautiously followed Bobby through the living room.

"Where's the trapdoor?" Morgan whispered.

"The plans say somewhere under the stairs," Bobby softly replied. "We gotta search for the panel."

"Wonderful," Morgan said.

O'Brien placed fresh brews in front of Lebeche and Daniels. They stood at the bar of The Central Booking Saloon, watching New York 1, an all-news TV station, with silent dread. Caputo and Dixon, Levin and Flynn, sat spaced along the bar, flat beers warming on the counter as they watched with growing alarm the breaking news about the murders of Barnicle, Tuzio, Hanratty, and Farrell.

Then the alarm turned to panic when stock footage of the Empire State Building came on the screen. "In what could be a related matter," the Asian newscaster announced, "a man identified as Constantine Zeke, an ex-cop who worked for Gibraltar Security in Brooklyn, has been identified by Manhattan homicide detectives as the man arrested in the Empire State Building this evening for stabbing to death a fellow Gibraltar operative named Richard Kuzak. Sources say Zeke is cooperating with authorities in an unfolding corruption scandal. . . ."

Silence prevailed in The Central Booking Saloon until the men at the bar heard the sound of a gun being cocked behind them, followed by the sounds of a basketball being dribbled. The shocked cops turned and saw Patrick Emmet standing there. Walters and his father were with him. Patrick held his gun on the cops at the bar.

"Now, let's nice and slowly put all the guns on the bar, guys," Patrick said, training his service revolver with confident authority. He pinned his badge on his PAL jacket.

The stunned three-quarters cops complied, placing their service revolvers on the bar.

"What, are we making a Spike Lee movie here?" Daniels said, attempting humor amid the shock.

"Walters, collect the guns for me," Patrick said to the tall teenager. Walters moved quickly along the bar collecting the guns, placing them in a gym bag, patting down each livid cop and finding concealed "drop" guns, used to plant on potential perps, on two of them. "And then identify the ones who robbed you."

"Your name is gonna be shit on the job, asshole," Lebeche said to Patrick. "I got your badge number stenciled in my brain."

When Walters got to Lebeche and Daniels, he said, "Remember me?"

"I don't watch *Soul Train,*" Daniels said.

"You star in *Gorillas in the Mist?*" asked Lebeche.

"You guys helped me celebrate my father's birthday," Walters said. "That ring a bell?"

He yanked Daniels off the stool first, hit him with a right hand that flattened his nose into a bloody pulp. He followed with a left hook to the rib cage that dropped Daniels in a heap.

Lebeche ran toward the rear of the bar, and Walters's father followed, grabbing him. He slammed Lebeche onto the top of the pool table and drove a right hand into his face, cheekbones and the nose cracking.

"I'm the boy's father, fellas," the father said. "Now, I want an apology for my boy, and then I want my goddamned birthday money."

He hit him a second blow to the face, Lebeche's head lolling on the green felt.

"Easy, guys," Patrick shouted. "I want them to be able to stand when they're in front of the judge."

After some trial and error, Bobby finally found the right panel in the oak stairwell wall. Easing it open, he silently signaled for Forrest Morgan to follow him. They descended to the bottom of the soundless stone stairs and paused for one deep final breath. Bobby and Morgan exchanged a pensive look and then quickly burst into the twenty-by-twenty-foot underground bunker, waving guns.

"Dorothea, get down," Bobby yelled.

Bobby and Morgan were instantly blinded by the spotlight behind the heavy armchair where John Shine sat. Bobby and Morgan tried to aim in that direction, but in the blinding light they could not get a clear shot.

Shine was only momentarily startled. He dropped quickly to the floor, firing a pistol he pulled from his waistband. Bobby and Morgan dove in different directions, hitting the floor, returning fire into the blinding halo of light.

"Oh, my God!" screamed Dr. Perez, dragging Dorothea from the couch to the floor with him.

Shine grimaced with back pain but scrambled for cover behind the armchair and shot again at Bobby. Morgan fired at the spotlight, blowing it out, leaving just the overhead lights and a table lamp illuminating the room.

Shine fired three rounds toward Bobby and Morgan, keeping them pinned down. Bobby let loose with a return barrage of shots in his general direction, but the rounds lodged harmlessly like spitballs into the soft cushions of the big chair. Shine popped up from behind the chair to fire, and Bobby shot him, the bullet tearing through his left arm, blood splattering the wall behind him. Shine grunted loudly and disappeared behind the chair again.

Forrest Morgan rolled behind a coffee table, under a softly shining lamp and ripped off several shots from his 9 mm Glock automatic. The room went momentarily silent, and then Shine popped out like a defiant target in a shooting gallery and fired back at Forrest Morgan. A bullet tore into Morgan's right shoulder and sent a pink fog misting across the lamplight. A second bullet exploded into Morgan's left thigh, and he stumbled backward, pulling the lamp off the end table as he fell, the lightbulb exploding, casting deeper shadows into the dim room.

Bobby crawled on his belly toward the armchair, firing three more times. Two bullets zinged over his head, and he lay flat for a moment on the deep pile carpet, frantically reloading his spent revolver.

"Dorothea, I'm here," Bobby shouted, drowning out the sound of the reloading. "It's Bobby. I'm here, Dorothea . . ."

"You're not Bobby," Dorothea said in her faint singsongy voice. "Bobby is dead. You leave my daddy alone . . ."

And then Dorothea stood, frail and disturbed, and sauntered through the room, bumping into furniture, falling to one knee, getting back up, desperately reaching for the walls, as if searching for something.

"Get down, Dorothea," Shine screamed.

"Dorothea it *is* me, *Bobby*," he shouted, and rose to a half crouch to try to get to her. Dorothea looked at him, her eyes blinking, as if trying to decide if she were dreaming or awake.

Shine fired at Bobby, but the bullet whizzed by him, shattering a vase filled with flowers. Bobby fell flat to the floor.

"Bobby?" Dorothea said, the amphetamine making her progressively more lucid. "Daddy? Is that really Bobby, Daddy?"

"No, Dorothea, he's lying," Shine shouted.

"I'm not lying, Dorothea," Bobby said softly. " *'Ya tebe kohayu.'* St. Peter's Church. The red light on the top of the Empire State Building."

"He's telling you the truth, lady," Morgan shouted. "He don't do that often, but he is now. He is Bobby Emmet . . ."

"Bobby," Dorothea whispered. Then Bobby heard her sigh softly, like a lost kitten's sad lament.

"Get down, Dorothea," Bobby shouted, as he searched the room for John Shine. Dorothea continued to grope at the walls, knocking down a calendar and a wall clock.

"Bobby . . ." she said.

And then Dorothea found what she'd been looking for—the light switch! She swiped it in a downward motion, and suddenly the room went completely dark. A darkness as total as Bobby'd ever known.

John Shine began to laugh as Bobby tried to adjust to the menacing blackness.

"She's been in the dark for a year and a half," Shine said, moving confidently in the accustomed gloom. "She doesn't even know who she is, never mind who you are. Only I know who she really is."

Bobby could tell that Shine was still moving in the dark, arrogantly familiar with the layout. There were no windows, so not even a dull glow found its way into the sunken dungeon.

"I know more than you think I know, John," Bobby said, eager to keep Shine talking until he could track the sound of his voice to get his hands on him.

"Like what for instance?" Shine said, his voice coming at Bobby from his left side now. "What do you think you know?"

"I know you ran the whole three-quarters pension operation," Bobby said. "That you ordered Tom Larkin killed because he figured out you had an architect named Barbara Lacy murdered in my apartment and then had her cremated and made to look like it was Dorothea. Then you had Sandy Fraser killed because she was finally going to tell me her child's father was really Gerald Stone . . ."

"I wish the fuck you woulda told *me* this shit," Morgan shouted from the gloom.

"Sandy . . ." Dorothea said from the darkness. "Daddy, did you really hurt Sandy?"

"He had her killed, Dorothea," Bobby said.

"You're good, Bobby," Shine said, and this time his voice came from yet another part of the room. "But then again, *I* taught you."

Bobby could not get his bearings. He could hear Dr. Perez saying prayers in Spanish in the dark and Forrest Morgan moaning in pain.

"You ain't goin' nowhere, Shine," Morgan shouted. "So give this crazy-assed shit up, man."

"Oh, be quiet, you insignificant dust mite," Shine said. "Can't you see there is a serious tête-à-tête going on here between teacher and student? Show some respect."

"Fuck you, psycho," Morgan shouted.

"I also know you were never married, John," Bobby said. "That there was never any boating accident."

This brought a long silence from the pitch dark.

"But I know about the woman," Bobby said. "The diplomat's wife. Slomowicz's wife. Whose maiden name was 'Dubrow.' "

"That is quite enough," Shine said, his voice suddenly sharp with anger.

"And that she was recalled back to the Ukraine after they discovered the affair she had with you," Bobby said. "But she was pregnant, with your child. With Dorothea."

"Enough!" Shine angrily boomed, his voice closer now.

"Then after the Iron Curtain fell, you searched for them, didn't you?" Bobby said, listening to Shine shuffle in the dark. "Moira Farrell helped you get a visa. You even traveled to the Ukraine. Came up empty . . ."

"You have no idea how much pain, the fucking *heartache* I lived with all those years," Shine said softly, almost as if hoping for understanding.

"Then one day a couple of years ago little Dorothea showed up at your doorstep, as a beautiful grown-up woman," Bobby said, searching for a reply in the dense murk. "Like a war baby.

A Cold War baby. She looked you up because her outcast mother had always told her about her real father in America. A mother who died after years of being disgraced and ostracized back home. Dorothea told me how her mother had lived a terrible, lonely life. That she lived only to educate Dorothea, to pass on all that she knew to her daughter, who might someday have a life. She never told me why there was no father. Now I know why. Her mother was considered a cheap, cheating, traitorous wife who had embarrassed her diplomat husband and her country by having a *baby* by some lowbred American cop.''

"You make it sound so tawdry,'' Shine said, and Bobby could hear him moving a chair in front of him in the dark. "But I loved that woman all my life. Loved my daughter I never knew . . .''

"Then Dorothea came in search of her father in America and found a crackpot,'' Bobby said. "A man incapable of having another woman or another child and who chose instead to exploit everyone in power until he had the power himself.''

"How come you never told me none of this shit, Bobby, man,'' Forrest Morgan shouted. "I would have brought me a net and six-pack of shrinks.''

"It would have been so perfect,'' Shine said, reflectively. "But you had to come sniffing around. I only asked Dorothea to amuse you, have dinner with you, to find out what you knew about me and her. To play along with this joke on my friend and keep it a secret that she was my daughter. At least until I learned what you knew about the business I was involved in. And then, the silly girl—just like her lovely, silly mother—she fell in love with a New York cop. I pleaded with her. Begged her to drop you. But she said she was going to marry you. I couldn't let that happen now, could I? I couldn't let *my* Dorothea be taken away from me again. The only way to get her away from you, and you away from me and my little operation, was to arrange for both of you to disappear.''

"You call twenty million dollars a little operation?'' Bobby said.

"That was only this year's take, Bobby, baby,'' Shine said with a proud laugh. "The Stone campaign has already spent twenty from last year's take . . .''

"I'll be double goddamned,'' Morgan said from the darkness.

"Not much to own a New York governor, huh?'' Shine said, still chuckling. "Mr. Emerson, who coined the phrase 'man in the street,' advised people like us to 'hitch your wagon to a star,' Bobby. I did."

"And in case Stone tries to renege on his promises, you arranged for another ace in the hole," Bobby said. "A card from your own deck, when you used Barnicle and Moira Farrell to set up Sandy Fraser with Gerald Stone, Mr. Family Values. Talked her into having horny Stone's baby so you could blackmail him for as long as he held office."

"Sandy was an attractive woman who wasn't getting any younger," Shine said. "She wanted a child. She found Stone attractive. She was more than willing to use *him*. He was willing to use *her* for his own pleasure, the hypocritical prick. So why shouldn't I use two users? I would know how to control a man like that. Tell him what laws to sign, which ones to veto, who to pardon, who to hire and fire. What programs to fund, which ones to cancel . . . even when to run for *president*."

"You are one outta-space motherfucker," Forrest Morgan said. "What the fuck kind of drugs you on?"

"Just like you blackmailed the doctors on the pension boards with videotapes of murdered hookers," Bobby said, gripping his pistol. "You were going to use Sandy's kid as blackmail against a family-values politician. Problem was, Sandy wound up loving the kid more than the greedy plan. She wanted out. You wouldn't allow that."

Bobby felt a cold circle of steel on the back of his skull as Shine knelt over him with the gun. Shine removed Bobby's gun from his hand and slid it across the floor.

"Couldn't," Shine said softly, and then sighed. "Just like I couldn't let Dorothea continue with you, Bobby. I couldn't lose her again. So I kept Dorothea here with me. Safe. From you and all the others. Helping her forget . . ."

"Like Kate Clementine's uncle," Bobby said.

"I understood him," Shine said. "Yes, I could relate to how much he loved his niece; that he wanted to protect her from this fucked-up world."

"You loved Dorothea so much that you had Sandy killed; Dorothea's only friend," Bobby said.

"Daddy, did you have Sandy killed?" Dorothea demanded, her voice stronger now.

"And now it's a shame you got in my way, Bobby. I never

wanted to have to kill you myself. I tried to have you taken care of a half-dozen times. But in the end, you really must rely on yourself. You were a dear friend and a more than worthy enemy. But look what being an honest cop got you. Jail. Now, like your father, death. Emerson said, 'Good men must not obey the laws too well.' Now, Bobby, it's over. I gotta go."

He heard Shine's gun cock.

"Daddy, did you kill Sandy?" Dorothea said.

"Get down, Dorothea," Shine said. "We'll be leaving soon."

"You know what my favorite Emerson quote is, John?" Bobby said, trying anything to keep Shine talking.

"No," Shine said eagerly. "Which one?"

"He said, 'I hate quotations.' "

Suddenly Dorothea switched on the lights and screamed, "Bobby! Daddy!"

In the blinding glare, Bobby swung a wild hand at a stunned John Shine, knocking his gun out of his hand. Bobby smacked him hard enough to tumble him to the floor. Morgan trained his gun in Shine's direction and fired. Empty. "Motherfucker!" Morgan shouted and hurled the gun at Shine, hitting him in the chest. Shine groaned, and Bobby lunged at his shadowy form. Shine hit Bobby with a crunching right hand to the temple that made Bobby see a burst of tiny dancing sparkles. Bobby threw a left hook into the bottom of Shine's spinal column, making him wail with anguish. But, ever in terrible pain, Shine kept scrambling for his pistol. Bobby rolled across the floor toward his own gun.

Shine reached his gun first.

He swung, took dead aim at Bobby Emmet, and squeezed the trigger as Dorothea Dubrow lurched from the light switch by the wall, in between the two men.

"No, Daddy!" Dorothea shouted.

"No!" Bobby shouted. "Dorothea, No!"

John Shine fired.

"Bobby," she whispered.

Dorothea Dubrow absorbed the bullet intended for Bobby Emmet. The impact sent her sprawling across Bobby's lap. Perez, from his prone position, kicked Bobby's gun toward him. Bobby snatched it up. The bullet that Dorothea had just taken had left Bobby emotionally numb. Bobby fired past the dying Dorothea with a reflexive, mechanical response. His bullet entered Shine's forehead like a rivet. Shine remained in a seated position for three more suspended seconds, his astonished eyes at first refusing to accept the death that had already arrived. Then he slowly collapsed to the floor.

Dorothea Dubrow lay on Bobby Emmet's legs, heavier than the weight of the rest of the world, her chest torn cruelly open, her eyes forever closed.

56

Tuesday

In the predawn on election day, Gerald Stone came alone to meet Bobby Emmet on the empty beach at Prince's Bay in Staten Island.

Bobby had called the gubernatorial candidate's private number during the night and told an aide that Stone had better come meet him that morning. He gave him the time and place on the deserted beach near Wolfe's Pond Park.

"The councilman is much too busy to meet with anyone on election day morning," the aide said.

"Tell him it's about little Donald," Bobby said. "He'll understand. If he doesn't see me about the kid, tell him to watch with his wife, his kids, and the rest of the state on the morning news."

The aide had obviously passed on the message because at five AM sharp a blue Chevy Blazer pulled alongside Bobby's Jeep in the parking lot near the sea. Bobby watched the gulls wheel on an awakening sky as the waves rolled in like installments of a very deep and endless sadness. Bobby was weak, stained with the mental images of Dorothea's death. He had been grilled by cops for two hours, and finally Izzy Gleason told them to arrest him or cut him loose.

They let him go with a promise to the state attorney general's office that he would testify about the whole three-quarters opera-

tion and all the deaths that surrounded it. The cops that Patrick
had neutralized in The Central Booking Saloon were arrested by
Internal Affairs, the collars credited to Forrest Morgan.

Morgan had arranged for Sandy Fraser's aunt in New Jersey to
get custody of Sandy's son. While in the nanny's house, Bobby
retrieved a photograph of Sandy holding Donald.

Bobby unfolded an early four-star edition of the morning's
Daily News. The text of Max Roth's column, along with his photo
logo and an EXCLUSIVE banner, began on page one, a tabloid
editorial decision made only when the paper has something truly
big. The main front-page headline screamed out at the city:
COP SHOCK!

Roth's column carried a subhead: Emmet Walks as Rogue
Cops Talk.

In the end, Bobby Emmet did what he always did best—
he busted a bunch of bad guys. This time the bad guys were
dressed in blue with shiny badges, badges they abused to
frame Emmet for the murder of the woman he loved.

A murder he never committed.

The woman, Dorothea Dubrow, didn't even die until last
night, as Emmet, accompanied by Internal Affairs detective
Forrest Morgan, closed in on her abductors in the subcellar
of a Windy Tip beach house owned by a deranged, disgruntled, delusional ex-cop named John Shine. Shine was the secret mastermind behind a rogue cop pension racket that is
now being called the Three-Quarters Crew.

In searching for Dubrow, to clear his sullied name, Bobby
Emmet has cracked open the biggest police corruption scandal of the decade.

Emmet has untangled a web of political conspiracy, murder, revenge, greed, kidnapping, blackmail, municipal loot-
ing, and outrageous abuse of power. This morning, corrupt
politicians are cowering in their miserable back rooms, waiting for the indictments to fall like trapdoors on the gallows.

All over town, all day long, greedy defense lawyers will be
rubbing their hands together in glee as dirty cops race to cop
pleas faster than DAs can impanel grand juries. Last night
the "Three-Quarters Crew" cops were diming on each other
like terrified school kids, each desperate to save his miserable

behind from the life of an ex-cop in the joint. A life that almost killed Bobby Emmet a half-dozen times in 18 months of what he calls "cop in the can."

But today Bobby Emmet walks as a free man, today Bobby Emmet goes home to his kid with his head held high and . . .

Bobby knew the rest of the story, especially the part about Dorothea and Sandy. He folded the paper and now held the photograph of Sandy and Donald in his hand as he watched a nervous-looking Gerald Stone, dressed in jeans and windbreaker, walk across the sand to the picnic table where Bobby sat facing the sea.

"The news is already starting to break," Stone said quietly, looking out at the foaming waves. "It's all so awful. Every paper and news station in town wants a statement."

Bobby placed the photograph of little Donald on the table and stared silently at Gerald Stone. Bobby's eyes were tired and raw, glittering with a barely controlled anger. Stone looked from Bobby down at the picture of a smiling Donald in the arms of a proud and beaming Sandy Fraser. Stone nodded as if he were identifying a perp in a mug-shot book.

"I knew he was my kid," Stone said. "But try to understand. I was afraid if I acknowledged him, I'd lose all my other kids. My wife. My career . . ."

Bobby picked up the photograph and put it in his own shirt pocket.

"You don't have a career anymore," Bobby said.

"Please, I had no idea about all the things they did," Stone pleaded. "To you. Your girlfriend. To Sandy. I was a victim, too. Me, I've been used, too. . . ."

Bobby got up and looked Gerald Stone in the eyes, the wind off the ocean twirling Stone's hair. Bobby was surprised that he had no desire to kill him. If this was maturity, he didn't like it.

"I'll support the kid: money, schools, medical, college, every-thing," Stone said, desperately. "What do you want from me? What? Tell me what you want."

"It's over," Bobby said, and walked to his Jeep, leaving Stone alone on the shore.

*   *   *

On the morning news, gubernatorial candidate Gerald Stone stunned the media when he called a hasty press conference and announced he was withdrawing from the Republican primary for personal reasons and family considerations. Even if he was nominated, he would not accept.

Epilogue

Because Maggie had completed so much extra school credit over the summer, Connie relented and let her take the whole week after Thanksgiving off from school. This gave Bobby, Maggie, and Patrick eleven full days to take *The Fifth Amendment* down to Miami to visit Grandma.

Patrick was celebrating his promotion to the rank of detective, third grade, assigned to Brooklyn PMD, Public Morals Division, for his participation in busting open the three-quarters pension scam.

Izzy Gleason had just left the boat, after dropping off Bobby's pistol carry permit and his private investigator's license. "Bobby Emmet, P.I.," Gleason had said before leaving to make arrangements to see his own kids for Thanksgiving.

"Prisoner of Izzy," Bobby said, reminding himself that he still owed Izzy Gleason two years of indentured servitude for getting him out of jail and having all charges against him dropped. That grim prospect was softened when Izzy also gave him ten thousand dollars in cash, ten percent of the one hundred thousand dollars Hector Perez paid to have Gleason work out his plea bargain, where in exchange for his testimony he would receive five years probation and a thousand hours community service in a city hospital.

"Where's Venus?" Bobby had asked.

"As soon as she learned enough English, she told me I had a

filthy fuckin' mouth," he said. "Last week, after I got the charges thrown out against the prick nutritionist owner of the fat farm, she took off. With him. Can you believe this ingrate? But I found a new one, Betty, Beatrice . . . Whatever her name is, she might have a beak like a bald eagle, but her body is as tight as a hand- ball, and all she needs is a little rhinoplasty. . . ."

Max Roth was almost certain to be nominated for all the top journalism awards for his series called "The Three-Quarters Crew."

Forrest Morgan headed a task force that rounded up what was left of the pension scam. Sol Diamond stepped down as Brooklyn DA and was being investigated by the state attorney general's office for his part in the illegal financing of the Stone for Gover- nor Campaign. The city was investigating hundreds of fraudu- lently purchased three-quarters medical pensions of ex-police officers. For Sale signs started going up along the beach in Windy Tip as cops facing heavy jail time scrambled for bail and lawyers' fees. Izzy was trying to land a few as clients. The prosecution's new star witness, Constantine Zeke, turned on his fellow cops. Two of the cops, Lebeche and Daniels, were fingered for the murder of Tom Larkin. Caputo and Dixon were charged with the murder of Sandy Fraser. O'Brien, Levin, and Flynn were charged with racketeering, fraud, extortion, tax evasion, and a host of other related felonies.

Bobby Emmet buried Dorothea Dubrow in a simple ceremony in Evergreen Cemetery in a plot on a soft green hill with a clear view of the blinking red light of the Empire State Building.

Now, as a splendid trip approached, Bobby stood on *The Fifth Amendment* with the river wind blowing in his hair. Herbie Rabi- nowitz had painted the entire boat by hand as a repayment for Bobby's getting the Queens bookmakers off his back with a sit down to which he'd secretly brought a pile of Herbie's brother's money. The deal was that Herbie would never bet action again in the borough of Queens.

Bobby turned when he heard his daughter's voice and saw Maggie skipping along the walkway toward *The Fifth Amendment*.

"Hi, Bobby," came a chorus from the three sweater-clad women sipping hot cider on the Chinese junk at the next slip.

Maggie looked at the beautiful women waving to her father

and smiled. "Been busy with a tough case, huh, old man?" Maggie said.

"Just being neighborly," Bobby said, mildly abashed.

Maggie rushed up the gangplank, and Bobby picked her up in his arms. "Let's take this tub out to sea," Bobby said.

Patrick came down from the fly deck and kissed Maggie. "Grandma is gonna cook the biggest turkey you ever saw," Patrick said.

"Can we stop in Coney Island for a hot dog on the way, Dad?" Maggie asked.

"We can do anything we want," Bobby said as he untied the lines and started the twin engines. Maggie sat in the pilot's seat as they backed out into the river and headed downtown toward the open sea.

About the Author

Denis Hamill is the author of *Stomping Ground* and *Machine.*
He has been a columnist for *New York* magazine, the *Los
Angeles Herald Examiner,* and the *Boston Herald American.* A
resident of New York City, Denis currently writes a column
for the *New York Daily News.* He is at work on a new novel.